NEVER LET ME DOWN AGAIN

A JOHN MILTON THRILLER

MARK DAWSON

PROLOGUE

EIGHTEEN YEARS AGO

Major Connor Gordon convened the men in the tented area that would, at least, offer a little shelter from the brutal heat of the late afternoon Iraqi sun. Gordon—nicknamed 'Flash' by the men for obvious reasons—had only returned from the recce of the town of al-Majar al-Kabir yesterday. Camp Abu Naji was near to the town in an elevated position to give the troops inside a decent look at the dusty buildings in the valley below. The base was protected from direct attack by a range of measures, with overwatch of the surrounding area provided by carefully sited towers around its perimeter, each manned by at least two soldiers.

It had been a relief to pass through the main gate and into an enclave, where the only viable threat was from occasional mortars or, if it was a really bad day, a salvo of well-aimed rockets. Al-Majar al-Kabir had been something else entirely; still at boiling point following the battle that had taken place there last week, the locals were paranoid—with good reason—that the British were going to return in force and take revenge for the murder of the six military policemen who had been trapped in a police station there. Flash and the others had posed as RMPs, including the distinctive scarlet berets, knowing full well that to be uncovered as Special Forces soldiers thirsty for revenge would lead to another confrontation and the certainty of bloodshed.

The men arrived and sat in the canvas chairs that had been arranged around a large screen. There were sixteen men in the troop, and eight of them were present: Hardcastle, a bandage around his bicep from where he had been grazed by a random bullet; Heywood, nicknamed Chimney on account of the number of cigarettes he smoked; Sullivan; Black; Greenslade; Cameron. Captain John Milton—the troop commander—sat at the back of the tent, a scowl on his face that Flash had seen before. He knew what it portended, too: trouble.

George Rippon, the MI6 spook who had been assigned to the base in the aftermath of the massacre, went to the table to wake his laptop and collected the clicker to move between his slides. He looked over at Flash and nodded that he was ready to start.

Flash stood and clapped his hands. "All right, lads, pay attention. George is going to run you through what we know and tell you what's going to happen next."

Flash gestured that Rippon should continue and took his seat once again. Rippon pressed the clicker, and a satellite image of the town filled the screen.

"Thanks to you, we now have excellent intel on the current state of play inside the town. As you might expect, the locals are concerned that there will be reprisals for what happened last week."

"No shit," Black commented.

"Shut it, Cilla," Flash said, using the nickname he knew that he hated.

Rippon continued. "As you know, the army entrusted security in the town to the local Shiite militia. Our intelligence suggests that the militia in the town is part of the Badr Brigade—these are men who have been trained in Iran. They are heavily armed and affiliated with Ayatollah Muhammad Abdelhossein, a prominent cleric who only returned from exile in Iran in the last month. The locals have been reluctant to criticise the militia, but those who did said they were outlaws."

Rippon clicked, and the image of the town was replaced by a grainy image of a man captured by a telephoto lens. He was wearing a black turban and robe and was surrounded by other men in similar garb. "This is Abdelhossein. We have confirmed that he is currently in the town and living at this house."

Rippon clicked, and a picture of a small two-storey house replaced the photograph of the cleric.

Sullivan leaned forward. "Where's that?"

"Near the Haj Jalil Mosque."

Rippon clicked again, and the image was replaced by something entirely more macabre: the decapitated body of a man hung upside down from a bridge with a sign attached to the front of his *dishdāshah*.

"This is Fareed Abbas—the local elder who spoke to us about Abdelhossein. He was abducted from his home last night and murdered. The militia beheaded him and hung his body from the bridge on the outskirts of town."

"The sign they've stuck to him," Cilla said. "What does it say?"

"Death to the British," Rippon translated.

The men chuntered angrily as Rippon clicked back to the satellite image of the town.

Milton raised his hand. "How confident are we that Abdelhossein is at that house?"

"Very," Rippon said. "We've had UAVs on station since last night. He was seen going in just before ten, after the murder, and he hasn't been out since."

"So when do we go in and take him out?"

Rippon shook his head. "We don't."

"But we know he gave the order," Milton protested. "We know it was him."

"I realise that, but we have very clear orders. We are not to engage."

A ripple of anger passed through the room.

"Lads," Flash said, both palms raised, "settle down."

"He gave the order to attack the station," Milton continued, ticking the facts off on his fingers. "We know where he lives. We could go in, pick him up and be out in twenty minutes. We could have him in a cell here in time for tea."

"*Fuck* picking him up," Sullivan said. "Put a Claymore under the fucker's car."

Hardcastle shook his head. "Why bother? Get a drone to put a Hellfire up his arse."

"Chaps," Rippon said and, when they continued to talk over him, he looked to Flash for support.

"Shut the fuck up and listen!"

"You have very clear orders," Rippon said. "You are *not* to go back into the town, and you are *not* to engage, not under *any* circumstances. The battle last week accounted for more than a hundred Iraqi dead. The determination has been made that taking out Abdelhossein now would destabilise the town even more than it already is."

"Who made the decision?" Milton said.

"It's political," Rippon said, "with a capital *P*."

Milton didn't let it go. "So we forget what happened?"

"No, we don't. You're right—we *do* know who was responsible, and he will be brought to justice. The order has been given to pacify the town, but to do it properly this time—in numbers. 1 Para are going back in, and this time it's going to be done right. They'll find Abdelhossein, and he'll be arrested and given a fair trial. We can't afford for this to look like a kangaroo court. The locals need to know that there's due process and that we'll follow it." Rippon turned to Flash. "Thank you, Connor."

Flash stood. "Dismissed. Foxtrot Oscar, all of you."

FLASH FOUND Milton in the mess. It was an informal area with large trestle tables and a smoking area covered with camouflage netting. Milton had helped himself to a bottle of whisky that one of the lads had smuggled in by persuading the lads at Brize to look the other way in exchange for a four-pack of beer. Milton poured a shot into the black plastic cup from his water bottle.

"What the fuck was that, Flash?"

It was only when they were alone that Flash let Milton call him by his nickname. In front of the men, it was always 'boss.'

"I don't know," he said.

Flash took out his own cup, and Milton poured a measure for him, too. "It's bullshit. You know it and I know it."

"You don't think I'm frustrated?"

Milton went on as if Flash hadn't spoken. "Because if we wait, you know what'll happen—right? Abdelhossein will disappear." He snapped his fingers. "*Gone*. Back to Iran."

"And we'll find him again."

"Like bin Laden? *That's* going well."

"We'll find him," Flash repeated.

"But we know where he is now, Flash. *Right now*. Give me a couple of the lads, and I'll go and sort it out. I can be in and out without anyone seeing."

"You can't. He's guarded."

"There wouldn't have to be a firefight. We wait until it's dark and do it surgically. You know it can be done."

"And *you* know we can't do it."

"Yeah, yeah, I know—because the pencil pushers are worried about upsetting the locals. Give me a break."

They both knocked back their whiskies.

"Another," Flash said, holding out his cup.

Milton poured for them both. "Six Redcaps murdered on his orders. *Six*. You know what gets me? How are we going to tell their wives and kids, their mothers and fathers, their mates, that we knew *exactly* where the man who ordered their deaths was hiding and we didn't do a thing about it?"

They drank again.

"None of this *bothers* you?"

"Of course it bothers me, you prick," he snapped. "But you heard what he said. They've stood us down."

"I heard it. I just don't know if it's an order I can accept."

Milton reached for the bottle, but Flash reached across and stopped him, grabbing his wrist. "We're on the same page here, right? We both agree it's an outrageous liberty, but we also know that there's *nothing* we can do. Okay?"

Milton turned and stared at him. His eyes were the palest of blues, icy cold. "Let go of my wrist, Flash."

"There's nothing—"

"—we can do," he finished.

"Say it."

"There's nothing we can do. We have our orders. Now let go of my wrist."

Flash released him. Milton poured for them both again, touched his cup to Flash's, and sank his in one hit.

"Another?"

"No, thanks. And you should go easy." He stood. "I'm going to walk the perimeter. I need to stretch my legs. I'll see you tonight."

Flash didn't feel like more whisky and left it on the white plastic picnic table. He opened the door and stepped into the heat. He needed a little exercise to clear his head and, despite the burning sun, he started on a walk around the perimeter of the base.

He was restless and couldn't get the conversation with Milton out of his head. Milton had been in Iraq longer than most and had had a rough time of it recently. He and three others had been dropped behind enemy lines at the start of the invasion. Flash had done all the high-altitude low-opening jump training, but had not served with an Air Troop and was happy leaving all the HALO shenanigans to them. Milton's squadron had been searching for Saddam's Scuds to paint them with targeting lasers so that the fly boys could drop bombs on them. There had been an incident out near the Tigris when Milton's patrol had tracked down a launcher and called in an airstrike. The Americans had sent a Warthog, but the bomb went astray, landing on a *madrassa* and wiping it—and the children playing outside—from the face of the earth. Flash had debriefed Milton upon his arrival at the camp. Milton had shrugged it off, but Flash hadn't bought his reaction for a minute; he could tell that it had affected him, but with Milton saying he was fine and no shrink to say otherwise, Flash had had no choice but to allow him to continue with his tour.

Milton was angry. Flash had seen it then, and he had seen it this afternoon, too. He was angry, and violence swirled behind those blue eyes.

He reached the tower that marked the northeastern extent of the camp and turned back. He decided that he wasn't happy with how the conversation had ended, and made his way to the mess.

He had thought that Milton would still be at the bar. Sullivan and Cilla were drinking, but Milton wasn't with them.

Sullivan had a tin of Red Stripe. "What's up, boss?"

"Have you seen Milton?"

"Not for a while. Why?"

Flash told him it was nothing and, with a sick feeling in his stomach, he went to the accommodation. Milton wasn't there, either.

Flash pushed his way outside, took out his phone and called the main gate. "Has anyone gone in or out of the camp in the last hour?"

"Hold on, sir," the guard commander replied. "Let me check the book."

Flash knew what the answer would be.

"It says here there *has* been a departure. Captain Milton—he went out twenty minutes ago."

"On his own?"

"Wait." Flash could hear the sound of a robust conversation. "Yes, sir. On his own."

"Why did you let somebody out on their own? You know the rules on escorts and protection."

"I didn't see him go. The two lads on the barrier said they had no choice."

"Yes, they *fucking* did. Nobody goes out on their own, no matter who they are or who they *think* they are."

"Young lad here says Captain Milton threatened them. Said if they didn't let him out, or if they said anything after he'd gone, he'd beat the shit out of them both. Do I raise the alarm, sir?"

"Absolutely not. Get rid of the entry in the book and say fuck all about it. I'll deal with this."

Flash jogged across the dusty ground to the mess. Sullivan and Cilla were still there.

"Get the others," he said. "All of them."

"Flash? What's the matter?"

"Milton's left camp. I think he's gone to get Abdelhossein."

"On his own?"

"It would appear so. We need to go and make sure he doesn't get himself killed."

PART I

MONDAY

1

John Milton's time in Okinawa had been as pleasant as he had hoped. These were Japan's 'sunshine isles,' and they could not have been more different to the regimented order of Tokyo. The suits of commuting salarymen were swapped here for *kariyushi*, brightly coloured shirts that reminded Milton of Hawaii. He had spent a week looking around the main island before flying to Ishigaki. He had visited a different beach every day, each of them resplendent with powdery white sand and crystal-clear waters in which it was possible to see little sharks and manta rays as they cruised just offshore. He had managed to husband enough of his money so that he didn't need to work, nursing his funds with cheap accommodation in a *ryokan* and eating with the locals rather than suffer the markups that the tourists were happy to pay. He had been here for eight days now, exercising in the morning and then reading on the beach and listening to music until the sun dipped down beneath the horizon at dusk.

He had felt closer to a drink in Tokyo than he had for years, and had resolved to attend a meeting every day in order to find his balance again. There were plenty to choose from, most of them attended by US sailors from the nearby base. His Wednesday evening meeting was in a gazebo at the north end of Chatan beach, close to the Hilton. He checked his watch as he made his way to the gazebo, the sand warm between his toes. He had struggled to find the venue the first time, the familiar AA sign just visible in the darkening light. He took a folding chair from the stack at the rear of the gazebo and sat down at the back of the small congregation of men and women. It was a rich mixture of colour and age, a collection scraped from all strata of society and united only by their addictions. There were the usual unlikely alcoholics: the well-turned-out men and women who would have looked more at home at a tennis club or on a golf course. They sat among those who more readily fulfilled the stereotype of the drunk: red noses and bloodshot eyes, the unwashed and unwanted.

The secretary opened the meeting, ran through the opening formalities and then handed the floor to the speaker who had been asked to share her story. Milton looked at her: she was white, in her late seventies, soft-shoed and dressed in faded floral patterns that were appropriate for her vintage. Nothing ostentatious; just practical, inexpensive attire.

"My name is Judith-Ann," she said, "and I am an alcoholic."

The others welcomed her in one voice.

"I've been coming to meetings for years," she said in a soft Glaswegian accent. "I've had a problem with drink for as long as I can remember. Back when I was a wee lass in Glasgow, I used to take little sips out of the bottles I found in my mum and dad's drinks cabinet. By the time I was old enough to drink, I was going out on Fridays and Saturdays and drinking away all the money I'd made at work that week. I'd wake up the next day, often covered in sick or... or worse, and I'd tell myself that that was the last time, that I would go straight from now on. Of course, that lasted for a few days until the weekend came around, and then I did it all again."

There were murmurs of recognition. Milton reminded himself to listen for the similarities and not the differences, and they came easily enough. He had been thinking about the pattern of his drinking lately, and had recalled an unhealthy appetite even as a schoolboy at Fettes. His thirst had been deepened by the death of his parents and then again as he joined the army, and he had wholeheartedly thrown himself into the culture of going out and ransacking whichever garrison town was unfortunate enough to host him and his mates that night. It had raced out of control from then, providing him with the oblivion to forget the things that he had seen and done as a soldier and then, after that, in the Group.

"Lately," Judith-Ann continued, "I've found that I've needed to come more than ever. I was diagnosed with cancer six months ago, and that's obviously been a kick in the teeth, but it's not the reason. The doctors said that I might last a year if they gave me chemotherapy, but I'm old and I've had a good life, and I'm not sure that's the right thing for me to do. I'm philosophical about coming to the end of things, and I *had* decided that I'd tell them no, but then, just after that, my lad went missing. He's a human rights campaigner back home in Scotland. He's a good boy—always calls me twice a week, Wednesdays and Sundays, but then, just like that, the calls stopped. I sent him emails and didn't get a reply. I wrote a letter—the same. I eventually managed to speak to his girlfriend, and she said she doesn't know where he is either.

"My view on things has changed—I have to stay alive long enough so that I can find out where he is. Obviously, throughout all this I've been thinking about how a drink or two would help me to calm down, but then I think of the forty-three years that I've been coming to these Rooms, and that's been enough to keep me on the straight and narrow. I think that's what I wanted to share tonight—life is going to throw problems at us, and we're going to think that a drink will help solve them, but it won't. I'm staying sober because I know that if I don't, then I won't have the chemo and I'll stop looking for my wee Alan, and, if I do *that*, I'll die without ever seeing his sweet face again." She took a breath, her eyes shining with unshed tears. "That's all I wanted to say. It works if you work it..."

"... so work it 'cause you're worth it," the others—except Milton—finished for her.

The secretary opened the floor to those who wanted to share their own experiences. Milton's eyes fell to the floor, just as they always did at such moments, but he found himself dwelling on the woman's story and wondering if there was anything that he could do to help.

2

Milton stayed on after the meeting and helped stack the chairs at the back of the gazebo. He kept to himself, nodded farewell to the secretary and started to make his way up the beach to the promenade. He was intending to jog back to his accommodation, but, as he took the steps that climbed up from the sand, he saw the old woman. She was lighting a joint, her hand cupped around the flame to protect it from the gentle breeze that blew in off the East China Sea.

"Is that such a good idea?" he said.

She turned to him with a frown that lifted as she saw his smile and recognised him from the meeting. "Aye, I know it's probably stupid, but the odd toke isn't going to make a difference in the long run, and it helps with the pain."

"Thank you for your share," he said. "I needed to hear it today."

"How long have you been in?"

"A few years."

"And how's it going?"

"I've had a rocky month or two. There was a moment

when I was very close to throwing it away. I'm just trying to find some peace again. You know what it's like."

"I do," she said. "Forty-three years and it still feels like I'm hanging on by my fingernails."

She drew down on the joint, tipped her head to the side and blew out a jet of smoke. "You want some?"

"Not for me."

"Normal smoke?"

"Okay."

She took out a cigarette, and Milton put it to his lips, ducking his head all the way down so that she could light it for him.

"Which way are you going?" she asked him.

Milton pointed to the south. "Chatan. I'm staying in a hostel there. What about you?"

"I'm getting the bus."

"Would you mind if I walked with you?"

"Not at all."

They set off, following the promenade toward the athletics and baseball stadia. The temperature dropped quickly as the evening set in, and Judith-Ann took a shawl from her bag and wrapped it around her shoulders. Milton tried to guess her age and settled on late seventies. She walked with determined purpose, although it was obvious that the treatment to hold back her cancer had weakened her.

"You're English," she said as they passed a statue of a stretching figure set atop a tall pedestal.

"That's right."

"You're far from home."

"I am," he said. "But not quite as far as you."

"Aye, I lived in Scotland, but my home's here now. Been here for twenty years."

"What do you do?"

"I'm a missionary."

"A nun?"

"No. Other team. Reformed faith, not that it matters. What about you? You're hardly a tourist, are you?"

"Why do you say that?"

She stopped on the pretext of looking into the swimming pool, but Milton suspected that she needed to gather her strength. "Man of your age staying in a hostel?"

"Just passing through."

"Passing through to where?"

"Don't know yet."

She drew down on the joint again, and the two of them continued on their way. They walked silently, measuring one another.

"What's your name?" she asked.

"Eric," Milton said, still getting used to the sound of his new pseudonym.

"You didn't share at the meeting."

"I'm more of a listener than a talker."

"You'll get more out of it if you share."

"So everyone tells me."

They walked on, taking the footbridge across the Shirahi River.

"Tell me about your son."

She looked over at him. "Why?"

"I might be able to help."

She looked over at him, suddenly dubious. "And how would you be able to do that?"

"I used to be a policeman," he lied. "I'm retired now."

"I don't have any money," Judith-Ann said. "You can save the sales pitch."

"No," Milton said. "It's not like that. I don't need cash."

"You just like helping people?"

He heard her scepticism and guessed that she had already been shaken down by scam artists ready to cash in on a worried mother's fears.

"It's part of my recovery," he said, picking a path that would allow him to limit questions that might require him to tell a more elaborate lie. "I can't make amends to some of the people I hurt when I was drinking, so I try to balance things by helping others."

"Sounds very karmic," she said and then, after glancing over at him again, shook her head and apologised. "I'm sorry. I don't mean to scoff."

"I wouldn't blame you if you did. Scepticism's not a bad thing."

"More's the pity," she said. "What are you doing now?"

"Not much," Milton said. "Why?"

"You hungry? There's a lovely little local place around the corner. Good food and cheap, too. Are you really interested in helping?"

"I am."

"So I'll tell you about Alan."

3

Jimmy Bolton was uncomfortable. The evening's event had not been cheap, but, he reminded himself, he was playing for a reward that was worth having. You had to speculate to accumulate; that was what Caesar had told him. He'd also told him that he'd have to fake it until he'd made it, justification for the fifteen hundred quid that he'd blown on clothes. The sharp suit he was wearing made him feel like an imposter, just like the double-cuff shirts that he still struggled to pin down in the morning. Caesar had admonished him for the little signs of unease—the tug of the cuffs, the straightening of the lapels—but he couldn't help it. Jimmy had been born into poverty, and it was only by dint of his hard work and tenacity that he had risen as high as he had. The trappings of success did not fit him easily.

He remembered the conversation with Caesar before he had come out here for the meeting. "You're not a bogger with bailer twine for a belt anymore," he'd said. "If you want to *look* the part, then *act* the part." Jimmy had asked what was wrong with how he looked. "You're *so* uncultivated."

Caesar could be catty and harsh. "If you weren't so fearful about it, I'd come with you and keep you right."

That was *never* going to happen. Jimmy reminded Caesar that it was easier for him, that while he could be out and proud in a place like Glasgow, it wasn't an option in the islands. Caesar had disagreed and insisted that he would have to be true to himself in the end. Jimmy had told him that he was being unreasonable and, as was becoming more and more frequent these days, they had argued to stalemate.

Caesar seemed unwilling to take the hint. He'd poked and sniped at Bolton's reluctance to be seen in his company, but Jimmy knew how distracting it would be to have his sexuality out in the open; not just distracting, he corrected himself, but *fatal*. So, when Jimmy went home to the islands —like now—he went alone. Too much work had been done to take chances.

Jimmy bumped up the steps onto the tiny schoolhouse stage to begin his introduction.

"Thanks for coming out," he said, making an effort to smile even though he hated the way it made him look. "Typical Hebridean summer weather."

There was a muted grumble of agreement. He knew that plenty of those in the crowd remembered him as the son of a cattle farmer, an overconfident upstart who had bantered his way around the markets, regaling his elders with his overfamiliar cheek.

"We're on the cusp of an election," he said. "We have councils that ignore the islanders, we have our biggest communities riddled with blow-ins who care only about making a few pounds from renting their houses to tourists, we have our distilleries in the hands of Far Eastern companies who only care about how much money they can squeeze out of them, and we have an assembly at Holyrood more interested in the east coast than the west, with all its polluting oil and gas."

There was a ripple of applause from the eighty or so who sat before him. It gave him a little jolt of confidence, and he gripped the microphone like the chanter of the pipes, lowering it and raising his voice instead.

"What we desperately need is local indigenous industry. We need employment for our bairns so, when they grow up, there's something on the Hebrides for them. Something that belongs to *us*; something that'll keep them from going to the mainland and nae coming back. We need opportunities for them so that they can live as we've lived, to toughen with the salt air and the barren hills. We can harness that hardship, that work ethic, and turn it to our advantage."

The applause grew louder.

Jimmy stood taller. "That's why I want to introduce you to a friend of mine. Johnston Hannah has the energy—literally, if you'll excuse the pun—to make a real difference around here. This is a man bringing prosperity to our area, grabbing the breeze and turning it to pounds, shillings and pence. A true Scotsman, an entrepreneur and an all-round decent spud. Jonty—get yourself up here."

The crowd clapped harder as Hannah mounted the steps. Jimmy stepped back and allowed him the limelight.

"What a welcome," Hannah began, as if he were at an American caucus instead of a parochial meeting. "My goodness, what a fine introduction—thank you, Jimmy." Hannah drew Jimmy into an uncomfortable hug, ignoring the fact that they had been sitting next to one another just moments earlier. "You know me," he continued. "I'm just a laddie who grew up in Tobermory, got a bit lucky in Glasgow, and came home to give a wee bit back."

"Good man, Jonty!" shouted an old woman from the audience.

"I love these islands," he said, waving his arm around as if encompassing all of the Hebrides. "And I have a plan for them. A proposal. And best of all, given where we are, it won't cost you a single penny."

There was a chuckle from the gathering.

"I made a few quid from the fish farms. You know that. If supermarkets are going to stock salmon, they might as well have Scots Highland salmon, aye?"

"Too right!" a man called up from the back of the room.

"Because that's natural, isn't it? We grow the fish up here, we smoke it here, we create jobs here, we sell it in Glasgow, and it gets shipped all over the world."

There was another ripple of applause.

"So, I found myself asking, what *else* is like that? What else is unique to our beautiful environment, our fantastic scenery, our long northern daylight?"

"The bloody weather, Jonty!" shouted the man at the back of the room.

Jimmy kept his smile to himself. He had hired the man on the mainland, then briefed him and planted him close to the back so that everyone would hear his enthusiastic comments.

"Got it in one," Hannah said. "The weather." He paused for effect, and the crowd leaned in. "We've got plenty of it. And it's *pish!*"

There was surprised laughter at that. The old folks would not tolerate real swearing, but they still enjoyed a modicum of roguery. Hannah turned to Jimmy. "And what do we do with pish weather, Jimmy?"

Jimmy leaned into the microphone. "We shelter."

"But why? Why would we turn our back on all that

Atlantic energy? Why, when we have the greatest natural resource blowing our bonnets off, would we run for the houses? Why, when we've plastic washing up on our beautiful beaches and diesel spilling in our sea and contaminating our fish—the fish we depend on to make a living, by the way—why would we not take all that clean energy and turn it into a few quid? You probably know that I have an interest in the wind farm north of Lewis. Fifty turbines producing millions of kilowatt hours of clean energy. Each turbine has eighty-metre-long blades that produce enough electricity to power a home for thirty-six hours with just a single rotation. Think about that—one spin, and everything in your house is powered for a day and a half. And think about how many spins those big old rotors get through every hour."

The nods and mutters of appreciation needed less of a prompt now. Hannah prepared himself for the sales pitch.

"So," he said, "what I propose to do is this. You might have heard that the government has proposed another wind farm, out west of St. Kilda. It's deep out there, but there's technology coming that'll allow us to anchor the turbines even in waters that go down as far as they do. And I'm throwing my hat into the ring for that lease. Just like I did before, I'll create yet more employment here, in the Western Isles, to give your wee lads and lassies jobs in the biggest growth industry on the planet. I propose that we take the resources that God gave us, and we turn them to the good of this community and others just like it. I propose we *literally* harness the wind, the sun, the tide—even the rain—to make us healthy, wealthy and the envy of Scotland!"

The applause was lusty and spontaneous.

Hannah leaned forward. "We'll build the most efficient wind farms in Europe. The *best* in the world. We'll train local engineers to install and maintain them. We'll give them high-paid, secure incomes. We'll bring professionals to the west—architects, engineers, designers. They'll bring their families. They'll settle in our beautiful communities, and instead of raping the seabed for polluting carbon and fossil fuels, like our friends on the east coast do to the North Sea, we'll plant trees and mitigate their mistakes. Instead of our villages being taken up by landlords who'll let the homes out to southerners, forcing up prices so that locals can't live there anymore, we'll fill those homes with people who live in the communities and want to see them prosper. We'll farm the wind instead of the scrub, we'll become the green envy of the planet—and all we'll use is what the good Lord gave us!"

Jimmy took the microphone, determined not to be forgotten in the excitement. "So, what do you say, folks? Will you support Jonty in securing a future for our children?"

"We will!" called the shill at the back.

"Aye," took up a woman.

"Then you need to make sure you elect councillors who will support the proposal. We've got a list at the back of the room. Feel free to take a copy for yourself. Vote for them, tell your friends about them, pass the message on. We can do this, ladies and gentlemen. Give Jonty a chance to make a real difference, like he made a difference up on Lewis three years ago. Thank you for coming—and goodnight."

The clapping might have stopped there had the delivery not been as compelling—had there not been people paid to stand and cheer. Instead, though, the locals had been whipped to a perfect peak. Any councillors who might have objected to Hannah's proposal would now have to give careful consideration to changing their opinion if they wanted to win their elections.

Jimmy closed his eyes and allowed himself to breathe.

Months of work in the books and thousands of quid spent.

He was *nearly* there.

So long as he didn't get caught.

4

There was socialising to do after the event. Johnston Hannah had no appetite for it—the islanders were small-minded provincials with an overinflated sense of their own importance, and boring to boot—but he knew that he had to keep up the façade. He needed their support and, with that in mind, he had to persuade them that he really was *the* man of the people that he had suggested. The image had been cooked up by the public relations people in Edinburgh, and, although it was tedious, he couldn't deny that it had served him well so far. He was rich beyond reason, and, while not exactly hiding it—his was an aspirational story, after all—he made sure not to glory in it, especially when coming to poor, benighted places like this. He was humble to a fault, made lavish donations to charity and had established his own foundation to help those local children with the ability to get to university but lacking the finance to do it.

He said goodbye to Bolton, extricating himself before his obsequiousness became too cloying, went back to the hotel and poured out a miniature whisky from the minibar.

His telephone buzzed before he had the chance to take a sip.

"Hello?"

"It's me," said Donnie Chen.

"What's up?"

"We've lost another of the men."

"What? Lost? How?"

"There was a supply run. He ran."

"Where?"

"Tobermory."

"Jesus," Hannah said. "We can't have him wandering around. What if he gets picked up?"

"I'll find him," Chen said. "I'm just telling you—in case."

Hannah had known that he couldn't employ locals for this stage of the project. It wasn't strictly on the up and up, and a good way to ensure that rumours didn't spread was to employ men who wouldn't complain if they were billeted away from the mainland and, even if they managed to make it ashore, didn't speak English. The leading member of Hannah's consortium was a Chinese investor, and he had proposed Chen as the manning agent until the job was done. The labour for the project had then been gathered from questionable quarters, men who were desperate to avoid Dungavel Immigration Removal Centre and eager to be deployed on a remote island that no Home Office employee would sensibly volunteer to inspect. Illegals were flighty by definition, and that was before they experienced the conditions in which they would be expected to work.

"That's the third man we've lost."

"And the last."

"Please tell me you're not going to have a problem hitting the deadline? We need the test to go ahead."

"The test will happen."

"You've got the cable connected?"

"Yes."

"Good, because if we can't prove the cable works across the seabed, the investors pull out."

"I know that, Johnston."

Hannah would have bollocked any other employee who had spoken to him so informally, but Chen was not like anyone else with whom he had ever worked before. Hannah had heard from his contacts that he had once been a cage fighter, long before cage fighting became cool. Hannah had been out to the Flannans and then St. Kilda and had seen the bruises on the arms and faces of the men. Chen had a short temper and high expectations, and it didn't need a genius to work out that he enforced his standards with his fists. Hannah had begun to avoid face-to-face meetings after that.

"What about the turbine?"

"We'll raise it the night before."

"And you're sure no one will be able to see it?"

"From the other island?" said Chen. "There's no one there. We've checked."

"Good," Hannah said. "We'll get the blades turning, capture the data, prove the technology works and get the bloody thing down again. We've got two days."

Chen hung up, leaving Hannah staring at his phone.

He was aware that the risk he was taking was substantial. He needed the test to prove to the consortium that the experimental technology they were relying upon to win the bid would send enough power to the grid without losing efficiency along the cable. Most existing offshore wind farms transmitted their power using older systems that led to energy loss when the turbines were located too far out at sea. The new technology used high-voltage transmission that was more efficient. But the cable had been laid illegally, and they had no permission to erect the turbine, just as had been the case for the first test on the Flannans. It was an intractable problem: his would-be investors demanded proof, yet the only way to get that proof was to break the law.

Hannah sipped the whisky and reminded himself that they had made progress. He just needed to hold his nerve. With Jimmy Bolton in his pocket, the locals warming to the plan and the wind at his back—figuratively and literally—he could be up and running in months. Chen might have been ruthless, but he was efficient. Hannah needed that, because he was *close*. Two days was all it would take. If everything went to plan, that would be all he needed to get the hedge fund equity released. Then Bolton could concentrate on winning the lease, and they could get on with making money.

Hannah tossed the phone onto the bed and took another sip of his whisky.

Not just money, he corrected himself. He had that already. He was a millionaire several times over.

Serious money.

5

The restaurant was called Arigato, and, rather incongruously, the awning advertised apparel together with dining. Milton followed Judith-Ann inside and waited as she conversed with the owner in fluent Japanese. It was a small place, with paper lanterns swaying in the wind outside, paper drapes in shades of white and cream over the windows, and a menu that was chalked up on a board behind the counter. There were six small tables inside, with more seating in the car park outside. The kitchen, which looked to be miniature, was behind the counter and separated by a thin wall.

"He's closing up," Judith-Ann said, "but he knows me, and he's said he's happy to serve us."

"You come here a lot?"

"It's one of the places we come to after the meetings. He's done good business out of us over the years."

They sat at a table in the window, and the owner, a gruff, bald-headed man dressed in a white smock, came over and took their order. Milton ordered a bowl of hot soba noodles with dashi broth, and Judith-Ann chose deep-fried chicken meatballs.

Milton waited for the owner to make his way back to the kitchen to prepare their order. "Tell me about your son."

"What do you want to know?"

"What does he do for a living?"

"He's an activist," she said. "A campaigner. Like me, I suppose, in his own way. I shouldn't be too surprised he turned out the way he did. He's the son of a church minister and an impressionable young woman who ended up being a missionary. He's kind and well meaning."

"Where was he when he disappeared?"

"The Western Highlands," she said. "Where he was born. He was living in Oban, on the coast. It turned out he was seeing this woman from there—pretty lassie named Helena—and they'd got a place together. He kept that quiet —I didn't know she even existed until she got in touch with me after he disappeared."

"And she doesn't know where he went?"

"No."

The owner of the restaurant returned with appetisers: *sobagaki* and *yakitori* served with a sweet *tsuyu* sauce.

Judith-Ann wound some of the noodles around her chopstick and dipped them in the sauce. Milton did the same.

"You said Alan's a campaigner," Milton said. "What was he campaigning against?"

She shook her head. "He never told me. I asked Helena, and she said it was something to do with human rights. She said he'd been back and forth to Harris a few times."

"Harris?"

"Lewis and Harris. The main island in the Outer Hebrides."

"What about the police? Have they been told?"

"Aye. Helena reported him missing after the first couple of days. They opened a file on him, but they haven't found anything. I called them, and they said that he's a grown man and he'd come back if he wanted to—they were brushing me off, basically."

"What do you think happened?"

"I've come to think of him as passed," she said sadly. "But that's maybe just how I cope with the fact that I don't know the truth."

"Do you have any pictures?"

"I have some photos at home. Why? Do you really think you can help?"

"Maybe," he said. "Do you think we could meet tomorrow? I'd like to have a think about it."

"Aye," she said. "I'm coming to the meeting in the morning. Will you be there?"

"I can be," he said.

She smiled. "I'll bring the photos then."

6

They enjoyed a pleasant meal together, and then—after an hour and a half—they went their separate ways. It wasn't far to the hostel, but he went back to the waterfront so that he could walk a little farther and consider what he had been told and what he might do next. He knew that the Group was looking for him, and that would have been reason enough to stay as far away from the United Kingdom as possible. But, on the other hand, he had a new alias and excellent papers to back it up. Provided he was careful—and he was *always* careful—there was no reason to think that he would be putting himself at any greater risk by travelling to the Hebrides.

His thoughts moved on to whether the mystery of a vanished son was something that he was equipped to address. He was not an investigator; his talents had been directed more toward ending people than finding them. But then he thought of Judith-Ann and knew that he was likely her last chance of finding out what had happened to her son. He considered the debts he owed and the impossibility of making amends to those he had wronged. He spent his travels looking for opportunities to balance his ledger, and this was as good a chance as any.

There was another reason for travelling, too. He had an old friend in the area, a man to whom he owed a debt of gratitude that had never really been repaid. Milton had recalled him several months ago and, in an idle moment, had Googled his name. It turned out that he had set up a business in Oban. It was a coincidence, and, the more Milton thought about it, the more he concluded that it was felicitous.

Someone was telling him something.

He reached the *ryokan*, took off his boots at the entrance and replaced them with a pair of slippers. He went through to his room, undressed and put on the *yukata*, the bathing robe that he had been given on his arrival. The *ryokan* had communal bathing facilities, and Milton made his way there, parted the blue curtain that denoted the male area, removed the robe and slipped into the water. It was hot, warmed by the volcanic hot spring, and thick with minerals. The tradition was to bathe nude; Milton was pleased that the bath was empty, given that he had read that his tattoos might suggest an association with organised crime that could have been awkward to explain away.

He slid through the water to the edge of the bath and looked out at the view over the sea. He closed his eyes and concentrated on the feeling of the hot water on his skin. He had been tired when he had arrived here, but a week's relaxation had fortified him, and he felt ready to move on. Judith-Ann was a deserving case—a good woman who had been dealt a bad hand, both by illness and the worry of a missing child—and he doubted that there would be anyone else who would be able to help her before she died.

He knew, as he gazed out onto the gloaming, that he would try to find her son.

PART II

TUESDAY

7

Milton woke the next morning with a sense of clarity and purpose: he was content that his time in Japan was at an end, and that it was time to move on. He wanted to do something worthy with whatever he decided to do next, and hoped that Judith-Ann would still want him to find her son. It wouldn't make a difference to his decision, just to his destination: he would either make his way to the Scottish Highlands or, if he decided that the search for the missing man was not something that he should involve himself in, or she had changed her mind about it, then he would pick somewhere else and head there instead. He had a knack for finding trouble; most people did everything they could to avoid it, but he went out of his way to put himself squarely in its way. There would be someone who needed his help.

Milton was travelling light, as was his preference. He packed his meagre collection of things—three paperbacks, a change of clothes and a toothbrush—into his bag and went to collect his shoes at the door. The proprietor of the *ryokan* was sweeping fallen leaves from the path outside and bowed her head as Milton approached.

"*Arigatō*," Milton said, returning the bow.

"*Dōitashimashite*," the woman replied.

Milton put his EarPods into his ears, connected them to his phone, selected a Primal Scream playlist and set it to play. The opening beats of 'Rocks' began, and, invigorated by the prospect of work to do, Milton set off for the beach and the morning's meeting.

MILTON TOOK a seat at the back of the gazebo and listened to the share from an American ex-pat who reported heavy alcohol consumption during his time in the military. Judith-Ann was at the front, and Milton waited for her on the beach at the conclusion of the meeting.

"Good morning, Eric," she said. "How are you?"

"Very good," he said.

She noticed his pack. "Going somewhere?"

He nodded. "It's time I was on my way. Maybe to Scotland if you'd still like me to help look for your son." She started to respond, then swallowed. Milton saw that her eyes were shining with tears again. "What is it?"

"Why ever would you *do* something like that? I've been thinking about what we talked about last night, and I don't know why you'd agree to go halfway round the world looking for someone you don't even know."

He smiled gently. "I've been in Japan long enough," he said. "I like to keep moving, and I've been meaning to go to the Highlands. I have an old friend there whom I'd like to see. If I can combine a visit with the chance to do a good deed, so much the better. I told you—it's the way I work the Steps."

"Well," she said, "I won't argue with you. But I am grateful—it's a very kind thing to do."

Milton told her to forget it. "What do you have for me?"

"Some bits and pieces."

She reached into her bag and took out a copy of a photograph. It looked as if it had been taken at her son's graduation. He was wearing a suit with a black gown and mortarboard and had a fake scroll clasped in both hands. He was fresh faced, with bright eyes and a wide smile.

"How long ago was this taken?"

"Three years ago," she said. "He was thirty. He went back to university to get a law degree. He hasn't changed much since then, at least not as far as I know."

"Do you mind if I take this?"

"Of course not."

Milton slipped it between the pages of the copy of *Jude the Obscure* that he was reading.

"What else?"

"I spoke with the police at the time he went missing. They told me that they'd looked into his movements and that they couldn't find anything that would give them reason to think that something suspicious had happened."

"What did they say they thought had happened, then?"

"They looked into Alan's medical history. He had mental problems when he was younger. He dropped out of university the first time he went, and I didn't see him for over a year. It wasn't unusual for him to up sticks and go without telling anyone. They decided that was what it was—a relapse."

"But you don't think it's that?"

She shook her head. "He got on top of it—he had his medication, and it kept him level."

"He couldn't have gone off his meds?"

"No," she said. "I asked Helena. His girlfriend. He was definitely taking his pills. She's sure of it."

"You mentioned her yesterday," he said. "What else did she say?"

"Not as much as I would've liked. She told me they met at a pub in the town and found out they liked the same things. Things developed quickly between them, and he moved in with her. She still has all his stuff—I told her to keep it until he came back again. That was when I thought he was *going* to come back." She paused. "You'll go and talk to her?"

"Probably not a bad place to start."

"I don't think she told me everything," she said. "It's not that I think she was lying to me—I didn't get that impression at all. I just think she was holding something back. I think she was scared."

"Why? Of what?"

"She said that Alan was investigating some dangerous people. She wouldn't tell me any more than that. We had three conversations in all, and I could tell that she was reluctant to talk to me by the third one. I'd said that I was going to hire someone to look into what had happened—she didn't say anything, but I got the impression that she wasn't keen about that at all."

"Do you have an address for her?"

She handed him a piece of paper upon which she had noted down a few of the pertinent details about her son, including Helena's address in Oban. Milton slid that next to the photograph.

"Thank you," he said. "Is there anything else you think I

should know?"

"Not about Alan," she said. "About me, really. The doctors say that I have three or four months left before... well, you know—the cancer. If you can find anything out about Alan before then, you'll help me to go without having that worry on my mind. Even if something's happened to him—it's the *not* knowing that's the worst of it."

"I understand," Milton said. "I'll do my best."

She reached down to her handbag, unclipped it and reached inside. Before Milton could say anything to stop her, she brought out a plastic bag that had been tied around something the shape of a small brick. She opened the bag and took out a wad of banknotes.

"No," Milton said. "You don't need to—"

"I *want* to," she interrupted him. "It's not as much as I'd like, but it'll be enough to cover the cost of your flight."

"No," Milton said again more firmly. "I'm going to the Highlands anyway to see my friend. It's no problem at all to look for Alan while I'm there."

"But I don't need the money," she said.

Milton reached out with both hands, placing them around hers and the money. "Nor do I. And you *might* need it. Please. I'm not doing this because I want paying; I'm doing it because it's the right thing to do."

And, he thought to himself, *because it'll give me a chance to add another mark on the right side of my ledger, something else to balance against all the blood that I've spilled.*

"You're a good man, Eric," she said. "God bless you."

Milton smiled awkwardly at her misguided praise, then gently let go of her hands. "I've booked a flight this afternoon," he said. "I'll be in Scotland the day after tomorrow. I'll let you know the moment I find anything out."

"God bless you," she said.

Milton swung his pack onto his shoulder. “Goodbye,” he said. “I’ll be in touch.”

8

Milton stepped out of the taxi and paused on the pavement to take a final look at Japan. He had mixed feelings: on the one hand, he had enjoyed his time here; on the other, he was leaving behind Sakura and the possibility that the two of them might have had a relationship.

He dismissed his second thoughts.

A relationship? What was he thinking?

He had already ruled that out after he had reunited her with her son and then disappeared from their lives. People like him did not deserve to have a normal life. He could have pretended that domesticity was possible, but he knew that was folly. He had to keep moving, from place to place, never staying in one location for longer than necessary. There were people looking for him, and they would use those for whom Milton had affection as leverage against him. To pretend otherwise was selfish, and he knew those moments of weakness when he might have buckled were symptoms of his addiction. But he was stronger now; he wouldn't succumb.

He watched as the taxi edged into the slow-moving knot of traffic outside the drop-off for the terminal, then turned and went inside. He had thirty hours of travel ahead of him. He was booked on a JAL flight from Naha to Haneda and then a transfer to Narita International. There would follow an eleven-hour red-eye to Doha and then a final eight hours to Dublin. He had considered flying into Glasgow or Edinburgh, but had decided against it. He was already taking a risk in returning to the United Kingdom, and there was no need to exacerbate that risk by using an airport within its jurisdiction. Far better to land in an adjoining country and then look to cross the border at a point where surveillance would be less intrusive. Milton already had an idea how that might be done, but would give it additional thought during his flights.

He looked up at the departure board and saw, to his annoyance, that the flight had been delayed by three hours. He went to the JAL desk and confirmed it; the harassed-looking staff member told him that the inbound flight was late. Milton thanked her and moved away from the desk, biting his lip as he considered how best to spend the unexpected time. It was lunchtime, and, doubtful that anything particularly nutritious would be served on the short hop to the mainland, he decided to fill up now. There were plenty of restaurants in the food court, but Milton—in homage to his stay in Japan—decided to have sushi. He took a seat next to the conveyor belt and grabbed a selection of covered dishes as they slowly went by. He chose a plate of edamame, a vegetable maki and peppered tuna, and started to eat.

He opened Google Maps and typed in Alan Caine's last known address. Oban was a town on the west coast of Scotland, a hundred miles northwest of Glasgow. He opened Wikipedia and skimmed the details. It was a small resort on the coast with the locals relying on tourism to help them make their way. It was set on the edge of the Firth of Lorn, the bay reaching out in a horseshoe shape and shielded by the island of Kerrera and, beyond that, the larger Isle of Mull.

Milton popped the tuna into his mouth. It was charred, given a piquant edge by intense seasoning, and delicious. He looked back to his phone. Judith-Ann had said that her son had been working on Harris before he disappeared. Milton cleared the search box and typed that in. The map swung up and to the left, showing an island west of the mainland. Harris was, in fact, the Isle of Lewis and Harris, a large island divided by mountains at the northwestern extremity of the British Isles. Milton ran his finger down the coast, reading the names of the little townships—Lickisto, Geocrab, Manish, Flodabay, Ardvay, Finsbay, Lingerbay—and remembered what Flash had told him as he had recuperated in the hospital after what had happened in al-Majar al-Kabir. He had said that he had been born on Harris, and that he was going to return and set up in business there. Milton navigated to the website that he had found previously. Outer Hebrides Adventures offered tourists the opportunity to sail out to the remote islands—St. Kilda, the Flannans—and enjoy the spectacular scenery and the abundant wildlife. There were pictures of Flash: in a kilt accepting an award for the Best Outdoor Experience at the 2011 Scottish Thistle Awards, a tacky trophy clasped between his two meaty paws, behind the console of a rigid inflatable, staring meaningfully into the middle distance.

It had to be providence, Milton decided. He could go and look for the missing man and drop in on his old friend at the same time.

Flash had been a bitter man at the end of his service,

and Milton knew that he held him responsible for what had happened. Milton had been furious to have been blamed, too ashamed to admit that what had happened *was* his fault. He had been a different man in those days—impetuous and reckless—and, although he had always told himself that he had gone back into the town because he wasn't prepared to let the murder of six Redcaps go unavenged, he knew now that he was driven by his anger and not the need for justice. Milton's selfishness had come at a high price for Flash and the others. They had risked their lives to save Milton. Flash had been shot in the battle that followed and had lost his career as a result.

Flash had been right: Milton *had* let him down, and this was a chance to make amends.

Milton grabbed a plate of eel and cucumber from the conveyor belt. He was going to need to make enough money to support himself while he was out there. He navigated to the website of a catering industry recruitment agency that he had used before and looked for suitable positions. There were plenty—ranging from a job at a grill in KFC to a position of commis chef at the Royal Botanic Gardens in Edinburgh—but one, in particular, caught his eye.

The Harris Hotel and Restaurant, the premier hotel on the Isle of Harris, has an exciting role for a person to join the team for its grand reopening. The new chef de partie will be passionate, experienced, and familiar with a wide range of culinary techniques. In return we can offer you an opportunity to grow and develop your talent, creativity, skill and passion as a chef. This position comes complete with accommodation and is close to a beautiful sandy beach warmed by the Gulf Stream. Pay commensurate with experience.

It sounded as if it would be worth a punt. Milton filled

out the application form for the job. It took him ten minutes and, once he was done, he hit send.

9

Charles 'Caesar' Connolly ran a nail bar and beauty salon in Glasgow's West End. It wasn't necessary for him to actually do the filing and polishing anymore—these days, he had staff for all that—but he *did* enjoy coming into the salon for a coffee and a natter and to take the bookings of particular clients. He had been sharing tittle-tattle with his favourites—the ones who had come to him from the start—for donkey's years. He particularly liked the sassy lassies who gave him the salacious gossip he could share with Jimmy.

Political gossip. The kind that might prove useful to his boyfriend.

Alexandra had loads of it. Caesar wasn't sure what she did for a living apart from that she was some sort of back-room journalist with Scottish Television, and that she spent plenty of time at Holyrood hobnobbing with the political set. Caesar always took her booking himself and thoroughly enjoyed the hour that they would spend together. She had lovely hands and a foul mouth, the *perfect* combination.

He guided her to the table and pulled back the chair so that she could sit.

"Are you *never* going to tell me who your secret squeeze is?" she said.

"Maybe one day you'll meet him," said Caesar conspiratorially.

"Where?"

"At work. But you wouldn't know he was my bit of rough."

She cocked an eyebrow. "Really? Is he in telly?"

"Not even warm."

"A journalist, then?"

"Cold. Very cold."

"A cameraman?"

"*Please.*"

"A pap?"

"Freezing."

She lit on the answer with glee. "Politics!"

"Roasting! But that's all I'm saying." He drew an imaginary zip across his mouth. "My lips are sealed."

"That's no fun."

"I've already said too much." He gave her a wink and got to work on her nails with an emery board. "What about you? Any scandal in parliament?"

"Nothing interesting," she said.

"I'll be the judge of that, darling."

She grinned. "Wind."

"What?"

"I told you it was dull. Have you heard about the new wind farm they want to build out past St. Kilda?"

It *did* ring a bell with something Jimmy had told him, but he decided there was no point in telling her that. "No."

"Well, they are. They've invited tenders. The winner gets picked by the Crown Estate."

"The Queen owns the seabed?"

"I know. Isn't it *outrageous*?"

"So what's interesting about it?"

"The money," she said. "These leases come up once in a blue moon, and they cause a feeding frenzy. I've heard there are four bidders for this one: one group from Denmark, another from Germany, one from Sweden and one homegrown."

"Who's that?"

"Johnston Hannah—have you heard of him?"

Jimmy was working for Hannah.

"Of course," he said, hiding his interest.

"The word is that the Danes are going to win. The thing is, you know how popular Hannah is with the locals up there, *and* he has friends in government—they're all going to lose their shit when the contract goes abroad. There's millions at stake, apparently."

"You're right," Caesar said. "Dull. You must have something more salacious than that?"

She did, wittering on aimlessly about an affair between two mid-ranking government ministers, but Caesar barely heard her. He was thinking about what she had said about Johnston Hannah and his bid to build another wind farm and how grateful Jimmy would be when he passed the information on.

PART III

WEDNESDAY

10

Johnston Hannah always stayed in the Balmoral Hotel whenever he came to Edinburgh. It was one of the better places in the city, centrally located on Princes Street and with a Michelin-starred restaurant that was a joy to visit compared to the dull and dismal grub that he was forced to endure when he was out on the Hebrides. Hannah had a couple of very busy days ahead of him. He had been offered a piece of land that looked ripe for development within spitting distance of Holyrood; he had scheduled a visit to look it over tomorrow, and then there was a meeting with the bank. His diary was already full, but he had found time to see Lukas Jensen for a debrief. The scientist was responsible for the prototype cabling technology that the consortium was planning to use to bring the electricity from the turbines to the mainland, and had agreed to meet so that they could discuss progress.

Hannah went down to the brasserie and took a table at the edge of the room. He ordered a full Scottish breakfast from the waiter and checked his watch. He had arranged to meet Jensen at eight, and it was already ten minutes past. He insisted on punctuality, and its lack was a sure way to rouse his temper.

It had been a long, *long* journey to reach this point. The plan had always been to test the cable from the Flannans. The islands, eighteen miles to the west of Harris, were close enough to be practical, offered a landing stage to unload their gear and the seclusion that ought to mean that the test was not observed. But the island had special ecological status, and Hannah had known that it would be pointless to try to get dispensation for the test: it would have meant jumping through endless bureaucratic hoops that would have taken months, if not years, to manage. They had gone ahead in secret, and the test had been successful.

That ought to have been the end of it, but one of the partners in the consortium—a Dutch hedge fund—had baulked, saying that the cable run needed to be longer. And so, Hannah had changed location, moving the test seventy miles southwest to St. Kilda, much nearer to the site of the eventual wind farm. Boreray—the most easterly island in the archipelago—had promised the isolation to test the cable without being seen and, at eighty miles from the landing point on Harris, enough of a run to assuage any residual fears that the technology would not work over longer distances.

Hannah looked out through the window and saw Jensen hurrying along Princes Street. The scientist came inside and made his way across the brasserie to where Hannah was sitting.

"You're late," Hannah said.

"I'm sorry. I've been working on the data. I got distracted."

Hannah waved the excuse away. "I don't care about any of that, Lukas. All I care about is that you're ready." He paused and, when Jensen didn't answer, he prompted, "Are you?"

Jensen fidgeted with the ring on his finger. "Not quite."

"What does *that* mean? The test is supposed to be on Friday."

"That's too soon," Jensen said. "The turbine isn't up yet, and we don't have the cable in place."

Hannah closed his fists and took a breath to control his temper. "We need the test out of the way," he said. "There are no funds until we can demonstrate that we can transmit the electricity to shore."

"I understand that," Jensen said, trying to placate him. "We're working as fast as we can. But we don't want to rush it, either. We'll make mistakes if we go too fast, and I'm not sure we can afford that."

We can't afford *anything*, Hannah thought, flashing to the precarious state of his own finances. He had always been a gambler and, so far in his career, he had picked more winners than losers. This particular gamble had the biggest upside, but with that potential reward came enormous risk. He had put everything into this and, if it went wrong, he was finished. It would be ruinous. There would be no second act for him.

Hannah unclenched his fists and forced a smile, his lips tight against his teeth. "What do you need to make sure that it goes ahead?"

"It's the workers," Jensen said. "They're slow."

"We don't have a choice," Hannah said. "You know we can't use locals—we're not supposed to be there. There's no possible way we'd be able to keep it quiet if we used labour from the mainland."

"Doing everything by hand is like pulling teeth. They

need to dig the pit, pour the foundations, lift the tower and secure it... It takes time."

"We can't use heavy equipment. We can't get it there."

"And we don't even have the gear box yet."

"What?"

"The gear box. It changes the slow motion from the blades into the faster motion of the axle, which then drives the generator."

"I know what it does," Hannah snapped. "What do you mean you don't have it?"

"It was damaged when they took it down. It can't be fixed. I ordered a new one."

"I wasn't told."

"I didn't want to worry you."

"So where's the replacement?"

"It was delayed. It's due in Tobermory on Sunday. If we can get it to the island on Monday, we should be able to get it fitted and erect the turbine so that we can run the test on Tuesday."

Hannah suddenly felt very tired. He lowered his head and scrubbed his forehead with his fist. "Fine," he said. "Tuesday, but it can't be later than that."

"Relax," Jensen said. "It'll work."

Relax? Jensen had no idea. Hannah felt like telling him what it was like to juggle the elements of a project that was as complex and capricious as this one: there was the labour —all illegal—and the brutal Chinese gang-master who marshalled it; there was the hourly worry that someone would spot what they were doing on the island; there was making sure that Jensen had everything that he needed. Those were the *current* tasks, but they weren't the extent of his responsibilities. He was also responsible for securing the lease from the Crown Estate, and that was going to require some very careful politicking on Jimmy Bolton's part; Hannah had never *quite* conquered the fear that he had erred in appointing him over the other agencies who had pitched for the work.

He took out his wallet, put a twenty on the table to cover the bill, stood up and took his jacket from the back of the chair. "Tuesday," he told Jensen. "Tuesday and no more delays."

11

The eight-hour flight between Doha and Dublin stretched on interminably. Milton had booked a ticket in economy and, to his relief, had found that he had the row to himself. He had paid for an hour of the internet and, on checking his email, saw to his satisfaction that he had received a reply to his job application. A woman by the name of Chrissie O'Sullivan said that she would be pleased to meet him to discuss the role. Milton answered that he would arrive on Harris the day after tomorrow, and that he was looking forward to learning more.

He stretched out, ate a rather plasticky meal and then started to watch a movie. It was no good. The film was brainless and should have been distracting, but he was unable to quieten his mind. He hadn't thought of Flash for years, and now the prospect of visiting him had exhumed memories that he had buried.

He took off the cheap headphones and switched off the screen. It wasn't hard to remember what had happened in al-Majar al-Kabir, nor the guilt that he felt for his impetuous decision, one that had had consequences not just for those Iraqis responsible for the murders of the Redcaps, but also for the men who had bailed him out of the mess that he had caused.

Milton had driven into the town disguised as a redcap. He had located the house where Ayatollah Muhammad Abdelhossein was said to be hiding and, by chance, had seen him speaking to another man in the yard. Milton had left the car and closed in on him, shooting him twice in the torso and then once in the head. The second man had pulled a pistol, and Milton had downed him, too, and then the guard who had been roused by the muffled reports of the suppressed rounds. The three men had fallen in less than fifteen seconds, and, even if there had been any witnesses, Milton would have been able to effect his escape before they would have been able to do anything to stop him.

That should have been the end of it. Milton had made his way back to the car only to find that the engine would not start. He had tried again and again, with the same lack of success. Someone had raised the alarm and, before Milton could abandon the car and attempt to exfiltrate on foot, locals started to arrive. He had known that the odds of successfully fleeing the area without a vehicle were minimal; he had a decent amount of ammunition, but he knew he would eventually be outgunned.

With no other options, he had taken cover in Abdelhossein's house, barricading the door and firing a warning shot above the heads of the two men who were first to try to get inside. He remembered vividly how he had felt: there was satisfaction that he had delivered justice to the dead men, irritation for not checking that the car was reliable, and fear for the fate that he knew awaited him. He had seen the picture of the local elder who had been murdered and hung upside down from the bridge into town. That was how he would meet his end, too.

A mob of thirty or forty locals had formed around the property. Milton fired out of the window to keep them back, but he knew he could only delay the moment that they stormed the building. He would have contacted the base for backup, but had foolishly left his satphone in the car. The mob started to throw stones and bricks and anything else they could lay their hands on, the missiles smashing the windows and thudding into the rooms inside. Milton heard the rattle of the door at the rear of the property and fired through it, a scream of pain confirming that the bullet had found its mark. Two men tried the front door at the same time, and Milton fired on them, too, watching through the gap at the foot of the door as their feet went left and right, one man on either side of the entrance as they waited to try again. A Molotov cocktail sailed through the smashed window and shattered over the floor, burning petrol spilling across the cheap furniture and starting fires that Milton had no chance of extinguishing. Another followed, and then another. They were going to try to burn him out.

Milton knew he was finished and, not prepared to be captured and paraded on TV, had put his service pistol against his temple and started to squeeze the trigger. He would have pulled it, too, were it not for the loud rumble that he heard over the jeers and yells from the mob. He recognised it at once: Warriors. The Quick Reaction Force had arrived just in time to save his arse. He risked a glance through the window and saw a pair of Warriors come to a stop; their turrets swivelled so that their 30mm cannons and 7.62mm chain guns were pointing at the crowd. Two more

Warriors halted behind them and, as Milton watched, the rear doors opened to allow their complements of infantry to deploy. Milton realised with a jolt that this was not the camp's standing QRF when he saw Chimney, Sullivan, Cilla, Greenslade, Cameron and Flash bundle out of the back of the nearest vehicle.

They fired into the air, forcing the crowd back. Milton took his chance, hurrying to the door and yelling that he was inside. Flash called back, and, with the men covering him, Milton exited the building and retreated to the safety of the waiting Warrior. The convoy had retreated, small-arms fire rattling off the armour and Molotovs spilling their burning fuel over them.

Milton remembered the way that Flash had looked at him: he was furious, but, beneath it, Milton knew he understood. They all did.

Milton was brought out of his reverie by the clink and clatter of the drinks trolley. "Can I get you a drink, sir?" said the steward.

"No, thanks," Milton said. "I'm fine."

There were always going to be consequences for what Milton had done that afternoon, but they had not been as he had expected. There was discipline, but not for him; Flash was court-martialled for disobeying a lawful command. Milton, on the other hand, had eventually been approached by Control and recruited to Group Fifteen. The incident had been discussed at length during the selection process, and Milton had learned, much later, that his ruthless cold-bloodedness had trumped his disobedience. Control told him that he had seen something of himself in Milton and that that had been the decisive factor in his decision to recruit him. Milton had been excited at the time, but, with the benefit of hindsight, what he had done in al-Majar al-Kabir had led to adverse consequences for both him and Flash. Milton had never apologised to him for that; this was a rare example of someone to whom he could admit his error and seek to make amends, and, while it would have been going too far to say that he looked forward to it, the opportunity was one that he intended to take.

12

Caesar was excited. His snatched moments with Jimmy had become fewer as Jimmy's career encroached on their lives, and he had felt his boyfriend pulling away from him over the course of the last few months. There had always been a reluctance to meet in public places, but lately it had become much worse. Jimmy had refused to have even the slightest physical contact in hotel bars or restaurants, and then, when that wasn't insulation enough, he had said that he wasn't comfortable being seen out with him at all. Caesar decided it was a combination of grandiosity and paranoia: Glasgow took no notice of him, Edinburgh had never even *heard* of him, yet Jimmy was convinced that the career that he had built could come crashing down around his ears in an instant if people found out that he was queer. They had argued the last time they had seen each other, and Jimmy had promised Caesar that it would be different this time.

Caesar had booked a room in the Blythswood Square Hotel. It was near to Glasgow city centre, just a short walk from Sauchiehall Street, and was about as nice a place as could be booked here. Caesar was going to suggest that they go for a meal and then out to a pub, with the—probably—vain hope that he could persuade Jimmy to end up at the Riding Room or Katie's Bar or one of the other bars in Merchant City.

Caesar was fixing his hair in the bathroom when he heard a knock at the door.

"Hold on."

He hurried across to the full-length mirror to check his reflection and, satisfied that he looked good, went to open the door.

Jimmy was standing in the corridor. His suit was dishevelled, and he looked tired.

"Look at the state of you," Caesar said, reaching out to smooth out the jacket.

Jimmy brushed Caesar's hand away. "Leave off." He came into the room, closing the door with his heel.

"What's up?" Caesar said.

Jimmy shook his head. "I've had a *bitch* of a day."

Caesar stopped him with his hands on his shoulders and reached in to kiss him; Jimmy turned and offered him his cheek instead of his lips.

"What?"

"I told you—*awful* day."

Jimmy crossed the room and sat on the bed, prising off his left shoe and then his right. He flopped back onto the mattress and then raised his head and squinted across the room.

"What's that you're wearing?"

Caesar bristled. "What?"

"Nothing," Jimmy said.

He probably realised it was not the most politic thing to say, but it was too late, as usual.

"You don't like what I'm wearing?"

"I didn't mean that. I like it."

"Bollocks. You think the shirt's a bit gay, and the trousers are a *total* giveaway."

"No, Caesar. I don't think that. Stop overreacting. I just wondered where you'd got it."

"*Bullshit*. You think I look too gay to be seen walking around with because you're too scared to tell anyone you're queer. And that's *my* fault, so *I* need to dress like a farmer—just like *you* do."

Jimmy sat up and patted the bed next to him. "You're being melodramatic. Come and sit down here."

Caesar put his hand on his hip and looked down at him with as much disdain as he could muster. "'*Melodramatic*'?"

"I'm sorry. I'm tired and we've got off on the wrong foot. It's my fault. Can we start again? Come and give me a cuddle."

Caesar pouted, then relented and sat down on the edge of the bed. "Are we going out?"

"Can't we just get room service and have a night in?"

"No, Jimmy. I want to go out and dance. Restaurant, pub, club. I want to get drunk."

"I'm *destroyed*," Jimmy groaned.

Caesar got up. "When was the last time we went out together?"

"We're together all the time."

"In the closet."

"What's that supposed to mean?"

"In, in, in. The only time we're actually seen together in public is when we're out of the bloody country."

"Don't start."

"Nothing's ever going to change, is it? I'm just supposed

to help you get to where you want to get to, and then that'll be that."

"What does that mean?"

"I dress you. I advise you. I talk through your options with you. There's about a million things I'd rather do."

"Then don't do it."

"Right, then. Fine. Have it your way—I won't."

He grabbed his jacket from the back of the chair and put it on.

"What are you doing?" Jimmy said.

"Going out dancing."

Caesar knew that Jimmy would realise what that meant, and that it would make him jealous. Jimmy already knew little enough about Caesar's movements while he was away on the islands, and Caesar knew that he couldn't stand the thought of him flirting with other men.

"Come on," Jimmy wheedled. "I like you getting involved in business. Your advice is important to me. I'm serious."

Caesar knew he was being played. His boyfriend was pulling out a lobbyist's tricks, trying to make him feel special. "I don't believe you."

"It's true. You know I couldn't do it without you."

Caesar tilted his head to one side. "You need me?"

Jimmy sighed. "I need you."

Caesar decided to tease him a little. "So you'd like a little bit of information, then?"

"Always."

"Johnston Hannah."

"What about him?"

"You were pitching for his business, weren't you? The wind farm?"

"That's right."

"You might like this, then."

"Get to the point, Caesar."

"He's not going to be a very happy man. I heard that one of the rival bidders is going to be preferred. The Danes, I think. Or the Swedes. One of the Scandis, anyway."

"Who told you that?"

"A wee birdie."

"Stop being coy," he snapped. "Who was it?"

"What's got you so agitated? Ask nicely and I'll tell you."

Jimmy made an effort to smile. "I'm sorry. Please, Caesar, who told you that?"

"One of my regulars. A journalist."

"How reliable is she?"

"Usually pretty good. I've given you plenty of nuggets from her. Why? Is it relevant to you?"

Jimmy took a beat too long to answer. "Not directly," he said, "but it might be useful. Can you find out anything else?"

Caesar enjoyed having something that he wanted and decided to draw it out a little. "I could try. I scratch your back and you scratch mine?"

"What do you want?"

"Dinner at Cail Bruich would be a good place to start. And we can see where we go after that."

PART IV

FRIDAY

13

The catamaran sped across the Atlantic, with Ballycastle to stern and Islay ahead of it. The craft cut through the surf and spray blew back into the boat on the wind. The tang of the salt was fresh on Milton's lips, and he knew that it would work its way into his clothes and stay there until he washed them. He didn't care; it felt good. He sat back in the hard, uncomfortable chair and watched the gulls that wheeled around in the sky atop their wake. It had been a long two days of travel, but he had been under no illusions. Getting to the Hebrides would be a trek, and his devotion to anonymity made his route more scenic than it might otherwise have been.

He had landed in Dublin, spent a night at an old lady's bed and breakfast without being able to understand a single word she said, then got a lift with her son, who was headed north. Equally unintelligible, the man had yammered on endlessly all the way to Sligo, from where Milton had caught a bus to Enniskillen in the North. A pleasant night led to an unpleasant, stop-filled journey to Derry. He could have made the trip to Scotland from there, but, for the first time since Dublin, he knew that identification would be demanded. He was confident that the passport that had been put together for him in Bali was robust, but he preferred to cross the border into Scotland without leaving any digital footprints. Milton knew that Control was looking for him, and, in the event that Group Three had picked him up after his departure from Japan, he was keen to have his trail go cold. He doubted anyone would think to look for him on a windswept, Atlantic outpost.

Milton hitched to Ballycastle and booked a tour of the whisky distilleries on the island of Islay. The catamaran had departed the dock ninety minutes ago, and now they were on the final stretch of the voyage, with Port Ellen ahead of them.

The tour guide struggled along the pitching deck of the catamaran until he was alongside Milton. "You sure I can't tempt you?" He held out a small paper cup in his left hand and a silver hip flask in the other. "Islay whisky. Very peaty."

"I'm fine," Milton said with a smile.

It was the third time the man had been by to tempt him with what he described as a 'wee dram.' He evidently found Milton's refusals perplexing. "Really?" he said, not quite ready to give up. "It's a good one."

"It's kind of you to offer, but, really, no, thanks."

"What's up?" said the man in the seat immediately behind Milton, his accent drawn out by the alcohol. "Do you not drink or something?"

"Used to," Milton replied.

"But not now?"

"That's right."

The guide looked bemused. "So why did you book on a tour of the distilleries?"

"I'm interested in how they make the whisky," he said. "The process. I'm in the process of setting up my own distillery in England."

"A distiller who doesn't drink?" the man behind him said with a splutter of indignation.

"My wife's the expert when it comes to tasting," Milton explained. "I'm all about the logistics."

The guide nodded his understanding, told Milton he hoped he was inspired by the tour, and retreated to the rear where the other members of the party did not share Milton's reticence. They started to sing. Milton was pleased that they did not press him to join in with that, either.

THEY DISEMBARKED AT PORT ELLEN, the men staggering away to the Laphroaig distillery. Milton followed for a while, falling back to the rear of the group. Then, when he was confident that he would be able to slip away without being noticed, he ducked into a hotel for a coffee and booked a taxi to take him across the island to the tiny airport. He went to the desk and bought the tickets he would need to complete his journey. He needed two connecting flights: one from Glasgow to Benbecula and another from Benbecula to Stornoway.

The flight to Glasgow was due to depart in fifteen minutes. He hurried through the relaxed security onto the tarmac, climbed into the twin-propellor plane and took a seat at the window. They took off, passing over the Sound of Islay and cutting between Islay and the rugged, rocky outcrop of Jura, the Paps of Jura mountains rising up to the right as they passed by. Milton looked down to watch a pod of porpoises below, cutting through the surf with effortless grace and ease.

Milton allowed himself to relax and enjoy the rest of the trip.

14

The final leg of the journey was by taxi, the driver picking Milton up at Stornoway airport and then following the single-track road that skirted the coastline of the Isle of Harris. Luskentyre appeared out of the sea mist after an hour: a place with a job on offer and evidently a lot of sheep. The area was gradually revealed as they drove: the gentle hills, the crescents of pure white sand that made for some of the best beaches in the world, the craggy coastline. The Atlantic swallowed the island on all sides, a deep blue that—to the west—stretched all the way to Canada.

"You can drop me here," Milton told the driver.

He felt like stretching his legs and walking the rest of the way. He waited for the taxi to disappear back in the direction from which it had arrived and listened. He could hear no other traffic. He breathed in deeply, the stress leaving him as he exhaled. There was an attraction to this kind of silence; he found peace in the Rooms, but he knew he would be able to find it—deeper, perhaps—here, too. His modus operandi of late had been to busy himself beyond thought, to work so hard that there was room for nothing else. Crowding out the phantoms of his past life with labour and then stifling the ghosts with exhaustion had brought some success, but he knew he was just treading water. Maybe this would offer a more effective balm. And if it did not? He could always return to the noise and mania of South America or somewhere else.

Milton followed the road. There were no signposts, but then they were almost irrelevant with so little choice in terms of destination. Two cyclists whirred by, no other traffic beside them save a herd of sheep that ambled across the tarmac ahead. Two cows wandered over to a post-and-rail fence, but largely ignored him as their attention was taken by grass that hadn't yet been eaten. He kept going and, fifteen minutes later, dropped his rucksack and stared at what he hoped might be his new workplace.

THE HARRIS HOTEL AND RESTAURANT was painted on an old sheet of timber and hung on a dry-stone wall. The building beyond was large, with two wings, four tall chimney stacks and a large single-storey extension that looked to have been added recently. It was painted mostly in white with black tiles. An agricultural building was to the left of the building, a long barn with a corrugated iron roof that was also painted white. There was a wooden gate in the wall, and the approach to the entrance was made by way of a gravelled track. Beyond the building Milton could see that more construction had been taking place; there were piles of concrete blocks, and he could just make out the end of a static caravan around the edge of the gable wall.

Milton pushed the gate and walked down the path. The extension was ahead, its leaded windows covered with black paper that had been fixed to the inside. The front door was locked. Milton rapped his fist against the glass.

He heard footsteps and then a voice. "Can I help you?"

It was a woman; Irish, he thought, not Scots.

"I'm the chef. I applied for the job. You emailed me yesterday."

"You're English." It was a statement, not a question.

"I just arrived from Ireland, actually."

"But you're English."

"Is that a problem?"

"Go round the back," she said. "I can't get the bloody door open."

Milton lifted his bag and made his way around the property. The evidence of construction was much more apparent here. There was a small digger, piles of material and a second pile of blackened debris that looked as if it had been burned at one point or another. The caravan was there, together with an identical one that Milton hadn't been able to see, and, beyond them, a short garden led to a wall before the terrain started to climb to a rocky outcrop.

Milton was pensive. He hadn't expected a fanfare, but he had a sinking feeling that the reception might be tricky. The rear door to the building opened, and a stunning-looking woman in her late thirties stepped out to meet him.

She looked him up and down. "You've a good tan for having come from Ireland."

"I've been overseas."

"Have you now?" She squinted at him. "Doing what?"

"Cooking," Milton said, which was not, strictly, a lie. It *had* been hot in Okinawa.

"You said you were qualified?"

"No," he corrected. "I said I was experienced."

"No formal qualifications, then?"

"I'm self-taught."

She walked away, and Milton could think of nothing else to do but follow.

"Where's the kitchen?" he said.

"It's nearly finished," she said, leading him up the path toward the caravan. "And this is where you'll be staying."

"So I've got the job?"

"Probation until you've proven you're not all mouth and no trousers. I'm sure you said you were qualified."

"I could get the email for you if that would help."

"Never mind. Have a look at the van. Let me know if it's not good enough."

Milton looked at the caravan. It wasn't in good shape. One of the windows was cracked, and the other had lost its glass altogether, the space covered by what looked like a sheet of flimsy plastic. The door looked to be hanging off one hinge.

She watched his reaction. "Too rough for you?"

"Don't be so hard on yourself," Milton said with a smile.

He yanked back on the stiff door and left his potential employer outside with her mouth wide open.

15

The caravan was *very* basic: there was a deep pile carpet, mildewed at the edges; heavy velvet curtains covered the windows; the seats were adorned with a fanfare of flowers that, once colourful, had long been faded by the sunlight; there was a hob with two burners and a grill above it; a small fridge; a toilet that might charitably be described as 'bucket and chuck it'; and a bed that could be fashioned from the bench seats. It was clean enough for his purposes, though, and would serve him as a base while he was here.

Milton left his rucksack and decided to go and find the woman so that he could introduce himself properly. He hopped down from the caravan and crossed the open space to the building. It was obvious that a very substantial rebuild had taken place. The roof was new, with fresh black tiles that glistened in the evening sun. The walls looked to have been newly laid, with new window frames and doors. Some of the fabric was older and, from the occasional black marks on the existing brick and beneath the eaves, Milton guessed that the building had been damaged by fire.

The door that the woman had used was open. Milton went through it and found himself in the kitchen. It was far from finished. There was a stainless-steel countertop standing on its side next to a half-assembled frame and no power sockets; the walls had been tracked with a first fix of wiring, but the cables stuck out of the junction boxes unattached. There was a fryer, a hotplate, four large sinks and an extractor hood, but beyond that... nothing.

"Not much to look at, aye?"

Milton turned to find a small man with a thin moustache standing in the doorway between the kitchen and what he imagined was the dining room.

"What happened here?" Milton said.

"She hasn't told you?"

"All I know is that the hotel was looking for a chef."

"And that's you, pal?"

"I was hoping it might be."

The man gestured with an arm. "There was a fire," he said. "Eighteen months ago. Started in here—chip pan. Burned down most of the hotel. The builders left two weeks ago."

Milton pointed to one of the rectangular holes in the plaster. "Without finishing?"

"Money ran out," the man said with a shrug. "I think she'll be wanting you to finish it. What's your name?"

"Eric," he said. "You?"

"Bobby."

"And what do you do?"

"I look after the bar. They finished that first, but it got messed up again last night."

"How?"

"Wee spot of bother. I'll show you."

Milton followed him through the door and found

himself behind a serving counter with a cash register and dishwasher crates full of glasses, bottles and plates. On the other side of the counter, a potentially cosy taproom had been wrecked.

"It's not normally like this," Bobby said.

"What happened?"

"Couple of the regulars had a wee tiff over a woman. Busted each other up."

"And where are they now?"

"Frankie McCauley buggered off home. Stewie Lyons is over there."

Bobby pointed. Milton saw a bundle on the far side of the room. "He's got a pulse?"

"Aye. He's okay—breathing and everything. He was just pished up and had a few bangs on the head. I left him to sleep it off."

Milton walked over to the man and leaned down to take a look. There was blood on his head, but it had dried.

"How long ago did all of this happen?"

"It was probably two o'clock this morning before all was said and done."

A door shut behind them. Milton turned to see the woman from before. "Jesus, Bobby," she said. "Stewie's *still* there?"

"Sorry, boss. I was just about to wake him up."

"Nice clientele," Milton said, smiling at the woman.

"It's not normally like that," she said defensively.

"That's what Bobby said."

"We just reopened, and things got a little... exuberant."

"That's one way to put it."

"Sure it's not too rough for you?"

"I think I'll manage. But I still don't know your name."

"Chrissie. And you're Eric."

"I am."

"Hello, Eric." That appeared to be the extent of the pleasantries as far as she was concerned. "It's just the electrics to do in the kitchen. Colin McSweeney is coming over to finish off. You can help him."

Chrissie folded her arms and moved to the side. Milton slid through to the kitchen.

"Get him up and out of here," he heard her say to Bobby.

"I will."

"And if you let *anything* like that happen again, you can catch the next ferry."

The door swung closed, and Milton ignored the rest of the muffled conversation. He found a toolbox on the floor and set about bolting the countertop together. Music started in the bar, and, eventually, he heard groaning and then an angry commotion. He put down the screwdriver and returned to find the man was *much* larger when upright than he had appeared on the floor. Bobby was trying to show him to the door, and, apparently, he hadn't taken kindly to it.

"Come on, Stewie. Calm down."

The man growled and jabbed a finger at Chrissie. Milton couldn't make out what he was saying, but he could tell it wasn't pleasant.

"Just get the hell *out*," Chrissie shouted.

The man bellowed something at her, his bloodied face revealing a gash above his eye. Milton raised the hatch in the counter and stepped out. The man saw him and, immediately assessing him as the most dangerous of the trio, turned to face him.

Bobby pulled Chrissie back; she shook him off.

"Get out, Stewie!" she yelled at the man. *"Now!"*

The man leered, took a step toward her and raised his fist. Milton grabbed Bobby by the shoulder and yanked him backwards, then stepped in front of Chrissie. The man squared up to him and threw a wild haymaker. Milton ducked beneath it and, as the man was unbalanced, kicked into his knee from the side, collapsing the joint and crashing him down to the stone floor. Milton backed away, hoping that might be enough for his opponent to realise that it would be wise to stay down. He did not and, instead, staggered back to his feet. He favoured his good leg as he fired out another wild slash, missing by a mile as Milton dodged out of the way. Milton stepped back into range and threw a hook into the man's midriff. He doubled over, winded, and Milton brought his knee up so that it cracked into the side of his head. Lyons's eyes rolled back into his head and—just moments after regaining consciousness—he was back on the floor again, staring up at the lights.

"That's just bloody brilliant," Chrissie moaned. "We get him on his feet for the first time in twelve hours and you knock him out again."

"You're welcome," said Milton.

She faced up to him. "Get this straight, sunshine. I'm not some helpless wee girl needs some Brit to come in and wave his dick around. I'd have got that eejit out the door handy enough if you'd just stuck to your kitchen. Right?"

Milton looked at her, thought again how pretty she was, and shrugged. "You won't mind dragging him outside yourself, then," he said, making his way back to the kitchen to continue with putting the counters together.

"What did you say you were again?" she called after him.

"I'm a cook."

"And I'm the Queen of Sheba," she muttered.

16

Milton looked around his rudimentary accommodation. The place smelt about as fresh as a boot locker. He had slept in far worse, but he set about clearing his quarters into the basic, functional, tidy arrangement that he preferred. He swabbed the walls, scraped the carpet with a dustpan and brush and cleaned out the single cupboard. He disinfected the basin with bleach he found in the kitchen and went outside to the outhouse toilet to flush it away.

"What's that?"

He turned to see Chrissie staring at the two bin liners of clutter that he had bagged up for disposal. She was standing on the step to the other caravan; he noted that hers had steps, while his required a leap akin to that of a long-haul lorry cab.

"Rubbish," he said. "You can have a look if you like—see if there's anything you want to keep."

"Good of you."

"Is yours the nicer of the two?"

"Are you still complaining?"

"Not at all. It'll do just fine."

She held a box of menthols in her left hand and clutched a lighter in her right. "Most men aren't so fussy. Do you need a pinny and some marigolds?"

"I think I'm done now."

Chrissie stepped down from her caravan, came over to his and leaned inside. "Very fragrant. Are all your fatigues perfectly pressed in the wardrobe?"

Milton noted the jab. She stared hard at him. He knew what she would be thinking: ex-military. She would be wondering if he had ever served in the Six Counties. The scrub of the caravan, the lack of personal possessions, the intolerance of clutter and his usefulness with his fists would have betrayed him. Still, he thought, the reaction taught him a lot about his new employer and gave him an idea of the subjects he would be wise to approach with care.

"Smoke?" she asked, thumbing a cigarette out of the pack.

"I'm all right."

"You into clean living?"

"How do you mean?"

"I mean do you abstain from fun stuff."

"Like what?"

She raised a suggestive eyebrow, then, as he smiled at her, hunted for a way out of the conversation that she had started. It was the first time that Milton had noticed her become unsure of herself.

"Drink, drugs, fags," she said. "What are your vices?"

"I don't drink. I don't do drugs. I *do* smoke, but I'm not a fan of menthols."

"Suit yourself."

She put the cigarette to her lips and lit it.

Milton nodded to the hotel. "It's nice."

"It is now," she said. "Ten bedrooms, all en-suite. The restaurant ought to be nice if the chef can be trusted."

"He can," Milton said. "Who are you catering to?"

"The guests? Tourists. You've got the beach just over the way, and we're offering trips out to the islands—the Flannans and St. Kilda and the like—for those who want to go and see the birds."

"Whales?"

"Aye," she said, "and dolphins, too. You're pretty much guaranteed to see them. We bought a boat so we could do it all ourselves. It's tied up in Tarbert at the moment on account of the fact that we don't have anyone to drive it. I don't suppose you'd know how to do that?"

There it was again: she'd definitely pegged him as ex-military. "Not really my thing," he said. "I think you'd rather I concentrate on the kitchen. What about grouse?"

"We're looking to offer that. Got the gear; just need to work out how best to go about it."

She drew down on the cigarette and, for a moment, there was contented silence.

He nodded at the building. "When was the fire?"

"Eighteen months ago. I'd only moved in the week before—worst luck ever. We were planning the reopening, and then we almost lost everything. Bobby tell you what happened?"

"Chip pan fire."

She snorted. "Did he tell you who left it on the hob?"

"He didn't."

"Not surprising. I probably should've let him go after that, but I didn't have the heart. He's mostly useless, but he's been here a long time, and no one else is going to give him a job."

"Is it yours? The business, I mean? You said 'we' nearly lost everything."

She looked pained for a moment. "I've got an interest in it, but it's not mine."

Milton could see from her reaction that that was one of the subjects he would be best to avoid. "You've done a good job with the rebuild. And it's in a beautiful spot. When are you planning on opening?"

"When can you have the kitchen ready?"

"A day or two," Milton said. "It looks worse than it is."

"That'll work." She sucked on her cigarette, exhaled and looked at him through the haze of smoke. "You carry on with your cleaning. So long as you can fix up the kitchen and cook, that's all I need to know."

PART V

SATURDAY

17

Jimmy snored like a hog. Caesar had long since given up shoving and poking him. He had thrown books and shoes at him at the start of their relationship, and nothing made a blind bit of difference. Jimmy had complained that it was a genetic affliction. Caesar had pleaded with him to see a doctor. Jimmy had said no and told him if he didn't like it, then he should sleep somewhere else. There had been row after row after row. Caesar realised now that the snoring was symptomatic of so much that was wrong about how things were.

It was all on Jimmy's terms.

Talk of work was confined to *Jimmy's* problems, *Jimmy's* connivances, *Jimmy's* lofty ideals of what his career might entail. The expensive retainers, the glamorous clients, the important work, the wealth, the lavish house in the Highlands with a swimming pool... they were all *his*. There would be a sauna and steam room for Caesar, Jimmy had promised, stroking his boyfriend's eyebrow, before the snorting and grunting began anew.

Caesar had tried to rationalise it: the suggestion that the

house might have some of the things he wanted had been the first indication of a commitment despite Caesar having to wrestle it out of him. Was it *likely*, though? Jimmy was always banging on about his plans to build: the career, the home, his profile. He'd explained that he wanted to be the hero of the islands; the wee lad made good who'd had petals thrown down on the path before him every time he went home. But he never did ask about the salon, about the complications of running a business in difficult economic times, about the problems that Caesar faced with staff.

Caesar's sleeplessness mutated into irritability and then, finally, into anger. He elbowed Jimmy in the ribs.

"What is it?" he mumbled.

"Wake up. It's late."

Jimmy rolled over and covered his head with his pillow.

"Wake up."

"Why?"

"There's something I want to talk to you about."

"What?" Jimmy replied, his voice muffled by the pillow.

"I had someone from immigration in the salon yesterday."

Nothing.

"Did you not hear me? *Jimmy?* I thought I was about to get arrested."

Jimmy took the pillow away and looked across the bed to him. "Why?"

"They were in to take away one of my staff."

"Why?"

"She was a foreigner."

"*Please* say she had her papers."

"They asked for them."

"And what did you say?"

"I said I didn't have any. She said she had experience, so I gave her a chair."

"No, Caesar. You didn't do that. Please tell me you're winding me up."

"Aye," he said. "I did. She was good. I got her to do a demo, and then I gave her a chair."

"What about national insurance?"

"She wasn't even there a month. What's the problem? It's not like they arrested *me* or anything."

"What's the *problem?* Do you realise how that could impact on me?"

"How it could impact on *you?* What about me?"

"Here we go again," Jimmy muttered.

"I'm serious. How would it possibly have any impact on a man who doesn't even want to be seen in public with me?"

"How stupid are you, Caesar?"

"Excuse me?"

"I work in politics. The papers would love it if they found out."

"You're a lobbyist, Jimmy. You grease the wheels. The papers wouldn't give a fiddler's fondle about a relationship they couldn't prove even if they wanted to."

"Piss off, you sad little queen."

Jimmy rolled out of bed and crossed to the bathroom. He shut and locked the door and, moments later, Caesar heard the sound of the shower. Caesar got up, too, and went to the table. He was hungry and flipped through the room service menu to see if there was anything that tempted him for breakfast. Nothing. He put the menu down and looked at Jimmy's bag. He pulled the zip and reached in to pull out a sheaf of paper. The top sheet bore an emboldened title: HANNAH ENTERPRISES. He flipped the first page and found a subheading: SCOTWIND OFFSHORE WIND LEASING ROUND.

His heart began to race a little. He thought of what Alexandra had told him about Johnston Hannah and his plans for another wind farm. He flicked through the pages. There was a lot of technical information that might have been written in Dutch for all the sense he could make of it: kilowatt hours, capacity, blade speed, gearing, transmission. He flicked through to the end and then turned the document over. He recognised Jimmy's handwriting on the reverse. He had noted down a series of names—Dayton, McCloud, Rowley, Taggart, Barney—and then crossed them through and added, after each, a sum of money.

One name had not been crossed out: Watson.

Caesar didn't know anyone with that name.

The shower was turned off, and Jimmy came to the door of the bathroom and opened it a crack. "I'm sorry," he called out. "You're right. That was insensitive."

There was something else in the bag. Caesar reached inside again and took out a thick wad of cash. He looked at the note on the top of the bundle. It was a fifty. He turned the wad on its side and riffled the edge. There had to be a hundred notes there. Five grand? More? He reached into the bag again and took out another wad and then another. Fifteen thousand? What did Jimmy have fifteen thousand quid in cash doing in his bag?

"Caesar?" Jimmy called out. "I'm sorry."

Caesar looked at the thick wedges of money laid out on the bed.

"I shouldn't have said that," Jimmy said. "I'm a total dick."

"Aye," he said. "You shouldn't have. And you are."

"I'm starving," Jimmy replied, as if the argument and the

slur were forgotten. "You want breakfast? Let's splash out and have it in the room. Get the menu—order whatever you want."

Caesar closed his eyes and felt the anger drain out of him. It was the final straw. He had told Jimmy what he wanted—a normal relationship, not a clandestine fling—and Jimmy seemed set against giving it to him. Caesar was calm, thinking about the money on the bed. He knew what it was for and what it could do for him.

"Breakfast in the room, then?" Jimmy called. "That okay? Can you order me the fruit pancakes?"

Caesar reached for his phone, opened the voice recorder and set it to record. He turned the phone upside down so that the screen was hidden. "That's fine," he said. "Are you busy today?"

"Very. The diary's packed."

"With what?"

"Have to do some advocacy for a bloke to bring some business up home. Potentially a lot of jobs. A few meetings to grease the wheels. That kind of thing."

"What wheels?"

"The usual," he said, irritatingly vague. "Getting the players onside. Never you mind about it. It's politics. It's all about scratching backs."

Caesar didn't bristle at the deflection, not this time. He had decided that the two of them were through and, now that he had reached that conclusion, Caesar was going to make Jimmy pay for the months Caesar had wasted while he waited for Jimmy to do what he always should have done.

Jimmy opened the door of the bathroom and towelled himself dry.

Caesar sat up and gestured to the money. "What's all this cash for?"

"What? You've been going through my bag?"

"There's a lot here. Fifteen thousand? What's it for, Jimmy?"

Caesar could see the way Jimmy's mind worked: there was confusion at first, then anger at being discovered, then desperation as he tried to find an excuse that would allow him to explain it all away.

"That's none of your business."

"You've been bribing people." He phrased it as a statement, not a question, and underlined his conviction by brandishing the list of names. "You've been paying people off, haven't you?"

Jimmy crossed the room and swiped the paper. "You're so *naïve*. You have no idea how the world works."

"This is for scratching backs, is it? Greasing the wheels?"

"Don't look so outraged. This kind of thing happens all the time. It's how you get things done."

"Isn't bribery illegal?"

He snorted. "It's only bribery if you get caught."

Caesar had all he needed now; he could allow himself the pleasure of sticking the knife in. "I thought you were a lobbyist. You're not, though, are you? You're just Johnston Hannah's bagman."

Jimmy went back into the bathroom and ran a tap. Caesar reached for the TV remote, switching on the breakfast news. Jimmy came out of the bathroom and went to the pile of clothes that he had discarded on the chair last night. He pulled on his socks and trousers and began to button up his shirt. Caesar stared at the TV, refusing even to look at him. Jimmy finished tying his laces. He took his jacket and put it on.

"I think this has run its course, don't you?"

Caesar said nothing.

"Can you pass me my bag?"

"Get it yourself."

"Petulant little queen."

He picked up the bag, made his way to the door, opened it and then turned back. He was about to say something else when a room service trolley arrived. Jimmy pushed past the member of staff, his head down, and disappeared down the corridor.

Caesar reached for his phone, ended the recording and then played it back to make sure that he had what he needed.

He did.

Now he just had to decide how best to twist the knife.

18

The electrician was a man called Colin McSweeney, and he arrived just after eleven with a roll-up dangling between his lips. He tossed the cigarette aside and got to work on the electrics, whistling tunelessly to himself as he installed the control box and then wired in the empty plug sockets and lights. Milton attempted to make conversation, but was quickly rebuffed by the monosyllabic responses that he received. He took the hint and got on with finishing the set-up and testing the appliances as the power was connected.

It took Milton all day to get everything ready, but, once he was finished, he took satisfaction from what he had done. He had worked in enough kitchens over the years to know how best to prepare his *mise en place*. He repositioned the workspaces, allowing him to slide used tools from the chopping station into the basin. He allocated separate areas for vegetable and meat preparation, put the deep fryer near the meat section and the space for fish prep closer to the waste bin to make it easier to get rid of the waste.

Chrissie observed his progress without comment. Milton could not tell whether she approved or not, but worked to the assumption that she was vocal enough to pipe up if she was unhappy. He sensed an almost grudging appreciation of his skills, but she had yet to taste anything that he had made.

The bar had been curiously quiet. Milton had quickly come to the conclusion that Bobby was far from the shiniest button in the box. He was lazy, too, and Milton had decided that he would have him earn the salary that he presumed he was getting from Chrissie and put him to work. Bobby had bristled at first—the idea of taking direction from the new boy had obviously been unwelcome—but Milton just fixed him with his dead-eyed stare, and any resentment that Bobby might have felt just melted away. Milton had a way about him—years of military discipline, both taking it and handing it out, had seeped into him over the years—and people tended to do what he asked. Once Bobby had realised that Milton was *telling* him and not just *asking*, things had settled down nicely. Milton had him wiping and mopping, cleaning the shelves for the drinks and cutting logs for the fire in the bar. Bobby quickly grew accustomed to the new regime, to the point at which he even asked Milton what he would like him to do next.

Chrissie drove around the island in her old van, striking deals—at least that was what she said—with local businesses for vegetables, privately butchered meat and freshly caught fish. She left Milton with lists of the ingredients that he was likely to receive on any given day, and seemed to adopt a frosty contentedness with progress until he posed the obvious question.

"When can we expect some customers?"

"When will you be ready, Gordon Ramsay?"

Milton looked around at the newly finished kitchen. "I'm ready now if you can get the supplies in."

"Right, then. We'll open tonight. I'll spread the word, and we'll see how good your cooking is."

19

Milton used a metal rod with a fork on the end that was shaped like a snake's tongue to skewer every last morsel of white flesh from the crab he had just boiled. The small pile of meat paled in comparison to the effort required to extract it, but cooking shellfish was not new to him, and he enjoyed the labour. He had seared and sealed the haddock, some of which he had set up in a rudimentary smoker outside. Chrissie had watched silently as he had worked under his own initiative with Bobby deputed to act as his sous-chef when business in the bar was quiet.

The reopening was tonight, and Chrissie had made no attempt to hide her anxiety. She had fretted and worried all day, checking that Milton had everything he needed, questioning his qualifications for a crowd that included local dignitaries, checking the bar was ready and then returning to the kitchen to start the interrogation all over again. Bobby had taken a bicycle and had spent the afternoon circumnavigating the island and sticking flyers on lampposts and tree trunks and shoving them through the letterboxes of the locals. There was a Facebook group for the island, and Chrissie had posted the announcement of the grand reopening there, too.

The publicity drive seemed to have paid off. Milton heard the hubbub as the guests began to arrive and, putting his head through the door into the bar, noted the effort Chrissie was making in order to make everyone welcome. He had not experienced the same hospitality or warmth from her; now, she was all hugs and air kisses and shimmering welcomes while wearing a sparkly dress with heels. Milton had wondered how she had managed to get from her caravan to the restaurant without sinking the stilettos into the soft ground. Perhaps Bobby had offered her a piggyback.

Milton had prepared a simple menu for the evening. There was seafood chowder, homemade crab cakes and slaw, pan-fried scallops, a homemade chunky fishfinger, fish goujons and seaweed roast potatoes. He had kept it as simple as he could, since it would just be him in the kitchen when it really mattered. Bobby was busy in the bar, and Chrissie was welcoming the customers. Milton had concluded that there was no point in asking Chrissie to pay for another pair of hands to help, so he had done his best to make sure he would be able to manage.

A teenage girl from Tarbert had been recruited as waitress, and, with sweat beading on her brow, she began delivering the tickets to the kitchen. Milton struggled to decipher her writing at first, but now, after thirty minutes of the service, he had an idea what she meant. He insisted that she wipe the perspiration from her hands before she carried anything through to the dining room; she had dropped two plates already, and only the hubbub from the other room and Milton's swift work with the sweeping brush had concealed her clumsiness from Chrissie.

She backed into the kitchen now, knocking the door open with her backside and handing three more tickets to Milton. He looked at them: two scallops, two crab cakes, two chowders.

"On it," he called out.

TWENTY-FIVE COVERS later and with a sink full of plates and bowls, Chrissie shimmied in with a rare smile. "Seems you *can* cook," she said. "Why don't you come out to the bar for a moment and take a little bit of credit."

He gestured to the washing-up. "I don't need that. I'd rather get stuck into this."

"I'll send Bobby."

Milton could see that she was a little drunk, her lips coloured red by her choice of wine. "I'm fine. It's really not necessary."

"Ah c'mon," she insisted. "Bobby! *Bobby!* Come in here."

"Really," Milton protested. "It's not my thing..."

Bobby appeared, flustered and obviously under pressure.

Milton spoke to him firmly: "Back to the bar. False alarm."

Bobby, confused—it was practically his default setting—was turning when Chrissie stepped over and grabbed his arm.

"Bobby—washing up. Eric—bar. *Now.*"

She flicked her hand, directing each of her staff in opposite directions. Milton relented for fear of making a scene and led the way into the bar. He emerged into the cosy lounge, and the guests turned to him and began to applaud. Milton could not have felt more uncomfortable. His whites were stained, his brow was damp from the heat of the kitchen, and attention had always been something that he fought hard to avoid.

Chrissie poured a glass of something sparkling and pushed it into his hand.

"No, thanks."

"Just the one glass," she said and turned to the assembled gathering. "Our chef—Eric. Not bad, even if he is English." There came a rumble of polite laughter and more applause. Chrissie waited for the hubbub to die down. "I want to thank you all for coming. As you know, the last year has been difficult. The fire was devastating, and the rebuild has been a struggle for almost the whole time. I would've given up if it weren't for the love and support that's been shown to me by everyone here and the others on the island. I just wanted to mark the occasion by telling you all that I'm grateful, and I couldn't have done it without you."

One of the men at the front of the room stood and raised his glass. "Three cheers for Chrissie," he said. "Hip hip!"

The others joined in with him. Milton turned to look at Chrissie and saw that she was blushing and that her eyes were damp. She had put up an impressive front, but it was obvious to everyone now that the hotel, and the work that she had undertaken to bring it to this point, had been a labour of love.

The second cheer rang out as the front door opened. Milton was watching Chrissie and saw a flash of something in her eyes. Her face darkened, and she immediately ignored the final toast and made her way quickly back to the kitchen. Milton gazed through the small crowd at the newcomer. The man who was standing in the doorway looked as if he might have been there all evening. He was dressed in a tweed suit, and Milton assumed that he had just been outside for a smoke. He lifted a menu and gave it a long look, then made his way to the bar.

He cocked a finger to bring Milton over to him. "What Malbecs do you have?"

"Let me get the barman for you," Milton said, turning to the swing door.

"You're the chef?"

"That's right."

"And you don't know the wine list?"

Milton paused, but decided against replying for fear of spoiling the evening. He carried on through the door and saw that Chrissie wasn't there. Bobby was busy with the dishes.

"Someone for you at the bar."

"Can't you?"

"Better if you take care of him," Milton said. "He's got an attitude, and I don't want to lose my rag with him."

Milton tossed a dishcloth over so that Bobby could wipe the suds from his hands and held the door open for him. He rolled up his sleeves, went to the sink and started on one of the pans that he had used to make the sauce. He looked out the window and saw the burning tip of a cigarette in the space that separated the back of the kitchen from the caravans. It flared, casting a little extra light on Chrissie's face as she inhaled.

Milton was still scrubbing the pot when he heard a pop. The lights went out—all of them, all at once—and he heard drunken cheers from the bar. He opened the door and saw that the lights were out there, too.

"What happened?" Bobby said.

"Something's tripped the board."

The room was lit by the flashlights from phones held up by the guests.

"I told her not to use Colin," Bobby said. "I *told* her, and she told me to mind my business."

"He didn't strike me as the best electrician I've ever seen."

"He's pissed most of the time, and the rest of the time he's just incompetent. God knows what mess he's made of it."

"I'll have a look," Milton said.

PART VI

SUNDAY

20

Milton woke at five in the morning, pulled back the scabby curtain and wiped away the thick layer of condensation on the window. It didn't make the view any clearer. He dressed and opened the door, then leaned out. It wasn't condensation; it was fog. He couldn't even see as far as the outhouse, such was the thickness of the mist that had descended overnight.

He had looked at the circuit box last night, but had been unable to find the fault. The main RCD had been tripped, and it flipped back and broke the circuit again as soon as he reset it. There was evidently a problem with the work that the electrician had done yesterday in the kitchen, but Milton knew it would be a fool's errand to try to diagnose the fault in the dark. Chrissie had agreed and phoned McSweeney, telling him that unless he came around to fix it first thing in the morning, she would not be held responsible for what she did to him. He lived on Skye and promised that he would be on the first ferry.

Chrissie had told Milton that everything would be sorted, but that he would need to go to the docks for fresh fish. He took out his phone and selected the map. There were ten miles between Luskentyre and Tarbert, and Chrissie had said that Milton could take her van. The Volkswagen Caddy Cargo had evidently been used during the rebuild despite the refrigeration unit that she had installed in the back for the food that she collected from the wholesaler. Milton swept the stones and wood shavings out of the back and then went to the front of the vehicle and patted the dirty carpet until his fingers brushed against the keys. He lowered himself into the driver's seat, started the engine and pulled out. He had rarely seen such thick fog, and he picked his way down the narrow road with caution.

He reached Tarbert and followed the road to the dock. He parked the van in an empty car park, listening to the mournful boom of a foghorn from somewhere on the headland nearby. The pier had a handrail splitting the fishermen's quay from the commercial ferry walkway; it served as a useful guide into the whiteout as Milton strained to see the industry that he could hear. He followed the quay with his hand on the rail until he could make out a small fishing boat that was unloading pots and fish boxes.

"Morning," Milton called out.

"Hello," replied a cheery voice. "Can I help you?"

"I'm from the hotel at Luskentyre."

"Aye," said a chubby-faced, dark-haired man in his twenties. "Chrissie said someone would be down. Surprised you still came, mind, in all this."

"It was a bit of an adventure," Milton admitted. "At least the roads are quiet."

"Heard you opened again last night."

"That's right."

"How was it?"

"Good—until the electricity went out. The electrician did a poor job from the looks of things. He's supposed to be coming over to fix it today."

"She used Colin McSweeney, didn't she?"

"That's right."

"He won't be over today, then. The ferries have all been cancelled. They won't come out in this."

"Right," Milton said. "I doubt I need to get any fish, then."

"We'll be here tomorrow, same time."

Milton made to move off, then stopped as a thought struck him. "Can I ask you a question?"

"Aye."

"Do you live on Harris?"

"All my life. Why?"

"I'm looking for someone. I think he was out here a few weeks ago. I know it's a long shot, but would you look at a photo?"

"No problem."

Milton took the photograph that Judith-Ann had given him of her son and handed it to the fisherman.

"Don't recognise him," he said. "Let me show my old man." He turned to the boat and called down, "Here—Dad. Look at this photo."

An older man with a thick white beard and rheumy eyes clambered up the ladder to the quay and took the photograph. He looked at it and shook his head. "Never seen him before. Who is he?"

"Alan Caine," Milton said. "He went missing a month or so ago."

"Sorry," the man said. "Can't help you."

"Thanks for looking." Milton took the photograph again. He was about to turn when he thought of something else. "I'm sorry to be a pest—can I ask you something else?"

The younger man nodded.

"A friend of mine came to Harris fifteen years ago," Milton said. "Might even be a bit longer than that. Connor Gordon. Big bloke with red hair and a temper. He was going to set up a business here the last I heard from him."

The younger man chuckled. "Sounds like Flash."

Milton looked at the fisherman with surprise. "That's right. Do you know him?"

"*Everyone* knows him," the older man said. "He's a hothead, especially when he's had too much to drink. He has a business out on the water—you can book him to take you out to see the whales."

"Do you know where I can find him?"

"He used to have a bothy here," the older man said, "but I haven't seen him for a while. I heard he moved to Mull."

The younger man scratched his head. "Isn't his office in Tobermory?"

"Aye," the older man said with a nod. "Keeps his boats in the harbour there, too. Meets the tourists straight off the ferry and away they go."

Milton frowned with frustration. He wanted to get started with his search for Alan Caine, and had planned to find Flash first to take advantage of his local knowledge. It looked as if he wouldn't be needed in the kitchen until the electricity was fixed, but there was no way to get over to Mull until the weather improved and the ferry started again.

The older man flicked the dog-end of his roll-up into the water. "You want to head over there now?"

"Sorry?"

"We're heading south around Skye and the Small Isles to

check some pots. We could give you a ride to Mull and then bring you back at first light tomorrow."

"I'll have to check with my boss. When are you casting off?"

"About an hour. We won't wait, though. Make sure you're here by then if you want to come."

MILTON FOLLOWED the road back around the island to Luskentyre. He parked the van and made his way over to Chrissie's caravan. The curtains were still drawn. He knocked on the door.

"This'd better be important, Bobby."

"It's Eric."

"Oh. What do you want?"

"The ferry's cancelled. The fog's too thick."

"You woke me up to tell me that?"

"The forecast has it here all day. The electrician won't be able to get over."

"Shit," she groaned.

"We'll be closed, then?"

"Can't very well run a restaurant with no power, can we?"

"No," he said. "In that case, could you do without me until tomorrow?"

"You get a day off. Take it today if you want."

"Thanks. I just wanted to check it was all right."

"You'll not be paid."

"Of course. I'm going to go to Mull if you need anything."

"You said the ferry was cancelled."

"A couple of fishermen said they'd take me."

"Do whatever you want," she said. "Leave the van for me,

though. There's an old motorbike in the barn. The key's in the ignition. Take that."

"Thanks. I'll see you tomorrow morning."

There was no reply. She must have hit the bottle hard last night, Milton thought. He left her to it.

21

Milton went into the barn at the back of the hotel and found the motorcycle that Chrissie had told him he could borrow. The key was in the ignition, just as Chrissie had promised, and there was a helmet resting on the seat. Milton put it on, straddled the bike and started the engine. It vibrated from left to right and back again and sounded to be in reasonable condition. He opened the throttle and brought the bike out of the barn, resting it on its stand as he went back to close the doors. He thought he saw the curtains twitch in Chrissie's window as he straddled the bike again and set off.

THE FOG HAD LIFTED a little by the time that he returned to the dock, and it allowed him a better view. The quay accommodated a number of fishing boats that had been tied up to metal mooring hoops, lobster pots stacked in their bilges and rope coiled neatly in their bows. Milton left the bike in the car park and made his way back to the two fishermen to whom he had spoken earlier. They were just getting ready to cast off.

"You're back," the younger one called up to him. "Jump down."

Milton did, reaching out to brace himself against the side of the trawler's wheelhouse.

"Welcome aboard the *Working Girl*," the man said.

Milton rapped his knuckles against the gunwale. "That's her name?"

"Aye. My dad's been taking her out for the last twenty-five years. She's never let us down once."

"Let's hope that continues," Milton said.

"What's your name?"

"Eric."

"I'm Will McCullum," the man said, putting out a hand. "And that's my dad. Dougie."

The old man was coiling rope in the bottom of the boat. He stood and shook Milton's hand. "Welcome aboard," he said.

"How much do I owe you for the fuel?"

"Don't worry about it."

"Really? I don't mind paying."

"You can help out. Not shy of a bit of hard work?"

"Not at all."

The old man winked. "We'll see."

THE *WORKING GIRL* sailed out of Tarbert and turned south, following the coastline until they reached Leverburgh and then turning again into the open sea that lay between Harris and Skye. Dougie and Will had put on orange and yellow oilskins, and they had found another set for Milton in the below-deck storage cupboard. The boat's engine chugged happily, pushing them forward with enough speed to cut through the gentle waves and sending spray back onto the deck. The fog had continued to lift a little, and visibility was up to a hundred feet or so. Harris had been visible when they were close to shore, but now it had quickly faded away into the grey.

Will came out of the wheelhouse, bracing himself against the structure as he made his way to Milton.

"You okay?"

"Fine," Milton said.

"Not seasick?"

"Not yet."

Will smiled. "We'll see. It's due to be choppier on the way back."

Milton gestured to the water. "What are you after?"

"Langoustine and lobster mostly. They live in burrows in the mud at the bottom. We bait the creels with herring and tempt them out. The smaller ones can get out through the netting mesh, and we bring up the big ones."

A gull kept pace with them just above the deck. There was a box full of herring scraps that they would use to bait the pots, and Will took a piece and held it out in a gloved hand. The gull descended, expertly navigating the stiff breeze until it was close enough to take the fish before climbing steeply above them.

Dougie put his head out of the doorway and called out, "You ready?"

"Aye," Will shouted back.

"What are we doing?" Milton said.

"Shooting the pots. I'll show you."

Will went back to check the lobster creels stacked at the

stern of the boat. He checked that they were securely tied together with two orange buoys at the end.

"Mind your feet on the lines," he warned.

The first pot was thrown into the water, and the rest were dragged after it, sliding up a ramp and disappearing over the stern, pursued by the next and then the next. The pots shot out at ferocious speed along the flat floor of the small boat, each of them separated by three or four metres of line. Milton could see why Dougie and Will kept repeating their warnings to be careful; if a coil of rope snared a leg, the man attached to it would be overboard and underwater before he could do anything about it. He would be drowned within seconds.

The last pot plunged beneath the surface, and the two buoys followed, floating on the top and marking the location of the pots below.

"How long do you leave them out?" Milton asked.

"They'll stay down today, and we'll pick them up on the way back."

"Is that it?" Milton said.

"No," Will replied. "We've got some to pick up before we get to Mull."

22

Caesar leafed through his appointments diary, ignoring the chatter between the beauticians and their customers and the noise of the nail driers.

It had been a dreadful morning. He had allowed his anger with Jimmy to fester and, even though he knew it was unhealthy and he would be much better advised to forget all about him and just move on, he *couldn't*. He was not used to being snubbed, especially by the likes of *him*. The more he thought about it, the more annoyed with himself he became; why had he allowed himself to be put in a position where he could be rejected in the first place? That made him angrier, which made him question himself all over again. It was a vicious circle—a doom loop—and it was all because of Jimmy.

He wasn't going to stand for it. He looked at the names and phone numbers in the diary and ran his forefinger down the page until he found the entry that he had been looking for. The idea had come to him the moment he had seen the money inside Jimmy's bag, and he hadn't been able to get it out of his head ever since. Jimmy needed to know that Caesar was not some little fancy piece to be used and then thrown aside. There were consequences for bad behaviour. He would teach him to behave with respect.

He punched the number into the salon phone and waited for the call to connect.

"This is Alexandra Marshall from STV," the recorded message said. "I can't answer now, but please leave a message, and I'll get back to you as soon as I can."

"Alexandra," he said, "it's Caesar from Caesar's Palace nail and beauty salon. I've got something I think you might be interested in. Give me a buzz. I think you'll be interested. Maybe we could get a glass of something to talk it over?"

23

Dougie had opened up the throttle after they had deposited the empty creels, and they had cruised for four hours before he cut the engines. The *Working Girl* slowed to a lazy drift, and, as Milton went forward, he saw a red buoy bobbing in the waves ahead of them.

He pointed. "That's yours?"

"Aye," Dougie said. "This is where it gets harder."

Milton looked out over the sea: there were islands to both port and starboard. "Where are we?"

Dougie pointed to an island on the port side of the boat. "That's the Isle of Eigg," he said. He pointed to starboard. "And that's the Isle of Muck."

The scenery was stunning. Milton stood, hands on hips, and took it all in. He saw waterfalls, green rolling hills from which the cloud seemed to tumble, and the remote settlements where he knew the pace of life would be dictated absolutely by the weather. Dougie waited until the *Working Girl* was closer to the buoy and then used a pole with a grapple on the end to snag the line and pull it in. Will reached down and brought the buoy up, unclipped the line and fastened it to a drum that was, in turn, connected to a winch.

"What do we do?" Milton asked.

"Haul them up, bring them on deck, empty them, stack them. Once we're finished, we'll send them down again."

They set to work. Dougie operated the winch, and the rope was yanked up and out of the water. The first pot broke the surface and struck the side of the boat. Dougie stopped the winch so that his son could haul the pot over the side and onto the deck. The rope was unfastened, and the creel was opened up. There were two lobsters inside. Will reached in for the smaller of the two. He measured it with a ruler and shook his head.

"Too small?" Milton called out.

"Yep. A little fellow like this one can go back in. We'll see him another day."

He tossed the lobster over the side, then reached in for the second. This one was much bigger. Will said that he was a keeper and there was no need to measure. He took two small elastic bands from a box on the deck and used them to secure the lobster's pincers. He dropped it into a large tray and dragged the pot to the back of the boat.

"Your turn," Dougie called to Milton.

The old man powered up the winch again, and the next pot on the line broke the surface. Milton reached over the side, snagged the mesh with his fingers and pulled it up. Milton unlatched the door and reached inside, grabbing the shellfish around the carapace. The long antennae swept across the back of his hand as he held it up. It, too, was large. Will secured the pincers, and Milton dropped it into the tray.

It was three o'clock in the afternoon—eight hours after they had set out—when Dougie announced their destination was on the port bow. They had landed one thousand pounds worth of crustaceans, and they needed to get them onto the dock to be sold. Milton had been glad of the workout. He had used muscles that no kitchen work or hike over an island could exercise, and was ready for a hot drink and a long soak in a bath. He had enjoyed the haul and hurl of the lobster creels as pot after pot was retrieved, emptied, rebaited and returned to the seabed, but he was feeling it now.

Tobermory, when it revealed itself through the fog, reminded Milton of a children's poster painting. The colours of the buildings were vibrant, and the bay before it was crammed with the masts and rigging of fishing and commercial boats. It was the stuff of holiday postcards, all set beneath a glowering brow of dense, towering forest. Dougie steered the boat to the stone pier and tossed up a mooring rope to a man who tied it to a bollard.

"You'll feel at home here," Will said.

"Why?"

"Everyone's English," he said, with a wry smile. "They're taking over the place."

"Do you know where I'll be able to find Flash?"

"You haven't been here before?"

"Never."

"There's a chandlery and a branch of the Clydesdale Bank. The Mull Museum is between them, and I think he has one of the rooms above it."

They iced the catch and, with Will on the pier and Dougie and Milton on the deck, they transferred all of the crates. Milton climbed the wrought-iron ladder, accepting

Will's hand as he reached the top. Dougie followed and fished his cigarettes from the inside of his waterproof jacket. The old man offered one to Milton, and he accepted.

Milton put the cigarette to his lips and lit it from the old man's lighter. "What time will you set off tomorrow?"

"Four in the morning," Dougie said. "So not too many pints tonight, all right? We'll pull up and replace the pots again and have you back in Harris by lunchtime."

"Where's the best place to stay?"

"Och, you'll be spoiled for choice. Come off the pier and take a left. You've got guest houses all the way along."

"The Tobermory Hotel's nice, too," Will said.

"Aye," his father agreed, "but you'll need a shilling or two to stay there. It's not cheap."

Milton drew down on the cigarette and exhaled. "Thanks," he said. "I'll see you tomorrow."

Dougie looked at his watch. "If Flash's not in his office, he'll be boozing. Try the MacDonald Arms. Down the street and on the right."

"Thanks."

"Good luck. Fingers crossed he's in a good mood."

24

Milton walked down Main Street until he found the Mull Museum. There was a door next to it that looked to offer access to the rooms above. A notice on the door advertised OUTER HEBRIDES ADVENTURES. Milton tried the door, but it was locked. He cupped his hand over the glass and peered inside. A flight of stairs ascended to the first floor, and at its foot there was a pile of post. Either Flash had become sloppy in the years since Milton had known him, or he hadn't been here for a while.

He went to the pub that Dougie had suggested. The MacDonald Arms was a simple building, the walls painted blue with the window frames and door painted in white. It was open, but, as Milton glanced into the taproom, he couldn't see Flash. He waited for a moment in the event that he might be in the bathroom, but there was no sign of him.

He came outside again and stepped around a car that had pulled up with two kayaks—one red and one yellow—strapped to its roof. He decided to scout the small town, and climbed a ramp that ascended the hill that backed onto the main street. Argyle Terrace, running atop the cliff, was home to a line of two-storey houses, their gardens on the other side of the road. The hill continued to ascend beyond the houses, quickly cloaked by the thick wood that Milton had seen from the *Working Girl*. Milton followed the road north until he found a vantage point that looked down on the marina. He looked down, wondering where to begin. A man was working on the pontoons below, wheeling a barrow over the floating timber walkway to load a large rigid inflatable vessel tied up to the outside spit. The man was big in comparison to the others around him. Milton couldn't see his face, but he knew him straight away. He was sure it was Flash.

Milton followed a steep road down the side of the hill to the quay. Flash had moved on by the time he arrived, but he was easy enough to spot. He was making his way around the seafront, heading in the direction of the pub that Milton had just visited. Milton followed at a leisurely pace, keeping a good distance between them so he could observe without being spotted himself. Flash turned into the pub, and Milton picked up his pace. By the time Milton arrived, Flash was at the counter, waiting to be served.

Milton found that he was nervous. It had been a long time since the two of them had seen each other, and they hadn't parted on the best of terms.

He took a breath and stepped a little nearer. "Hello, sir."

The big man turned around slowly. *"Milton?"*

"Fancy seeing you here."

The barman looked up, concerned. His gaze landed first on Milton, then Flash.

"It's okay," Milton said to him with a smile. "We're old friends."

Flash stared at him. "Is that right?"

"Good to see you, too."

"What are you doing here?"

"Just passing through."

"Really? This is a coincidence?"

"No. I thought I'd try to find you. You told me that you were going to come home. You know... after..."

Flash held his eye. "After they binned me?"

"Yes," Milton said, seeing that time hadn't healed all of the wounds that had been inflicted in the dusty street outside Muhammad Abdelhossein's hideaway.

"I don't believe you," Flash said.

"You don't believe what?"

"This isn't a social call."

Milton was confused. "Why else would I be here?"

Flash snorted with bitter laughter. "Please," he said. "Don't treat me like a fool."

Milton was perplexed. There was no handshake and no hug; Flash just stared at him. Milton could tell that Flash had been drinking—he could smell the alcohol coming off him—but having a few in the tank didn't explain the suspicious way that Flash looked at him, or why he seemed to think Milton was here because of some agenda.

The big man was still staring at him. "Get it over with, Milton. Say what you've got to say and then piss off. I'm not done for the day yet."

"Can I get you a drink?"

Flash still seemed baffled. "Why?"

"For old times," Milton said patiently. "You still drink Guinness?"

"Aye," Flash replied.

"Go and find a table, then. I'll get a round in."

Flash walked over to the empty table in the window. Milton watched, remembering the time they had served together. He hadn't been expecting a fulsome welcome, but this awkwardness had taken him by surprise. Milton had always suspected that Flash resented the fact that Milton's career had been allowed to continue; he knew, too, that Flash blamed him for his own career coming to an end. It wasn't an unreasonable position to take. Milton had hoped that time might have repaired some of the damage, but now he questioned his judgement. Maybe not.

"What'll you have?" the barman said.

"A pint of Guinness for my friend," Milton said. "And a coffee for me."

25

Milton and Flash sat in the bay window of the pub. They had a view of Tobermory Harbour, beautiful in the early evening sun.

Flash took a sip of his Guinness. "This is pretty ripe," he said. "Even for them."

Milton had no idea what he meant, but decided the only thing to do was play along. "What is?"

"Sending you. What is it—they don't think I'll follow it through, so they send someone who knows me?" He sipped his pint. "I heard the rumours. Seems they were right."

"What rumours? What are you talking about?"

"That you went on to more interesting things."

Milton shifted uncomfortably. "After the Regiment? I can't—"

"Don't worry," Flash interrupted. "You can't tell me about it—I know the drill. National security and all that bollocks. Look—you can fuck off back to London and tell them that they didn't need to send you. It's not necessary. I'm too far into this mess to back out of it now. I'm up to my neck in shit. I just hope it's worth it."

Milton had served with plenty of men who had chips on their shoulders, but he had never pegged Flash as one of them. He guessed that life after the Regiment had not been generous to him, and could see how that might lead to melancholy and bitterness. There were reasons for Flash's antipathy; after all, he had paid a heavy price for saving Milton's life. But he appeared to be ascribing a motive for Milton's visit that made no sense.

Milton fixed him with a steady stare. "I don't know what you're talking about. I'm not here on behalf of anyone else. I'm here to look for a young lad who went missing a few weeks ago. You told me that you were going to settle in the Islands once you got out. I remembered what you said, so I asked around and found you."

Flash stared at him; Milton could see that he was reassessing, perhaps considering whether or not he should trust him. He looked away, winced—in embarrassment, perhaps—then shook his head. "Whatever."

Milton was curious what had caused Flash to react the way he had, but there was no profit in delving into that now. It seemed like a chance to start the conversation anew.

"What have you been doing with yourself?"

"Since they binned me?"

Milton nodded.

"You said you'd been asking around."

"You take people out to see the whales."

"Aye," he said.

Milton grimaced; the conversation was like pulling teeth. He sipped at his coffee as Flash drank down half of the Guinness.

There was an awkward silence before Flash spoke again. "What's with the coffee? I'm not good enough to share a beer with?"

"I don't drink," Milton said.

Flash scoffed. "Bullshit. You used to be the only one who could keep up with me."

"I liked it a little too much," Milton said.

"You counting tokens or what?"

He nodded. "That's right."

"I've an old pal over in Oban, he's like a fucking slot machine. He craves them wee coins. Nearly twenty years he has. Never stops telling me about it, like I should slap him on the back every time he has an orange juice instead of a proper drink." He finished his Guinness and pointed to the bar. "You sure?"

"I'm fine."

Flash got to his feet and crossed the room. Milton watched him as he bantered with the barmaid. Milton didn't like talking about his addiction outside the Rooms, and, in this instance, he was left with the very firm impression that Flash would not understand. Flash had always been a heavy drinker, and Milton could see from the ruddy cheeks and the bloodshot eyes that the intervening years had not seen a reduction in his appetite. Milton was not minded to diagnose others, but he had always seen plenty of his own vulnerabilities in Flash and wouldn't have been surprised if they shared the same affliction. Flash, though, would not have appreciated the suggestion.

Flash returned with a bottle of Famous Grouse and a tumbler. He put both on the table. He laid a finger against the bottle. "I told her it'd save me the hardship of getting up and down if she just gave it to me. One of the benefits of people thinking you're a cripple."

He opened the bottle and poured a shot.

"I might be here for a few weeks," Milton said. "I've found a job on Harris."

"Aye? Doing what?"

"I'm a cook."

"Get away. I remember you destroying field rations."

"I've been practising since then," Milton replied, hopeful that a little of the old regimental banter might return. "I even got a round of applause last night."

"Where on Harris?"

"At the hotel next to Luskentyre beach."

"Chrissie O'Sullivan's place? I heard that burned down."

"It's been refurbished. It opened again last night."

Flash knocked back his tumbler and poured again. "Look, pal, you can say that you're a cook and maybe some people will believe it, but I wasn't born yesterday. Give me a bloody break. I mean—look at you. You didn't get that tan in Scotland."

"No, I didn't. I was in Okinawa."

"And you just *happened* to come to the Western Isles?"

"I told you," Milton said. "I'm looking for a missing man."

Flash drank again. Milton doubted it had even touched the sides. Flash was a huge man, but four doubles in short order were having their effect. "Be straight with me, Milton."

"I *am* being straight."

"You joined the spooks, didn't you?"

Milton shook his head. "Come on. Even if that *were* true, you know I wouldn't be able to talk about it."

Flash snorted. "I'm not as patient as I used to be. Tell me the truth or piss off."

"I met an old woman in Japan. She's dying. She wants to know where her son is before she goes."

Flash's eyes were deadening with the effects of the drink. "And who's he?"

"A human rights campaigner. He went missing in the islands."

Flash's forehead creased, his cheeks reddening a little. "Where?" he asked.

"One of the Hebrides."

Flash replied a little too rapidly for Milton's liking. "Which one?"

"He was last seen on Harris. Did you hear anything about it?"

"Not a dickie bird," Flash said, his voice slurred.

"I could do with some help from someone with local knowledge. I was hoping that you might be able to point me in the right direction."

"Too busy. Find someone else."

His tone was becoming abrasive, fuelled by the drams or his memories from before, and Milton decided that meeting had been a bad idea. Flash was either unwilling or unable to help, and seeing him again had not been what he had hoped.

Milton got up. "It's been good to see you. Take care of yourself."

He offered his hand. Flash shook it and, without saying another word, poured himself another drink and looked out through the window to the early evening lights that sparkled around the pretty harbour.

MILTON MADE his way to the Tobermory Hotel. It was on Main Street and appeared to have been converted from a terrace of fishermen's cottages. He went to the front door and paused, turning to look at the view. The bay was opposite, and, with the tide out, a stretch of muddy foreshore had been exposed. Small boats rested on the mud, waiting for the high tide to float them once again. The headland rose on the right and left, with the multicoloured façades of the buildings along the quay still bright even in the dusk.

He had been up for hours and was exhausted; he hoped that they had a room. The conversation with Flash had unsettled him. Time had not been kind to his old squadron commander, and some of the things that he had said—or implied—had made no sense. He tried to put it out of his mind. He smelled of salt and sweat and needed a bath, a long soak in hot water, enough to scrub himself clean and soothe the aches and pains of age.

26

The offices of the Crown Estate Scotland were on Simpson Loan in Edinburgh. Jimmy Bolton knew the city well, especially this part of the city, and had suggested a familiar curry house as the venue for his meeting with Jack Watson. The Chaskaa Indian was on the western side of the Meadows, and Jimmy took the opportunity to walk there so that he could clear his head. He followed North Meadow Walk and stopped at the Prince Albert Sundial, looking at the lights in the windows of the tall tenements that faced the green space and settling his tactics for the meeting so that he would appear as natural as possible. Watson was a difficult operator, and his support was essential; Jimmy knew that there would be serious problems if he took a position against the plan.

The last few days' work had been challenging. Part of the problem was that Hannah's plans spanned more than one council area. That had necessitated trips to Stornoway, Balivanich and Castlebay. Jimmy had been working on the councillors individually for weeks, buttering them up when he could, threatening them when he couldn't, and bribing them when all else failed.

It had gone to plan so far. The list of names on the back of the project prospectus had mostly been struck through. The councillors were on board, and the inhabitants of the islands had been amped up by the promise of thousands of jobs and cheap electricity, all delivered by a local company rather than faceless corporations from Scandinavia. But those successes, while important, would mean nothing without Watson's backing. Jimmy knew he was going to have to be at his absolute best.

He took a deep breath, brushed a hand down the lapels of his bespoke suit, and continued on his way.

WATSON WAS ALREADY SEATED at a table at the back of the restaurant. Jimmy had asked for that particular table; it was away from the door and the windows, and they were unlikely to be observed there. Given that the conversation had the potential to be difficult, that was a good thing. Jimmy gave the waiter his coat and crossed the quiet room to the table.

"Jack," he said with his biggest smile.

Watson looked up, but didn't stand. "Jimmy, nice to see you."

"I'm not late, am I?"

"No. I'm just a little early."

Jimmy offered his hand and, although Watson took it, he didn't smile. He had always been a stone in Jimmy's shoe. He was in his sixties, wizened and with skin that had been blasted dry by his first career as a captain on the ferries, and had built up a reputation as a recalcitrant bastard.

The waiter pulled the chair out, and Jimmy sat down.

"Would you like to order drinks?" the waiter asked.

Jimmy handed the wine list to Watson. "What'll you have, Jack?"

"Nothing for me."

Jimmy made sure to keep the smile on his face, doing all he could to stay nice and relaxed. Watson had always been a cold fish, but there was a froideur here that was a real cause for concern. Jimmy got the impression that Watson had come against his better judgement; Jimmy was going to need to proceed carefully. He ordered a bottle of Kingfisher together with poppadoms and pickles and waited for the waiter to make his way to the bar before opening the conversation.

"Thanks for coming to see me, Jack."

"I'm only here because I knew your father."

"I know. And I do appreciate it."

"How is he?"

Jimmy found as pleasant a smile as he could. "He's plodding on."

"I heard he had a heart attack."

"Had several."

"It'll take more than that to get rid of him. He always was as tough as old boots."

The fact was, Jimmy would have been pleased if one of those emergencies had carried the old bastard off. Jock Bolton was a traditional—meaning bigoted—old bawbag who had made Jimmy's life a living hell ever since he had come out to him and his mother twenty years earlier. There had been nasty little digs about never having grandkids, about how he had no idea how a hard Highland upbringing could lead to a result like *that*, and he made no effort to hide the fact that he now considered Jimmy's sister, Ruth, to be his favourite. Jimmy was self-aware enough to know that one of the things that motivated him—perhaps the thing that drove him most of all—was the desire to prove his father wrong. Jock had told him, even as a boy, that he wouldn't amount to much and, now that he was a 'poof'—his word—he was even more sure of that. Jimmy would show him. Money wasn't the most important thing in his life, but it was as good a way as any to keep score.

"So," Jimmy said, "did you have a chance to look through the proposal?"

"Aye," Watson said. "I did."

"And?"

"What do you want me to say? It's decent."

Jimmy kept smiling, the effort causing the muscles in his cheeks to ache. "What does that mean?"

"Everyone knows those areas west of the islands are probably the best spots in the world to build a wind farm. It stands to reason that sites with all that going for them are going to be fought over, and that's exactly what's happening here."

"How many bids have you had?"

Watson smiled indulgently. "Now then, Jimmy, you know I can't tell you that. It's a sealed process. That's confidential."

"Can you give me any idea at all?"

"The biggest companies in the world are involved. The Danes, the Americans, the Germans, the English. They all want a piece of it. Mr. Hannah has his hat in the ring, just like the others. We'll decide whether his bid matches up with the competition when we assess them."

"When will that be?"

"Soon."

The waiter returned with Jimmy's beer, two plates and a

tray that was stacked with poppadoms and chutneys. It was a useful pause; Jimmy had known that Watson would be a tough sell, but his reticence—and the implicit suggestion that Jimmy should be careful with how much harder he pushed—was troubling. Hannah had made it very, very clear; he had to get a positive answer from the Crown Estate. Jimmy had sold his relationship with Watson as a benefit when he had pitched Hannah for the contract to promote the scheme; he had oversold their closeness, but he had needed the business, and he didn't think he would have secured it without suggesting that he could pull levers that were impossible for others.

He couldn't afford to fail now.

The waiter took their orders and went back to the kitchen.

"Look, Jack—can I speak freely?"

"Aye."

"The bid from Hannah might not be the biggest, but it needs to be given equal consideration to the others. It's local, for a start. Local money and local people behind it."

"Local money? Really? I don't think it'll breach any confidences if I tell you that the source of the funding will be a key question. Mr. Hannah is a rich man. We know that. By the standards of the Highlands, he's as rich as Croesus. But that's just by local standards. The other bids are backed by vast corporations with practically unlimited funding. How's Hannah going to manage if it's found that the cost of installing the wind farms is more expensive than we thought?"

"There are contingencies in place."

"Where's the money coming from? It's not all his, is it?"

"It's a consortium."

"Go on. Who's involved?"

"That's confidential."

"Aye. Well, if the only thing you get to take back to Mr. Hannah after tonight's dinner is that he'll need to be a lot clearer about that sort of thing, then I'd say it would've been worth however much you're charging him to break bread with me."

Jimmy glanced away quickly, then down at the poppadoms and their luminous chutneys. He had hoped that he would be able to persuade Watson of the good sense in backing Hannah's bid by dint of personality, but that was always going to be a stretch. He was going to have to resort to older, grubbier tactics.

"How else could we improve the odds that the bid is preferred?"

"What do you mean?"

"What could I do so that you'd recommend it to go forward?"

He shook his head. "I'm not following."

He was going to make him say it. "Look—I think we can both agree that there's a big PR win in having the lease awarded to a regional company. A good Highlands company employing local men and women. I've got a budget to promote the bid. Serious money. How much would it take to make you part of the team?"

Watson nibbled a poppadom, then brushed the crumbs away from the corner of his mouth. He stared at Jimmy and held his eye as he said, in a quiet voice, "A hundred."

Jimmy swallowed. Hannah had only authorised him to go up to twenty-five.

"Seventy-five?"

Watson shook his head. "Got to be a hundred, Jimmy."

Jimmy had told Hannah that it might cost more, but he

hadn't budged. Jimmy ran the sums in his head. If he could bring Hannah up to seventy-five, he could fund the balance from the two hundred that Hannah had agreed to pay him once the bid had been preferred.

"Fine," he said. "One hundred. But it's contingent on getting the bid over the line."

Watson gazed at Jimmy without so much as a flicker, and Jimmy knew that he had made a serious misjudgement.

"You should be ashamed of yourself. My God."

Jimmy smiled and held up his hands. "Come on, Jack. Don't pretend that this is the first time you've taken money for doing the right thing."

Watson shook his head, pushed his chair back and stood. "If your father knew what you've become, it'd break his heart. You can't buy me. I'm paid to protect Scottish interests, to make sure that the people we do business with are the right sorts who'll share our visions and goals. Tonight has been disappointing on many levels, but at least it's not been a total waste. I know now, for sure, that Hannah is not concerned about playing by the rules, and that, beyond all doubt, tells me that working with him would not be the right thing to do."

"Have you even looked at the proposal?" Jimmy said, desperately clutching at straws. "It'll bring jobs to the area. Thousands of jobs and cheap, clean energy that'll make us the envy of the country. I don't see how anyone could possibly object to that."

"If the proposal is as good as you say, then buying influence would not have been necessary, would it?"

"I'm not trying to buy influence," he protested. "I'm just trying to make sure that the bid is given the consideration it deserves. Look—"

"No," Watson said, "*you* look. I know what you've been

doing, and you won't buy me like you've bought up the local councillors. You're not the first to try, and you'll not be the last, but you won't be changing my mind. I can't be bought. Now—I've lost my appetite. Goodnight."

Watson swiped his jacket from the back of his chair and made his way to the door.

27

Across town, Caesar took off his coat and scanned the bar for Alexandra. She was sitting in a booth at the side of the room and looked fabulous. The high table afforded her the opportunity to show her ankles to the suits and boots gathered at the bar. Caesar approached with a broad smile, administered three air kisses and took the stool opposite her.

There was a bottle of pink bubbles wedged into an ice bucket at her side, and she tapped a finger against the neck. "Want a glass?"

"Yes, please."

She poured as they chatted about the men at the bar, his business, her hair and outfit. She made a show of how pleased she was to see him, and how she was happy to treat him to the bubbles, but Caesar was too wise to take it all *that* seriously. The booze would be expensed, and she was only here because he had tempted her with the prospect of a scoop.

She brought the small talk to an end. "So? What's this juicy gossip you wanted to tell me about?"

He leaned closer and lowered his voice to a conspiratorial whisper. "What if I were to tell you that there's a man in the West Highlands who's bribing councillors to get them on board with a project he's working on out on the islands?"

She shrugged. "I'd say it wasn't all that interesting."

"Seriously?"

"What's new about bribing councillors, Caesar? Doesn't that happen all the time?"

He worked to keep the smile on his face. "I'm surprised."

"Okay, I'll play along. Who's bribing them?"

"Jimmy Bolton."

"Never heard of him."

"He's a lobbyist."

"Still never heard of him. Should I have?"

"No, but..."

She shrugged. "Look, I'm sorry to break it to you, darling, but there's no way my editor is going to release me from the rota to look into something like that. You'd be better off going to one of the local rags. They'd probably have a look at it for you."

"And then *they* get the scoop. I thought you'd be all over something like this."

"It's just not all that sexy." She shrugged. "What can I say?"

Caesar had hoped to hold back some of his information in the hope of squeezing out a little more cash, but he could see that approach was not going to work. He was going to have to go all-in.

"What if I said the man Bolton was working for was a local hero?"

"Depends who it is."

"A businessman. A man with factories up and down the west coast. Employs hundreds of people."

"You have to tell me his name."

Caesar had quaffed two glasses by now, and he was desperate. "Johnston Hannah."

That brought her up short. "Really? Might be a little more interesting."

She was a good actress, but Caesar had learned how to read people after speaking to so many customers in the salon, and he could see that she was excited.

"He's funding the bribes, and Bolton's paying them. I told you I had a big fish for you."

"What about proof?"

"I've got a recording. I got Bolton to tell me about it."

"How'd you manage that? Do you know him?"

Caesar aimed a meaningful pout in her direction.

"*Oh*," she said. "You and he were..."

"In a relationship," Caesar finished. "Past tense. I don't give two shits about him now—he glides through life like he's the only person who matters. Fuck that, darling. Fuck *that*."

Alexandra finished her drink and set the flute back down on the table. "Does that mean you'll be interviewed for the piece?"

"Absolutely," he said. "Photos, too?"

"I should think so."

"Just give me plenty of notice," he said. "I'll want to look my best when I put the knife in."

"I'm sure we'll be able to do that," she said.

"I suppose you'd like to listen to it?"

"Do you have it with you?"

He took out his phone and laid it on the table. "I do."

PART VII

MONDAY

28

Flash woke on the bedroll on the floor of his office with a thick head, the taste of stale whisky in his mouth and the suspicion that he had behaved badly. It took a moment to connect the uneasy feeling to the facts, but gradually the conversation with Milton came back to him.

He had stayed in the bar after Milton had departed and had finished most of the rest of the whisky. His foul mood had deepened, and things had come to a head with the two lads on the opposite table, who he knew had been looking at him and making remarks at his expense. He'd shared a few abrasive words with them on the way out; they'd followed him into the street, and Flash thought he could remember cuffing them both. The scabbed blood on his knuckles confirmed that he had.

He cursed himself. His paranoia had got the better of him. *Again*. It had been a shock to see Milton after all these years. Could he be on the level? Was it really reasonable to think he'd come to find him with no agenda other than to ask for his help? Flash couldn't shake the suspicion that

Milton was here because of something else and that he had not treated him to the full truth. He screwed up his eyes and tried to remember what Milton had said about the missing man. How likely was that? What was a man like Milton—a *killer*—doing helping an old woman find her missing son? That didn't match with what Flash remembered of him. It didn't match at all.

He lay back and allowed the doubts to multiply. He thought of the cargo he had come to collect and wondered if that was why Milton was here: he'd come to check on him, to make sure that he followed through with what he had agreed to in the face of all the misery that he had seen.

The gear box. It still needed to be shipped a hundred miles west into the North Atlantic.

He got up, kneading his temples with his knuckles. He felt sick, and the forecast for a choppy sea was hardly auspicious. He went through to the bathroom and relieved himself. He looked in the cracked mirror and thought how old he looked, how beaten-up and knackered. Things had been different when he had served with Milton. He had been young, fit and strong. He allowed himself to wonder how things might have been different if it hadn't been for Milton's fuck-up and what it had cost to save his life. He wondered if he should mention the encounter to Chen, but then he worried that might be more trouble than it was worth.

And if what Milton had said about the missing man was true... well, Flash could think of a few men who had gone missing in the islands over the course of the last few months, but he found it difficult to draw a line between them and Milton. But if there *was* a line? Flash knew what Milton was capable of, and the thought of him nosing around in his business was cause for serious concern.

29

Alexandra dropped a pair of Nurofen tablets on her tongue and swallowed them down with what was left of her pint of water. She felt dreadful. She had stayed in the bar with Caesar all evening, and—as far as she could recall—they had worked their way through three bottles of fizz. *Three!* She had kept the booze coming in the hope that he might be persuaded to email her the recording that he had made of Jimmy Bolton's confession. They had both been drunk by the end of the evening, but, to her irritation, he had remained steadfast: she could have the recording, he said, and he would go on the record, just as soon as she had arranged a contract for the story. She had asked him how much he wanted, and he had told her that the figure would need to have five zeroes. She knew that she was going to have to corroborate some of what he had told her before she took it to her editor. He would just tell her to piss off if she went to him with what she had now.

A colleague had interviewed Johnston Hannah for a puff piece in the *Herald* not long before, and Alexandra called her to see if she could be persuaded to let her have his number. It took a little persuasion, and the promise of a night out at her expense, but she was successful. She tapped the number and waited for it to connect.

"Hello?"

"Who's this?"

"My name is Alexandra Marshall."

"Do I know you?"

"No, Mr. Hannah. We haven't spoken before. I'm a journalist."

"I see. What can I do for you?"

"I'm calling about the Scotwind project. I understand that you're involved with a consortium looking to get the lease?"

"I am," he said. "Are you writing about it?"

"That's right."

"Happy to help. What do you need?"

Hannah had a reputation for vanity, and she wasn't surprised that his first instinct was that her call was an opportunity to get his name in the papers.

"I'm just going to record the conversation—is that okay?"

"Of course," he said.

"That's great—thank you." She tapped the screen to record the call. "Okay—we're recording. I suppose I'm interested in the process that you're going through at the moment. Would I be right in thinking that you've employed a lobbyist to help?"

"We have. That's fairly standard, though. There's a lot of people you need to impress in a bid like this."

"His name is James Bolton, yes? From James Bolton Associates in Edinburgh?"

"That's right. Why are you interested in him? Like I said, there's nothing particularly unusual about it."

"I'm sure that's right," she said. "It's just that I spoke with someone who knows Mr. Bolton last night. He says he has evidence that Bolton has been bribing people to support your bid."

His denunciation was a little too automatic. "That's ridiculous."

"It's obviously a very serious allegation," she said.

"And complete rubbish."

"I wouldn't have brought this to you if I didn't have any evidence, but I do. I heard a recorded conversation with Mr. Bolton confessing that he's been paying large sums of money to local councillors on your behalf. Tens of thousands of pounds. I wanted to give you the chance to comment."

Hannah started to speak, then took a breath. Alexandra could imagine him trying to compose himself. "I think the best thing to do is to contact my press secretary. All I'll say now is that I don't know anything about that at all. Mr. Bolton is contracted to work on our bid, but he has a wide degree of latitude as to how he goes about his duties. If what you're saying is true—and I really can't comment on that either way—then it's obviously very serious, and you can be assured that I'll look into it right away."

"Could we meet? I'd like to talk to you about it in more detail."

"I'm afraid I'm tied up with the bid and my other businesses," he said. "But please do contact my press secretary—the details are on the website. I'd better leave it there for now—thanks for calling. Goodbye."

30

Milton hitched a ride back to Harris aboard the *Working Girl.* They shot creels off the coast of Mull and pulled up the ones that they had dropped near Leverburgh the day before during their outward voyage. They chugged into the harbour at Tarbert, and Milton felt obligated to at least offer to pay his share of the fuel. The older McCullum shook his head, said that Milton had worked more than hard enough for that to be unnecessary, and that they would be happy to offer him a place on the boat again if he needed to go anywhere else. Milton thanked them both and rode the bike back to the hotel.

He arrived in the early afternoon. Bobby was bashing around in the bar as Milton walked around the building to the caravans. As he rounded the gable of the hotel, he saw Chrissie standing with her back to him, facing a half-built wall. Beside her was a wheelbarrow filled with cement. She had laid four full courses on the wall of the terrace she was building. She had stopped work, and Milton could see that her shoulders were shaking. He cleared his throat.

She straightened up, her hand going to her face before she turned to him. "You came back, then," she said.

He could see that her eyes were wet from crying. "I did." He decided against asking her what was the matter. "Any joy with the electrics?"

She shook her head. "McSweeney let me down. He says he's booked up until next week, and he can't come out until then. I told him he needs to finish the jobs that he's already been paid for, but he wouldn't budge. I told him to do one. He won't be back. Bobby says he knows someone who can help, but they won't be here until tomorrow."

Milton nodded down at the wall. "You've been busy."

"Someone has to be. It's not going to build itself."

Milton looked at the pile of concrete blocks. He went over to them and picked up a trowel. He dipped it in the mix and spread it atop the blocks that she had already laid. He lifted a block from the pile and placed it gently in the cement. He lifted another block, sliced up the spillage and deposited it in the barrow, then knocked and bumped the block into position with the handle.

"What are you doing?"

"Giving you a hand," he said. "Your plumb line was a little off."

"Up yours," she said, although, for once, there was no heat there.

Milton needed to move along the wall to keep going, but Chrissie just stood in silence, blocking the way. He could feel her watching him. He flicked his hip gently to bump her along, still refusing to look into her face; she chuckled at him.

"Got any music?" he said, crouching down to collect another block.

"In the van."

She disappeared for five minutes and, when she returned, he saw that she had applied a little make-up. Her eyes were still puffy, but the interval had allowed her to recover her composure.

"How much do you reckon we could do before it gets dark?" she asked him as she picked up the spare trowel.

THEY WORKED on the wall until dusk. Chrissie connected her phone to a Bluetooth speaker and put herself in charge of the music. She had excellent taste—The Miracles, The Marvelettes, The Supremes—and Milton found he was enjoying himself. Building the wall was therapeutic, the music was good and, although neither of them said much, he was content in her company.

"We'd better stop," she said at last. "You can only lay so many courses before the weight starts squeezing the wet mortar out. The last thing I want is a wonky wall."

"Still got half an hour of light," Milton suggested. "Want me to start clearing the ground for the terrace?"

"Go on, then, Bob the Builder," she said. "You do that. I'll be back in a minute."

Milton lifted the shovel and began to turn over the hard earth. It looked as if rubble and debris had been dumped here at some point and then covered over with earth that had then, in turn, seen a growth of weeds. Milton drove the blade down, scooped out a load of rocks, and dumped them into the wheelbarrow. He turned back and dug down again, loosening a load of bricks that were still mortared together.

Chrissie came out of the kitchen door with two bottles of Corona, slices of lime sticking out of the necks.

Milton winced. "Water for me," he said.

Chrissie looked crestfallen. Milton watched her face and worried that she might have been volatile enough to take his rejection as a personal slight. Her brow lowered into a frown.

"It's a necessity for me," Milton explained quickly. "It's not that I wouldn't *like* to."

She went back into the kitchen and returned with an iced bottle of water in one hand and the two Coronas in the other. She gave the water to Milton, and they sat down with their backs against the side of his caravan, facing the terrace rather than one another. One of the beers was already half-empty; she put it to her lips and sank the rest.

"Sorry," she said.

"For what?"

"I'm an angry wee bitch sometimes."

"Forget it," he said, cranking off the cap and drinking deeply.

"It's been a hard few months."

"I bet."

"The fire was a disaster."

"And now look at it," he said. "You've done a fantastic job."

"I suppose so," she said, allowing herself a smile of satisfaction. "It's not too bad. At least I've found a brickie."

"I'm happy to throw a few blocks around."

"Brickie, cook, bouncer—is there anything you can't do?"

"Not so good with beer."

She looked at him slyly. "What about delivery driver?"

"What do you need?"

"I've got an oven on order from a supplier on the mainland," she said.

"You've already got a perfectly good oven."

"This one smokes meat, too. It'll be better than that contraption you set up outside when we opened. I'll be honest, I saw that and had nightmares about the place going up again."

"Give me a little credit," he protested.

She winked at him. "I always wanted the restaurant to be known for its fish—we can get it fresh off the docks, so it makes sense to be able to smoke it in house, too. The oven arrived last week, but they won't deliver it. They want me to go and pick it up."

"Where on the mainland?"

"Oban," she said.

Milton remembered what Judith-Ann had said. Alan had settled in Oban and had been living with a girl there. He had written down her address in his book.

"Not a problem," he said. "I can go and get it tomorrow if you like? If the electrician's not coming until then..."

"That would be great. You won't be able to get there and back in a day, though."

"That's settled, then. I'll make sure I'm back first thing the day after."

"Take my van," she said. "I doubt I'll be up if you catch the first ferry."

Chrissie took out a packet of cigarettes and held them out.

"Menthols?" he said, looking dubiously at the packet.

"Normal," she said.

Milton took a cigarette and lit it. Chrissie did the same and, for a moment, they sat together side by side and stared out at the sloping hill that led down to the beach, the sea and, beyond, the island of Taransay.

She turned her head toward him. "So what's your story? Really?" She ducked her shoulder and nudged into him with it; they didn't look at one another, but, for the first time, they were at ease.

"I think you have the gist of it."

"Maybe. We'll not get into all *that*, though."

Milton knew exactly to what she was referring: she was Irish; he was English. Milton had spent enough time in Northern Ireland to know how to determine what way the wind blew; the subtle tells, names, appearances, the pronunciation of certain letters all served to betray one's political belonging. She had pegged him right from the start as ex-military, and he could tell that she leaned toward the Republican point of view. The idea of British forces in Ulster would have been something upon which they would not be able to agree.

"I left the army a long time ago," he said. "Nearly twenty years. I've been travelling around the world ever since. I'll find a job, earn enough money to support myself, and use whatever I can save up to fund a little travel before I move on somewhere else."

"You're a hippie, then? That's what you're saying?"

He smiled. "That's not quite the word I'd use to describe myself."

"Dropout?"

"Free spirit," he said. "That'll do."

"That's what I thought—hippie."

She scrolled through a Spotify playlist on her phone to select a song. The speaker burst into life, and Milton recognised The Proclaimers.

"*No,*" he protested.

"Come on," she said, grinning. "It's a classic!"

Milton decided not to quibble. They sat as the sun fell, amid the rubble of the half-built terrace, and took it in turns to choose songs. There was a contentedness to the evening, and, as Chrissie worked her way through a third and then a fourth beer, she kept up a steady conversation while Milton, mostly, just listened. He knew two things: he and his boss would never be more than a whisker away from a serious misunderstanding, and he would spend the night in her caravan.

31

The island of Boreray was a rocky outcrop seventy miles west of Harris. It was the northernmost island in the St. Kilda archipelago, a long-extinct volcano that now studded the Atlantic with four islands: Boreray, Hirta, Dun and Soay. The islands were all steep and jagged, and this one soared out of the surf to a peak of a thousand feet at Mullach an Eilein. It was a lonely and desolate place, and Flash would have struggled to think of somewhere more isolated. It was also spectacular and would have offered a quiet place to meditate were it not for the activity that he knew was busily taking place on the western side of the island. Flash had facilitated much of that activity himself, delivering men and material and watching as the preparatory work for the test went on.

He looked back into the stern of his boat—the *Perseverance*—at the crates that he had collected from Tobermory. He didn't know what was inside, just that it was the last delivery that he had been scheduled to make. They would run the test, hope that the results were acceptable and then, either way, strike the equipment and do whatever they could to ensure that the evidence of their presence was removed. It would be just the same as what had happened on the Flannans; Flash had assumed that test had been successful, and had been surprised when Chen had told him that they would need to recreate it here, on Boreray, even farther out. Flash hadn't asked why, knowing that he wouldn't be told. Chen had always made it very plain that his was not to reason why.

The gannets were returning to the cliffs to roost as Flash aimed the boat toward the dock. Other birds—puffins, guillemots, fulmar, razorbills and kittiwakes—whirled overhead, squawking loudly as the boat drew nearer. The slab of rock was a natural platform for a landing stage. It reached out into the ocean with a steep incline above it that led up to the grassy amphitheatre. Spray had crashed over the rock for millennia, and now the surface was treacherous with lichens and seaweed. They had drilled cleats into the granite to hold the boat in place, and a further series of cleats all the way up the incline so that a guide rope could be attached. Flash radioed to the camp, said that he was approaching and that he would need assistance to get the gear box off the boat and transferred up to the site.

He saw the first of the workers peek over the edge and look down as Flash gently opened the throttle to combat the current that nudged him away from the stage. The wind was down, and the sea was calm enough for the landing to be about as free of drama as he could have wished for. He brought the *Perseverance* alongside as the man—a Pole called Andrzej—strapped himself into the climbing harness and made his way backwards down the slope. Flash tossed over the coiled mooring line, and Andrzej tied it to the cleat. Flash tossed over a second line to ensure the boat stayed close to the rock.

Five more men waited at the top of the steps. They were unimpressive, doing what they were told to do out of fear rather than conviction. The work they did was based on a squalid transaction: hard labour in exchange for poor, illegal wages. The conditions in which they lived and worked were appalling; Flash had pointed that out to Chen just after he had started here, but he had been told that it was none of his business. The men had been recruited so that the job could be finished as quickly as possible; that, Chen had told him, was all he had to worry about.

Flash went to the prow and gestured to the men watching at the top of the slope.

"Don't just stand there," he shouted up to them. "Send the trolley down."

His sympathy often manifested in anger at their lack of self-worth and their inability to think for themselves. They were like sheep, complicit in their own maltreatment. They were drawn from Eastern Europe—two Albanians, two Poles and a Romanian—all of them united by the poverty that had driven them halfway across the continent. There had been others: the Polish lad who had been there one day and not the next, and the Moldovan who had slipped on the landing stage in the Flannans and fallen between the *Perseverance* and the rock. His body had been sucked beneath the hull before they could get to it and was last seen drifting face down out into the Atlantic. Flash had wanted to go and collect the poor bastard so that he could be buried properly, but Chen had said no.

The men set to work above and, after a moment, a four-wheeled trolley was lowered down the slope. It comprised a metal sled that was around six feet long by three feet wide with a caged top, and the rope that was fixed to the hoop at the front found its way up the slope to a diesel-operated capstan winch. The trolley reached the bottom of the slope, and Andrzej reached across to open the top.

Flash took the first case, heaved it onto his shoulder and then crossed the deck so that he could push it up onto the platform. Vitalie the Romanian backed down to the bottom to join Andrzej, and the two of them lifted the case and lowered it into the cage. Flash unloaded the next case, and then the next; in five minutes they had transferred the gear box onto the trolley, and the cage was closed and locked. Vitalie yelled up to the men at the top of the slope, and the winch was switched on, slowly dragging the cargo to the top.

Flash disembarked, grabbed the sodden rope and pulled himself up, hand over hand, placing each foot carefully so as not to slip and fall. He was heavy, but, perhaps in response to the injury to his leg, he had maintained all of his upper-body strength, and the ascent was easily within his ability. He crested the top of the slope just as the men had unloaded the gear box. Behind the natural amphitheatre formed of grassy slopes, the ground fell away to the crashing sea many hundreds of metres below. Chen was stalking across the meadow and reached Flash as he undid the harness and let it drop down to his feet.

The big man jabbed a finger at the crates. "You get it?"

"I did."

"It was waiting for you on the dock?"

"Aye."

"Anyone see you with it?"

"Lots of people," he said. "But no one knows what's inside. Don't worry."

Chen grunted his satisfaction. Flash found himself thinking about Milton again, and wondered anew about their meeting. It couldn't have been a coincidence, and he didn't believe the story that Milton had just happened to end up in the Hebrides and had decided to pop to Tobermory on the off chance that the two of them might bump into one another. If he was right about that—that Milton had lied to him—then what reason was there for him being there that *wasn't* connected to the turbine? He deliberated again whether he should mention it to Chen, but decided again that there was nothing to profit from doing that. He didn't like him, and he knew that the feeling was mutual. They had managed to function together so far, ensuring that by restricting themselves to business and nothing else. Flash was suspicious, but had no evidence that Milton's purpose was nefarious. Perhaps it *was* just a chance meeting, after all. Flash knew that Chen was the kind of man who would err on the side of caution when suspecting a threat, and that might not be great for Milton.

Chen made his way over to the cases that they had just unloaded. Flash watched him open each one and take a long look inside, but he did not take anything out. Chen's role was discipline and security, and the actual inspection and assembly of the gear box would be down to the two technicians. Flash assumed that they would already be up by the site of the turbine, waiting to get started.

Chen closed the lid of the last case and fastened the clips to secure it. He stood and turned to Flash.

"Go back," he said. "I don't need you now."

"The turbine?"

"It is in hand. The test will be soon. We will need you to move the gear off the island again when that is done. Go rest. You look like shit."

Flash stared at Chen. He hated taking direction from him, but that was what he was paid to do. He couldn't argue that he looked rough, though; the hangover would only be cured one way, and he made his way back to the slope with the intention of heading back to Harris, where he might partake of a glass or two to set him right.

Chen must have read his mind. "No drinking for you today," he called back over his shoulder. "You drink too much."

Flash stopped. Anger spat and fizzed and his fists clenched. If he had been younger, he would have been able to give Chen a run for his money. But now? Probably not. Chen was big and strong and fast; he would have Flash on his arse before he could say Mao Tse Tung. More than that, his orders had been clear: Flash was to do whatever it took to test the turbine and the cable.

Whatever it took.

32

They were in Milton's caravan. Chrissie sat on top of him, naked, her hands together in the dip in his chest, and stopped moving.

"Were you in Ireland?"

"What?" he said, surprised at her sudden ability to change gear.

"Were you deployed to Ireland?" she repeated.

"Northern Ireland?"

"Aye," she said, rolling off him and taking the sheets with her.

"Yes. I was."

There was silence for a long time.

"What were you in?" she said eventually.

"Do you really want to talk about it?"

"Just tell me you weren't a Para."

Milton thought for a moment. He had not been a member of the Parachute Regiment, although he had served with many men who had. Their involvement in the Bloody Sunday massacre made them the military unit that the Republicans hated the most.

"I wasn't a Para."

Milton lay where he was, looking at the moisture on the ceiling, and waited.

"I should have brought my fags," she said.

"I'll get them for you if you want?"

"I'd prefer if you levelled with me."

He knew that she was dying to learn more about his background; she had evidently taken the opportunity to ask provided by the comfortable post-coital atmosphere.

"What do you want to know?"

"Did you kill anyone?"

"In Ireland?"

"Yes."

"Did you lose someone?"

She was quiet for several seconds. "My dad."

"By the British?"

"Yes," she said.

"Was he involved?"

"Yes. But they could have arrested him."

"When was this?"

"Eighty-two."

"Well before my time," Milton said truthfully.

"It was in Derry."

"I wasn't deployed to Derry."

"Did you kill anyone, though?"

"I fired my weapon on more than one occasion. I don't know whether I hit anyone, though, so I can't say. It's possible."

She was silent again, but didn't recoil.

"Want me to get the smokes?" he said.

"They're on the side as you go in."

Milton grabbed a towel, wrapped it around his waist,

opened the door and hopped down. It was a cold night, and the sweat became icy on his skin as he crossed the space to her caravan. The door was open when he tried the handle, and he opened it and climbed inside. The interior was similar to Milton's, although much less tidy. The bed was unmade, and clothes had been left to spill out of the wardrobe and onto the floor. Milton saw a framed picture on the floor; it was face down and looked as if it had been stamped on. Milton picked it up and turned it over. The photograph inside the frame was of Chrissie and a man dressed for the races. Chrissie was wearing a decorative hat and a purple dress that showed off her figure. He turned his attention to the man; he looked familiar, and Milton wondered if he had seen him before. He put the frame back on the floor, found the cigarettes and crossed back to the other caravan.

"Got them," he said, holding up the pack.

He noticed the expression on her face: it was as if she had seen a ghost.

"What is it?"

She mastered it and smiled. "Nothing."

He got back into bed and reached over her for his lighter. He opened the pack and tapped out two cigarettes; he lit one and handed it to her, then lit the second.

She held up the photograph of Alan Caine. "Who's this?"

"Been going through my things?"

"I was flicking through the book," she said, holding up his copy of *Jude the Obscure*. "This fell out."

"It's someone I'm looking for."

"Who is he?"

"His name's Alan Caine. I met his mother when I was in Japan. He went missing around here a month ago. She has cancer and wants to know what happened to him before she dies. I said I'd look."

"Just like that?"

"I was looking to move on, and I've been meaning to come to the Hebrides for as long as I can remember. It was the excuse I was looking for."

"That's why you're here?"

"The main reason, yes."

"Why didn't you tell me?"

"I didn't think it was relevant. I needed a job, and you had one on offer. I'll make sure I do it well and, when I have time off, I'll look for him."

He tensed, expecting her to press him, but she let it pass. They lay back for a moment, both staring up at the ceiling.

"You've been asking all the questions," he said. "My turn."

"Go on, then. What do you want to know?"

"You're not from here."

"Very observant."

"So? Why did you come?"

She sighed. "The usual. A man."

Milton thought of the framed picture that he had found on the floor. "What happened?"

"He wasn't what I thought he was."

She rolled over and flicked the butt of the cigarette out of the folding window, then fell back against him again. It was clear that she didn't want to talk about it.

"Are you still going to Oban tomorrow?"

"For the oven? That was the plan. I was going to stay overnight and be back as early as I could after that."

"Not an expensive hotel," she said.

"I'll sleep in the van."

"I was kidding," she said. "We can stretch to the Premier

Inn. Bring me the receipt, and we can expense it. We should have the electricity fixed by the time you're back."

She put her hands on his chest again.

"Again?" he asked her.

"You won't be here tomorrow," she said. "Best make the most of this evening."

33

Jimmy Bolton parked his car outside the Oban Bay Hotel, but didn't switch off the engine. He laced his fingers around the top of the wheel and stared out of the windscreen at the bay and the Isle of Mull. He had been summoned to a meeting, and he was nervous. All of his hard work on the turbine project—*months* of it—was in danger of going up in smoke, and he needed to think of a strategy to give him a little additional time. That was what he needed, he told himself. He needed a week or two to figure out what to do next. The only problem was that Johnston Hannah was not renowned for his patience, and Jimmy knew that he was going to be upset when he learned just how much of a setback the meeting with Watson had been.

Jimmy had been fretting about that all day. His record with the local councillors and industry figures in the islands stood in stark contrast to the abject failure of his attempt to win the Crown Estate to his cause. It was galling: the successes that he had won were important, but they were insignificant when compared to the decisions that he still needed to secure. It wouldn't matter how well Hannah was regarded on the islands if the body responsible for selecting the winning bidders for the seabed leases was not prepared to play ball. And, Bolton feared, his approach had not just been unsuccessful; his misjudgement of Watson had caused serious—potentially fatal—damage.

Hannah had called him yesterday evening for an update, and Bolton had bluffed his way through the conversation. He knew he was kicking the can down the road, but he had persuaded himself that if he could just get a little extra time, then he would find a way to either persuade Watson to cooperate, or bypass him and find someone else to give him what he wanted.

But Hannah had not played ball; he had said that he was in Oban, tonight, and that he wanted to see Bolton for a face-to-face. Prevarication as a strategy was not going to work for much longer. Jimmy had driven across the country from Edinburgh, more tense and anxious with every passing mile.

He switched off the engine, pulled down the sun visor and checked his reflection, and then, with a deep breath, opened the door and stepped outside into the crisp evening air.

HANNAH WAS SITTING ALONE at a table as Jimmy came inside. A bottle of white was upturned in the cooler, and he looked angry. Jimmy looked at his watch, fearful that he had the time wrong, and Hannah had been waiting for him, but he wasn't late.

"Evening," he said as he slid into an empty chair. Hannah glowered at him. "You okay?"

"Long day," Hannah said. "Difficult day."

Jimmy smiled, but didn't know where to start. There was an awkward silence.

"Jimmy? What have you got for me? What happened with Watson?"

Jimmy swallowed, his mouth dry. "There are some challenges," he said carefully. "I'll get to that. The locals are all onside. The Western Isles council bought in—they'll pass a motion in support whenever we ask them. The MP is on board, too. He's very keen on the local employment angle, rather than giving the jobs to the Scandinavians. Easy win for him."

"Especially when he's getting paid, too."

"That doesn't hurt."

"How much have we spent so far?"

"Between all of them? A hundred and fifty."

Hannah closed his eyes and gave a little shake of his head. Jimmy found that confusing; a hundred and fifty ought to have been a drop in the bucket to someone as rich as Hannah.

"And Watson?"

"There are some challenges," Jimmy said again. He couldn't put it off any longer. "I heard on the grapevine that the Crown Estate already had favourite bidders—the Norwegians and the Danes, apparently, not a word about us—so I set up a meeting with him. I wanted to find out from the horse's mouth what the situation was."

"And?"

"There's some work to do," Jimmy admitted.

"What work? A straight answer, please, for once. If you have a problem—an issue, a fuck-up, a 'challenge,' whatever you want to call it—you need to let me know *now*."

The waitress ambled over, providing a useful distraction and a chance for Jimmy to get his thoughts in order. He ordered a gin and tonic, and Hannah indicated that he wanted a second bottle.

Hannah stared hard at Jimmy until she had gone back to the bar. "Be honest. What happened?"

"Right," Jimmy said. "Okay. Watson said he had a big concern: the source of your funding for the project. I told him you had a consortium behind you, but he said that they'd need details. I said that the details would be supplied in due course. I couldn't very well say anything else—I don't know where the funding is coming from, do I?"

"I can take care of that," Hannah said. "Is that it?"

Jimmy's mouth felt even drier. "Watson is not playing ball."

"But you said he wouldn't be a problem. You said he was a friend of the family."

"I said he was a friend of my *father*."

"That's why I chose you, Jimmy. You said you had the connections we'd need. I could've gone to a bigger lobbying outfit, but you persuaded me that they'd wave it through if you were involved. Why do I get the feeling that's changed?"

"It *hasn't* changed," Jimmy said, sensing that Hannah was edging toward an explosion of temper.

"You said he could be bought," Hannah said.

"I thought he could."

"Did you try?"

"Yes."

"How much?"

"Fifty."

"And?"

"He told me I should be ashamed of myself."

"So offer more."

"I don't know if that'll work."

"Everyone has a price."

Jimmy winced. "I don't know about him."

"It's funny you should tell me this now. I had a phone call this morning from a journalist. Alexandra Marshall. I dug up a little information. She works for STV. Do you know her?"

"No."

"She said she'd heard that you've been bribing people to get them onside."

Jimmy's mouth fell open. "How would she know that?"

"She said she'd heard a recording of you confessing to it."

Jimmy gaped. "*What?*"

"Are you saying that isn't true?"

"Of course it's not true."

He denied it volubly, but, even as he did, he thought of Caesar. He remembered the argument in their hotel room and the weird direction that Caesar had forced the conversation to take. He was a duplicitous bastard, but surely he wouldn't have lowered himself to recording what Jimmy had said. *Surely.*

"Are you sure?" Hannah said.

"I'm sure," Jimmy said. "I'd never talk about something as sensitive as that with anyone who couldn't be trusted."

"What about the councillors? What if she starts digging around in the islands?"

Jimmy ignored the roiling in his stomach. "They'd be pretty stupid to admit to taking the money. They'd just incriminate themselves, wouldn't they?"

The waitress brought over another bottle of wine and a large gin and tonic. Hannah filled his glass, knocked it back and filled it again.

"I don't know, Jimmy. Seems like there's a lot of stupidity going around. Maybe it's catching." Hannah's voice was thin and taut. "Let me sum up. Something you've said or done has been passed to a journalist, and now they're asking me questions about paying off people to get the bid approved. And, worse, the most important man we need to get on our side, the man who was the only reason I appointed you in the first place, has turned down our money, and who knows what consequences there will be from that. This couldn't be any worse. Apart from the press—which is bad enough, Jimmy, *more* than bad enough—you've managed to turn Watson against us. And if that's right—if the bid has been tainted—how do we get shortlisted?"

Jimmy scrubbed his forehead until the answer came to him. "Run the test, show them how much more efficient the cabling is, show them how you can minimise the size of the turbines for the same output."

"Maybe," Hannah said.

"You were always going to play the environmental card," Jimmy said. "Double down on it. Get them on board that way."

"That does beg a question, though, Jimmy—if it all comes down to the test, what do I need you for? I mean, rather than make this process as *easy* as you promised, you've somehow managed to make it more *difficult*. Haven't you?" Hannah took the bottle from the bucket and left three twenty-pound notes on the table. "I'll finish this in my room."

"What are you saying, Johnston? Where does this leave us?"

"If anyone asks about money being paid out, I'll say you were acting without my knowledge or authority. As soon as I found out—today, in other words—I terminated our arrangement. Maybe I should report it myself."

"But you *knew* what I was doing. You provided the money."

"No, I didn't," Hannah said. "You paid in cash, and I made sure that there's no trail from me to you. If they ask, I'll explain that your retainer included a bonus payable upon winning the bid. All I can say is that you must have been speculating with your own cash because you knew you'd make more if you got what we wanted. I don't know, Jimmy—that'll be something you'll have to explain to the police if it comes to that." He turned to leave, then paused. "But I will say this, before I go—you wanted to know about the consortium. I didn't tell you because some of the people involved are what you might consider unsavoury. Not the sort of people you'd want to get on the wrong side of, so you'd be wise to make sure the issue with the press goes away without any blowback on us. Find out where she got that story and deal with it. Understand?"

He finished his glass, stood it down and left the table. Jimmy felt sick to his stomach as Hannah made his way out of the room.

34

Hannah went up to his hotel room, shut the door and took off his shoes. He had managed to hide his fear in front of Bolton, masking it with anger that the man's incompetence had made the process more complicated than it ought to have been. But, now that he was alone, there was no fooling himself: he was afraid.

He looked at his watch: just before ten. Wu Yongkang had arranged to speak to him on the hour, and Hannah knew that Wu was not a man to keep waiting. He was the man behind Manticore, the Chinese hedge fund that was responsible for the majority of the investment in the project. He went over to the bureau, opened his laptop and opened the encrypted chat application that Yongkang had insisted that they use. He waited until the clock ticked over to 22:00 and then typed out his first message.

>> Hello.

The cursor flashed for a moment, and then it changed to show that a reply was being composed.

>> Update, please.

>> The test is scheduled for tomorrow or the next day.

Everything is in place. The equipment has all been delivered and is being set up now.

>> Will you be there?

>> I'll be at the receiving station.

>> Good. I will expect a full report as soon as it is available.

>> Understood.

Hannah stared at the screen as Yongkang typed again.

>> What about the lease?

Hannah swallowed. There it was. There was no way the question could be ducked, and Wu had demonstrated a preternatural ability to sniff out lies and evasions before. Better to rip the plaster right off now rather than draw it out.

>> We have a problem.

>> I had heard the same.

Hannah stared at the sentence and the cursor that flashed beneath it, waiting for his response. How had Yongkang found out already?

>> How much do you know?

>> I know that your agent is a fool.

>> I only found out tonight.

>> Then you are a fool, too. It is unacceptable. The project cannot be jeopardised by incompetence.

>> It's not all bad. We have local support.

>> It will mean nothing if we do not win the bid.

Hannah squeezed his hands into fists. His skin was damp with sweat.

>> What do you want me to do?

>> Nothing. You have done enough. No more mistakes. Chen will deal with it.

Hannah stared at the screen, waiting for Yongkang to tell him what that meant. The cursor blinked stubbornly, but there was no further message.

Hannah typed instead.

>> What will you do?

He stared at the screen, waiting for a response, but, instead, the app reported that the conversation had come to an end.

PART VIII

TUESDAY

35

It was six in the morning, and Control checked her blood sugar for the first time. She took out her phone and opened the app that recorded her levels. There was a small sensor inserted just beneath the skin of her upper arm that continuously analysed her glucose levels, sending the data to her phone. Her level was a little lower than she would have liked, and she took out a packet of glucose tablets and popped them in her mouth one at a time, chewing and swallowing each. The tablets were fast acting and would rebalance the sugar until she checked again at lunch. Her diabetes had been something with which she had had to contend ever since she had been a child. It might have been a problem as she ascended the ranks of the intelligence services, but she was as fastidious about keeping an eye on her health as she was about everything else in her life, both professional and personal. She was the first woman to hold the position of Control of Group Fifteen, and she intended to make a success of it. There was not the slightest chance that she would allow her illness to have any impact on her performance.

She put the iPhone back in her handbag and reached for the intercom on her desk. The device was a relic—practically an antique—but it, and several other similar curios that she hadn't been able to dispense with, were links between her and her predecessors as Control. There had only been three: Harry Mackintosh, who had been murdered by Beatrix Rose's daughter, Isabella; Michael Pope, who was AWOL with Isabella Rose; and her. Pope had not been in post for long enough to make changes from Mackintosh's way of doing things, and, since Mackintosh had been in place since the Group's formation during the Cold War, there were certain ways of doing things that had almost become institutional habits. One of those habits—the assigning of the red-lined files that marked out the Group's work—was relevant this morning. She had three files to assign, and an agent waiting outside to collect them.

She pressed the button on the intercom.

"Yes, ma'am," said her aide-de-camp, Benjamin Weaver.

"Send in Number Twelve, please."

Control looked up as the door to the office opened, and Number Twelve made his way inside. He was six three and powerfully built and had served in the Special Boat Squadron before his transfer. He had been blooded as a Group agent in Guatemala several months earlier when a momentary distraction during that assignment had allowed his target to wound him with a hidden blade. The tip had sliced across his cheek, and a pale sickle-shaped scar had been left, its track white against his black skin. Control expected perfection and had been irritated by Twelve's negligence but, since the target had been neutralised and the subsequent files he had been given had been actioned without issue, she had written off the mistake as the lapse of a beginner and allowed his career within the Group to continue.

She gestured to the chair on the other side of her desk. "Take a seat, please, Twelve."

He unbuttoned his jacket and sat, crossing one leg over the other.

"I've read the report from your trip to Alaska. Well done."

"Thank you, ma'am."

"You didn't have any problems?"

"None. It was exactly as I'd been briefed."

"Clean work. That's the standard we need to set. In and out and no one the wiser. Very good."

Twelve nodded. He had been active long enough to know that Control was parsimonious with her praise. She had torn strips off him after his sloppy first assignment and had made it clear that he was on an extended probation because of it. He had done enough now to relieve her concerns, and, while she did not want him to relax—relaxation often meant death in a business such as theirs—she wanted him to know that she was satisfied with the standard that he had set.

"I have something else for you," she said.

She reached into the leather in-box and withdrew the three files. They were lined in red and closed with a red ribbon. That treatment was another affectation of Harry Mackintosh, and despite a preference for a paperless office, she had decided that it was something that might be kept. There was something solid about the files and, given the men and women whose names were found on the covers had been marked for death, it felt right that there should be something real to mark their selection rather than just incorporeal packages of data.

She handed the files to Twelve. He scanned the details on the front pages and inclined his head. "Scotland, ma'am?"

"That's right. The RAF will fly you up to Lossiemouth and then back again. Pick up your gear from the quartermaster on the way out."

"Yes, ma'am. Anything else I need to know?"

"Not really, Twelve. It's all in the files. Three targets, all civilians, none of whom ought to detain you for too long. Group One has agents in theatre already, and the targets are under surveillance."

He stood and collected the files from the desk. "Thank you, ma'am."

36

Milton got up at six and went for a run. He followed the single-lane track for five miles, following the line of the coast, and then turned back and retraced his steps. He stripped down to his shorts, walked down the pristine white beach and strode out into the sea. The water was intensely cold and beautifully clear. Milton swam out for a hundred yards, watching a pod of dolphins as they crested the gentle waves between him and Taransay. He kicked down beneath the surface, reached the bottom and grabbed handfuls of the fine sand, letting the grains fall between his fingers as he surfaced and struck back toward the shore.

Water streamed off his skin as he collected his clothes and jogged back to the caravan. He took a tepid shower, dressed in clean clothes and went back outside to the spot where Chrissie kept her van. He dropped into the driver's seat and closed the door. He had a lot of travel ahead of him and then, when he reached Oban, the prospect of beginning his investigation into the disappearance of Judith-Ann's son.

Milton started the engine and, with a glance back to the caravans, he put the van into gear and pulled away.

HE DROVE to Tarbert and took the ferry for the two-hour crossing to Uig in Skye. He went up to the deck and found a quiet spot where he could think. He hadn't made any progress with the search for Alan Caine yet. He had hoped that Flash might be able to assist, but he had written that off now. If he was going to find him, he was going to have to do it himself.

He took out the copy of *Jude the Obscure* and checked the details that Judith-Ann had provided: Alan's girlfriend was called Helena, and she lived at 2 Albany Terrace, George Street, in Oban. She had sent Judith-Ann a letter following Alan's disappearance, and her return address had been written on the back of the envelope. Beyond the vague information contained in the letter, and the similarly sketchy information that had been provided when the two women spoke on the telephone, there had been no other communication with her. Milton hoped that she still lived at the address.

THE JOURNEY TOOK SIX HOURS, and it was one in the afternoon when Milton finally drove into Oban and found the industrial estate where he was due to collect the smoker. The proprietor of the business was expecting him, and the unit was waiting on a pallet. The two of them lifted the oven and carefully slid it into the back of the van. Milton thanked him, turned the van around and drove into the town. He had the rest of the day to start his search.

He followed the satnav to the Oban Bay Hotel, parked the van and made his way into the lobby. It was tastefully elegant in tartan drapes and leather recliners, and the receptionist, dressed in a tartan that matched the curtains, was polite and accommodating.

"I've reserved a room," Milton said.

"Your name, sir?"

"Eric Blair."

"Ah, yes. Hello, Mr. Blair. We have you for one night?"

"Yes, please."

"I have one on the second floor. Lovely view out to sea."

"Perfect," he said.

The man handed Milton a paper wallet with the key inside. "Breakfast starts at six in the restaurant. The lift is over there to the right."

Milton thanked him and took the lift to the second floor.

HE FRESHENED UP, plotted the route from the hotel to Helena's address, and set off. It was a ten-minute walk following the promenade. Oban was a pleasant enough town: Milton passed an austere church that had been blasted by the fierce winds, a large Gothic building that accommodated the Alexandra Hotel, and newer holiday apartments that advertised sea views and private parking. The saltire flew proudly from several buildings and was displayed in the windows of others, a rebuke to the union and a reminder that plenty of the locals would be happier with an independent Scotland.

George Street was behind the ferry terminal, and the

address that Helena had provided was above a pub—the Tartan Tavern—and the Oban Youth Café. The latter building, with a faded sign and a wheelie bin left in the doorway, looked to have been abandoned. Access to the first and second floors was by way of an open corridor to the right of the café. Milton was about to make his way inside when the door at the end opened, and a woman stepped outside. She turned to close and lock the door; Milton looked up at the building and guessed that there could only be space for a couple of flats. Unless Helena had moved since corresponding with Judith-Ann, there had to be a decent chance that he was looking at her.

She turned and made her way out of the corridor and onto the street. She was in her early thirties, with blonde hair that she wore in a bob and a pair of thick-rimmed hipster glasses that would have been more at home in Hoxton than the Highlands.

Milton stepped into her way and smiled. "Excuse me. Are you Helena?"

She stopped. There was confusion on her face, but, as she looked at him, that quickly became fear. She stepped around him and started walking again, more quickly this time.

Milton followed. "I'm sorry. I don't mean to frighten you."

"Leave me alone," she said, without turning around.

"It's about Alan."

"Didn't you hear me? Leave me alone, or I'll call the police."

"His mother sent me. Judith-Ann. You spoke to her after he went missing."

"What?"

"She hasn't heard from him for weeks."

She stopped and turned to face him. "I don't want to get involved in that—not again."

Milton frowned. "Why? What happened?"

"Alan was in trouble because of the work he was doing. I've kept my head down. I've got a life to live, and I don't want to rock the boat. I'm sorry."

The girl was evidently frightened.

"Judith-Ann is sick," Milton said gently.

She frowned. "No—not when I spoke to her."

"She has cancer. She wants to know what happened to her son before she dies. Can you help? Please—I just need you to answer a few questions. I don't know what you're worried about, but I promise that whatever you tell me stays between us. You won't get into trouble. You have my word."

She looked as if she was ready to turn away, but she didn't. "How long does she have?"

"I got the impression that it isn't long—weeks."

She bit her lip and then breathed in deeply, in and out. "Okay," she said. "We can talk. But not here."

37

Helena led Milton onto the High Street, a collection of local businesses, empty units and charity shops. She took him to the Vita Café, a building with a garish red and green colour scheme and windows that overlooked the harbour. It appeared that Helena knew the girl behind the counter; they exchanged smiles, and the waitress told her to find a table and that she would be over to take her order shortly.

There was an empty space at the counter that ran along the window, but Helena declined it and led the way to the back of the room, where it would be harder for them to be noticed by anyone who might be passing on the pavement outside. Milton saw again that she was scared.

They both sat down.

"You didn't tell me your name," she said.

"Eric Blair. And you're Helena...?"

"Atkinson," she finished for him. "Are you working for Judith-Ann?"

"How do you mean?"

"As a... well, as a detective or something like that?"

"Not in any official capacity."

"What, then?"

"As a good deed, I suppose."

"Doesn't she live in Japan?"

"That's right."

"And you agreed to come halfway around the world just to look for him?"

"I was coming anyway. And it seemed like the right thing to do."

The waitress came to the table to take their order. Helena ordered a mint tea, and Milton took a coffee, handing the waitress a ten-pound note to cover the bill. The waitress went to prepare their drinks.

Helena chewed on her lip. "What do you want to know?"

"Do you know what happened to him?"

"I spoke to Judith-Ann about that."

"I know you did, and she's grateful. But it would be very helpful if you'd go over it again with me."

She paused, looking at him carefully. "How much do you know about what he was doing?"

"Not much. Judith-Ann said she lost contact with him a month ago. He used to call her once a week, but then he stopped. She tried calling him, and he never picked up."

"A month ago," she said with a nod. "That's about right."

"What happened?"

"He went out one day, and he never came back. He was working on an investigation. He didn't tell me what it was, just that it was important."

The waitress returned with their drinks and set them down on the table.

Milton waited until she went back to the counter. "What kind of investigation?"

"Alan worked for Migrant Help—have you heard of them?"

"I don't think so."

"They run campaigns to help illegal immigrants. He got a tip that Eastern Europeans were being brought in to work on something out on the islands."

"Where?"

"The Flannans—they're twenty-five miles west of Harris. Uninhabited. He went out there a week before he disappeared; he hired a boat from the harbour."

"With a skipper?"

"No," she said. "He was always on the water. He wouldn't have needed anyone to take him."

"Did he find anything?"

She shook her head. "I don't know, but whatever it was, it got him into trouble. This one night, a couple of days before he went missing, he came to my place covered in blood. He said someone had jumped him—he said they put him in the back of a van and drove him out to Gallanach. They told him that he was going to get killed if he kept putting his nose into other people's business. They beat him up pretty badly to make sure he got the message and left him to walk back."

"Did he speak to the police?"

"Aye, and they said they'd investigate it, but they didn't. And it didn't stop him. Just made him more determined. He said he was going to go back again, I told him that was a stupid idea, and we had a row about it. A pretty bad one. He said he didn't want to see me anymore." She paused, looked out to sea and then down to the surface of the table. "I was angry at the time, but, the more I think about it, the more I think he wanted to split up because he didn't want *me* to get into trouble."

"Because of the people who beat him up?"

She ran her finger around the rim of her teacup and nodded.

"Go on," Milton said.

"I never saw him again. I got this, though." She took out her phone and opened her messages. She read one aloud: "'I'm leaving Scotland and moving to London. Have a good life.'"

"Does that sound like him?"

She shook her head emphatically. "Alan is many things, but he's not a coward. He would never have sent something like that by text. He would've said it to my face."

"So what happened to him? What do you think?

"I don't know. I went to the police and reported him missing. They went to his flat and got inside. Most of his stuff was gone. They said that, as far as they were concerned, he'd told me that he was moving and that was what he must've done. They said there was nothing to investigate." She paused and glanced down at the table, then met Milton's eyes again. "He had mental issues, too."

"Yes. His mother said he took medication for them."

"He did. I don't think that had anything to do with it, but the police were looking for excuses not to look, and that was a pretty good one."

Milton drummed his fingers against the tabletop. He had hoped for a little more to go on from Helena. He had somewhere to investigate now—the Flannans—but that sounded as if it might be something of a wild goose chase. If there had been something happening on those islands and Alan had discovered it—and then disappeared *because* of it—then the chances that it was still there were slim. It was a month ago. Milton would make arrangements to go and have a look around, but it felt as if the avenues open to him to discover what had happened to the missing man had started to shrink.

Helena laid her phone down on the table, and Milton noticed the screensaver. He pointed. "Is that the two of you?"

She smiled sadly. "Yes," she said.

"Can I have a look?"

She unlocked the screen, opened the gallery and found the photograph. Milton looked at it: Alan and Helena were standing on a beach, their arms around one another, Alan's right hand holding the phone up so that the selfie could be taken.

"We were on Taransay," she said. "You can kayak over from Harris."

Milton looked at the picture more closely, concentrating on Alan. He was wearing a blue technical jacket with the logo of the manufacturer—Rooster—printed across the middle. He wore a woollen beanie, and he had spread sunblock across his nose and cheeks.

"Could I send this to myself? It'll be useful to have a recent image."

"Of course," she said.

He tapped on the photo, added it to a text message, and sent it.

Helena looked at him. "There's another reason I don't think the message was from him," she said. "He left some things at my place. Clothes, books, some records that we both liked."

"He couldn't just have left them and gone?"

"It's possible," she said, "but he left his laptop, too. He's not rich—neither of us are. Who'd leave town without saying goodbye properly and without coming to pick up their laptop?"

Milton sat up a little straighter. "Do you still have it?"

She shook her head. "I gave it to someone who I thought might be able to help."

"Who?"

"A journalist," she said. "I wanted someone to look into what had happened to Alan, and he's got a reputation."

"For what?"

She chuckled to herself and then picked her words carefully. "He's very single-minded."

Milton could tell she was being diplomatic. "Do you think you could introduce him to me?"

38

Helena called the journalist and said that she would like to talk to him about Alan's case. He was evidently happy to do that, and the two of them agreed to meet in the bar of Milton's hotel.

"What's his name?" Milton asked as they walked along the promenade.

"Ox," she said.

"Ox?"

"You'll see why when you meet him."

"Anything else I need to know?"

"He can be difficult."

"How?"

She checked her watch. "It's three. He's probably been drinking for a couple of hours by now. He can get a little"—she paused, looking for the right word—"a little *cantankerous*."

"I'll bear that in mind," Milton said.

~

HELENA LED the way to a table in the window, took off her coat and draped it over the back of one of the chairs. She glanced around the bar.

"He's not here yet. I'm just going to use the bathroom."

"Can I get you a drink?"

"I'm fine," she said.

Milton went to the bar to get a glass of water and waited for the barman. A rugby match was showing on a big screen that hung from the wall, but Milton's attention was taken by an elderly couple who came in from the lobby. The two of them were dressed in cheap jackets that did not look like they would be much of a match for the Scottish elements. They approached the barman and held out a sheaf of leaflets. Milton couldn't make out what they asked, but could see that, whatever it was, the barman was not happy with their request. He shook his head, refusing whatever it was they had asked of him, and pointed to the door. The couple ignored him, made their way to the tables and started to hand out their leaflets.

"Come on," the barman protested. "I said no."

The couple paid no attention to him. They nodded apologetically to each person they approached, gesturing to a photograph on the leaflets that they laid out on the tables. They received dour shakes of the head in return.

The barman reached them. "I'm sorry," he said to the man to whom they had just given a leaflet. "I told them no."

The barman tried to get behind the couple so that he could usher them to the door, but they resisted and shuffled over to Milton instead.

"Please," the man said. "Our son. He..."

"Disappear," the woman finished for him.

The man nodded. "He disappear."

He held out a leaflet, and Milton took it. He looked down and saw a picture of a man in his late teens or early twenties.

"You know him?" the man asked hopefully.

"When did he disappear?"

"Four weeks," said the woman. "No call for four weeks."

"Where are you from?"

"Kraków. In Poland."

The fact that Milton had showed an interest appeared to have overwhelmed them both.

"He is good boy," the man said, blinking back tears. "He would not... just go."

Milton looked from the man to the woman—husband and wife, surely—and could see that they had been to hell and back. The man, in particular, had suffered; his face drooped to one side with what might have been a stress-induced palsy.

"Come on, now," the barman said, making a shooing gesture with both hands. "Time to leave."

"I'm talking to them," Milton said.

"Aye, but—"

"I'm talking to them." Milton glared at the barman and, pinned in his icy-cold gaze, the man lost the rest of his protest.

The father took Milton's elbow. "You know him?"

Milton gently removed his hand. "What was your son doing here?"

"He is coming to Scotland for working."

"What kind of work?"

The man shrugged. "He say they come to Oban; then he stop making SMS; then he stop sending money."

Milton laid his finger next to a cellphone number on the leaflet. "Is this your number?"

The woman nodded enthusiastically. "Please call if you know anything."

"I will. I hope you find him."

The barman manoeuvred himself behind the couple and, with his arms out wide and looking at Milton helplessly, he ushered them to the door, warning them that he would call the police if they came back again. Helena came back from the bathroom and took her place at the table. Milton told the barman that he would like a glass of water and, once it had been poured, he crossed back to join her.

"Everything okay?" she asked him.

Milton took the sheet of paper and laid it out on the table before her. "Have you seen this man before?"

She looked at it and shook her head. "Only on the leaflet. They've been pinned up around town. Why?"

"His parents were just in here. They said he was working here and went missing."

"And you think that might be connected to Alan?"

"Alan was looking into migrant labour. It could be a coincidence, but I've never put much store in that."

Helena started to reply when she looked over his shoulder to the door. Milton turned and saw a very large man standing outside, disengaging himself from the Polish couple and backing into the bar.

"Is that him?" Milton said.

Helena nodded. "That's Ox."

"You were right," Milton said. "I can see why they call him that."

39

Ox was *big*. He had broad shoulders—Milton suspected a lot of time spent on a bench press—together with thighs like tree trunks and arms that filled the sleeves of his shirt to the point of stretching. Milton guessed that he was in his thirties. He was the only patron in the bar not wearing a collar; instead, he was decked out in a pair of scruffy trainers, jeans and a polo shirt. Helena raised a hand to attract his attention, and the big man came over to their table.

"Afternoon," he said, his voice a gruff rumble. He turned to Milton. "This who you wanted me to meet?"

"Yes," she said.

Milton stood and extended a hand. "Eric Blair."

Ox delivered what for most people would be a bone-cracking shake. Milton squeezed back and held the big man's gaze, determined not to show any signs of discomfort. They locked eyes for a moment before Ox chuckled, nodded appreciatively and released his grip.

"Good to meet you," Milton said. "Thanks for coming."

"Helena says you want to talk to me about Alan."

"That's right."

Ox regarded him with a creased brow. "Why—are you a lawyer?"

"No."

"What then?"

"He's here because of Alan's mother," Helena said.

"She's dying," Milton elaborated. "She's worried about him. I said I'd see if I could find him."

"Private investigator, then."

Milton shook his head. "I met her when I was on holiday. I said I'd have a look for her."

"Just like that? Come on, man. I dinnae think so."

"I was sceptical, too," Helena said. "Just hear him out—what harm can it do?"

Ox looked from him to Helena and back again. "Tell you what, pal. You go and get me a drink so we can have a little chat, and then we'll see what's what."

Milton nodded. "What'll you have?"

"Corona. Two bottles—ta."

Milton got up and made his way to the bar. He found that the barman had already opened the two bottles in anticipation of the order.

"He's a regular, then?" Milton asked.

"Most days," the barman said. "He comes here because the guests don't know who he is and they leave him alone. The locals give him a hard time, and he isn't the best of company anymore."

Milton turned back and saw that Ox had made himself comfortable in the chair that he had just vacated. He was watching rugby on the screen that had been fixed to the wall, his long legs stretched out in front of him and crossed at the ankle.

"Who is he?"

"Dougie Oxendale. You don't recognise him?"

"I don't."

"He was a prop forward. Fifty caps for Scotland before he got a bang on the head. Concussion, they said. Changed him completely—he used to be a teddy bear, but not now. If you want my advice, you'll not annoy him."

"Someone the size of that? You don't need to tell me twice."

Milton took the drinks and returned to the table. Ox shuffled in his seat, his eyes on the screen. "Pathetic."

Milton sat. "Sorry?"

He waved a hand at the match. "Laziness lost them that."

Milton looked up and saw that the match had come to an end: the winners celebrated while the losers sat on their haunches, gasping for breath.

"Did you play?" Milton said.

"Aye," Ox said. "You?"

"Years ago."

"I used to play for Scotland."

"Really?"

"Aye. And you know what my proudest moment was?"

"I'm guessing it was at Twickenham."

"Scored two tries," he said, eyeing Milton as if daring him to comment.

"Well done," Milton said. "I'm more of a football man."

"What? Yer aff yer heid, pal. Game for sissies." He took a bottle and gulped down half of it. "I had a word with Helena. She thinks you might be on the level, but she's got a kind heart and I don't, so I'll make up my own mind if that's all right with you."

"Absolutely."

"What do you want to know?"

"You looked into Alan's disappearance."

"I covered the story."

"For the newspapers?"

"Aye. I'm freelance, normally. I do the rugby and a bit of football. This was my first for the news desk."

"Which paper?"

"Got this one in *The Scotsman*."

"I read the stories from when he went missing," Milton said. "There was nothing about what he was doing here."

"Correct," Ox said. "That's because he never really said. What's your name again?"

"Eric."

"See, Eric, a place like this—Oban, the islands, all *that*—you get the tourists coming up here and all they can see are the landscapes and the wildlife and all the good stuff. But that's not all of it. There are things happening up here that people don't want others to find out—the things that happen in the shadows. Know what I mean?"

"Like what?"

"Like how all the local heroes are actually shits."

"I'm not following."

"See those foreigners who were just in here?"

"The Poles?"

"Aye. Lost their son, didn't they? Thing is, he wasn't the first to disappear. There was another one the week before. Moldovan lad called Fiodr. Alan had been digging into what had happened to him."

"Another migrant?"

"Aye. That's two of them gone missing."

"What work were they doing?"

"A very good question. Nobody knows. But I spoke to Fiodr's girlfriend, and she's sure he was working for that bastard Hannah."

"Who?"

"Highland Hannah," Helena added.

"Johnston Hannah. Employs hundreds up here on his fish farms. Loads of jobs, loads of money. And a total and utter gobshite."

Milton frowned. "The migrants were working on fish farms?"

"That's where Fiodr started, but his girlfriend says he got moved somewhere else. She didn't know where, except that it was offshore."

"Did she know what he was doing?"

He shrugged. "Therein lies the mystery. I think that's what Alan was trying to find out. And maybe he did. Maybe that's why he's missing—like the lads he was trying to find."

Milton thought for a moment. "Have you spoken to the people Alan worked for?"

"Migrant Help. Aye. They were useless."

"Alan preferred to work alone," Helena explained. "He didn't always get on with others. He'd put the case together and then give it to them to prosecute when it was done."

"And he had a pretty good track record," Ox said. "There was a bloke in Glasgow who had a dozen car washes staffed by Romanians who were getting paid pennies and then giving it all back to him as rent for the shitty houses he put them up in."

Helena nodded. "He helped prosecute a gang running pop-up brothels, too."

"So he had enemies," Milton said.

Helena nodded.

"I thought that, too," Ox said. "I looked, but I couldn't get anywhere, and now I've done about as much as I can. There comes a point when you have to admit your limitations. I'm a sports reporter. I've never done an investigation like this before."

"You've still made progress," Milton said.

"Don't patronise me," Ox said. "I haven't. I know Alan had enemies, but I don't think it's got anything to do with them. It's Hannah. I know it is. You hear rumours about a bloke like that, but getting detail is like trying to nail jelly to the wall."

"What rumours?"

"It's something on the islands. He owns Amhuinnsuidhe Castle on Harris—just finished renovating it, and I wondered whether they might have been involved in that. But no—that was local craftsmen, and they said nothing happened there that wasn't like it ought to be. Then I heard stories about Hannah hiring boats from Tobermory out to the islands—trips that had nothing to do with tourists—and I started asking about that, but everyone was tight-lipped. They either don't know what's going on or they're too afraid to say. Either way, I cannae stand the smug git. Lords it up like he owns the place—it's the same for anywhere here, the islands... like he's some sort of prodigal son bringing prosperity to all us poor wee bastards."

Milton finished his water, taking the moment to look at Ox. The big man looked as if he was cross all the time, his heavy brows lowered in a permanent scowl, but Milton suspected that at least some of his present anger was because he had been thwarted in his attempt to find out what had happened to Alan Caine. He had a dogged determination to him, and Milton decided that—if handled carefully—he would be a useful ally to have.

"I don't mind looking into him," Milton said.

"What makes you think you'd get anywhere I haven't?"

"You said you hadn't done this before," Milton said. "I have. And I can be persuasive. If you think he's got something to hide, maybe it's just a case of needing someone with fresh eyes."

Ox finished the second bottle and shrugged. "Don't suppose it can hurt."

"Helena says that you have Alan's laptop."

"Aye," he said. "Most of the folders on it are locked, though. I cannae get into them."

"Do you think I could borrow it for a day or two?"

"Why would you get any further than me? You said you're not a cop or an investigator?"

"I'm not. But I know someone who's handy at dealing with those kinds of problems."

"Oh, aye—a hacker or something?"

Milton smiled. "Or something."

"I'll let you have a look at it," Ox said, "but it'll have to stay at my place. I'm not letting you run off with it."

"Do you have the internet?"

"This isn't the bloody Third World, pal. Of course I do."

"Then your place will be fine."

40

Ox led the way through the town to Stevenson Street. They reached a row of shops—a chemist, a bookseller and a butcher—and he stopped.

"I'm up there," he said, pointing to the floors above the retail units.

Milton looked. There looked to be two main floors, with further space in the roof. The view in the opposite direction looked out over Oban Bay, with a vista that included the isles of Kerrera and Mull. Milton guessed that the panorama from up in the property would be spectacular. Ox opened a door next to the bookshop and led the way up a double flight of stairs to the first floor. There were two flats off the landing, and Ox opened the door on the right. A hallway led into the property.

"Kitchen's down there," he said, pointing. "Put the kettle on. I'll get the laptop."

Milton and Helena went through to the kitchen and listened to the groan of the stairs as Ox climbed up to the second floor. Milton looked around: the room was sparse, with a juicer, a steamer and a small fridge. The cooker was old, and the bread on top of the bread bin was mouldy. The property looked as if it might be expensive, but, that apart, his impression was that Ox was just scraping by. Milton took the kettle and filled it from the tap. He lit the gas hob and put the kettle atop the burner to boil.

Ox returned with a laptop that he set down on the kitchen table. "Sorry," he said, gesturing around the room. "I don't get visitors."

That didn't surprise Milton at all. Ox was a daunting presence, and his imposing size, combined with his gruff attitude, would not have encouraged thoughts of friendship. He plugged a power cable into the computer and put the plug at the other end into a wall socket. The machine was an old MacBook, and the fan whirred noisily as it started.

"Too old for an AirPort card," he muttered. "We'll have to wire it in."

Ox took an ethernet cable and slotted it into the port on the side. The kettle whistled as the water came up to heat. Ox waved a hand in the direction of one of the cupboards and said that there was coffee and tea inside, and that the milk—assuming it was still good—was in the fridge. Helena got up to attend to the refreshments, finding three chipped mugs and then discovering that Ox was, in fact, out of coffee and made tea instead.

The computer took an age to boot but, when it was finally finished, Ox clumsily navigated to a folder that bore the icon of a padlock. Ox double-clicked, and a dialogue appeared asking for a password.

Milton turned to where Helena was preparing the drinks. "You have no idea what he might have used?"

She dunked a tea bag and shook her head. "None at all. He'd never tell me something like that."

Milton gestured to the laptop. "Can I have a look?"

Ox nodded, moving the machine across the table so that Milton could get to it. He opened the email client and clicked to compose a new email. He typed in the email address that Ziggy Penn used and dragged the folder and dropped it into the email.

Ox squinted at the screen. "Who are you sending it to?"

"Like I said," Milton replied. "A friend of mine who's very good at getting into things like this. I doubt it'll take him long."

Milton pressed send, and the email disappeared.

"Here you are," Helena said, putting two cups of tea on the table. "We can have these while we wait."

41

Gallan Head was a promontory at the tip of the Isle of Lewis and the most northwesterly point in the United Kingdom. The area had once been the site of a Ministry of Defence surveillance station, with radar equipment pointed out to sea in search of the Soviet navy. It had all been decommissioned and handed over to a community trust that was planning to open an observatory where the sea and the sky could be studied without interference from nearby buildings or people.

Hannah had other plans for it.

He had flown by helicopter from Oban to Stornoway that afternoon and had then driven the forty miles from the eastern to the western side of the island. It was nearly midnight now, and those clear skies for which the area was renowned were very much in evidence. Hannah looked up; without the light pollution that scarred the heavens above towns and cities, it was as if every star in the sky was visible. Hannah's proposal wouldn't affect that in any meaningful way. The cables from the wind farm would come ashore here and then be routed to the grid. There would be work to be done, of course, but it wasn't as if he were proposing an extensive build. The tree huggers could have their site back once he was finished.

The cable from the Flannan Isles had been brought ashore here prior to the first test, and they were using the promontory for the same purpose again tonight. Boreray was almost one hundred kilometres to the southwest, and they had spent the last several days laying the cable and ensuring that it was secured in place for the test. The cable broke the surface due west of their present position, snaked up the side of the cliff and then trailed the remaining few hundred metres to the monitoring station. Yongkang had arranged for the cable to be laid, hiring a specialist boat and crew who had not objected to doing most of the work at night. The cable had come ashore three days ago and had been hidden until this evening, when it was brought up to the headland and connected to the scanner.

The unit had been towed here by a Land Rover once it was dark. It looked like a large Winnebago with extending boxes that concertinaed out from the sides, everything propped up by hydraulic legs. He climbed the steps, opened the door and looked inside. Screens and monitors flickered all over the walls, displaying information that he could not begin to decipher. There were fold-down desks on either side where the two technicians tapped keyboards and adjusted knobs and dials and sliders. Hannah fleetingly wondered how much of it was for effect; after all, there was just a single cable carrying data from a single turbine; how complicated could it really be?

The engineer responsible for the development of the cable was a German called Lukas Jensen. He was standing at the back of the scanner.

"How long to go?" Hannah asked him.

"The wind's good," Jensen said. "We're just bringing it online."

"How long will it take?"

"Ninety minutes of intermittent testing and then thirty minutes to strike the vehicle. We'll be gone in a couple of hours."

They were isolated up here, but it wasn't impossible that they might be seen. Hannah had given thought to a cover story and had settled on the suggestion that they were here to measure pollution levels. It might stand up to questions from a local, but he doubted that even the dimmest villager would be fooled if they noticed the cable that ran from the truck to the cliff and then over the side to the water below.

Jensen unhooked a VHF radio microphone and pressed the button to transmit. "Turnstone, this is Redshank. Come in, Turnstone. Over."

The radio crackled to life. "This is Turnstone. Receiving you loud and clear, Redshank. Go ahead. Over."

"Roger. Report on met conditions. Over."

"Wind speed is a sustained and steady seven metres per second per hour. We're good to go. Over."

"Okay, Turnstone. Spin it up. Over."

"I confirm spin it up. Over."

"Correct. Out."

Hannah hadn't slept well after his exchange with Yongkang, and today's endeavours had been stressful. He had been feeling a little ragged, but now, with the future of the enterprise dependent upon a successful test, he was sustained by adrenaline and caffeine from the flasks of coffee that were stowed in the back of the Land Rover outside.

The radio crackled. "We're up to speed. Stand by."

Jensen had explained the benefits that his new technology provided, but Hannah's eyes had always glazed over as soon as he went beyond the fact that it offered significant reductions in transmission loss. The jargon was baffling and beyond him. Hannah was happy to know that reduced losses in the new cable design would enable them to use smaller turbines to deliver the same power to the grid that much bigger turbines could manage by way of standard cables. Smaller turbines cost less to install and required less maintenance. Technically and financially, it was a win-win.

"Test beginning in five, four, three, two, one."

Hannah watched the screens.

Nothing happened.

"Well?" Hannah said.

Jensen picked up the radio again.

"Turnstone, this is Redshank. Confirm release. Over."

"This is Turnstone. Release confirmed. Over."

"Roger. Out."

Jensen stared at the screen.

"What's happening?" Hannah said.

Jensen ignored him and turned to the technician on the right. "Check the connection to the scanner."

The technician pulled on his coat and scampered from the van.

"What did you say this would be?" Hannah griped. "'Very straightforward.'"

The door opened, and the technician came back inside. "All looks good," he muttered, peering up in hope at the blank monitor.

"'All looks good,'" Hannah said. "But if it all looks good, then where's the bloody signal? Fifty fucking thousand quid this is costing us and not a blip on your wee telly!"

"It may not be the cable," Jensen said. "It might be the

turbine itself. There are any number of things that could be at fault. That's why—"

"*No*," Hannah spat. "Don't you dare go on about your daft suggestion that we spend a week at this. You'd have us spend a quarter of a million quid and *still* end up with not so much as enough juice to light a bulb."

The technician pointed to the screen. "Look!"

They all looked up. The screen had come to life. Three columns—one red, one yellow and the other blue—told Hannah that there was life in the project, and potentially his empire.

"What's it mean?"

"There's a signal," Jensen said.

"Definitely from the turbine?"

"Definitely."

"Definitely from the turbine on Boreray?"

"Do you have any others?"

"How strong is it?"

"We don't measure in strength. We determine the feed of potential power and the loss between the turbine and the receiving station."

"So is it good or bad?"

"Just a minute." Jensen went from station to station, watching the screens and then picking up the radio again. "Turnstone, this is Redshank. Please send through base station output."

Jensen turned to another screen: a circle ticked up, changing colour as it did so and reminding Hannah of a broadband speed test.

"Well?" Hannah said.

"Minimal loss. It looks good. Very good indeed."

Hannah felt relief flood through him. "Great," he said. "Just great. Send the data to me now."

"Not yet. We need to take a dozen measurements to test how robust it is. It'll be fine now—just be patient."

Hannah opened the door and stepped down onto the windswept promontory. He reached into his pocket for his pewter hip flask and took a swig. He turned to the west and looked out over the sea in the direction of the islands. It was too dark to see anything now, but that didn't matter. He knew the blades were turning, the turbine was producing electricity, and the cable was transmitting most of it.

On cue, the breeze picked up.

Hannah held up the flask in a toast. "Thank you," he said. "You might just have made my fortune."

42

It took three hours and several cups of tea before the computer beeped with the sound of an inbound message. Milton woke the screen and clicked the email. Ziggy had included just one word of reply—VOILA—and, beneath it, he had attached the folder, but now without the lock. He double-clicked the folder, and a host of files was revealed: Word documents, spreadsheets, JPEGs, videos. The naming convention was chronological, with nothing that might give an idea of what each file might contain.

Milton moved the mouse to the first .mp4 and double-clicked. A video played. It had obviously been taken from some distance on a phone. The person who had taken the video was up a slope from a group of men who were labouring at something. It looked as if the person shooting the video was sheltering behind rocks; the ground descended steeply to what looked like a sheer cliff edge.

"Do you know where that is?"

"One of the islands," Ox said.

"Which one?"

He shrugged. "Could be any of them. Look at the pictures—maybe that'll make it clearer."

There were more than a hundred photographs. They scanned through them, watching as the landscape changed: beach, to cliffs, to a small loch that reflected the clouds overhead. Milton clicked again; the subsequent shot was of a tall lighthouse painted white. The camera had been placed at the foot of a slope that climbed up to the building.

Helena sat up a little. "I know where that is."

"So do I," Ox said.

"Where?" Milton said.

"That's the Flannan Island lighthouse," Ox said.

Helena nodded emphatically. "Alan took me."

"Are you sure?"

"Positive."

"When?"

"Weeks ago," she said. "Before all this. We went out on a whale-watching boat. He said he wanted to show it to me because it was so spectacular."

"What's on the island?" Milton asked.

"Thousands of birds," she said. "No one lives there anymore."

"The lighthouse?"

"It's been automated for forty years," Ox said. "Keep going through them."

Milton clicked on another video. A man was pointing and shouting orders, but the audio was too poor to make anything out.

"Who's that?" Ox thought aloud.

"I've never seen him before," Helena said.

Milton assumed that Caine had captured the video himself. The camera angle jerked suddenly as he retreated behind the boulder. The footage stopped.

"Open another," Ox said.

Milton double-tapped a subfolder, and another selection of images appeared. He opened the first image, and they saw men in a line, facing the camera, being addressed by the man from before. It made Milton think of a field briefing. Milton clicked the next shot and then the next. Each shot had the dark-haired man in a slightly different position, as if he were delivering orders while walking back and forth. Milton clicked on the final file. The image revealed was a shot of another man, this one mooring a rigid inflatable boat to a cleat fixed to the wall of a natural stone landing stage. The man was looking toward the camera, and his face was visible.

"Recognise him?" Ox said.

"No," Helena replied.

Milton was silent.

He recognised him, but, for now, he thought it best to keep that to himself.

43

Number Twelve bumped the car over the lip of the ramp and parked where he was directed by a member of the ferry's crew responsible for loading the vehicle deck. He switched off the engine and stepped out into the echoing space as two large lorries muscled their way aboard. He went around to the boot, opened it, and took out the leather bag that he had found inside when he had picked the car up from the public car park near Tesco. The quartermaster had left it there for him and had stocked it with everything that he would need: the bag contained a Glock 17 and ammunition, together with a small pouch that contained a dispenser and two ampoules with clear fluid inside. The fluid was a solution that contained a cardiotoxin that increased the flow of calcium ions through the cardiac muscle, inevitably leading to heart failure. As was usually the case with these assignments, Twelve had been given leeway to act according to the circumstances that presented themselves on the ground; the preference was for death that appeared natural, but, when that was not possible, a handgun was permitted. The only requirements were that the target was eliminated and that Twelve faded away afterwards without being seen.

He left the car and climbed up to the cafeteria. The MV *Loch Seaforth* was the largest ferry that operated between the mainland and the islands, and was due to complete the voyage to Stornoway on the Isle of Lewis in just over three hours. It looked as if it was going to be a quiet crossing; the car deck was a quarter full and there was no queue as Twelve bought a smoked salmon bagel and a cup of coffee. He went over to one of the empty tables and sat down, pretending to read the copy of *The Scotsman* that he had bought before collecting his car. He looked over the top of the page at the men, women and children who ambled through the cafeteria. The target was a sixty-three-year-old man called Jack Watson. Twelve had memorised Watson's photograph and was sure that he would recognise him. Group One had put him under loose surveillance and had confirmed that he had driven from Edinburgh to Ullapool earlier that afternoon, and that he had purchased a return ticket to Stornoway. He had been briefed that Watson was going to be speaking to local councillors tomorrow morning about a proposed seabed lease off the coast of the islands. The suggestion was that a series of wind farms were to be erected and that Watson was involved in that decision. Twelve didn't know any more than that, nor did he want—or need—to know. He had everything he needed: his target's photograph, the means to eliminate him, and the order to do so.

He didn't have to wait long.

An older man climbed up from the deck below and went to the counter to order a coffee. Twelve compared him with the photograph that he had hidden inside the pages of the newspaper and satisfied himself that it was the right man.

Watson was dressed in a tweed jacket, a pair of jeans that were a little too baggy for him, sturdy shoes and a tartan cap. He stopped at the counter, bought a coffee and took it out to the stern observation deck.

Number Twelve collected his coffee and followed. It was dark, with the lights of Ullapool visible against the dark shoulder of land that was quickly disappearing behind them. The wake was churned up, a white track that was picked out by the glow of the moon. The deck was taken up by fifty or sixty red-painted metal chairs, none of which was occupied. Watson continued to the stern and stood at the rail. A section of the vehicle deck, used to stow the trucks and larger vehicles, was directly below. Watson stood there for five minutes, then went to the port side, where a barrier that sloped away from the boat warded against passengers falling overboard. Twelve stayed on the other side of the deck and wondered whether this was an opportunity. There was a security camera fixed to the superstructure and aimed back to the deck, but Twelve was confident that, if it was working, it would not be monitored. It might be relevant in the hours after someone went overboard; the footage would be checked for confirmation, and that would raise issues with identification. Twelve decided against it. He was black, and he hadn't seen any other passengers of the same colour as him. He'd be too easy to identify after the fact. Better to wait until they landed and do it on the island, as he had planned.

He headed back into the warmth of the cafeteria and sat down where he could observe the doors. He unzipped his coat and found a table where he could drink the rest of his coffee. The boat really *was* quiet; he scanned quickly, left to right, and counted just three other people taking refreshments: a young man in a suit, an elderly woman who was doing a crossword puzzle, and a middle-aged man who was looking at something on his phone.

A man appeared from the bathroom and ambled toward the door to the observation deck. The man who had been looking at his phone glanced up, and Twelve noticed the two of them exchange a look.

Twelve finished his coffee and went over to drop the empty cup in the bin. He came back behind the man with the phone in the hope that he might be able to see what he was looking at, but the man had laid his device face down on the table. He returned to his seat and took out his own phone, opening the camera and switching to video. He pressed to record and, under the pretence of looking at the screen, swivelled the lens so that he could film the other man.

He looked back at the doors to the observation deck just in time to notice sudden movement from outside. He looked through the doors, blinded a little by the reflection of the artificial lights in the glass, but, before he could discern anything, the man from the bathroom returned. He walked easily, with a nonchalance that said he was supposed to be there and that there was nothing that was out of the ordinary. The doors hissed aside; he came inside; the doors closed behind him. Twelve paid him more attention this time: he was in his thirties or forties, Asian, and, despite being of average height, he was bulkier than normal. Twelve angled the phone to ensure that he had footage of the man as he walked to the counter, casually ordered a coffee, and then took it down to the car deck.

Twelve waited a moment.

The second man—also Asian—rose and followed the first.

Twelve waited another thirty seconds to make sure that

the two men did not return. He stood, went to the doors and passed out onto the observation deck.

Watson had been standing by the rail, but there was no one there now.

Twelve looked for another way that the man could have left the deck, but saw none; the only way in or out was through the door that he—and the man from the bathroom—had just used.

He went to the rail and looked down into the churn of the sea. The waves were three or four feet high, a rolling seascape of ups and downs that would have made it difficult to spot anyone in the water even if it had been light. There was no sign of Watson.

He kept his face neutral as he went back into the cafeteria and took out his phone. He found the footage that he had recorded and reviewed it: he had a clear shot of the man from the bathroom and a profile shot of the man he now suspected of being his lookout. Twelve's phone was standard issue for Group Fifteen agents, technology developed by Group Six that used a VPN to encrypt internet traffic to and from the central servers. He uploaded the footage so that it could be accessed by the analysts in Group One and typed a quick flare requesting immediate identification of the two men at the time-codes he supplied. He pressed send, waited for the file to complete its upload, and then put his phone away again.

He went to order a second coffee, half expecting to hear the blasts of the ship's horn that would announce a man overboard.

There was nothing.

PART IX

WEDNESDAY

44

Milton woke up before dawn, got straight out of bed and, with an hour to kill before he needed to leave to catch the first ferry from Uig to Tarbert, decided to indulge himself with a bath. He ran the taps and emptied the small bottle of soap into the churn of the water. He had ordered a copy of *The Scotsman*, and it had been left in a bag that had been hung on the handle of his door. He collected it, left it on the side of the bath and slid into the hot water.

He allowed his mind to drift back to what he had discovered with Ox and Helena yesterday. He had emailed himself the pictures that they had found on Alan Caine's computer, and he flicked through them now. He examined each, looking for anything that might help him to understand what the man had been investigating, before swiping onto the photograph that he had been unable to get out of his head: the shot of a large man mooring a rigid inflatable boat to a landing dock. The man was looking just to the left of the camera, but his features were clear and unmistakeable.

It was Flash.

What was he doing on the island? His business was taking tourists out on his boats, but it didn't begin to explain what he was doing there. How was he involved?

He put his phone down and removed the newspaper from its plastic sheath. He looked at the front page and skimmed a story about Oxfam appealing for more volunteers to work in its Scottish shops. Another story concerned the launch of a new nationalist party, and another set out possible progress on the campaign for a second independence referendum. Milton read them and turned to the second page.

He frowned. The story at the top of the page—Treasure Trove Unearthed in Scottish Castle Fetches £250,000 at Auction—told of a haul of valuable antiques that had been found during the restoration of Amhuinnsuidhe Castle on the Isle of Harris. The story would not normally have been of interest to Milton, save that he remembered the unusual name of the property. There was a picture of the castle's owner standing next to a table that bore the paintings, crested dinner services and silverware that had been discovered.

Milton recognised the man from the framed photograph that he had found face down in Chrissie's caravan. The caption beneath the photograph confirmed his recollection. It was Johnston Hannah.

Milton stared at the picture. Hannah was handsome and confident in front of the lens, as if having his photograph taken for a newspaper was something that happened to him every day.

Ox had suggested that the migrant workers who had gone missing had been working for Hannah at the time of their disappearances.

How did Chrissie know him?

Milton found himself wondering. How had she come to own the hotel? She said it wasn't hers, so whose *was* it? He took his phone, opened the website for the Registers of Scotland and entered the property's details. The title register and plan downloaded, and Milton opened them. The hotel had been purchased for one and a half million pounds two years earlier, but not by Chrissie. The owner was listed as Amhuinnsuidhe Investment (Holdings) Limited, a company with a registered address in Panama. Milton dug around to see if he could find out anything else about the company, but Panama required only limited information about corporations and their officers, and there was nothing to see.

The prospect of speaking to Chrissie about Hannah did not fill him with enthusiasm—she was testy at the best of times, and he was sure she would not react well to his probing into her affairs—but there was no option. Ox was convinced that Hannah was involved in the disappearance of the workers whom Caine had likely been investigating; it wasn't unreasonable to think that he might be able to offer some answers.

45

Twelve had set his alarm for seven, but he was awake before it had the chance to sound. He had booked himself into the Sandwick Bay hotel in Stornoway upon his arrival on the Isle of Lewis. It was a modest place that would serve as a useful base as he worked out what had happened on the ferry the previous evening. He relieved himself, showered and changed into fresh clothes and then took out his laptop and sat down. He piggybacked onto his phone and opened the secure portal to London.

Group One had been busy, and there were two files waiting for his review. Twelve looked at the first file. There were three pictures of the same man: he was clean shaven in two of them and wore a thick beard in the third. Twelve recognised him: it was the man who had gone from the toilet to the observation deck on the ferry. He read through the dossier of information that accompanied the pictures: the man's name was Huang Xin, and he was forty-three years old. He had left school to enrol in the Guangzhou Military Region Special Forces Unit, graduating with honours. Huang's records indicated that he had been active against the Uyghurs in Xinjiang province and had been awarded the Heroic Exemplar Medal for meritorious service.

Twelve opened the second file and saw a similar dossier, this one with pictures of the man who had posted watch over the deck from the cafeteria. His name was Donnie Chen, and he was born in Wugong, a small militarised town in Shaanxi Province. He had also served in the People's Liberation Army in Xinjiang until being transferred to Beijing to enrol in the elite Military Diplomatic Academy. He was assigned the legend of "Zhang Shengmin" and was subsequently recorded as present during a handful of suspected state-sponsored assassinations. He had risen to the rank of major and was reported to have been responsible for several hits in Taiwan.

Why had two PLA operators been assigned to murder a man who worked for the Crown Estate in Scotland?

Twelve read the files more thoroughly before closing them and opening an email to Control. He reported what had happened on the ferry, referred to the suspected identities of the assassin and his handler, and requested an update to the terms of his assignment. He sent the email, folded up the laptop and put it back into the shielded bag that protected it from wireless infiltration.

He would proceed with attending to his second and third targets until he was told otherwise. Both were due to be in Glasgow this afternoon. Twelve would have breakfast, check out of the hotel, take the ferry back to the mainland and start his preparation.

46

Milton checked out of the hotel and went looking for an outdoor clothes shop. He found one on Argyll Street, went inside and waited for the woman behind the counter to finish serving the couple ahead of him.

"Thanks for waiting," she said to him as the couple edged between Milton and a display of sunglasses and left the shop. "What can I do for you?"

"I'm going on a trip out to the islands," he said.

"Which?"

"The Flannans."

"That's quite a trek."

"I know," he said, with a self-deprecating chuckle. "I'm hoping to see the puffins."

"You won't be able to miss them," she said. "Big colony of them. You want to get yourself kitted out?"

"I do. What will the weather be like out there at this time of year?"

"The same as the rest of the year," she said with a wink. "Cold and blowy."

Milton walked around the shop and put together the gear that he would have chosen for an expedition in conditions that were likely to be unpredictable. He took a winter sleeping bag with liner, a Gortex sleeping bag cover, then added a Thermos bottle, technical underwear, mid-layers, a windproof jacket and shell pants, a down jacket, mittens, liner gloves, wool socks, liner socks, a scarf and a woollen hat. He added sunglasses, a head torch and a rucksack large enough to stow everything. He went to the counter for it all to be rung up.

"How are you getting out there?"

"A friend has a boat."

"You'll want to check the forecast," she warned. "There's a storm coming in. Nasty one, they say. You won't want to be out there when it hits."

"Thanks," he said. "I'll take care."

MILTON WATCHED from the observation deck as the ferry approached Tarbert. He had driven to Uig in silence, his thoughts busy with what he had discovered on Alan Caine's laptop. At least he had a direction in which to lead the investigation now; the problem was that now he was even more concerned with what he might find.

The captain encouraged drivers to return to their vehicles. Milton flicked his second cigarette overboard and went down to the car deck. The ferry bumped into the dock, and the ramp was lowered. Milton was three rows back and waited for the cars in front to roll over the ramp and onto the dock before reaching to switch on his own engine. The starter clicked, but the engine would not start. He turned on the dome light in the cab and tried again; the light stayed on, suggesting that the problem wasn't with the battery. The cars behind him were waved through by the stevedores in their orange tabards as Milton popped the bonnet and went out to have a look.

"You okay?" asked one of the crew.

"Fine," Milton said. "I think the starter motor needs some encouragement."

"Aye," the man said. "Let me know if you need a hand."

Milton went around to the back of the van and took out the tyre lever he had seen there earlier. He went back to the front of the van and used the lever to tap firmly against the motor. He suspected that the contacts were stuck, and hoped that, with a little encouragement, they could be unstuck. He climbed back into the cab and turned the key. This time, the engine turned over and caught.

He rolled out and passed the line of traffic waiting to board for the voyage back to Uig. The vehicle at the front of the line caught his eye. It was a normal-looking four-by-four, but it was towing an unusual trailer behind it. He hadn't seen anything quite like it before: it had expanding sides, hydraulic supports, a satellite dish folded down on the roof and flaps for what he assumed were external plug-in points. It was a dirty white rather than the green that might have suggested that it was military. Milton knew well that this part of Scotland thronged with members of the armed forces, particularly with regard to the naval hardware that sailed in and out of the Firth of Forth. The trailer had no markings, though, and he fleetingly wondered whether it might be a mobile medical unit or a library for the use of islanders. The driver edged ahead, manoeuvring onto the ramp and carefully rolling it onto the deck.

47

Milton got back to Harris in the early afternoon and drove across the island to the hotel. He parked at the rear of the building and went round to Chrissie's caravan. It was quiet, and there was no answer when he knocked. The kitchen door was open, and Milton crossed the yard and went inside. Bobby had filled the sink with soapy water and was washing the glasses by hand.

"Afternoon," he said.

"Afternoon."

"Where's the boss?"

"She didn't tell you?"

"She didn't. What's going on?"

"She's gone to Glasgow."

"Why?"

"Don't ask me—she wouldn't tell the likes of me her business."

"When did she say she'll be back?"

"Tomorrow."

Milton pointed to the oven; its display was still dead. "What about the electrician?"

"He's coming in an hour. We're closed for tonight, though."

"I've got a smoker in the back of the van, and I need to get it in here. Give me a hand, will you?"

Bobby finished the last of the glasses and left them to dry on the draining board. He followed Milton out to the van and, between them, they hauled the heavy oven into a space that had been cleared for it next to the dishwasher.

"I wanted to ask you something," Milton said as he removed the cardboard packaging. "You've lived on the island a while, haven't you?"

"Aye. All my life."

Milton gently pushed the oven back into its space. "Who owned the hotel before Chrissie?"

"John and Ruthie MacGovern. They'd had it for years and years. Before I was born, anyway."

"And Chrissie only recently came to the island?"

"That's right. She's not local. I mean—the accent gives that away, right?"

"Right," Milton said. "What happened? She just turned up?"

"John died, and Ruthie put the place up for auction. A lad I know was interested in buying it, turned up on the day ready to put in his offer, but he said he never got a sniff. There was a phone bidder, and they kept increasing the price until he couldn't go any higher. There was another bidder in the room—I think it was someone from the mainland—and it was him and the phone bidder left in it. My pal says that whoever it was on the phone had deep pockets, because there was never any hesitation on bidding up, even when they were well past what the place was supposed to have been worth."

"Who was the bidder?"

"Can I have a fag?" Bobby said. Milton took out his box and tossed it over. Bobby took a cigarette out, held it between his lips and lit it. "She'll kill me if she thinks I've been talking about her business behind her back."

"It can just be between us, then."

Milton followed as Bobby went outside. "Chrissie turned up a week later. No one had ever seen her before. It'd be fair to say she wasn't the most popular person on the island."

"Why?"

"The local lad she outbid is a good sort, and no one liked the idea of outsiders taking the place over. She worked hard, though. Tarted the place up and got it open again. Made a real effort to fit in with the community—she hired local when she could."

"Like you."

"Aye. And she made sure that the grub for the kitchen all came from local producers and told everyone that the atmosphere of the old place wouldn't get trashed. People were worried that it'd turn into some sort of theme hotel for Sassenachs who wanted to come up here for the grouse and the beaches, and she said that wouldn't happen. Everyone thought she was doing well. Then, on the first night, she made this speech and told everyone that she was a half owner and that the other half was owned by her husband. No one knew she even *had* a husband."

Milton could tell where Bobby was going. "And that was Johnston Hannah?"

"She told you?"

"She mentioned it," he lied. "It wasn't popular?"

"That's one way to describe it."

"I thought he was a local hero."

"He'd like you to *think* he is, but it's all hot air with him. He doesn't give back half as much as he tells people he does. There was a piece on him in the newspapers four or five years ago, back when he was starting to do well for himself. I don't understand exactly what he was doing, but he had some sort of tax dodge going where he was employed by some offshore operation that meant he could avoid the higher rate. This place, too—someone checked. It's owned by a company registered in Panama. *Panama*—I couldn't even show you where that was if you gave me a map. I'll bet you whatever you like that not all the tax generated here goes into the coffers in Edinburgh."

"He was here the night when the hotel reopened after the fire, wasn't he?"

"Aye," Bobby said. "The posh bastard who looked down his nose at you? That's him."

"What about him and Chrissie? Are they still married?"

"They split up while she was fixing the place up after the fire. He lives in a castle north of here. He drives down now and again, though, maybe to see how she's getting on. They used to row. You could hear it from miles away when he dropped in for one of his little visits."

"And the locals know he's out of the picture now?"

Bobby nodded. "You saw the reception she got when we opened. People have forgiven her since they know she's not involved with him anymore. They've got short memories when it comes to someone who'll let them drink cheap and feed them decent grub."

"But if they've split up..."

"Why does he still come?" Bobby finished for him. "I get the impression that he still has a thing for her. I think the split was her idea."

Milton nodded that he understood.

"I did wonder, you know," Bobby said.

"About what?"

Bobby winced, as if embarrassed about what he was going to say.

Milton helped him out. "About me and Chrissie?"

"Aye. Hannah's the jealous type. Look—I don't want to speak out of school or anything..."

"I won't be offended."

"There was another bloke, six months ago. One of the roofers who helped fix the place up. Chrissie had a fling with him over the summer. They seemed to be getting on well, but then he disappeared. Packed up his things and left —the roof was only half done."

"And you think Hannah had something to do with it?"

"I *know* he did," Bobby said. "Hannah came to visit a day or two later, and the two of them had one of their ding-dongs. She said she knew that Hannah had scared him off. I heard him admit it—and he said he'd do it again if there was anyone else. You and the last bloke are different. I know you can look after yourself, but that might not do you any good with someone like Hannah. A man like him, with as much money as he has, can pay for a couple of blokes to rough you up, toss you in the back of a van and get you off the island."

"I'm not scared of him."

"You should be—I am. He's dangerous. And he's got dangerous pals. You need to watch out for him. He's bad news."

48

Hannah walked along the beach, reaching down to collect the tennis ball that Nessie had deposited at his feet and launching it away again for the hound to chase. He clambered up the path to the cliff and paused to admire the view. Amhuinnsuidhe Castle was perched on the rocky outcrop at the southern end of the Isle of Harris. Its position allowed it to stand as sentry, watching over the ships that passed through Loch Leosavay and out to sea. Hannah stopped by the ancient cannons that were aimed out over the water and rested the palm of his hand against iron that had been warmed by the sun.

The castle loomed up behind him, built on the narrow strip of flat ground between the water and the hills that climbed up behind it. He had purchased it ten years ago and had spent most of the time since engaged in a continuous program of refurbishment. It had become a money pit, but Hannah was prepared to put up with that for the glory of being able to call it his home. It had fallen into such a state of disrepair that the owners had no longer been able to afford its upkeep. Hannah had taken it on with collapsed ceilings and rainwater that flooded through its eight-foot-thick walls, but now, after spending nearly two million on a series of extensive works, it was back to something approaching its former glory. He had made a business out of buying distressed assets, investing in them and selling them on for a profit. He had originally intended something similar for the castle, but, after living in it for a year, had decided that it was too precious to sell.

Hannah was watching the slow passage of a small boat out of Amhuinnsuidhe when Nessie turned around and started to growl. Hannah turned, too, and saw a man making his way from around the corner of the curtain wall.

"This is private property," Hannah said.

The man ignored him. He was dressed in an understated way that suggested quality: black jeans that appeared to have been pressed, boots that were polished to a high sheen, a black ribbed turtleneck sweater and a leather jacket, also black. He sported black Wayfarers, and his hair looked as if it had been recently trimmed. There was a little stubble on his jaw, but even that looked manicured.

"Did you hear me? Private property. Please, you have to leave."

"I don't think I will," the man said.

The dog growled, baring his fangs. Hannah reached down and attached the lead to his collar.

"Who are you?" he said. "Have we met?"

"No, we have not."

"Then look," Hannah said. "I'm afraid I'm very busy. I need—"

He stopped as he saw a second man. This one he recognised: it was Donnie Chen, the muscle responsible for making sure the immigrants did what they were told out on the islands.

"You know Mr. Chen," the first man said.

"I do."

"Good. My name is Chiang Zhou. I represent Mr. Yongkang, and I do not care if you are busy. You will cancel your plans so that we can speak."

Hannah felt a twist in his gut. He couldn't afford to say or do anything that would cause Yongkang to question his involvement; if he was to pull out, everyone else would follow, and Hannah would be left high and dry.

"I'm sorry," he said. "I spoke with Yongkang a couple of nights ago. Everything was fine."

"He is concerned with the progress of the project. He feels that you have been evasive."

"That's not true—"

"He feels that you have been evasive," Zhou repeated over Hannah's objection, "so he sent me to review your work. Shall we go inside?"

HANNAH LED the way through the courtyard and into the east range and the sitting room. Zhou and Chen followed and, when they reached their destination, they both sat in the armchairs next to the fireplace without being invited. Hannah was not blind; he was being shown that he was not in charge any longer, not even in his own home.

"We will be based here," Zhou said without preamble.

"We?"

"Chen will bring men to help."

"We don't need help," Hannah protested. "The work has already been done."

"I am not talking about the test."

"Then what?" He paused, realising what Zhou meant. "Oh. *That* kind of help."

"It is time to exert our influence. We cannot allow local difficulties to delay us. We must have a successful test—"

"We have that," Hannah said.

"So you say, and we will assume, for now, that you are correct. Now we must make sure that we have all the necessary approvals in place."

"I told Mr. Yongkang about that," Hannah said, as if that might win him better treatment. "There's just one man whom we need to persuade."

"Watson."

"That's right. We employed a lobbyist to take care of that for us, but he hasn't done his job properly."

Zhou tutted. "There is a saying in China: don't blame a mirror for your ugly face. I believe you would say that a bad workman blames his tools. It doesn't matter how we say it; the sentiment is the same. You chose Mr. Bolton as your representative. The responsibility for his failure lies with you."

"We can still persuade Watson," Hannah protested. "Everyone has a price."

Zhou shook his head. "The time for persuasion has passed. He was given a choice and he said no. That was his decision to make and his consequences to face."

"What does that mean?"

"It means, Mr. Hannah, that we don't have to worry about Mr. Watson anymore."

Hannah felt the muscles in his cheeks go slack as his mouth fell open. "What?"

"You *do* know how much money is at stake in this project?"

"Of course I know."

"So you'll understand how we couldn't allow this man to stand in the way of progress." Zhou shrugged. "We tried your way, Mr. Hannah. It didn't work. Chen took care of it."

49

Flash woke with a hammering on the door of his bothy. He had moved from Tobermory to this isolated spot when he had won this godforsaken job. Uigen was a tiny village, but it did come with one advantage for someone who was commuting out to the islands most days: it faced a bay and had its own small harbour from which he was able to come and go whenever he needed to work. One of the other benefits was that it was quiet, especially at—he checked his watch—seven in the evening.

The knocking continued. He got up from the sofa and made his way over to the door.

"What the hell is it?"

"Open the door. Need to talk."

He recognised Chen's voice and groaned.

"Hold on," he shouted, looking for his shoes.

He reached the door and unbolted it. Chen was standing outside.

"What is it?"

"You need to collect the men," he said without preamble.

"From where? Kilda?"

"Collect them from Kilda and take them to the Flannans."

"Tomorrow?"

"No. Now."

"It's getting late," Flash protested. "It'll be dark soon. You want me to take them *now*?"

"Yes—now. The sea is calm. Look."

Chen stepped aside so that Flash could look down the slope to the bay.

"That's an enclosed bay," he said. "It's not open water."

"The sea is calm."

Flash knew that there was no point in disputing it with Chen. The forecast was bad for the next forty-eight hours, but he wouldn't care about that.

"I don't like the idea of doing it at night."

"It *must* be tonight."

"Why are they going back to the Flannans? I thought we were done there."

"The excavations need to be filled in. We leave no trace —remember?"

"I remember."

Flash glanced through the door and saw that there were two other men waiting next to the jeep that Chen had used to drive here. Both men were almost as broad as they were tall and looked every bit as humourless. Each wore military-issue, non-rip combat fatigues and fireproof jackets, all in black.

"Who are they?" Flash said.

"Bao and Li Jie—they work for me. They will come with you on your second boat. You pick up the workers, take them to the island, then leave them there. You go back tomorrow when it is time to pick them up."

Flash turned to the two newcomers. "You know how to drive a boat?"

"They know," Chen said.

Flash believed him. He had spent most of his adult life around the military, and these two definitely had the martial look.

"Give me a minute to get changed."

He shut the door before Chen could complain and parted the net curtain to watch as the three men descended the path, went through the gate in the dry-stone wall and down to the jeep that had been left in the middle of the single-track lane. Flash did not want to go, but he knew better than to show dissent. Chen was unpredictable; Flash wasn't afraid of many people, but he *was* afraid of him. He changed into his warm clothes, pulled on his waterproof trousers, hooked the braces over his shoulders, and found his waterproof and windproof jacket. He took the keys for both RIBs from the hook by the door and went out to join the Chinese.

50

Alexandra checked her make-up in the mirror with her editor's parting warning ringing in her ears: "You've got three days, then you're back in the producer pool, and you'll be doing committee hearings. And don't spend a fortune or the bloody accountants will have me, and you'll never leave the office again."

She pouted and touched up her lipstick. She felt a rush of excitement at the prospect of her night's work. She was thankful that her editor was prepared to invest a little of her time investigating the allegation that Johnston Hannah—via his stooge, Jimmy Bolton—had been bribing local councillors in an attempt to muster up support for his move into renewable energy. Alexandra had listened with increasing excitement to the recording that Caesar had made of Bolton's unwitting confession. Bolton himself was small fry, the kind of catch that would be thrown back over the side for lack of interest, but the fact that he was working for Hannah made things very different. It was human nature for people to gloat at the demise of those who had previously been lionised; you could call it schadenfreude or mean-spiritedness, but it didn't really matter either way. It would be a big story, and it would be Alexandra's chance to advance her career. She meant to seize it.

She had always wanted to be a reporter, on air and delivering breaking stories, yet her working life had so far been confined to relentless early and late shifts, cutting together B-list stories for the middle or end of the nightly bulletin. Not once had her pleas for a screen test resulted in any action. She longed to stand in front of a boom mike and have the studio anchor throw to her at the scene of the biggest political story of the day. She was thirty-two now, and she knew that this might be her last chance to secure her break.

She wasn't about to let it pass.

She had spoken to Caesar and, with the promise that she was taking his scoop very seriously, had persuaded him to engage in a little subterfuge to put Bolton in a position where she could speak to him. Caesar himself had suggested that a direct approach would be unlikely to yield results. Bolton, he had explained, would panic if the allegations about what he had been doing for Hannah were put to him straight up; she would get more out of him if she got to know him first. He told her that Bolton was a dreadful gossip, especially when he was drunk, and working on him in a social setting would offer a better prospect of success.

Caesar had offered to set up the meeting. He and Bolton had had a tiff, he said, and Bolton was desperate to see him again. Caesar would tell him that they should have a drink to discuss their relationship. A venue had been agreed, and Alexandra would be there instead of him.

Her phone buzzed with the confirmation that her taxi

was waiting downstairs. She left the bathroom, grabbed her faux-fur shawl and handbag and made for the door of her flat.

She had work to do.

51

Jimmy looked at his watch for what must have been the tenth time in the last five minutes. It was ten fifteen already, and Caesar was hopelessly late. They had agreed on half nine in Chinaski's, and here he was, forty-five minutes later, feeling pathetic that he had put himself in a position where Caesar could make him look foolish. *Desperate* and foolish, he corrected himself. Desperate and foolish and *old*.

He looked out across the bar. It was one of the more fashionable venues in Glasgow, just off Sauchiehall Street, and Jimmy had thought it was just the sort of place that Caesar would have enjoyed. Jimmy had suggested it, too, pushing himself out of his comfort zone in an effort to show Caesar that he had changed. Fat lot of good that was going to do him, though, if he didn't even turn up. He glanced at the black guy who had just taken the stool at the other end of the bar; he was big, with muscles that pushed up against the short sleeves of his shirt. He was gorgeous, too; way out of Jimmy's league, but, as the man noticed that Jimmy was looking at him, he returned his gaze with a smile.

Jimmy looked away, embarrassed.

Jimmy had been surprised that Caesar had called. That wasn't what *usually* happened: whenever there was an argument, Caesar expected Jimmy to be the one to call and start the rapprochement. Jimmy had resisted that this time. He had started to accept that they had reached the end of the road, that Caesar would always want to move faster than he was comfortable with, and that the frustrations in their relationship would cause festering resentments. But then, just after lunch, Caesar had called and said that they should meet for a quiet drink and a chat, and all of Jimmy's sensible and mature decisions had gone out of the window.

Only for him to be stood up.

"Get you another?" the barman said.

"I'm fine," Jimmy replied. He had been nursing his Manhattan for half an hour and still had a third left.

"He stood you up?"

"What?"

"You look like you've been stood up."

"It's not a he," Jimmy snapped.

"Sorry," the barman said. "You're dressed up for a date in a gay bar. It seemed like a reasonable conclusion to reach."

"Well… don't!"

The barman raised his hands in surrender and backed away to serve a woman who was standing just to his right. Jimmy looked at his glass and considered picking it up and sinking it in one go and then going home. There was no point in prolonging the agony. Caesar had made it very clear what he thought of him, and he could think of no reason why he should—

The woman swept a hand across the counter of the bar in an absent-minded gesture and caught Jimmy's glass. It tipped over, sloshing what was left of his cocktail over the sleeve of his jacket.

"Oh my God!" she exclaimed. "I'm *so* sorry. I'm such a clumsy cow."

"It's fine," Jimmy said. "Just a wee splash."

"Hold on—let me get a napkin."

He was going to tell her that it was all right and she didn't have to, but she had already hurried over to the stack of cocktail napkins and swiped a handful of them. She came back and pressed one against Jimmy's sleeve, as if that were going to help.

"Really," he said. "It's hardly wet at all."

She started to mop up the liquid on the bar. "I can't believe I just did that," she said. "*Honestly.* I shouldn't be allowed out in public. What were you drinking? Was it a Manhattan?"

"It was. But you don't have to—"

She turned to the barman and, before Jimmy could complete his protest, she had ordered a fresh Manhattan for him and a pina colada for herself. The barman handed her a bowl of olives as he set about preparing the drinks.

"I'm Alexandra," she said, taking an olive and popping it into her mouth.

"Jimmy."

"Are you waiting for someone?"

"A friend," he said.

She winked at him coquettishly. "Girlfriend?"

Jimmy was going to say yes—anything to avoid admitting the truth to a stranger—but he felt a buzz of disappointment with himself that stopped him short; he and Caesar had split up *because* he had refused to answer those kinds of questions honestly, and, despite seeing the consequences of his continued denials, here he was, about to deny the truth again. He decided to stop pretending.

"Boyfriend, actually."

"Where is he?"

"I'm not sure," he said. "He's late."

"Same," she said. "I'm on a date, too. Looks like I've been stood up. He was supposed to be here thirty minutes ago."

"What a dog," he said.

"Welcome to Tinder—full of players and users and wasters. I'll keep you company until yours turns up if you like."

The barman finished the drinks. He set down napkins on the bar and rested the glasses on them.

"That'll be fifteen pounds," he said.

Jimmy reached for his wallet, but Alexandra held up a hand and, before he could protest, she had produced a bank card and held it against the reader. "No," she said. "I knocked it over. You're not paying for the replacement."

"Thank you. But you really don't have to."

She held up her drink, and Jimmy touched his glass to hers.

"Here's to shitty men," she said.

"Amen to that."

He sipped his drink and she did the same.

"What do you do?" he asked her.

She didn't answer. "Can I be honest with you?"

"I should hope so."

"I recognise you."

"You do? How?"

"You're Jimmy Bolton."

He frowned at that, suspicious that this was not quite the innocent encounter that it might have appeared at first. "How do you know that?"

She took out her purse, opened it and took out a business card. She laid it down on the counter and slid it across to him. He read it: ALEXANDRA MARSHALL and, beneath that, SCOTTISH TELEVISION.

"You've got to be kidding me," Jimmy said.

"Could I ask you a couple of questions?"

"This is a set-up?" The first domino fell and then the next. "Come *on*. Caesar did this? You've been working with *Caesar*?"

"This doesn't have to be antagonistic," she said, her hands raised in what might have been intended to be a placating gesture.

"You had my ex-boyfriend trick me into coming here, and now you say it doesn't have to be antagonistic? Seriously? Are you mental? This is outrageous."

"Fine, I'll just put it to you, then: have you been bribing local councillors to support Johnston Hannah's wind farm proposal?"

Jimmy realised that she was probably recording the conversation and, with that in mind, elected not to say another word. He got up and swiped his jacket from the hook beneath the counter where he had left it.

"I'm going to be running a story about it, Jimmy. It'd be better to say something now—get your side of things on the record."

"I have nothing to say," Jimmy replied.

"You know bribing local officials is a criminal offence, don't you? You know you could go to prison?"

Jimmy put on his coat and walked briskly to the exit.

Alexandra followed. "Fine," she said. "You can't say I didn't give you a chance. If you have second thoughts, you've got my card. Call me."

He pushed the door and hurried out onto the street.

Thankfully, she let him go.

52

Milton needed to wait until nightfall and, since the electrician had let them down again, he decided that he would see if he could fix the problem himself. He knew that the bothy up the road had power and, given that they shared the same transformer, the issue had to be local. He found the fuse box in a cupboard in the hall and concluded that the loss of supply was likely caused by one of three things: an overloaded circuit, a short circuit, or loose wiring. He checked the circuit breakers to ensure that none of them had tripped, and saw that they had not. He called for Bobby and told him to unplug everything in the kitchen. He reset the breaker, flipping it off and then on, and then had Bobby switch on the lights.

"They're on," he reported redundantly, since Milton could see that from the cupboard.

"We're going to reconnect the appliances one at a time," Milton said. "Start with the dishwasher."

Bobby did as he was told, shouted out that the unit was live and that the lights had stayed on.

"Try the freezer and the fridge."

Bobby connected the appliances and called out that they were working. The lights stayed steady.

"Now the oven."

"It's on," Bobby called.

Milton checked the lights and saw that they were unchanged.

"What's left?"

"The grill where you finish the food," Bobby suggested.

"The salamander," Milton corrected. "Go on. Try it."

The lights stayed on.

"What's left?" he called.

"The hotplate, the kettle, the chiller."

"Boil the kettle."

Milton heard the sound of running water, the *thunk* as the kettle was deposited onto its base plate and the click as Bobby switched it on.

The lights went out at once.

"They're out," Bobby shouted.

Milton killed the power to the circuit and took a screwdriver kit from the shelf. He went back into the kitchen and went to the outlet that powered the kettle. He took out his phone, selected the flashlight and had Bobby hold it so that there was enough light for him to see what he was doing. He unscrewed the cover plate and removed it and saw at once that the wiring inside was a mess. Bare wires were shorting against each other and the metal box. Milton could see and smell the charred insulation.

"What was the name of the electrician?"

"McSweeney."

"He's a cowboy." Milton pointed the screwdriver at the open socket. "If that's the standard of his work, I'm surprised the place hasn't burned down again. We're going to have to check it all."

"But not now?"

"No," Milton said. "We'll need daylight. We'll need to leave the power off."

"Do you think you can fix it?"

"Probably," Milton said.

"Chrissie will be pleased."

Milton put the screwdrivers back in the case and left them on the counter for the morning.

"I'll be off, then," Bobby said. "See you tomorrow."

"Hold on," Milton said. "Do you know where the key for the boat is?"

"What?"

"The boat Chrissie keeps at Tarbert. For whale watching. Do you know where she keeps the key?"

"In the office," he said. "Why?"

"I thought I might go out first thing."

"Does she know about that?"

"Of course she does," he said. "I wouldn't just take it."

"No, I'm not saying—"

"I used to be in the military, Bobby—I know what I'm doing."

"Okay. Hold on—I'll get it for you."

Bobby fetched the key for him,

"Where are you planning on going?"

"The Flannans," he said.

"You want to be careful out there."

"Really? Why's that?"

"You don't know the story?"

Milton said that he didn't.

"There used to be lighthouse keepers there. Three of them at a time. Once, a hundred years ago, all three of them disappeared. It was only discovered when the next crew went out to relieve them. Everything had been left as it should be in the lighthouse. There were meals on the table, candles that had burned down to the wicks. But they were gone. Vanished."

"What happened to them?"

"Depends who you ask," Bobby said, clearly enjoying himself. "Aliens. Ghosts."

"Neither sounds particularly likely."

"Aye," he said. "Most people think they were swept over the cliff by a storm, but all of them? At once? My mam used to scare me with the story whenever I was playing up."

"I'll bear it in mind," Milton said.

Bobby told him that he would see him in the morning and left. Milton went to his caravan and changed into the warmest clothes he had. He went back to the kitchen and took out the dish of lasagne he had made for opening night that hadn't all been sold. He took a fork and ate it, cold, while he waited for his phone to download an app with the nautical charts for the waters around the islands. He finished the dish as he plotted the best route for the evening's voyage.

53

Jimmy looked for a cab, but it was a busy night, and he struggled to get one to stop. He decided that he would take the subway and walked to Buchanan Street. It had started to rain while he was inside the bar, and he turned up the collar of his jacket to stop the drops from rolling down his neck.

He reached the entrance to the station and went down to the platform just as a train slowed to a halt. He boarded and took a seat, automatically reaching for his phone. He stopped himself; it was ridiculous, looking to see whether Caesar had contacted him when the evidence of his betrayal was as clear as day. No. He put the phone back in his pocket and checked his reflection in the window of the carriage. Caesar was history. Finished. Jimmy was a catch, whatever Caesar or anyone else might have to say. He'd had a bad run of luck—the situation with Johnston Hannah, the split with Caesar—but tonight could be the start of something new. Something better. Why should he just go home, alone, and mope about his misfortunes? No. That would get him nowhere. He would go out. Caesar had been complaining about that for as long as they had known each other, and perhaps—in that, at least—he had been right. What was the point of pretending to be something that he wasn't? He was a gay man. He would live in the open, as himself, and if people didn't like it? Tough. They would just have to deal with it.

He thought of the club on Glassford Street that Caesar was always going on about. He couldn't remember the name, but he thought he would be able to find it. The train was just rolling into St. Enoch station, and it was just a short stroll to the north from here. As he got to his feet, he saw a black man sitting on the opposite side of the carriage, beyond the vestibule area that lay between the doors. Jimmy recognised him: it was the man he had seen in the bar, the man who had been watching his encounter with the reporter. Jimmy looked at him properly for the first time. His clothes were designer, and his black leather shoes were well polished. He was handsome, with smooth skin and good teeth and hair that was cut close to the scalp and styled with precision. He was tall and muscular, with biceps that popped out of the sleeves of the T-shirt that he was wearing.

Jimmy reached the vestibule and grabbed for the overhead bar as the train jerked to a stop. The man got up, too. He saw Jimmy looking at him and smiled, a little blankly; Jimmy didn't think that he recognised him. The bar was popular with the gay crowd, and Jimmy wondered whether the man might be headed to the club, too. He would normally have considered him to be out of his league, but—fortified by his new attitude—he decided that there was nothing to lose in asking. Wouldn't that be the biggest 'fuck you' that Jimmy could deliver to Caesar? Jimmy would go to the club, but not with him. No. He knew that the guy was Caesar's type, and that he would be eaten up with jealousy if

Jimmy could get him to come with him. He'd get a picture and see to it that it found its way to that bitter little queen... see how he liked *that*.

He stepped down and started toward the exit, wondering what he should say to start a conversation. He turned off the platform and joined a queue of revellers waiting for the escalator and had still not decided when he felt a sharp sting against his shoulder. It was sudden, so quick and fleeting that it might almost have been possible to miss it. It felt like an insect bite, but that seemed unlikely on a cold, wet night in Glasgow. He saw movement to his left as the black man passed him on the outside and started to walk up the escalator, bypassing those who were being carried up on the right. The sting was quickly forgotten as Jimmy wondered whether to walk after him, or whether it might be a better idea to wait and see if he ended up in the club. Just because he had been in a bar that was popular with the gay crowd didn't mean that he was gay. It made more sense to wait. If he saw him in the club, he promised himself he would go over and introduce himself.

Jimmy shuffled along with the queue, and the escalator began to bear him to the surface.

54

Milton locked up the caravan and went down to where the motorbike was parked. He wheeled it out, straddled it and started the engine. The V7 burbled, and Milton opened the throttle. The night was a little windy, but the forecast was for a storm as the week continued. Milton knew that now would be the best opportunity he'd get to go out and explore the Flannans.

He reached the marina. There were two pontoons in East Loch: one at Tarbert, next to the distillery, and the other at Scalpay's North Harbour next to the pier where the fishing boats were berthed. There was space for fifty or sixty boats on the pontoons, and Milton followed the directions Bobby had provided until he found the boat with the hotel's name painted along the side. It was six metres long and bobbed happily against the side of the pontoon. He had fifty miles to cross from the marina to the islands. The RIB would be able to travel at forty or fifty miles an hour if he opened it all the way to its stops. He was capable enough to handle it at that speed, but, since he had all night to get to the islands, check them out and get back, there was no need to push things.

The boat had space for ten passengers in seats behind the driver's console. Milton jumped down, steadying himself against the gentle bucking with a hand against the fibreglass hull. He made sure the throttle was in neutral, lifted the choke lever on the side of the console and turned the key to start the engine. He untied the mooring rope and steered away from the pontoon, keeping his speed down low so as to exit the marina without making too much noise.

He took out his phone, selected the relevant Admiralty chart and checked his route. He would turn to starboard and follow the course taken by the Uig ferry, then peel off due south and follow the coast until he could turn northwest and head up through the tiny islands to the south of Harris. He looked out over the sea and saw, to his relief, that it wasn't too rough. The moon was full and cast its light over the water, a silvered stripe that rippled across the rolling waves. Milton reassessed his plan. The conditions were better than he had expected and, once he was in the open sea on the western side of the island, he would open the throttle a little more than he had first intended and see what the boat could do.

55

Jimmy had looked for the man from the bar, but it didn't appear that he was in the club. It felt strange to be in a place like this on his own, and he was older than most of the others here. He felt uncomfortable and decided that he would have a drink to save face and then make his way back home. He looked at the bottle of Sol that he had ordered and saw that it was nearly finished. He wondered whether he should have another, decided that he would need more than just one to make himself comfortable and concluded that his first plan had been the right one. It was time to go.

He got up from the stool next to the bar and promptly lost his balance and bumped into two men who were trying to attract the attention of the barman.

"Careful!" one of them complained.

"Sorry."

He tried to take a step, but found that his balance was still awry.

"Steady," the other man said, smirking at him.

"Pissed already," Jimmy said with what he hoped was a self-deprecating grin.

Jimmy went back to the bathroom, went into an empty cubicle and relieved himself. He went to the sink and looked at his reflection. He was definitely a little the worse for wear, and had to blink for a moment until his vision stopped gently swaying from side to side. His balance wasn't quite right, too, and he put both hands down against the edge of the sink until he was confident that he could stand without rocking back on his heels.

A man was standing at the next sink along. "You okay?"

"Fine."

But he didn't feel fine, and, as he stood there, he became aware of pain in his shoulder, right around the spot where he had felt the sting as he was waiting to leave the underground station. He undid the top three buttons of his shirt and reached a hand around, probing the skin with his fingers. There *was* something there: it felt like a hard little nodule just beneath the surface. He undid the rest of the buttons so that he could remove the shirt.

"At least buy me a drink first!" the man to his left said with a lascivious titter.

Jimmy swivelled so that he could look at his reflection in the glass. He saw a small circle of red, inflamed skin, no larger than a one-penny piece; at the centre of the circle was a tiny red pinprick.

The man to his left was watching with amusement. "You've been bitten."

Jimmy didn't answer, putting on his shirt and trying to fasten the buttons. It was difficult: they felt small and slippery, impossible between fingers that were suddenly clumsy. He closed his eyes and tried to concentrate. If only he didn't feel quite so smashed. How many had he had? He screwed up his face and tried to remember: one drink here plus those two Manhattans that he didn't finish. Surely that wasn't enough for him to feel as pissed as this? He turned on the tap, cupped his hands and filled them with cold water. He dunked his face, scrubbing at his eyes and trying to ward off the drunkenness a little longer. He dried himself and went back out to the bar.

He went to the cloakroom and handed over his ticket.

"You okay?" the girl behind the counter asked.

Jimmy nodded, although he really *did* feel drunk.

"Are you sure? You look out of it."

He tried to say something.

"What? I didn't catch that."

Speaking was suddenly difficult. It felt like he had wads of cotton wool jammed in his mouth. He tried again.

The girl raised the counter and came out with a stool. "Sit down."

Jimmy tried to step forward, lost his balance, reached out a hand for the bar, missed it, and toppled against it and then slid down to the floor. He blinked his eyes. Everything was blurred and, no matter what he did, he couldn't seem to clear it. He felt drowsy, too, and little waves of nausea came and went. He was aware that he was sitting down with his back against something hard. There were people around him; he looked up and saw concerned faces, their features swimming in and out of focus. He could hear the thumping of bass, loud enough to throb through his body. His chest felt as if someone were sitting on it, a heavy weight that wouldn't move, a pressure that lay over his heart and made it difficult to breathe.

"What's happening?" he tried to say.

"Have you taken something?"

He tried to speak, but couldn't say whether the noises he made were intelligible.

Someone spoke, but Jimmy couldn't make out the words.

What is happening to me?

He closed his eyes and tried to concentrate on enunciating each word. They were slippery in his mouth, difficult to work around his teeth; he knew he was making no sense, but there was nothing he could do about it.

He heard another voice: "Is he okay?"

"An ambulance is coming."

"He's fine. Just had too much to drink."

"No, it's not that. He's having a heart attack."

He looked up at the faces, his eyes passing from one to the other to the next, and saw the man from the bar. He was standing just behind the first row of people, his skin shining with the neon from the signs on the wall behind him. He was just watching, a cold implacability to his face that was at odds with the concern of some and the drunken curiosity of others.

Jimmy gasped for breath.

The pain in his chest got worse, as if his heart were in a vice and it was slowly and steadily being tightened. He looked up again, and the man was gone. He tried to find him, but he wasn't there. The room started to go dark; he lost his balance and toppled over onto his side. He heard muffled voices, someone calling out, but none of it lasted; the voices faded out, as if he were moving away from them, and then, finally, the darkness closed over him.

PART X

THURSDAY

56

Twelve waited until the target had been removed from the club on a stretcher and taken to the ambulance that waited outside. The paramedics had reported no sign of life when they arrived and, despite performing CPR, they had been unable to bring him back. Twelve had checked his watch and noted the time of death as just after midnight.

He was satisfied at how simple it had been. The dispenser had worked just as the technicians who designed it had promised. Twelve had waited for the right moment: a circumstance combining a crowd of people, a lack of CCTV and the obliviousness of the target to the threat he faced. The bar had been too public, especially after the attention that had been generated by the reporter's interrogation. The train carriage was bright and fitted with multiple cameras. The station, though, was perfect. There had been a crowd at the bottom of the escalator and only one camera that Twelve could see; the angle of its lens wouldn't have allowed it to catch the brief moment when the poison was deployed. The target was oblivious. Twelve had waited on the surface and then followed him into the club. He had no doubt that the compound would be effective, but standard operational parameters for an assignment like this required him to confirm efficacy. He had been able to do that.

He had dropped the dispenser in his pocket. It was small, able to fit into the palm of his hand, and much like the finger-prick devices that diabetics used to draw blood for testing. He had been careful to hold it with the applicator pointed down, touching it against the fleshy part of the target's shoulder and then pressing the trigger with his thumb. The dispenser had fired, stabbing a needle into the man's flesh and leaving the tiny pellet buried in the muscle. There were two micrograms of neurotoxin in the dose. The biochemists of Group Six had synthesised the poison and, although it would not be completely undetectable in a post-mortem toxicity screen, it was unusual enough that the pathologist would need to know to look for it. The target's file had reported that he had been under stress from his work and that there was a history of heart disease in his family; those two factors would suggest that the cause of his death was as obvious as it had appeared: cardiac arrest.

Twelve had seen security cameras in the club, but was not concerned. Even if he had been spotted in the bar and then the club, what would that mean? The two venues were close to one another, and the former was often the first port of call for the men who would end their nights in the latter. That Twelve and the target had been in both—that they had been on the train together—would be seen as nothing more than a coincidence.

The DJ announced that, due to tragic events, they would be closing early. Twelve made his way to the exit, bypassed the queue for the cloakroom, and stepped outside. It was half past twelve, and the Glaswegian sky was clear and icy cold. He walked away from the club and collected his car from the central car park where he had left it. He took out his phone, opened a browser window and saw that he was just a short drive away from the Premier Inn, where he had left his things.

He started the engine and pulled out, waiting at the exit as the ambulance with Jimmy Bolton's body drove by.

57

The flash of the lighthouse was visible across the dark water from miles away, a long finger of light that scoured from left to right and then, a moment later, reached out again. Milton had Googled the islands: they were marked on the maps as the Flannan Isles, although they were also known as the Seven Hunters. They had been uninhabited since the lighthouse had been automated in the early 1970s, left now to their abundant wildlife: the puffins and fulmars and petrels and gannets that chattered and croaked as Milton slowly chugged closer.

The chart that Milton had downloaded suggested that there were two landing stages: one on the southeastern side of the island and the other on the southwest. The lighthouse itself was to the north. Milton had examined a satellite image and knew that the island had a jagged coastline, with a number of narrow bays cutting into the rock. A series of man-made tracks led from the two landing stages to a central point where they merged and continued up to the lighthouse. A circle fifty feet to the south of the lighthouse was marked with an H that denoted the helipad; a helicopter was the only other way to reach such an isolated spot.

Milton was approaching from the east, and there was enough moonlight for him to be able to find the landing stage on that side of the island. It was man-made and looked old, most likely constructed to allow for the unloading of materials needed to build the lighthouse. A flight of steps had been carved into the rock, climbing from the water all the way up to the plateau above. Milton cut the engine and glided up to the platform. The rubber collar of the boat bumped up against the rock, and Milton, line in hand, took the opportunity to jump out. The surface was slippery with lichen and crusted with salt, and he had to put out his arms to balance.

Milton secured the line around an old cleat and took a moment to stop and listen. He could hear the sound of the waves breaking against the rocks, the bumping and jostling of the boat, and the clamour of the birds. He doubted whether he would have been able to hear anything that was out of the ordinary, but everything appeared to be just as it should.

The treads of the stairs had been eroded by the sea and the wind so that, in parts, it resembled a slope more than steps, and Milton was grateful for the rope that had been left to aid the ascent. He hauled himself up to the halfway point where the path switched back, the steps becoming a little more reliable as he continued up to the plateau.

A path that he had seen on the satellite imagery cut across the island in a sweeping route around to the lighthouse. It was an old railway track bed, and Milton guessed that it had been laid at the time the lighthouse had been constructed. The concrete casings cut through the jagged and uneven terrain and would have been useful for transporting material from the landing stages to the build site, together with supplies for the lighthouse keepers before they were no longer required. The island sloped up, but Milton was still able to see the top of the lighthouse over the summit, flashing its warning to any ships that might be straying too close to the islands. The sudden glare would have been more than enough to ruin Milton's night vision had he looked into it, but he was careful and made sure to keep his head down as he followed the track and clambered to the top of the rise.

He stopped.

What was that?

He could hear the crash of the waves and the calls from the birds, but there had been something else, too.

He held his breath, listening again.

The hum of an engine, somewhere to the north.

He climbed to the top of the hill and looked in that direction. Aside from the lighthouse, there was no illumination to be seen, just the undisturbed black mantle of the Atlantic. The moon was bright enough for him to see all of this part of the island from here, but there was no movement. Milton listened. He caught voices on the breeze, and the steady buzz of a machine.

The island was half a mile from one side to the other. The terrain was uneven and potentially treacherous, especially since he had decided he could not use his torch to light the way ahead. Milton estimated that it would take him ten minutes to reach the lighthouse from here if he moved slowly and deliberately. He decided to follow a more circuitous route that would allow him to check the rest of the island before the lighthouse, especially the western landing stage. If he was right and he was not alone on the rock, he wanted to make quite sure that there was no prospect that he could be penned against the edge of the northern cliffs by someone closing in on him from his six.

He crouched down low and started off.

58

The glare from the lighthouse reached out across the water again and again and again. The island had an eerie atmosphere to it. Milton remembered what Bobby had told him about the three lighthouse keepers who had disappeared. He had no time for suggestions of the supernatural, but, even so, the thick darkness and the knowledge that the island was miles from the mainland lent the outpost an ominous feeling.

The satellite imagery had revealed that the old track bed described an inverted Y, with the lighthouse at the foot of the stem and the two landing stages where the two arms terminated. Milton walked due west for two hundred metres until he met up with the downward-facing arm that led to the southwestern landing stage. This path also led down to the water, was as steep as the first and looked just as treacherous. A boat was tied up next to the stage, its mooring lines tugging against the cleats as the tide tried to pull it away from the island. It was a RIB, similar to the one that Milton had used, albeit a little smaller. Milton was tempted to clamber down to investigate, but knew that it had certainly deposited at least two people onto the island with him; he had no interest in being trapped at the bottom of the slope should those people return.

He knew, too, that his own boat risked discovery the longer he left it where it was; he mused on that for a moment, deciding that it was hidden from above by the darkness and the angle of the cliff and that there would be no reason for anyone to go to *that* stage if their own boat was here, on the other side of the island.

He concluded that it was safe to continue his search. He turned to the north, but, rather than take the track bed, he followed the cliff edge. On his right, the terrain climbed up to the peak upon which the lighthouse had been built. The regular flashes of light from the bulb lit the area, and Milton stayed down as low as he could to minimise his profile. A stone wall had been built around the lighthouse, and there was a one-storey building abutting the tower to one side. The main body of the building was at least twenty metres tall, with antennae bristling around its circumference and an array of solar panels to keep it charged.

The noise of the machinery that Milton thought that he had heard was no longer audible. He listened for it and, above the breaking of the waves, was rewarded with a shout and, a moment later, a shouted reply. He looked left, two hundred metres to the west, and saw the dark shapes of two men. They were standing shoulder to shoulder and looking out to sea. Both were smoking; Milton saw the red tips of the cigarettes glowing brighter every time the men inhaled.

Milton was at the edge of the main body of the island; there was a narrow isthmus and then another part of the island that was perhaps a quarter of the size. The isthmus was short and bordered on both sides by a steep drop to the crashing waves below. Milton flattened himself to the ground and slithered over the grass, trying to get close enough to observe the two men without giving himself away. He aimed for what looked like a large boulder between them and him that would offer him a little cover. He drew nearer and saw that he was mistaken; it *wasn't* a natural formation, but something that had been left and then covered with a tarpaulin. It was secured at each corner with a metal peg that had been driven into the ground. Milton grabbed one of the corners and heaved until the peg slid out of the earth. He lifted the tarp and folded it back just enough to reveal a cement mixer, a collection of shovels and pickaxes and stacked bags of sand and cement. Milton touched his hand against the mixer's engine; it was warm, as if recently active. It must have been what he had heard from across the island.

It made no sense. The island was supposed to be uninhabited, and Milton could discern no reason for the presence of building material. Could it be something to do with the lighthouse? But what? And why were two men here now, in the middle of the night? The only thing that he could think of was that they were here for the wildlife, but, given the context—the disappearance of Alan Caine and the immigrant workers and the evidence that they had been interested in this island—that seemed very unlikely indeed.

He heard the voices again and, as he peered around the side of the tarpaulin, he saw both men making their way up the slope toward him.

59

The light from the tower swung across the island. Milton crawled to a large boulder that stood at the edge of the island and pressed himself into its cover. He was stuck. He was out of sight for the moment, but that wouldn't last long if the men continued in the same direction, and he couldn't go back across the isthmus without being seen. He controlled his breathing and assessed the situation. It wasn't positive. He was outnumbered, with nothing beyond a fist-sized rock at his feet that he could use to defend himself. On the other hand, he didn't think the two men had any notion that he was here with them.

The men drew nearer, and Milton quickly realised that they were not speaking English. He waited, listening, and recognised an Asian language. He had worked throughout the region and, although he didn't speak it, he was about as confident as he could be that the two men were speaking Mandarin Chinese.

They certainly were *not* here for the birds.

The two of them drew closer and, staying low and

looking around the side of the boulder, he got a better look at them. They were both dressed in black, with tactical boots and black woollen hats. The man in front was big; Milton guessed he must have outweighed him by thirty pounds. The second man, while shorter, was also powerfully built.

The lighthouse flashed again.

Milton had hoped that they might bypass the covered equipment, leaving him free to stay in cover and out of sight, but the bigger man said something and diverted. He knelt down at the corner of the tarpaulin that Milton had pulled back and pointed to the dislodged peg. He said something to his comrade, pointing down at the loose flap. He put the peg back and used the heel of his boot to drive it back down into the ground.

Might they put the loose peg down to the wind? Milton hoped so; he wouldn't be able to move without being seen but, conversely, he didn't think they would notice him unless they began a proper search. He sucked his teeth. A low profile was possible for as long as the night lasted, but all bets would be off if they were still on the island when the sun came up.

He watched the two men as they spoke. They took flashlights from their pockets and switched them on, shielded cowls preventing the glow from lighting up too much of the slope. They swept the beams around them, splitting up so that the smaller man crossed the isthmus in the direction of the lighthouse. The big man investigated the tarpaulin and then started in Milton's direction.

Milton closed his hand around the rock. The big man would see him if he kept coming. Milton heard the crackle of a radio and watched as the man fished a receiver out of his pocket, turned his back to Milton and spoke into it.

Milton glanced across the isthmus to the lighthouse, wondering if there was any possibility that he could move out of range without being seen. The chances of crossing the open ground before he could find cover without being seen were slim, at best; the lighthouse confirmed that with another bright flash.

The big man was speaking English into the radio. "Have you seen anyone else tonight?"

The reply was heavy with static and difficult to make out. "No."

"Anyone else on the water?"

Again, the answer was negative.

The man put the radio away. He was just on the other side of the boulder now, and the sweep of the flashlight suggested that he was going to be thorough with his search. There was nothing else for it; Milton was going to have to take him out. The man muttered something in Mandarin and turned, the beam of light playing across the rough ground and then bouncing off the exposed granite of the island where the grass had died back.

Milton clutched the rock and balanced himself, ready to move.

The beam of light went past the boulder and off to the left.

The man followed it, coming into sight three or four metres away.

The lighthouse flashed.

Milton rose and threw a hook with the rock in his fist. The man must have seen him, for he managed to get an arm out and lean away just enough so that the rock caught a glancing blow against his head, an inch or two above his ear. It staggered him, forcing him down to one knee. Milton closed the distance between them, but, before he could strike out again, the man found a reserve of strength and speed that caught Milton by surprise. He powered at him, the point of his shoulder landing in Milton's gut and driving him back. Milton tried to arrest his backward momentum, but the man was too strong. Milton crashed into the boulder; the air was punched out of his lungs. The man closed his arms around Milton's torso, pinning his arms against his sides, and tried to get him into the air so that he could throw him to the ground. Milton locked his right foot around the man's left ankle, and, as the bigger man struggled to force it free, Milton raised his left knee into his groin.

The man gasped and let go.

Milton had the benefit of higher ground and raised his boot and kicked the man in the chest. The man stumbled back, his arms windmilling as he tried to maintain his balance. He went back one step, then another, then another and, as Milton descended the slope to close on him, the man's foot slid into something wet. It arrested his momentum and caused him to tip over. He landed on his back in something liquid. It wasn't water—the sound of the impact was a damp slap rather than a splash—and Milton, thinking of the bags of cement that he had seen, guessed that it must have been freshly poured concrete. The man cursed and tried to get back to his feet, but the concrete stopped him from finding any purchase.

He reached a hand into his pocket.

Milton lunged ahead and leapt onto him, one knee sliding on either side of his torso. It *was* fresh concrete and, although it was solidifying, Milton's weight pushed the man deeper into it. The man tried to withdraw his hand, and Milton, not prepared to stare into the barrel of a nine-millimetre, grabbed and pinned the man's wrist against his chest. They wrestled; the man was strong, but Milton was atop him, pushing down. He leaned forward, pressing with all his weight, and with his left hand he pushed the man's head around until he could force his mouth and nose beneath the surface.

Milton heard a shout. The second man had heard the struggle and was on his way. Milton leaned his forearm on the big man's head, staying atop him even as he bucked his hips in an attempt to get him off.

The lighthouse flashed.

The man struggled, jerking and thrashing.

Another shout.

The man went limp.

Milton held him down. He saw the light of the flashlight, close at hand. He reached into the man's jacket, found the pistol that he knew would be there, and yanked it away from the man's lifeless fingers. He aimed at the flashlight, nudged the pistol a little up and a little right, and fired three times in quick succession. The flashlight jerked up, then fell to the ground, the beam scattering left and right as it rolled down the slope.

Milton took a breath, the gun still trained on the part of the slope from where the second man had approached, and then scrambled away from the concrete, his elbows covered in the damp slop as he retreated onto the firmer ground. He stood and, the gun pointed out ahead of him, made his way slowly across the ground until he saw the body of the second man. He wasn't moving. The flashlight was on the ground, still lit, and Milton stooped to take it. He quickly cast the light over the two bodies to be sure that both were dead and, satisfied that they were, he dropped to his haunches and took a moment to regain his breath.

60

The bigger man was still face down in the viscous concrete, and his colleague was on the slope that led to the isthmus. Milton still had the pistol in his lap; he held it up in the beam of the flashlight and examined it. It was a QSZ-92 semi-automatic, the handgun favoured by South Blade, the Chinese equivalent of the Navy SEALs.

Could the dead men have been Chinese special forces? *Here?* How was that possible?

He saw something odd to his left, something else that shouldn't have been there, and reached out to pick it up. It was a cardboard cigarette carton wrapped in printed paper. He held the packet in his left hand and shone the torchlight onto it. The packet was red, branded with *Fajrant* and a health notice along the bottom: *Palenie zabija*.

Milton recognised the packet. He had smoked the brand before but, as far as he was aware, they were only available in Poland.

He thought back to the couple who had been looking for their son in Oban.

He had a feeling that he had stumbled upon something very bad indeed.

Milton got to his feet and went over to the man in the concrete. He grabbed him by the ankles, dug his heels into the earth and hauled. The concrete yielded him up with a wet slurp; Milton pulled harder, dragging him out of the mire and dumping him on the harder ground. He flipped him over and searched him. The wet mixture clung to his clothes and his face, hiding his features. Milton opened his jacket all the way and frisked him. He found the empty shoulder holster and, inside an interior pocket, the radio handset that he had used earlier, a set of keys, a deactivated cellphone, a packet of cigarettes and a lighter. He set them aside, patted him down for anything else and found nothing.

Milton stood and climbed back to where the second man had fallen. He had toppled onto his back and, as Milton shone the flashlight down onto him, he saw the bloody entry wound in his head where one of the bullets had punched through the skin and bone. Milton ignored that and searched him, finding a second Chinese-made handgun—this one a QSW-06 suppressed sidearm—together with a phone and not much else besides.

Milton stepped back and turned to face the slope down to the isthmus. He shone the flashlight over loose rocks and scree and picked his way over to the tarpaulin. He removed the pegs, including the one the man had stamped back into place earlier, and pulled the tarp out of the way. There were plenty of signs of activity: a barrow route had been carved into the grass and the moss, running from the cement mixer toward the west. Milton followed the track, past the wet bed of cement to another area that had been cleared and concreted over. It was five metres wide by five metres deep and, when he reached down to scrape its surface, he found that this one was set.

Milton knelt down to examine it more carefully and saw a series of metal fixing bolts that had been set into the concrete. There were six of them, arranged in a circular pattern with a diameter of a little over a metre. The concrete bed had been laid as a foundation, and the bolts were obviously used to fix something cylindrical to it.

But what?

Why would someone lay cement here, like this? Two separate patches, one of which had been poured by moonlight.

What were they building?

He crossed the isthmus and climbed up to the lighthouse. The way inside was through a door in the single-storey addition at the foot of the tower. The door was secured by way of a padlock. Milton found another rock and cracked it against the hasp until it snapped. He removed the lock, opened the door and went inside. The room beyond was dark, and Milton switched on the flashlight that he had taken from the dead man. It was a reasonably sized space that had recently been used to accommodate several people. Milton saw evidence of habitation: empty tins of food, discarded chocolate wrappers, plastic bottles of water. The place smelled fetid, too, of stale urine and worse. Milton continued inside, following a corridor into the body of the tower itself. He pushed another door open to find a filthy bathroom, and then, beyond that, a kitchen. A half-hearted attempt to clean up had been made, but Milton still found evidence of recent use. A bucket in the corner of the room had evidently been used for rubbish, and it had not been emptied; Milton took out more dirty food packaging and then, at the bottom, he found something else. He took it out and held it in the beam of the flashlight: it was a blue technical jacket with fleece on the inside and a polyurethane coating on the outside. The logo of the manufacturer—Rooster—was printed across the centre. Milton took out his phone and found the photograph of Alan Caine and Helena that she had been using as her screensaver. The jacket was the same.

Milton sighed. It wasn't conclusive, but it was enough. Alan had investigated what had been happening on the island and had died here. He thought of Judith-Ann, thousands of miles away, and was sorry for the sadness that he was going to cause her.

He looked at his watch. It was half past three, and he knew he still had an hour or two of work to complete before he could leave for the mainland. He shut the door, fastened it with the broken padlock and went back to the two dead bodies. He couldn't leave them here. He didn't think it would be possible to connect him with their deaths, but there was no point in making whatever subsequent investigation that might follow any easier than it needed to be. He edged to the lip of the cliff and looked down; the drop to the ocean was fifty metres at this point, with a surge of frothing water in the cleft between the two parts of the island. Milton turned the body of the larger man and rolled him over the edge, watching him fall out of sight and hearing—just—the sound of the splash over the breaking waves as he hit the water. Milton turned to the smaller man and did the same. Then, he peered carefully over the edge but saw nothing in the dark. The tide would pull them away from the rocks, and their bodies would be lost in the depths of the Atlantic.

Milton crossed the isthmus and retraced his steps to the landing dock where the two men had tied up their boat. He climbed down the wet, slippery stairs and boarded their

RIB. It had been manufactured by Zodiac and was of a design that was commonly used by the navy. Like his, it was constructed with an inflatable gunwale made of reinforced fabric. Propulsion was by way of dual-cylinder in-line diesel engines with a control console at the aft. Milton went to it and found a nautical chart clipped to a panel. The chart was protected from the water by a clear plastic sheath. Milton held the light over it and saw that the scale showed both the depth of the sea and the height of the various islands dotted across it. Two groups of islands had been ringed in red, and scrawled lines from both groups crossed the ocean and found land at the same spot in Harris. The group of islands at the top of the sheet were the Flannan Isles. Milton took the chart from the clip that fastened it to the holder and looked at the islands at the bottom of the page.

The label next to them read St. Kilda and, as Milton looked closer, he saw that one island had been ringed: Boreray.

61

Milton's watch showed half past six in the morning when he finally chugged into the marina. He drifted up to the pontoon, switched off the engines and secured the boat. Milton took his bag—containing the two phones, the radio, both pistols and Alan Caine's jacket—to the motorcycle. He recovered the keys from behind the loose brick where he had hidden them, straddled the bike and made his way across the island to the hotel.

He went around to the back and saw Chrissie sitting on the steps of her caravan. She had a cigarette clenched between her lips and stared at him with hard, angry eyes.

"Morning," he said.

"Where have you been?"

There was no point in lying. "Out on the boat."

"*My* boat?"

"Yes. I'm sorry—I know I should've asked."

"I know why you didn't."

"I couldn't ask—you weren't here."

"You didn't ask because you knew I'd say no."

"I'm sorry," he said again. "But it was important."

She spoke over him. "You know how I know?" she said, continuing before he could answer. "I got a call from the harbourmaster. He's a regular here. Good sort. He thought it was a bit strange to see my boat taken out to sea at night, so he called me to ask whether I knew anything about it. I called Bobby and that was that—it was you. I got the early ferry back this morning so I could find out what the fuck you were thinking." She stared at him, and, when he ignored the hint that it was his turn to speak, gestured angrily with her hand. "Go on, then—what was so important that you had to steal it?"

"The man I've been looking for."

"Alan Caine?"

"That's right. I spoke to his girlfriend when I went to Oban."

"You didn't tell me about that."

"I didn't think it was relevant. You wanted me to go and get the oven and I did. But since I was there..." He shrugged, and she gestured impatiently for him to go on. "Alan worked for a charity that investigates the exploitation of immigrants. The girlfriend had evidence that suggested that he was putting a case together that involved activity on the Flannan Isles."

He saw her stiffen. "Bobby said that was where you were going."

"Something's going on, Chrissie. I found evidence of construction."

"You get people fiddling away out there all the time. It's probably something to do with the wildlife."

He wasn't about to tell her about the men he had killed. "It wouldn't explain why Alan was interested."

"So why would he be?"

"I met a Polish couple in Oban. They were handing out leaflets in the hotel. They said their son came out here to work, and they can't get in touch with him."

"People go missing all the time."

"Maybe. But I think he was out on the island, too."

"How do you know that?"

Milton took the crumpled pack of cigarettes from his pocket. "I found this. They're Polish cigarettes. Both he *and* Alan disappearing when there's evidence that they've been on the same isolated island? That's not a coincidence."

Milton could see that she wasn't convinced. He could have persuaded her easily enough if he told her about the Chinese, maybe showed her the things he had confiscated from their bodies, but he suspected that wasn't something it would be in her best interests to know.

"Is that it?"

"That's why I took the boat. I wanted to have a look for myself, and the conditions won't make it possible once the storm comes in. The boat's back in the marina now. There's no damage. You can take the money for the fuel from my wages."

"Wages? You think you're getting paid? Are you out of your fucking mind? You stole from me."

"No, I borrowed—"

"You're not getting paid, Eric—or whatever your name is. You're fired. Pack up your stuff and sling your hook."

Milton didn't move. Instead, he fixed her with a steady gaze. "Do you think the missing lad worked for Johnston Hannah?"

That brought her up short. "How would I know that?"

"You used to know him well."

"Wee bastard Bobby says more than his prayers."

"It wasn't Bobby," Milton said, trying to spare him. "You've got a picture of him in your bedroom."

"Snooping through my stuff? What has my private life got to do with you? What has any of this got to do with you?" The blood had drained from her face. "Who *are* you? You turn up here out of the blue, start asking questions about my ex, for no reason? What are you really doing here?"

"I've told you everything you need to know."

"Go," she said, her hand trembling as she pointed to the gate. "Get out, *now*."

"I'm going," he said. "But let me give you a little advice. I don't know what Hannah is doing, but it looks very much as if two young men have lost their lives because of it. I think it might be more than two. I'm going to find out what happened to them. If you know anything, you'll be doing yourself a favour if you get it off your chest and tell me before I find out for myself."

"You're threatening me now?"

"I'm not. I'm telling you what's going to happen. I'm very single-minded about things like this—I won't stop looking until I know what happened. If you're involved, that might put you in my way, and that's not a place you really want to be. I like you, despite what you probably think of me, but that won't be a good enough reason for me to go around you. I'll go *through* you, Chrissie. Do you understand what I'm saying?"

"Get the *fuck* out of my hotel," she spat. "Go on—piss off, before I do what I should've done and called the police."

62

Milton packed up his things and closed the caravan door behind him. Chrissie was nowhere to be seen. Milton didn't regret that. He had said all that he wanted to say, and what happened next was up to her. She was a big girl, and, if she had anything to do with what Hannah had been doing, she would bear responsibility for what she chose to do next.

Clouds gathered overhead as Milton walked the ten miles to the harbour at Tarbert, and, by the time he reached the quay, a light drizzle was falling. His plan had been to take the hotel boat out to Boreray, but that was obviously going to be impossible now. As he approached the marina, though, he saw another way to reach his destination.

The *Working Girl* puttered around the corner, making for the harbour wall. Milton walked to meet it, watching as Dougie and Will McCullum, the two fisherman who had taken him to Oban, prepared to land. Will was at the wheel and performed a perfect three-point turn, gunning the engine into reverse and then forward again. There was no need for Milton to catch the lines—such was the practised routine of the berthing—but he tied up the stern and bow warps anyway.

"Morning," Milton called down.

Dougie squinted up at him. "You all right, son?"

"Not bad," Milton said. "Been out this morning?"

"Aye," Dougie said. "Just a quick run."

"I've a favour to ask."

"You need another ride."

"I do. I need to get to St. Kilda."

Will came out of the wheelhouse. "You know how far that is?"

"A hundred miles," Milton said. "I'd pay for your time and the diesel."

Dougie scratched his chin. "You know there's not much out there, right?"

"I do."

"So why would you want to go?"

"The wildlife," he lied. "I've not been to the Hebrides before, and I know I'll regret it if I don't make the effort to go. I'm not sure when I'll be back."

"It's certainly good for that," Dougie said. "Whales and dolphins, too. All sorts of birds."

"That's what I was hoping."

"And you know you can do a day trip from Oban? Your pal, Flash—that's his bag."

"I spoke to him about it," Milton lied again. "He's not going out until next week, and I'll be back home by then."

Dougie turned to his son. "What do you think?"

"We could lay some pots on the way there," Will said. "Pull them up on the way back?"

"We could," Dougie said.

"How much?" Milton asked.

Dougie threw the remains of his roll-up over the side.

"That's a hundred miles there and a hundred back. Two-hundred-mile round trip."

Milton reached into his pocket, took out the wad of notes that he had left and tossed them down. "Take whatever you think is reasonable."

Dougie started to peel bills off the wad, but stopped halfway and looked up. "Och," he said. "I'll not be taking all your cash." He tossed the rest of the wad back up to Milton. "I tell you what—Will's right. We can work all the way up and all the way back too." He held up the notes that he had taken. "This much to cover the diesel. If you agree to put your back into the work on the way, we'll call it quits. Okay?"

"That sounds fair," Milton said. "I'm not afraid to work."

"Aye," Dougie said with a wink. "We noticed."

"When can you go?"

Dougie looked at Will and shrugged. "Weather's not so great from tonight. It'll be bumpy today, but nothing we can't manage. We can probably get the boat turned around in a couple of hours—that any good for you?"

"I've got nowhere else to be," Milton said.

"You eaten yet?" Dougie asked him.

"Not yet."

"Go and get some breakfast," he suggested, pointing to the café behind them. "Nothing too greasy, mind. It's going to be rougher out there today than it was when we took you to Oban. A bowl of porridge. Something that'll be easy to keep down."

63

Milton followed Dougie's advice and got a bowl of plain porridge and a mug of coffee from the café. He could see the marina from the window, and he watched as the two fishermen fuelled the boat and prepared it for their westward trip. The porridge was warm and wholesome, and Milton finished it enthusiastically; he didn't know when he would have the chance to eat again and, while he didn't want to be so full so as to make it more likely he would bring it all up over the side of the boat, neither did he want to get out to St. Kilda and find he was hungry.

He thought about what he might find there. He had the two Chinese pistols in his bag, but hoped that he wouldn't have the need to use them. He was loath to put the two fishermen in harm's way and resolved that he would not take chances with their safety. A trip around the islands might be enough to see if there was any sign of activity; if there was, he would steal a boat later and make his way back there alone.

"How was it?"

Milton looked up. It was the old lady from behind the counter. "Delicious."

"You want another bowlful?"

Milton shook his head. "I'd better not. I'm out on a boat today, and I've been told it's going to be rough."

"Aye," she said. "You're going to have a bumpy time of it."

Milton replaced the spoon in the empty bowl, finished the last of his coffee and laid a five-pound note on the table. "Thank you," he said, holding up his hand when she asked if he wanted the change.

"Wait a moment," she said, and ducked into the kitchen.

Milton glanced through the window and saw that the McCullums looked to be almost ready to cast off. Milton checked his bag while he heard the woman busy herself with something in the kitchen.

She came back with a mug in her hand and put it down on the table. "Drink that," she said.

"What is it?"

"Ginger tea. Best thing to stop seasickness there is. My old man was a fisherman. He used to swear by it. I'd make him a cup before he went out, and he said it worked wonders."

Milton smiled, took the warm mug and drank the tea. It was fragrant with a spicy flavour, and he sank it in two long draughts.

"You're very kind," Milton said.

She waved his thanks away. "I hope it does the trick. Enjoy your trip."

WILL UNTIED the mooring ropes and tossed them to Milton, then jumped aboard as the boat started to drift away from the dock. Dougie fired up the engine from the wheelhouse, and the boat chugged out into the channel. They turned to starboard and followed the coast to the south for half an hour, just as Milton had last night when he had made the trip out to the Flannans.

They rounded the southern tip of the island and were met immediately by an enormous swell.

"You okay?" Will shouted over to Milton.

"All right so far," Milton called back.

"Just as well. This is us for the rest of the day."

"Stop jawing," Dougie complained. "We need to put some pots down."

Milton braced himself for a wet half hour's work on deck. Head down, he laboured to coil the ropes as he had been shown, careful to keep his and Will's feet clear, and then they began shooting. The cages fired off the afterdeck and into the ocean at breakneck speed. By the time he looked up again, the sun was halfway to its zenith.

64

Dougie stood at the bow, a pair of binoculars to his eyes as he scanned the rolling sea ahead of them. "There," he said, pointing.

Milton squinted out to the horizon. The sea pitched up and down, and it took him a moment to see the rocky fingers that reached above the swells. "That's it?"

"That's St. Kilda."

"What's out there?"

"Five islands in the archipelago, plus the sea stacks."

"How big are they?"

"Three or four square miles, all told."

"Inhabited?"

"Used to be, but not anymore. It's beautiful, but you wouldn't want to be out here when there's a storm blowing. The wind gets so strong there's stories of it blowing the cattle straight off the cliffs. Trees won't grow because of the salt in the air. It's just wildlife now. You got operators who bring twitchers out here to look at the eagles in the summer, but that's about it."

"Don't forget the military," Dougie called from the wheelhouse.

"Aye," his son agreed. "They're out here."

"Doing what?"

"The Hebrides Missile Range," Dougie said. "They run it from Benbecula. Radar station, too." The old man cracked a smile. "Looking for invaders."

"Speaking of which," Will said, "there's someone else out here with us. I think you might recognise him."

Will pointed to a smaller boat that had appeared from beneath a swell. It was a rigid inflatable with two big outboard engines on the back and, instead of heading for the larger of the islands in the archipelago, it had peeled off and was heading for the outcrop farthest to the east. Milton took the binoculars from Will and put them to his eyes. It took him a moment to find the boat and then get it in focus, but, when he did, he found his breath caught in his throat.

Flash was standing at the boat's console, both hands clasped around the wheel.

"Who is it?" Dougie called.

"Flash."

Milton followed with the binoculars. "Where's he going?"

Will shielded his eyes and squinted at the boat. "Looks like Boreray."

"Why would he go there?"

"No idea. It's just rocks and bird shit."

"I didn't think there was even a place to land," Dougie added.

Milton watched through the binoculars as Flash steered the RIB across the swells.

"Can you follow him?" he called out. "But don't make it look like you're following."

Milton knew that the request would sound strange, but Dougie made no comment upon it. He gave a nod, spun the wheel and picked out a path that mirrored the RIB without closing in on it. If Flash were to look back, he would see a lobster boat and think that they were out here to work.

The new direction brought them across the swells at an angle, and the boat rose and fell unpleasantly. Flash tracked around the island, passing the opportunity to land on a slab of rock to the southwest near one of the tall stacks and continuing around to the more sheltered eastern side. They lost him as he turned beneath an overhang that jutted out from the intimidating mass of rock and, when they gently rounded the same spot, five minutes later and a hundred yards farther out to sea, they saw that Flash had gone ashore on a narrow isthmus that jutted out into the swell.

"It wasn't like that the last time I was here," Dougie said.

Will took the binoculars. "It's been blasted."

"And that's not allowed?" Milton said.

"God, no. This is all protected. You can't go blowing it up."

Dougie put the engine in neutral and let the boat drift. "I can't land you," he said. "The swells are too strong. She'd crash into the rocks and that'd be that. Bottom of the ocean."

Milton looked at the gap between the *Working Girl* and the rock. "How much closer can you get?"

"Fifteen metres offshore," he mused. "Any closer than that and I'd start to get itchy."

"That'd be fine," Milton said. "I'll swim the rest."

"What?" Will said. "That's a stupid idea."

"I've got to get ashore," he said.

"So come back when it's calmer. Bring a Zodiac, like him."

"It's got to be today."

Dougie shook his head. "I still think it's a bad idea."

"I'm a strong swimmer. I think I could make it."

"Sure?" Will said.

"I'm sure," Milton said.

Dougie nodded. "It's your funeral."

"It might literally be your funeral," Will corrected.

"How are you going to get back?"

"On that," Milton said, pointing to the RIB as it bobbed and bucked on the swells.

"I'll tell you what we'll do," Dougie said. "We'll tie a rope around your waist and wait here until you're ashore, just in case you get into trouble. Assuming you make it, we'll head out here and fire out some pots. We're on the Gulf Stream here—might be able to land a few big ones." He looked at his watch. "Wind's picking up this evening. We'll need to be headed back by three. If you need us, get back down to that stage and make a song and dance until we see you."

"Perfect," Milton said. "Thank you."

65

Boreray was daunting up this close. The stacks of rock raced out of the water and climbed high into the crisp air, shrouded at the top by wisps of sea mist. Fulmars and puffins roosted in nooks and crannies all the way up. The rock was stained white with decades worth of guano so thick that even the elements couldn't scour it away. Milton took off his clothes and stashed them in his bag, making sure that the two handguns were hidden at the bottom. He took one of the ropes they used for the lobster pots and made a loop that was long enough for him to tie beneath his arms.

Will looked at him as if he were mad. "Are you sure about this?"

"I am. I'll get to the other side, and then could you throw my bag across?"

"What if it falls short?"

"I'll take off the rope when I get there—use that. You can haul it back and try again if it misses."

Will looked at the sea and shook his head. "It'll be freezing."

"I know. But it's not that far."

"Couldn't you just—I don't know—couldn't you just give him a call and arrange to meet him for a pint?"

Milton smiled, but didn't answer. He made sure that the rope was secure, checked that Will had the spare end, and, after thanking both men for their help, stepped onto the gunwale, took a breath, and launched himself into the water.

The cold hit him at once, an icy, bracing chill that sent jolts up his arms and legs. He cut through the water, kicked up hard and breached the surface, and then oriented himself. The huge stack loomed above him and, when he looked down, the water—even though it must have been ten metres deep—was as clear as crystal. A flock of puffins watched him curiously, then flapped away when he got too close.

The RIB bobbed up and down on the rising swells, and Milton started to stroke toward it. The current was not cooperative, the tide bouncing off the rocky outcrop and flowing back against him, and, for a moment, it seemed as if he wasn't going to be able to beat it. But then a large wave rolled over him from behind and, taking advantage of the sudden momentum, Milton kicked as hard as he could and closed the distance. His fingertips brushed against the collar of the RIB before the backwash pulled him away; he heard a shout of encouragement from the McCullums' boat, stroked hard again and grabbed onto a rubber handle. The waves tried to yank him away from the RIB, but Milton grabbed a second cleat and, kicking again, propelled himself out of the water and onto the gunwale.

He slithered onto the deck, the water pooling around him as he regained his breath. He licked his lips and tasted the salt, then ran his fingers through his hair to sluice the water off. He stood and raised a hand; Will and Dougie had apparently found the whole thing hilarious, the sounds of their laughter audible above the crash of the water. Milton untied the rope from around his torso and tossed it overboard so that Will could haul it back to the *Working Girl.* Will pulled it in, hand over hand, retied it around the straps of Milton's pack and got ready to throw it. Milton knew that there was a good chance that his bag would end up in the drink, and that, if that happened, the two handguns would be unreliable, at least until they had been given a chance to dry. He could have left the bag aboard the boat, but he couldn't say for sure that he wouldn't need a weapon—especially given what had happened on the Flannans—and he didn't want to run the risk that either of the fishermen might open the bag and find them.

"Ready?" Will called out.

Milton gave a thumbs up.

Will swung the bag back and forth to build momentum and then sent it flying across the gap between the two vessels. It fell a little short and bounced off the collar of the boat; Milton lunged and snagged it before it could fall into the drink. He gave another thumbs up before Dougie went back into the wheelhouse and fired up the engine. The *Working Girl* chugged away, turning back to the east and carving a path through the swells to a spot where they could lay some pots.

Milton unzipped his bag and dressed. He took the QSZ semi-auto, made sure it was ready to fire, and shoved it into the waistband of his jeans. He laced up his boots and disembarked from the vessel, taking a moment to review it from the relative security of the stone landing stage. It was manufactured by Zodiac Nautic and looked to be the exact same model and make as the one that he had seen at the Flannans last night.

He looked up the steep slope that led to the plateau above. A rope had been fastened to a rock at the top; Flash had evidently used it to help him ascend the slippery stone. Milton reached down for it, grabbed it with his left hand, anchored himself with it and then reached ahead with his right.

He planted his boots on the forty-five-degree slope and started to clamber up.

66

It was an effort to climb the slope even with the rope, and Milton was out of breath by the time he reached the top. He frowned: an industrial winch had been left there, long screws holding it in place against a flat rock. Milton crouched down so that he could look at it in more detail. It was reasonably new, although the scrapes and gouges along its housing suggested that it had been put to use.

Milton stood and took in his surroundings. Boreray was the shape of a diamond: a mile across its widest point and perhaps a mile and half from top to bottom. There were two stacks just offshore, vast rocky fingers that pointed to heaven. The cliffs were steep on all sides and no trees or anything that grew vertically; Milton knew that the weather here would be too inhospitable for any exposed vegetation. He saw a shelter that had been constructed from pieces of stone and guessed that it might have been used by the locals who had once visited from Hirta. The grass was cropped short everywhere he looked, and, as he tried to work out why, a sheep ambled out from behind the stone shelter and munched away, either unaware that Milton was there or uncaring.

Milton paused there and looked around, unable to do much other than inhale the extraordinary scenery. The noise was deafening as birds flocked to and from their nests. He turned back to the ocean and watched as the *Working Girl* found a spot to set down more pots. He could just make out the rattle of the anchor chain as its links went over the bow, plunging into the deep bay. A pod of passing dolphins crested the water, one after another, glistening as they leapt out of the heavy swells and continued on their way.

He looked for Flash, but there was no sign of him. He climbed up into the centre of the island, circling around onto its western face. A gully ran from south to north to a deeper gully that split the northernmost tip from the rest of the island. He reached the western edge and turned north, clambering up a slope of loose scree so that he might have a more elevated view.

There was another of the stone shelters at the crest of the ridge, and Milton aimed for it. He gained the ridge and was rewarded with an unobstructed view of the northern half of the island.

What he saw brought him up short. The slope descended to a plateau that, in turn, dropped away at the cliff. Two long metal tubes—each three or four metres long—had been laid flat, one next to the other. Next to them was the unmistakeable shape of a three-bladed rotor. A patch of grass had been cleared and a concrete foundation laid. Milton could see how it would all fit together: the two tubes would be attached and slotted into the concrete base, and the rotor and its associated nacelle would sit at the top.

It was a wind turbine.

The concrete foundation looked very similar to what Milton had seen on the Flannans. He looked at the cases stacked up next to the foundation and recognised them: he had seen Flash attending to them in Tobermory.

There was no cover between Milton's vantage point and the site of the turbine. The grassy meadow was wide open, with not even a boulder that Milton might have been able to hide behind. Milton looked for Flash, but couldn't see him. He reached around and pulled the pistol, holding it against his leg as he started to make his way to the plateau.

"Stay where you are."

The voice came from behind him.

"Get your hands up."

Milton did as he was told. He had the pistol in his right hand and raised it above his head.

"Turn around."

He did and turned to face Flash. He had a shotgun with the butt braced against his shoulder and his finger on the trigger. He must have seen him approach and taken cover behind the stone shelter.

"I knew it," Flash growled. "I fucking *knew* it."

"Easy."

"Easy?" He nodded to the pistol. "What's that about? I told you. You're here to top me."

"No."

"Toss it away from you."

Milton did, tossing the pistol a few feet away from him.

"Bumping into you in Tobermory was weird enough. But here? We're in the middle of the Atlantic."

Milton glanced around. "Are we alone?"

"Aye," Flash said. "Just me and you and your pals on the

lobster boat. What are you doing here? Tell me straight. You need to persuade me you're telling the truth. If I get itchy about it, you know what'll happen." He shouldered the shotgun. "Now—get moving."

67

Flash told Milton to walk down the slope to the disassembled turbine.

"You know what pisses me off?" Flash said from behind him as they walked. "You *lied* to me."

Milton could smell the booze on him. "When?"

"You said you'd just bumped into me. I knew you'd been sent. I *knew* it. What I couldn't work out was why they'd send *you*, but I get it now—it was bloody obvious. You've been involved right from the start... Maybe you put me up for it in the first place."

"Put you up for what?"

Flash snorted. "Yes, that's it. You lot would've known I had my business up here. They needed someone to ferry their labour around, and who better than someone like me, someone who already had a reason to be out on the water, someone they could manipulate and take advantage of. I just wanted a quiet life. That's not much to ask for, is it? Especially after the shitty hand I was dealt after I bailed you out. My boat, some peace and quiet, and just enough work to pay my way. But you exploited that. You took it away from me. After all I *did* for you."

"No, I didn't. Whatever it is you've got messed up in, it has nothing to do with me."

Flash didn't hear him or wasn't interested. "And now you don't need me anymore. The job's done. You know what happened last night with those poor bastards, and you've come to make sure I never say a word about it. What was the plan? Put a bullet in me and toss me into the drink?"

"It's not—"

"Shut up, Milton."

They reached the site of the turbine. The foundation looked as if it was of the same dimensions as the concrete pad that Milton had found on the Flannans last night. The two pieces of the tower were fashioned from round tubular steel, one fitting into the other. The height of the tower was about the same as the diameter of the circle its blades would make when they rotated. Milton wondered how the tower would have been erected without machinery, but then noticed hinged brackets in the concrete. The base of the tower would be fitted into the brackets and then hoisted aloft on a pivot, most likely pulled by winches.

Flash poked Milton in the back with the shotgun. "Put your bag down and step away from it."

Milton shucked the bag off his shoulder, lowered it to the ground and paced until he was next to the nearest piece of the tower. Milton heard Flash open the bag and tip its contents out.

"Where did you get that?"

"I can't see what you're talking about, Flash."

"Turn around, then!"

Milton did. Flash was holding up the second pistol.

"*Where?*"

Milton didn't know how much it would be safe to reveal. "I'll tell you," he said. "But you need to explain a few things to me, too."

Flash tossed the pistol aside and gestured with the shotgun. "Doesn't work like that, not while I have this in your face. Tell me now. Right now."

"The Flannans," Milton said. "Last night."

Flash's mouth fell open. "What?"

"There were two men there. Chinese. The guns were theirs. I took them."

The blood ran out of his face. "Shit," he said. "The men—where are they now?"

"I tossed them over the cliff."

"You killed them?"

Milton shrugged. "They tried to kill me."

"I don't understand," Flash said. "Why would you do that? That wasn't the plan. I did what you told me to do. Why are things changing now?" He paused, and then, as realisation dawned, fear shone in his face. "They'll suspect me! I was the last person to see them alive. I took them there. Jesus. Chen will kill me if he thinks I was involved."

"Flash," Milton said as calmly as he could manage, "you need to tell me what's going on."

The big man put his left hand to his face, holding the shotgun with his right. His aim drifted and, for a moment, Milton knew that he would have been able to disarm him. Flash was bigger than he was, but he wasn't as daunting as he had once been, and he was a little drunk. Milton could have taken him down easily enough, but he chose not to.

"I don't understand," Flash muttered again. "This wasn't what we agreed."

Milton spoke calmly and evenly. "Who do you think I'm working for?"

Anger flashed. "Don't play games."

"I'm not. Who do you think I work for?"

"The security services. MI6."

"No."

"I don't believe you. They told me you went into intelligence after you left the Regiment."

There was no point in denying that, but he could accept the suggestion without providing the specifics. "Ancient history. I used to work for them—sort of—but not now. Not for years."

"*Right*," he said sarcastically. "Here we are, the end of the world, and you just happen to bump into me? It's just us and the fucking birds. You expect me to believe that?"

"I had no idea that you would be here. I'm looking for a man who went missing a month ago. I followed a lead to the Flannans, and I found the two men, and then I found their boat—although I can see now that it's one of yours."

"So how do you get from there to here?"

"There was a chart on their boat. The Flannans were marked. So was this."

Flash snorted derisively. "Let's stop fucking around, aye? I'll tell you what this is all about and save you the bother. You went from the Regiment to intelligence. I know what blokes like you do. You take people out for them, don't you? Wet work. And now it's my turn. You're here to off me, but that's not going to happen, though, is it? Not now you're on the wrong side of this." He gestured with the shotgun again.

His anger sparked, and, for a moment, Milton thought he might actually pull the triggers.

"I met a woman in Japan," Milton insisted calmly. "I agreed to find out what happened to her son before she dies."

"*Bullshit!* Do you think I was born yesterday? You already

ruined my life once. At least do me the courtesy of telling me the truth."

"Let me prove it to you."

"How are you going to do that?"

"How do you keep in contact with the mainland when you're out here?"

"Satphone."

"Do you have it?"

"Of course."

"Can I have it?"

Flash stepped back, covered Milton with the shotgun held in his right hand with the stock braced against his chest, and reached into his pocket with his left. He withdrew a small black oblong with thick antennae protruding from the top and held it up.

"I'd like to make a call."

"To who?"

"To the woman," he said. "In Japan."

Flash tossed the satphone, and Milton caught it. "Go on, then."

"Her number is in the bag," Milton said. "I have a book in there—I wrote the number inside."

Flash kicked the bag closer to Milton and nodded down to it. "Fine. But if you do anything I don't like, I'll spray you all over the rocks."

68

Milton took out his copy of *Jude the Obscure* and thumbed to the blank pages at the back where he had written down Judith-Ann's details. He switched on the phone, waited for it to acquire a lock on the best-placed satellite, and tapped in the number. He looked across at the shotgun and realised that he was going to be in a tricky situation if she didn't answer.

The unit buzzed and clicked as the call was placed; it went silent for a moment before Milton heard it ring.

"Hello?"

"Hello. Judith-Ann?"

"Yes."

Milton pressed the button to switch on the speaker so that Flash could listen to the conversation.

"How are you?"

"Who's this?"

"Eric. We met—"

"Eric!" she said, cutting across him. "I didn't think I'd..." She paused. "I didn't think I'd hear from you again. Do you have news?"

"Maybe. I've made some progress."

Flash looked away. Milton thought he saw a sadness descend over him.

"What progress? Please, tell me—good or bad, I just want to know."

"Alan was looking for some people who'd come to Scotland from overseas and then went missing. I think he may have found some of them."

"In the Hebrides?"

"That's right."

"What about him? Do you know where he is?"

Milton heard the sound of another person talking to Judith-Ann.

"Is someone with you?"

"It's the nurse. I'm in the hospital."

"What's the matter?"

"Just the cancer—it's going faster than they said."

"Would you rather I spoke to you when you're alone?"

There was a pause. "They don't think I have long—days, they think. I can't put this off. Please—if you have something, tell me."

Milton stopped. He hadn't anticipated this call, and certainly not in these circumstances. He looked at Flash; the big man was gazing out to sea, all thought of covering Milton with the shotgun gone. The sadness on his face had curdled into shame.

"The people Alan was trying to help were involved with some dangerous criminals. I haven't found him yet, but I'm concerned that he might have come to harm because of what he found out about them."

"Come to harm? You think he was killed?"

Flash turned back and gave a single, slow nod of his head.

"I think that's possible," Milton said, picking his words carefully. "You need to be prepared for it."

"I've been prepared for that for weeks," she said. "But I need to know. I just need to know."

"I'll do my best to find him."

"God bless you, Eric. Thank you for phoning."

Milton clicked off, held up the phone and then tossed it over to Flash. "You need anything else?"

He looked away. "She could be in an office in London for all I know."

"She's an old woman with cancer in her last few weeks of life. I don't know what else I can do to prove it to you."

"Who's Eric?"

"The people you think I'm working for? They're looking for me. I don't use my own name. Eric is a pseudonym."

"This is nuts."

"You either believe me or you don't, but, if you don't, you're going to have to shoot me if you want to stop me going back to the mainland and telling the police what's happening out here."

Flash exhaled and shook his head. "What difference does it make?"

His shoulders slumped as he lowered the shotgun.

"Thank you," Milton said.

Flash took a hip flask from his pocket, put it to his lips and took a swig.

"You've got to come clean with me," Milton said. "What's been going on?"

"Aye," Flash said, wiping the back of his hand across his mouth. "Where do you want me to start?"

69

It had been a difficult morning. Johnston Hannah had tried to ignore the fact that the castle was accommodating unwelcome visitors. Zhou had installed himself in the library and, just when Hannah had hoped that he might be able to think of a way to send him on his way, he had seen from the security cameras on the front gate that more interlopers had arrived. The three Range Rovers, top-of-the-line models with blacked-out windows, had rolled along the drive, parked, and six men had stepped out. Zhou met them and led them along the path to the front door as if they owned the place. They had gone into the library for a meeting, and Hannah had waited by the closed door in the hope that he might hear something that would give him a clue about what he could expect. They spoke in Mandarin and, when they came out, they were grimly serious.

Hannah found the housekeeper and asked her to set up rooms for all of them, explaining that they were visitors here to enjoy the shooting and fishing. The woman had worked at the castle for years, and Hannah had kept her on when he'd purchased it. She was canny, though, and Hannah knew that she would see that the newcomers had very little in common with the men and women who typically stayed with them, but there was nothing that he could do about that.

He went down to the kitchen to make himself some lunch. He found a tray of lasagne in the fridge, slid it into the oven to warm up and cut himself a slice of bread to go with it. He was buttering the bread when he saw a copy of *The Scotsman* on the counter. He reached for it, unfolded it and set it out so that he could read it. There had been a series of articles on the renewables industry and the new seabed leases that were being offered, and he wondered idly whether the reporter might have written more. There was nothing on the front page, but, as he scanned it, his eye snagged on a story below the fold.

MAJOR SEARCH LAUNCHED AFTER MAN 'OVERBOARD' ON STORNOWAY FERRY

A extensive search operation took place over the weekend place following suspicions that a man had gone overboard from the Stornoway ferry. Maritime rescue teams initiated a hunt for Jack Watson upon realising his vehicle remained on the ferry after other passengers had left the 10.15pm Ullapool to Stornoway boat.

He picked up his phone and called Jimmy Bolton.

"Jimmy," he began, "have you seen the newspaper? I've—"

"Hello?"

The voice on the other end of the line was female.

"Who are you?" Hannah said.

"I'm Emily Bolton. Who are you?"

"Sorry—I'm trying to reach Jimmy. Could I speak to him?"

"I'm sorry. That won't be possible."

"It's rather urgent."

"That might be so, but I'm afraid Jimmy passed away last night."

Hannah's mouth fell open. "I'm sorry—what?"

"I know it'll come as a shock—it did for everyone—but I'm afraid it's true. He had a heart attack."

"But I saw him... I... No." He shook his head as if that might help to clear the cobwebs away. "That's not possible. I'm sorry—who are you again?"

"I'm his mother, love. Who are you?"

Hannah tried to end the call, but his fingers were suddenly clumsy and slick with sweat, and the screen didn't respond. He stabbed it again and again until, finally, the press registered and the woman's voice was gone. He put the phone down and suddenly felt dizzy. He laid his palms flat on the table, fingers splayed, feeling the cool surface against the abrupt clamminess of his skin. He closed his eyes and concentrated on breathing in and out, in and out, in and out. Watson and Bolton, both dead, within hours of one another.

He found Zhou in the library.

"What the hell have you done?" he said.

"What are you talking about?"

"What am I *talking* about? I just found out that Jack Watson's dead. He fell overboard on the ferry into Stornoway."

"Yes," Zhou said. "I said we would take care of it."

"But you *killed* him."

"And now the problem is gone."

"It's murder. *Murder.*"

"You rather clumsily tried to appeal to his venality, and

he said no. What happened is his own fault. He could have made a lot of money, but he decided against it. The project is too important to be held up by one man's morals."

"But—I mean, apart from anything else—the police? They'll investigate."

"The police haven't suggested that foul play was involved, have they?"

"No. But—"

"My men are professionals. There will be nothing that can link them to us. He fell overboard or jumped. That's it."

"What about Jimmy Bolton?"

Zhou cocked his head to one side. "What about him?"

"He's dead."

Zhou's lips kinked up at the side. "What?"

"He died of a heart attack last night."

Zhou paused for a moment to consider that. "Really?"

"Don't give me that," Hannah said. "That was you, wasn't it? Cleaning up. Right? He had to go, didn't he? Made you nervous."

"That had nothing to do with us."

"Bullshit." Hannah put his hand to his head. "Who's next? Me?"

"No one is next, and certainly not you—we need you."

Hannah shook his head. He found, for the first time since he had tied himself up with these fraudsters and shysters—and *murderers*—the clarity that should have shown him the folly of his greed. His choices were always going to have consequences; he needed to make another choice—a better one—now, and hope that it wasn't too late.

"You're the public face of our project, Mr. Hannah. Remember? The local man delivering jobs to his community. The prodigal son returning to his roots."

Hannah shook his head again, more vehemently. "Forget it. I'm done. I'm out. I can't be involved in anything like this."

"Like what, Mr. Hannah?"

"Murder!" He turned to leave.

Zhou stood. "Sit down."

"You killed them! I don't want anything to do with you. With *any* of it. I don't want any part of murder."

"Sit *down.*"

The chumminess was gone as quickly as if he had pressed a switch. His voice was cold and sharp, and it stung like a whip. Hannah slipped down into the armchair.

"You are already a part of it," Zhou said. "I don't know about Bolton—you can believe me or not, I don't care—but if our role in Mr. Watson's death were ever to come to light, then I can promise that you'll be implicated. You paid Mr. Bolton to bribe him and, when that didn't work, you killed him. It will be a simple enough thing to lay a trail that leads to your door."

"No. No—it had nothing to do with me."

"Really? Where were you when it happened?"

"I was..." He paused, knowing that the trap had just snapped shut around his ankle. "I... I..."

"You were here, by yourself, with no one to vouch for you. But maybe you weren't here. Maybe you were on that ferry. And *maybe* a witness saw a man matching your description and Mr. Watson having an argument. It will be a simple enough thing for us to arrange."

"No," he said. "You can threaten me, but it's not going to work. I'll take my chances."

He started to his feet but, before he could raise himself from the chair, he felt strong hands on his shoulders pressing him back down. He looked round and saw Chen standing behind him; he hadn't even noticed him come into the room.

Zhou steepled his fingers. "I can see that you have belatedly grown a conscience. That's a pity. Perhaps we need to bring someone else here to help you to focus on what you have agreed to do. Chen—please go and fetch Mr. Hannah's wife. She'll probably be at the hotel."

"No," Hannah protested. "Leave her out of it—she doesn't know anything."

"I'm sure she doesn't. But I'm sure having her here will help you make the right decisions."

70

There was no stopping Flash once he started to tell his story. Milton had seen that his conscience was weighing him down, and he was seizing the opportunity to lighten his load. Milton knew how that felt.

"It started three years ago. I can remember it like it was yesterday. I got a booking one Friday evening. A bloke from London said he wanted me to take him out so that he could go and watch the whales. He turned up on time, and I took him up north of Lewis. We saw minke and a pod of dolphins, but I could see he wasn't there for the wildlife."

"What was he interested in?"

"Me. Wanted to get the measure of me, see whether I was the sort of bloke who'd do what they'd need me to do. I must've passed the test, because he made the offer to me on the way back. I say it was an offer, but I know it wasn't. You don't say no to his type; I knew I didn't have a choice. He said he worked for the government. He didn't say exactly what department it was, but he told me it was national security and left me to fill in the blanks."

"MI6?"

"That's what I've come to think. He said he was involved in a project and that I was going to help him with it. He told me that I was going to be contacted by a Chinese man called Chen, who was going to ask me whether he could hire me and my boats for six months."

"To do what?"

"I was going to be a glorified marine taxi. Chen was involved in a consortium that had just won the seabed lease for the offshore wind farm north of Lewis. He was going to need someone with local knowledge to ferry them around while the turbines got built. The Chinese would pay very well, but I'd have to be exclusive to them and available on short notice. I told him no, I didn't like the sound of any of it, but he ignored me. He said the decision had already been made, and I had to go along with it."

Flash lowered himself to the ground and rested his back against one of the metal posts.

"It happened just the way he said it would. Chen rang me the next day. I'd got to thinking after I spoke to the spook, and I'd started to have reservations about the good sense in getting myself involved. Chen made me his offer. I told him I'd need to think about it and I'd get back to him. He wasn't happy, but he added another fifty grand to what he was willing to pay me and gave me until the end of the day to make up my mind. I'd only just put down the phone when I got a call from London. He tore a strip out of me. What was I doing? Who did I think I was? I obviously hadn't been paying attention. It wasn't a *choice*. Steps had been taken to make sure that Chen came to me, so I was to accept the offer and do whatever they told me to do or else I was going to find myself in the shit."

"Meaning?"

"Oh, he spelled it out for me. I did what I was told or

there was going to be an accident the next time I took tourists out and, if I survived it, I'd be prosecuted for negligence and put away. He didn't strike me as the kind of bloke to bluff about shit like that. I couldn't take the chance, so I called Chen back and told him we had a deal."

Milton listened quietly. He recognised that kind of proposal; he had made his fair share of them over the years. He felt a fresh sense of guilt and was reminded of the griminess that he had tried to scrub off in the years since he had left the Group. Flash was a good man. He had been badly treated by the military, but, through hard work and determination, he had provided himself with a second act. The spooks who had latched onto him wouldn't care a whit about that; they saw opportunity, they saw vulnerability, and they took advantage. Milton understood why Flash was angry and bitter.

"I'm sorry," Milton said.

"What for? You said you didn't work for them anymore."

"I don't, but I used to—or people like them. And I know how they work. You didn't deserve to be put into a situation like that. No one does."

Flash looked as if he was about to say something, but didn't; instead, he unscrewed the flask again and took another swig.

"Chen came in to the office to see me the next day," Flash said, chuckling bitterly. "We got started."

"Who else was involved?"

"Like I said—it was a consortium. The public face of it is a local entrepreneur who thinks he's the real deal, but everyone knows he's just a pound-shop Richard Branson."

"Johnston Hannah."

"You know him?"

"I haven't had the pleasure of a proper meeting yet, but I know him."

"Aye, well, *that's* not a surprise. He's bloody good at telling everyone how clever he is. I never really got to the bottom of who else was involved—there were Germans, Swedes, Danes—but the money's coming from China. Chen was the man on the ground—the project manager, I suppose. My job was to take him out there so that he could keep an eye on what was going on and report back to his boss. I'd been worried about it, but he didn't ask me to do anything that felt dodgy. I got over my worry and tried to see it for what it was—money for old rope. The contract was extended twice in the end. I worked for them just short of a year, until the turbines were all up, and then that was that."

"Chen?"

"Disappeared."

Flash drank again. Milton wished that he'd stop.

"But he came back?"

Flash nodded. "The government offered another package of leases, west of here, and the next day I got another call from London. Same bloke, same thing as before—Hannah's consortium was going to bid again, and they wanted to bring me back on board. The tree huggers were involved this time, and the turbines had to be smaller than the ones out at Lewis. The bloke said the leases would go to the bidders who could generate the electricity and then bring it back on shore as efficiently as possible. The consortium had got their hands on an experimental cable that didn't lose as much electricity along the way, but it was new technology, and the money men were going to need to see a successful test before they released the funds to support the bid. I thought it'd be like it had been before—easy street. I said yes. Chen called me the next week, and we started work the next Monday."

"Where? The Flannans?"

Flash nodded. "Originally. Chen had me picking up gear that arrived in Oban and Tobermory and moving it to the island. Building stuff—a mixer, tools, materials. Men, too. They used immigrants. Illegals who could be manipulated. None of them spoke English, and they were all vulnerable—they told them if they didn't do what they were told, they'd be deported. I picked them up off the beach in Northern Ireland and brought them up here."

"And this was to build a test turbine?" Milton said. He rapped his knuckles against the metal pole. "Like this?"

"It *was* that one. It's a quarter of the size of the ones they want to build, but it's big enough to run a meaningful test on the cable. That's what they said, anyway. I didn't get involved in all that, and I didn't ask questions. The way I saw it, the less I knew, the better."

"How did they get the tower and the rotors out there?"

"Helicopter," Flash said. "It was too risky to fly in and out more than they had to, but that was the only way they'd get the heavier stuff there. I brought the rest."

"And they had permission for this?"

Flash scoffed. "I asked once. I told Chen that I doubted whether they were allowed to build, and he said that I didn't have to worry, that the people he worked for had cleared it with the government, that it was all temporary and it'd all be made good once they were done. I never asked again. The turbine went up near to the lighthouse."

"I saw the groundwork last night. Why did they move it from there to here?"

"The consortium changed the requirements for the test. It's twenty-five miles from the Flannans to Harris. The wind farm will be on the other side of Kilda, over there." He waved an arm. "A hundred miles offshore. The cable worked from the Flannans, but they needed to see it work over the full distance. So we struck the turbine and moved everything over here. They erected the tower at night, tested it, and then took it down again."

"And no one saw?"

"Not as far as I know."

"Was it a success?"

"They don't tell me anything like that," Flash said. "I'm just the delivery boy. But they seemed happy, so my guess would be it did what they wanted it to."

"What about the labour?"

"Eastern Europeans. Half a dozen men. Hard workers. Good lads."

He looked away, and Milton could see there was more to tell.

"Where are they now, Flash?"

"The Flannans. I picked them up from here last night and took them over there. They had them sleeping in the lighthouse."

Milton shook his head. "They're not there."

Flash got up. He looked down the slope and extended an arm so that he was pointing down to the cliff and the water below. "You know what I was going to do today, John? Why I came up here? I was going to finish my whisky, enjoy being in nature, and then I was going to walk down there and jump. That's a long drop, and there are rocks at the bottom. The bloke from London said some of the things that I might see or they might ask me to do would be questionable, but that I needn't worry because I'd be given an amnesty once the business was taken care of. I thought he was exaggerating then. I don't now. He wasn't, and it's worse than I thought it could be. I can't prove what happened to those lads, but I *know*. I know what happened, and I helped Chen and his mates do it."

Milton knew, but he asked anyway. "What did they do?"

"One of the workers fell overboard when we were moving gear off the boat at the Flannans. Moldovan lad called Fiodr—I used to call him Messi on account of the Barcelona shirt he had on when I picked him up. He went under the boat and drowned. I told Chen that he had to get the police involved, but he said no. I called my bloke in London and said I was done, but he told me I had to keep going. Said it was too important to stop now. Made it *very* clear I didn't have a choice—it'd be made out that it was my fault what had happened if anything ever came out. What choice did I have?"

Milton said nothing; he could see how Flash had been artfully trapped into a situation from which there was no escape.

"And then a bloke started asking questions about what was happening," Flash said. "Might be the man you've been after."

"Alan Caine," Milton said. "He came out to the Flannans. Took photographs. There's one with you in it."

"And I should be worried about that?" Flash shrugged. "I'm past caring what happens to me."

"What happened to him?"

"The lads were in pieces after what happened to Fiodr. I'm guessing one of them got in touch with your pal and told him what was going on. When did he go missing?"

"A month ago," Milton said.

"It's about the same time. They would've killed him. Chen and his boys don't take risks and they don't leave loose ends. Same as the rest of the crew—they don't need them now, not since the test is finished, and they won't want to send them back to the mainland and have them run their mouths about what they've been up to. If you ask me, they're all dead. Most likely at the bottom of the Atlantic."

"I think they buried them on the island," Milton said. "There was fresh concrete there last night."

Flash looked away.

"You said Chen and his boys."

"Yes."

"How many?"

"It varied from day to day. There were four of them last night—five including him."

Two less now, Milton thought to himself.

Flash put the flask to his lips and drank. He exhaled, seemingly finished with his story.

"There's one thing I don't understand," Milton said. "Why would MI6 want you to help the Chinese?"

"What's their angle, you mean?" Flash shrugged his shoulders. "I've never been able to work that out."

Milton collected the two pistols and put them in his bag. Flash didn't protest. He seemed more interested in the contents of the hip flask.

"What are you going to do?" Milton said. "You can jump off the edge if you want—I doubt I could stop you if you've set your mind to it."

"What else is there? I've got blood on my hands."

"You're not responsible for what happened to the workers. You didn't know."

"I knew," he mumbled.

"They took advantage of you. They made it look as if you didn't have a choice, but that's wrong. You do."

"What? What could I *possibly* do to make up for all the misery I've caused?"

"Those men who were out here have families."

"You think I don't know that? I can't stop thinking about it."

"So give them justice."

"How? How could I do that?"

"Arrange a meeting with your friend from London. We need to understand how this fits together. Get him to come up here. That's the place to start."

71

Milton and Flash boarded the RIB and set off back to Harris. They drifted close to the *Working Girl*, and Milton yelled his thanks to the McCullums, calling over that he would ride back with Flash. They were busy hauling in the pots, and Milton could see that they had enjoyed a profitable trip. Will held up an enormous lobster and yelled that they would see him later.

Flash's phone buzzed as soon as the boat brought them within range of a mast. He took it out of his pocket and looked at the screen.

"Who is it?" Milton asked.

"Chen," Flash said. "Ten missed calls. I think we know what he wants."

Milton formulated a plan of action, shouting suggestions over the roar of the outboards and the crash of the hull as it slammed through the waves. They both agreed that it wouldn't be safe for Flash to go back to his bothy; there was a good chance that Chen would be looking for him and, if he was, that would be where he would start. Instead, Milton had suggested that they go back to the hotel. He knew more about Hannah now, and he wanted to speak to Chrissie again to see if there was anything else that she could tell him. In particular, Milton wanted to know where he lived.

"You think MI6 will come up here?" Flash called out.

"He will. Tell your man that Chen murdered the workers last night. Tell him you can't ignore your conscience, and you need to speak to him so that he can persuade you why you shouldn't go straight to the police. Don't take no for an answer."

"And that'll be enough?"

"Whatever they're doing up here, it's obviously important. They're not going to want to run the risk that you'll make a fuss and bring attention to everything. He'll come."

"And then?"

"And then you clear the air with him. Make sure it's somewhere public with good sight lines."

"The ferry to Uig?"

"I'd rather not be somewhere we can't easily get away from."

"Tobermory, then? The harbour?"

Milton considered it. "That'll work. Make sure the boat is fuelled. Can you bring extra?"

Flash nodded. "Aye. Where are you planning on going?"

"Back to the Flannans," he said. "But with reinforcements this time."

Flash skirted south around the deserted island of Taransay and picked out a spot on Luskentyre beach where they could run the boat aground. The sands were empty in both directions save for a man walking a dog away to the south. Flash killed the engines, and they coasted through the ever-shallowing water, the hull eventually scraping up against the bottom. Flash hopped down, drove a land anchor into the soft sand and tied up against it. There was an onshore breeze, and the tide was coming in, so he compensated by throwing a weight off the stern to keep the boat in deep enough water.

Milton vaulted over the side and waded through the surf to the beach.

Flash followed. "Who is she?"

"Hannah's ex-wife. She's one of the good ones."

"You think she knows anything about this?"

"I don't think so. She doesn't have much time for him now."

"What's she like?"

"Not afraid to speak her mind."

They reached the gorse and bracken that separated the beach from the road and the hotel beyond. He was about to cross the road when he saw the two four-by-fours parked outside. The cars were identical, and that—and the dark glass in the windows—suggested they did not belong to guests. He and Flash dropped down behind a thick clump of gorse and watched. The doors opened and four men stepped out. They were all of a type—muscular, medium height—and all wore black tactical jackets. Milton stayed down low, peering through the fronds of grass, and heard the man who had disembarked the car at the front call back in Mandarin.

"Shit," Flash said.

"Who's that? Chen?"

Flash nodded. "At the front. Why are they here? Because of you?"

"No," Milton said. "They have no way of knowing that I'm involved."

"The men on the Flannans—you killed them."

Milton shook his head. "You only took *them* out there, right?"

Flash nodded.

"So there were no witnesses. They can't know it was me. Not from that."

"What, then?"

Milton bit his lip and thought. Ox and Helena knew that he was investigating, but why would they have betrayed him? They wouldn't. That only left Flash, and Milton was sure that he had not had the opportunity to raise the alarm; unless, he thought, Flash had used the satphone while he was waiting to confront him on Boreray. That seemed unlikely. Flash had never been much of an actor, and Milton considered himself a good judge of character; he was as confident as he could be that Flash was not trying to pull the wool over his eyes.

"It must be because of Hannah," Milton said. "Stay down—we'll watch."

The men split up, two of them going to the front of the hotel and two to the back. Milton unslung his bag, unzipped it and took out the pistols. He gave one to Flash.

"Jesus," he said. "What are we getting into?"

"You're way beyond worrying about that. Just get ready to cover me."

They both stayed down low, hidden by the thick, spiky tufts of marram grass. Milton guessed there were fifty yards between their hiding place and the parked cars; he would be able to cover the distance in a few seconds and take cover behind them, but, by doing that, he was guaranteeing there would be a confrontation. He decided he didn't have a choice.

"We need to get over there," he hissed to Flash. "We'll disable the cars. You take the one to the left. I'll take the one to the right."

"And then?"

"We'll jump them."

Flash nodded his agreement.

They both heard an angry voice from the hotel, the sound of breaking glass, and then a woman's scream.

Milton gripped the butt of the pistol with his right hand and started to count down with the fingers of his left.

Three.

Two.

One.

"Now."

They both stood just as Chen reappeared from around the corner of the hotel.

He saw them.

He recognised Flash.

He was carrying a stubby submachine gun, and he raised it in their direction.

Milton dropped. *"Get down!"*

Chen sprayed a burst of rounds in their direction. Milton flattened himself on the sand and scrambled back behind the grass. Rounds *thwipped* through the air, none of them particularly close but dangerous enough to pin him down. He scrabbled around so that he could see Flash. The big man had found cover, too. He looked back to the hotel and peeked through the sedge as the other Chinese reappeared: two of them were on either side of Chrissie, dragging her toward the car at the front, and the third followed behind. She was struggling, but the two men were much too strong, and her toes dragged across the ground helplessly.

Chen must have caught sight of Milton; he fired again, but, this time, the rounds blasted into the dunes just ahead of him, and he was sprayed with sand.

"Where could they be going?" he called out to Flash.

"I don't know."

"We need to follow."

"How?"

"This road follows the coast—right?"

"Aye. They'll have to go south until they get to the main road. Then they could go inland or keep going down to Leverburgh."

"Take the boat," Milton said. "Stay on them for as long as you can. Send me your phone number—we'll keep an open line between us."

"How are you going to follow?"

"There's a motorbike in the store at the back of the hotel. I'll take that."

Milton heard the sound of car doors opening.

"Mr. Gordon," a man called from the direction of the hotel. It was Chen. "Mr. Gordon—you and your friend need to get up and come over here."

"I don't think so," Milton called back.

"Who are you?"

Milton didn't respond and heard the sound of conversation between Chen and one of the others. He raised the pistol and took aim through the grass. The Chinese operators were good; they had stayed on the other side of the cars, using the vehicles as cover. They obviously had military experience. Milton looked for options. He could have taken a shot at the tyres and was reasonably confident that he could strike them, but, if he did, they were just going to be caught in a firefight with an enemy who both outnumbered and outgunned them.

"Mr. Gordon," Chen called out again, "who's your friend?"

"I killed your men last night," Milton shouted back. "Two of them—on the Flannans."

The news must have concerned Chen, but he didn't

show it. One of the men got into the back of the second Range Rover with Chrissie, and another got into the driver's side as Chen covered the sedge with his submachine gun.

Chen and the fourth man edged over to the lead vehicle. "That was stupid," Chen called. "I will find out who you are. And, Mr. Gordon, you should have known better than to cross us. You are stupid, too."

"Not the first time I've been called that," Flash muttered, just loud enough for Milton to hear it.

"Get down to the boat," Milton hissed. "Get ready."

Flash did as he was told. Milton looked forward again as the fourth man got into the front of the lead vehicle, and both drivers started their engines. Chen fired another burst into the sedge, sending up half a dozen little plumes of sand and grit, and got into the back of the lead car. The drivers pulled out and raced away to the south.

"Go!" Milton yelled to Flash.

Milton broke cover and sprinted across the road.

72

Milton burst through the door into the store and took the keys for the motorcycle from the work desk where he had left them. He straddled the bike, started the engine and rolled out of the store. He reached the road and looked to the south; he couldn't see either vehicle. He took out his in-ear headphones and popped them in, called the number that Flash had texted him, then shoved the phone back in his pocket, pulling away as the call connected.

"Where are you?" Milton said over the grumble of the engine.

"Following the coast to the south."

Milton raced up to forty, following the single-track lane with a field of sheep on the left and the beach on the right.

"Can you see them?"

"I'm running right alongside."

Milton heard the sound of a muffled explosion over the sound of the boat's engines and then Flash's curse.

"What is it?"

"They're taking potshots at me."

Milton raced at sixty, pushing the bike as hard as he dared.

"What's your location?" he said.

"Just going by the camping place. A mile from the hotel. Where are you?"

"Following."

"What are you going to do?"

"Not sure yet," Milton said. "Just stay on them."

The road cleaved close to the bay, the light blue water separated by a slope of grass and rock. Milton was halfway around a sharp left-hander when he came on a Ford coming the other way. It was Bobby's car, and Milton caught a glimpse of his face—wide-eyed and mouth agape—as he swerved the bike to the right, threading the needle between the car and the guard rail with inches to spare. When Milton completed the corner, he was rewarded with a much longer view of the inlet and was able to follow a frothing wake until he saw Flash's boat.

"Milton," Flash said over the phone, "you still there?"

"I'm here," he said. "I'm behind you. I can see the boat. Where are they?"

"They've gone inland. I've lost them."

Milton cursed. "Where do you think they're going?"

"Tarbert? If they're going to get her off the island, they'll have to do it by boat."

"You said they've got access to a helicopter?"

"Aye," he said. "Boat or helicopter, then."

Milton reached the junction where the track had turned inland. The road—despite being the main east-west route across the island—was still just a single track, with passing places at regular intervals to the left and right. It climbed as he headed away from the coast, with granite outcrops bursting through the grass as they ascended the hill that dominated the interior of the island. Milton pushed the engine to seventy, feeling the vibrations between his legs as he hung on. He shot up a steeper incline between two jagged shoulders of rock that pressed in on him, cresting the blind summit and racing straight at the Range Rover that blocked the way ahead.

Shit!

Milton saw the two men on the other side of the vehicles, both aiming pistols down the road in his direction. Milton saw the muzzle flashes and, without thinking, yanked the handlebars around and steered off the road. The front wheel bounced over a loose slab of rock, and Milton struggled to stay upright, crashing down onto the uneven ground and ploughing a path between the rocks that lay strewn around. The men fired again, although Milton barely noticed as he tried to keep his balance. The bike was old and venerable and not designed for this kind of punishment. Milton managed to stay on the saddle for fifteen seconds before the front wheel caught in a cleft and the back end of the bike kicked up. Milton was thrown, flipping head over heels and splashing down into an icy-cold rill that ambled down the hillside. Milton rolled over, ignoring the spasm of pain from his hip and reaching for the pistol.

It was gone.

It must have been jostled free by the impact of his fall. He looked around for it, couldn't see it, looked back to the road in fear that the two men would come to finish what they had started. They had decided against it, though, and, as Milton breathed in and ignored the blare of pain, they got back into the black Range Rover and raced away to the east.

"Milton?"

Milton's EarPods were still in his ears, and his phone was thankfully still in his pocket.

"Milton? What's going on?"

"I lost them," Milton muttered. "They've gone."

73

The bike was a write-off: the front wheel was buckled, and the forks had been twisted out of shape. Milton left it where it was and tramped across the grass until he was back to the road. His shoulder ached, but Milton was confident that the damage, if any, was minimal.

He had left a trail of scorched rubber on the tarmac from where he had swerved the bike. He had arranged for Flash to meet him at the wall of the dam that separated Loch Fincastle from the sea. He jogged down the road that offered access to the facilities for the fishermen who were interested in the loch and waited as Flash brought the RIB in close enough for him to hop aboard.

"You okay?" Flash asked him.

"Bumps and bruises," Milton said. "It's nothing."

"What do you think that was all about?"

"Leverage," Milton said. "She was married to Hannah, and he still holds a candle for her. Maybe he's getting cold feet about whatever it is they've asked him to do, so they'll use her to keep him in line."

"Sounds like you know their MO."

"I do," Milton admitted. He looked out to the bay and the sea beyond. "The question is, where would they have taken her?"

"I don't know," Flash said.

"No idea?"

He shook his head. "Could be anywhere. They didn't tell me where they've been staying. They tell me where to pick them up, and I take care of it. That's all I know."

Milton exhaled. "I don't think we have much of a choice, then. We definitely need to speak to your contact in London. He'll know. We need to set up a meeting."

"Now?"

"We'll do it at the hotel," he said.

FLASH RAN the boat up the beach again and secured the land anchor. He stayed with it as Milton jogged up the dunes and across the road. Bobby was standing outside his car with his phone pressed to his ear. He lowered it as he saw Milton.

"What's going on?" he said. "Who were you chasing? Where's Chrissie?"

"She's been taken," Milton said. "It's something to do with her ex-husband."

"I was just calling the police," he said, holding up his phone.

"I wouldn't," Milton said. "Not yet, anyway."

"Why? You just said she's been taken."

"She has. And the men who have her won't leave her alive if the police track them down."

"So what do we do?"

"You just need to trust me," he said. "I'm going to find her."

Bobby exhaled, his shoulders slumping. "But won't I get into trouble? I mean, if I don't do anything?"

"What have you seen?" Milton said. "Two Range Rovers driving away from the hotel."

"And Chrissie isn't here," Bobby added. "Plus, her caravan door was left open, and everything has been turned upside down."

"Just close the door for now," Milton said, "and pretend you didn't see anything."

"I have to do *something*," he said. "I can't just sit here."

"You can help me," Milton said. "Chrissie said she's planning to have parties here who want to shoot grouse, right?"

"Aye."

"And she has equipment? Shotguns?"

"Aye."

"Show me the gun safe."

74

Zhou had locked Hannah into the guest bedroom. He had protested, but Zhou was adamant. Any illusion that Hannah had control over the course of events—that he had *ever* had control over them—was now gone. He was watching through the window as two of the black Range Rovers rolled down the drive and parked next to the house. Angry clouds had rolled in, and, as he watched the doors to the cars open and the occupants get out, there was a crack of lightning that split the sky and then a deep and ominous rumble of thunder. The men from the car walked briskly to the door, with two of them frogmarching a woman between them. Hannah squinted down at them, and, even though it was too dark to make out any detail, he recognised her.

It was Chrissie.

He went to the door and banged his fist against it. "Let me out of here!"

There was no answer; instead, he could hear muffled shouts of indignation. He heard footsteps on the stairs and then coming down the corridor. The key was turned in the lock, the door opened, and Chrissie was shoved inside. She stumbled and fell, landing on her knees. One of Chen's men glanced inside and then shut the door, locking it once more.

"Chrissie," Hannah said, reaching down to help her up.

She slapped his hand away. "Get off me."

"Are you okay? Did they—"

She cut over him. "What have you *done?*"

"Did they hurt you?"

"No," she said, getting back to her feet. "They just waved their guns in my face."

"I'm sorry."

"You'd better start telling me what this is all about. Like —right *now*, Jonty."

"You should never have been involved in this."

She crossed the room and looked out of the window. "But I *am*. So I think it's time you came clean with me. What in God's name is going on?"

He went to the bed and sat down on the edge. "What do you want to know?"

"Have you been using illegal immigrants out on the islands?"

"Of course not," he blustered. "Why would you say something like that?"

"Because I can't help feeling that this is all to do with that. I had a visit from the parents of a Polish lad five weeks ago. Their son went missing—they came out here looking for him."

"What does that have to do with me?"

"Jesus, Johnston, if you're going to deny it, you'll need to do better than that. There was a time, not so long ago, when you used to tell me everything about your businesses. Remember? When we were married? You've told me you've used immigrants before. In the factory—the fish, whatever it is that goes on there. Eastern Europeans, too, weren't they?"

"That was a long time ago."

"And a leopard doesn't change its spots."

"What did the parents say?"

"Their son came out here to work, and then they lost contact with him."

"What did you say?"

"Nothing, more's the pity. They left again before I could change my mind, and I wasn't able to find them. But they said they'd been working with a charity who helped people like their son, so I called them instead."

Hannah reached up with his hand and kneaded his forehead. "You didn't."

"I did, and they sent someone who'd been looking for them. His name is—or was—Alan."

"'*Was*'?"

"Like you don't know."

"I *don't.*"

She spoke with exaggerated patience. "Well, Alan went missing, too. I couldn't get in touch, and then, last week, someone came looking for him. He got a job at the restaurant. It was a coincidence that he ended up with us, I think, but I found out why he was here. Turns out he stole the hotel boat and took it out to the Flannans, and then, right after that, *this* happens."

He bit his lip rather than answer.

"Fine," she said, squaring up to him. "You don't want to tell me what's going on? Then you can tell the police."

"What?"

She stuck out her chin. "I went to Glasgow yesterday to tell them what I know. They've opened a file, and they're coming out to look around—you can deal with them instead."

"What have you *done*?" he mumbled.

"The right thing," she said. "It feels good. You should try it."

He heard the sound of footsteps outside and held a finger to his lips. "Keep your voice down."

Anger flashed in her eyes, but she spoke quietly. "Who are they?"

"I've been trying to win the bid for the new wind farm west of Kilda. There's a consortium, the same as before—it's Chinese, mostly, with a few others. The men who took you work for the main investor."

"And what does any of that have to do with immigrants? Were they working on the project?"

He nodded. "We had to run a test of a new cable from the islands to Harris. The Chinese supplied the labour. I don't know much more than that, but whatever this is about is to do with what's been happening out on the islands. This man who was looking for the investigator—who is he?"

"I'm not sure," she said. "He has a military background. He can look after himself. He was at the restaurant when they took me. He went after them."

"Why would he do that?" He frowned, realising. "You and him?"

"We're divorced, Johnston. I can do whatever I want."

He bit his lip again. "How much does he like you?"

"I don't know—why?"

"I mean, do you think he'd try to come and get you?"

"I doubt he even knows where I am." She sighed and shook her head. "I always knew you were bad news. I should never have stayed as long as I did, and now look where it's got me. Meeting you was the worst thing that's ever happened to me, and now it's going to get me killed."

"Don't say that. They're just using you for leverage. They need me. They said I'm the face of the consortium."

"You're not *that* naïve. What about when they don't need you anymore? What happens to us then?"

Thunder boomed outside, rattling the glass in the windowpane. Hannah didn't know how to answer her, so he turned to the window and stared out over the loch as the heavens opened and the storm broke.

75

Milton told Flash to take them to Tobermory. It was a hundred and twenty miles from Harris, and they arrived, tired and wet, at eleven. Flash tied up at one of the harbour pontoons while Milton went to book rooms for them both at the hotel he had stayed in before. The night porter recognised him from before and reported happily that they did have two rooms for the night. Milton paid for both and retired to the bar. They had two phone calls to make. Milton could deal with the first while he waited for Flash to arrive.

He dialled the number that Ox had given him.

"Hello?"

"It's Eric Blair. Any updates?"

"A little," he said. "I've looked through the data on the hard drive, and I think I've got a chronology of what happened. Your man Alan got a tip that an immigrant had died on one of the islands and started to dig into it."

"A tip?"

"Aye. An email. The IP address was on Harris."

"You found the IP address?"

"I'm not completely hopeless," Ox said. "Gmail keeps a record of it, then you pop it into this program, and you can find out where it came from."

"How specific is it? You said Harris—where on Harris?"

"Not enough IP addresses down there to be specific, I'm afraid. Harris, though. Not Lewis."

Milton could think of two possible senders of an email like that on Harris. It didn't really make much of a difference to what would happen next, save he knew that he would want to satisfy his curiosity. It could wait. "What else?"

"There's an email from Alan to the charity saying that he'd got a tip that he wanted to investigate, but nothing useful beyond that. I've looked through the photographs and video, but I don't recognise anyone—neither does Helena. What about you?"

"I've got something," Milton said. "Do you know anywhere you could get a hydraulic drill?"

"What?"

"The kind you'd use to dig up a road. This one would need to have a portable power pack."

"There's a tool hire place in town. Why would you need something like that?"

"You might have to trust me a little," Milton said. "I need to do some digging—literally—and I think we might end up finding something that'll lead to a very big story."

"Going to need more than that."

"Alan was investigating immigrant labour," Milton said. "I think he died because of what he found. Johnston Hannah is bidding for a lease to build another wind farm west of St. Kilda. He put up a small turbine on the Flannans—I think it was most likely for a test."

"The Flannans? Seriously? That's the middle of nowhere."

"I know," Milton said. "I've been out there. I'm going back tomorrow with someone else, but we need that equipment, and we could do with someone else to help us dig."

"That's not enough. Someone else?"

"A friend who's got caught up in Hannah's business. I'd rather tell you in person, Ox. It's serious, though. It might also be dangerous. I'm going, but I'd understand if it wasn't for you."

There was a pause. "I'll come," he said. "How would we get there?"

Milton looked up as Flash came into the lobby. "Can you get the ferry out to Tobermory for tomorrow morning?"

"Aye."

"I'll be able to handle the transportation from there. I'll let you know when to come."

Milton agreed with Ox that he would call again later and ended the call. Flash went to the bar and ordered fish and chips for both of them, with a pint for him and a glass of water for Milton. He paid and came to the table, slumping down in the chair opposite.

"I'm done in," he said.

"We're not finished yet. You need to call London."

Flash sighed. "You can't think of another way?"

Milton shook his head. "He'll know where the Chinese are holed up. That'll be where they've got Chrissie. We need to speak to him."

"How am I going to make him agree to come up here?"

"They don't want publicity for this. Just tell him you'll go to the press and you won't be able to keep him away."

Flash took out his phone, woke the screen and then stared at it. "I just want this behind me."

"This is how you do it. They've taken advantage of you. This is how you set it straight."

Flash drummed his fingers against the edge of the table and then gave a firm nod. "Okay," he said. "You're right."

He dialled the number and put the phone to his ear.

PART XI

FRIDAY

76

Control took off her coat and handed it to the attendant. The Athenaeum was not the sort of place that she would have chosen for a meeting, but Harding-Rolls had emailed earlier and suggested it. The club had only opened its membership to women earlier in the year, making a song and dance about it as if their conversion to the cause of inclusivity and equality was a virtue, and not an enduring stain of chauvinism that would require more to scrub off than an empty gesture so late in the day.

She was shown through into one of the private rooms off the main corridor. A fire had been lit in the grate, and Harding-Rolls and a second man were sitting in armchairs, the former with his feet propped up on a pouffe. Harding-Rolls turned his head as the attendant announced his guest, but did not stand. Instead, he waited for the man to step aside and then gestured to the chair next to his.

"Take a pew," he said.

Control sat in the chair between the two men. There was a decanter of whisky on a small hand table, a humidor of cigars and three glasses.

"Good evening," she said.

"Thanks for coming, Control. This is Sutton—I don't believe you've met before."

"We haven't," Control said, offering her hand.

Sutton was in his mid-thirties with a head of thick hair and a well-trimmed beard.

"He's working with me on the Scottish matter," he said. "He's relevant to the discussion, so I asked him to tag along."

"Very good."

Harding-Rolls reached for the bottle of whisky. "Can I tempt you with a tipple? It's from Jura—rather appropriate for what we need to discuss."

"No, thanks," she said. "I'm fine."

He sat up and poured himself a generous measure. Harding-Rolls was an austere man, in his early fifties although he looked older. He had salt-and-pepper hair that was always well coiffed, a ruddiness at the top of his cheeks that might have been brought on by the alcohol or the warmth from the fire, and eyes that shone dully, rarely sparkling with wit or humour. He was dressed in the standard uniform of the Whitehall mandarin: a blue suit, a light blue shirt and a red tie with an understated floral pattern. He had served the Queen in a variety of different roles prior to taking up his current post, most prominently as the ambassador to Turkey. Control had instigated her own research into his background and had found the usual hallmarks: independent school, PPE at Worcester College, a scholarship to Harvard. She assumed he had received the clichéd tap on the shoulder at Oxford that had ushered him into the civil service.

"What's the problem?" she said.

"I have new orders for you, and they're a little delicate. I thought it better that we do it face to face."

"Of course. There are a couple of things that I'd like to discuss with you, too."

"Fine," he said, sipping his drink. "You first."

"It's the three files that you wanted to have actioned. As you know, two of the subjects have been eliminated. James Bolton's death was made to look like natural causes. The coroner is unlikely to dig into it too deeply, and my agent was careful."

"Very good."

"But it's not him I'm concerned about. It's the second target—the man from the Crown Estate."

"Watson."

"He was killed two days ago, but not by us. My agent was scouting him when he saw a man throw him over the side of the ferry between Ullapool and Stornoway. He got images of the man and another man who was with him, and we cross-checked them. They're operatives from the Chinese Ministry of State Security."

"And you want to know why the Chinese are involved?"

"I think it might have been helpful to know that before I gave the file to my agent."

"Perhaps," Harding-Rolls said. "But, as I say, it's delicate." He turned to Sutton. "Do you want to do the honours?"

"We've been working on an operation up there that has already delivered spectacular results, and we're hopeful that we might be able to squeeze a little more juice out of it before the Chinese realise what we've been up to. How familiar are you with the background to the files?"

"Only what I was told—Bolton and Watson were involved in the bidding process for a new wind farm seabed lease."

"Quite so. And have you heard of Johnston Hannah?"

"The Scottish businessman?" she asked.

Sutton nodded.

"I know a little."

"Three years ago, Hannah led a consortium that was awarded the lease for the North Lewis wind farm. He makes a song and dance about how it's his project, but the truth of it is that he's just the figurehead. The money comes from China. Not directly, of course—they know we'd never allow them direct ownership in any of our infrastructure. It's hidden through the involvement of a large consortium of companies. Hannah doesn't know any of this. He thinks that the members of the consortium have come together because of him, but the Politburo is pulling the strings. He's just the front man."

"The carnival barker," Harding-Rolls added.

Control frowned. "Fine. But why are the Chinese interested in wind farms?"

"You know how close the North Lewis project is to Faslane?"

The penny dropped. "I see," she said. "This is so that they can surveil our submarines?"

Harding-Rolls sipped his drink and nodded. "So that they *think* they can."

Sutton continued. "They get the chance to build the farm and then install their tech in the towers. It's basic stuff—low-frequency active sonar systems, the kind of thing we used to tow behind our ships when we were looking for subsurface activity. But with a big enough array of them, pointed in the right direction, someone could be persuaded to think that they can keep an eye on everything going into and out of Gare Loch. That's the whole point of the at-sea deterrent—the enemy never knows where it is. The Chinese were prepared to take some pretty hefty risks to remove some of that uncertainty."

"Except that they didn't?"

"Of course they didn't. We want them to think that they're covered, of course, but it's manipulation. We've tapped their data—we can send them false signals whenever we want. Make them think one thing and then do the other. They think we've gone left, but, in fact, we've gone right."

"And we have someone manipulating things on their side?"

"We do," Sutton said. "An asset we've had in place for years. He pushed the idea in the first place. It didn't take much to get them on board, to be fair—they couldn't resist."

"I'm not surprised," Harding-Rolls said. "We'd be the same."

"And the new project?"

"The Chinese think they've sorted their coverage north of Harris," Sutton said, "all the way up to the Faroes. The new lease covers the seabed west of St. Kilda. Apart from allowing them the chance to surveil anything coming into Gare Loch from that direction, the Hebrides missile range is out there."

"They're greedy bastards," Harding-Rolls added. "We knew they'd swallow the bait, and they have. That's why it's *imperative* the consortium gets the green light. The new wind farm goes in, they sneak their tech into the towers again, and we manipulate it." He reached over to the humidor, opened the lid and took out a cigar. "Now—the reason we needed your help was that we had a couple of potential problems that we needed to iron out. Bolton was working for Hannah to secure local support for the bid, but he was indiscreet with what he was up to. It appears that a jealous partner decided to spill the beans on what he was doing to the press."

"And now Bolton's out of the picture," Control said. "What about the partner?"

"His name is Charles Connolly, also known as Caesar. Uppity little queen who runs a nail salon in Edinburgh. We have him under surveillance. I'd say it's fifty-fifty that his file ends up on your desk."

"And Watson?"

"Bolton was also responsible for liaising with the Crown Estate so that the bid was successful," Sutton said. "He tried to bribe Watson, and it went badly. Watson was going to report the approach to the police—obviously, we couldn't have that."

"And neither could the Chinese."

"Quite," Harding-Rolls said. "It seems that Hannah reported the mishap to them, and they got to Watson before your agent."

He took a cutter from his pocket and sliced off the end of the cigar. There were rules against smoking indoors, even in a place as antiquated as this, but Control was not surprised to see Harding-Rolls flout them. He put the cigar to his mouth, held the blue flame of a lighter to the tip and drew down on it until it was lit. He drew in a mouthful of smoke and let it drift out of his mouth.

Control decided that she had had enough. It was getting late, she didn't like either man, and it was time to leave. "You said you had something else you needed to discuss."

Sutton answered. "The bidding process for the new lease needs to at least *look* as if it is awarded to the best bidder. Hannah was encouraged to work with a new German company that has developed cable technology that will allow for more efficient transmission of the electricity from the wind farm to the mainland. The only issue was that the cable was untested, and the other members of the consortium—the ones Chinese intelligence have used to mask their involvement—demanded proof that it would work before they would commit to releasing the funds. Hannah conducted local tests to demonstrate efficacy—first on the Flannan Isles and then on St. Kilda. But both tests were completely illegal. He doesn't have planning permission for either of them, and he wouldn't get it—the environmentalists would be up in arms if they found out what they were doing—so they did it all in secret. The consortium were told that the tests were all bona fide, of course. The engineers needed transport to get from the mainland to the islands with their labour and equipment, and we arranged for a local man to win the contract. His name is Connor Gordon, although he also goes by the nickname of Flash, for obvious reasons. Ex-soldier. Major in the SAS, actually; had quite the career before he ran into trouble in the aftermath of the battle in al-Majar al-Kabir. We thought he'd be perfect. He moved to Harris to run a whale-watching business. He has several boats, and he knows the waters like the back of his hand."

"But?"

Harding-Rolls puffed on the cigar. "It seems that Gordon suffers from a guilty conscience. The Chinese brought in Eastern European labour to do the grunt work, and they've had a couple of accidents along the way. Gordon has struggled with that. He contacted Sutton this evening and said that unless we tell him where he can find the Chinese, he's finished."

"Why does he want to know where they are?"

"Hannah's ex-wife was abducted yesterday afternoon. We haven't spoken to our source in Beijing yet, but our assumption is that she's been taken as leverage over Hannah —he still has feelings for her, apparently."

"Why does Gordon care?"

"That we don't know," Sutton said.

"And where is she?"

"Hannah has a castle on Harris. Chinese intelligence has taken it over as their base of operations. She'll be there."

"Does Gordon know that?"

"Not yet. He demanded I go up there to meet him. Tomorrow, face to face, at the harbour in Tobermory."

"Hence why you wanted to see me."

"That's right," Harding-Rolls said. "We've considered the matter, and we've come to the conclusion that Mr. Gordon's usefulness has come to an end. His mental state isn't what it could be—we think he's unreliable. Obviously, the fact that he's an officer makes it a particularly difficult call, but the overall objective is simply too important to jeopardise because of one man, especially when we're so close to the finish line. We'd like you to do the necessary, and tomorrow seems like the perfect opportunity. You still have your agent in place?"

"I do," Control said. "But I think I might send another for backup. When are you proposing to travel?"

"I've got a driver outside waiting to take me. I'm aiming to be there in time for breakfast."

"I'll make sure my agents are in Tobermory in time for the meeting."

Harding-Rolls laid the cigar in an ashtray and took up his glass. "Very good," he said. "I knew I'd be able to count on you. I'll send Gordon's file straight away."

"Is there anything else?"

He sipped his whisky and set it down again. "No, I believe that's it."

Control stood, gave a final nod of farewell and walked from the room. She was already thinking about the addition to Twelve's orders and was sure that her decision to send another agent to assist was the right one. Three, Six, Nine and Ten were all operational, but she wouldn't have sent them even if they were available. The matter needed careful handling, and she would do Gordon the respect of sending her best. She gathered her coat from the cloakroom and hailed a cab from the street outside.

The driver opened his window. "Where to?"

"Vauxhall," she said, getting into the back.

She wouldn't take any chances. This had the potential to be more difficult than they had previously assessed, and, in the circumstances, she knew that there was only really one agent to call: she would send Number One.

77

Last night's storm had passed, although the radio had promised that another was due tonight. The sea was calm, as if gathering its strength. Milton knew they were running up against it; they needed to get to the Flannans, do what needed to be done there, and then return to the mainland, all before the weather turned on them. If the forecast was correct, it was going to be tight.

He sat in the prow of the boat as Flash navigated the Sound of Mull to Oban. He had only managed to get a couple of hours of sleep, his mind constantly running over the plan. There were all sorts of ways in which it could go wrong, but he couldn't think of any other way to find out where Chrissie had been taken. Johnston Hannah was tied up with the Chinese men for whom Flash had been working, and Milton was sure that Chrissie had been taken as a way of exerting their will over her ex-husband. That probably meant that she was safe, at least in the short term, although that did not mean that Milton was prepared to wait in order to try to win back her freedom. Flash, too, needed a resolution to his own predicament, and Milton's plan would allow him the best chance of finding that. There were flaws and vulnerabilities in what he had proposed, but it was the best that he had been able to come up with. It was all they had, and it would have to do.

He turned back to the console. Flash was gripping the wheel in both hands, a muscle in his cheek working as he clenched and unclenched his jaw. "Are you okay?"

"Been better," he called back.

"Did you sleep?"

"I don't sleep," he said. "I still get nightmares."

"From Iraq?"

"Don't you?"

Milton thought of the children outside the *madrassa*, just one of the memories that he had tried to drown in a flood of booze. "Now and again."

"You'd think they'd pass," Flash said. "It's been twenty years."

"Some things are difficult to shift."

They bounced over the waves.

"There's something I've been meaning to say," Milton said. "I don't think I ever said sorry for what happened."

Flash stared ahead and, for a moment, was silent.

"You saved my life, and then you sacrificed your career for mine. It should have been me who was disciplined, not you. You didn't deserve any of what happened."

"Probably not," he said at last. "I was angry for a long time—with you, with the army, with myself—but I've come to terms with it."

"I let you down, Flash. I wanted you to know that I'm sorry. And I'll never let you down again."

He turned his head to look at Milton. "You know what helped me get over it? You just had the balls to do what we all knew needed to be done. The order not to go and take out Abdelhossein was a disgrace. After what he did? They should have dropped a bomb on him and wiped him off the face of the earth. You were right with what you said about him running. Rippon told me—they had intelligence that the Iranians were already arranging to get him across the border, and, if that had happened, we'd have lost him. Taking him out was the right thing to do. And taking the fall for you was the right thing to do, too. I don't regret it. I'd do it again."

Flash turned back to look ahead, nudging the wheel so that they carved through an oncoming wave.

Milton was quiet for a moment. The Ninth Step required him to make direct amends to those he had harmed. He knew himself well enough to know that Flash's clemency would not be enough for him to absolve himself for what had happened, but acknowledging that he had been in the wrong was the right thing to do.

Flash glanced back at Milton. "You think this'll work?"

"I don't know. I'm open to suggestions if you can think of a better idea."

He shook his head. "I gave up trying to think of a way out of this weeks ago. At least this will get a reaction."

"It'll certainly do that," Milton said.

He turned back to the prow as they cut through the surf. Oban appeared on the horizon.

78

He was a big man, and he stood out among the other passengers who disembarked from the first British Airways CityFlyer flight of the day between London City and Glasgow. His skin was pale, his hair so blond as to be only a shade or two darker than white, and his eyes were blue. He was dressed in a suit today, so as to fit in with the legend that had been constructed for him: a sales executive from a Swedish company who designed and constructed aluminium window frames. The name on his passport was Stellan Nyqvist, but none of it was true. He was originally from Iceland, had served in the British army for eight years and had then been recruited to the clandestine agency that operated from a nondescript building on the banks of the Thames. His career with Group Fifteen had been a success, and Björn Thorsson had risen quickly through the ranks until he was the primary agent.

And now he had been sent to Scotland to help Number Twelve with a late addition to his assignment.

He passed through the arrivals lounge and made his way out into the car park. He had been given the key to an Audi

A8 and told that it would be left in the northwest corner of the space. He saw a possible candidate, blipped the key and was rewarded with a wink of the lights. He went around and opened the boot, unlatching the false floor and lifting it up. The space beneath would normally have been used for the spare wheel, but it was absent, and in its place was a simple canvas bag. Leaving the bag inside the boot so that he wasn't observed, he took out the equipment that the quartermaster had provided: a Glock 19 with a laser light, a high-capacity magazine and a sound and light suppressor; a CQD knife; AN/PVS-21 night-vision goggles that came with a ticket price of over £20,000; a burner phone; and a strip of paper with a cryptogram that he would use for secure communications.

He put the gear back into the bag, zipped it up and took it around to the front of the car with him. He tapped the address of the ferry terminal in Oban into the satnav, waited for it to plot his route, and then set off. He had a busy day ahead of him and no time to waste.

79

Flash guided them around Kerrera and rubbed off some of their speed as they cruised toward Oban. The buildings that lined the harbour revealed themselves through the early sea mist, and, as they drew closer, Milton saw that Ox was waiting for them on the quay.

"Morning," Milton called up as he tossed over a mooring line.

"Bloody *early* in the morning," Ox replied as he secured the line. "I'm not usually up for another couple of hours."

Milton clambered up the ladder.

"Is that your friend?" Ox said, nodding down to where Flash was clearing space for the cargo.

"It is," he said. "Ox—meet Flash. Flash—Ox."

Flash raised a hand in greeting and tossed up a second line for Milton to secure.

"Did you get what we needed?" Milton asked.

"Most of it."

The big man gestured to a collection of equipment that had been stacked on the quay. There were three pickaxes, three shovels, a hydraulic power pack and a breaker with a collection of new steels.

"Well done," Milton said.

"My mate asked what we needed it all for," Ox said. "The question crossed my mind, too."

"You're going to have to trust me on that," Milton said.

"I don't mean to be a dick about it, but I hardly know you from Adam. I'm going to need a little more if you want me to come with you."

Milton didn't want to say so much that Ox might get cold feet, yet he didn't want him to come without enough information to make an informed decision. "I think I know what happened to the missing men. Alan and the immigrants he was looking for."

"Right," Ox said tentatively. "Why do we need gear for digging?"

"I think they might have been murdered."

"And buried."

"That's right."

"On the Flannans?"

Milton nodded. "Are you still up for coming?"

Ox sighed. "I'm here, aren't I? In for a penny, I suppose."

"It'll be the biggest story you've ever covered. National news, not just up here—and it'll be yours to break."

"Hence why I'm up at this ungodly hour. What's the plan?"

"We need to shift all that gear into the boat," Milton said. "Then we're going back to Tobermory."

"Not the Flannans?"

"Afterwards," Milton said. "We're picking up someone else first."

80

Björn had arranged to meet Number Twelve on the ferry to Craignure. He went up to the cafeteria and watched the mainland recede into the distance, waiting for Twelve to find him. Björn had been involved in the man's selection, and knew a good deal about his background as a result of the process that had seen him transferred from the military. His name was Adam Duke, and he had built a superb résumé for himself during the time he had served in the Special Boat Squadron. Björn was aware that there had been the odd blemish on his record since his transfer to the Group, but that was hardly unique. It was one thing to work as a special forces soldier, operating as part of a team; it was quite another to undertake the typically lonely assignments that were handed across Control's desk. Mistakes were common. Björn's only stipulation was that they only be made once.

The door opened, and Björn turned to see Twelve making his way over to him.

"Number Twelve," Björn said.

Twelve sat down on the other side of the chipped and scratched table. "I wasn't expecting backup."

"Just precautionary."

"But the job went well—"

"It's not a reflection on your performance. Control's happy with your report."

"So?"

"Have you read the file on the new target?"

"Yes."

"She thinks we need to be careful with him. He's ex–special forces. Apart from the fact that we have at least two Chinese hitters running around, standard operating procedure requires a two-person minimum on an assignment with a target like that. I'm the second person."

Twelve shrugged. Björn could see that his pride had been hurt, but that was just his naivety, and it would be something that he would realise as folly as he built up his experience. Two agents were always better than one, especially with a target who might be difficult.

The ferry's horn sounded, a boom that rolled across the water to the approaching Isle of Mull.

"What happened to the first target?" Björn asked.

"It was a two-man team: one man watched while the other tossed him over the side."

"What about the men who killed him?"

"Huang and Zhukov," he said. "Not as professional as I would've expected."

"Why?"

"Apart from the fact that I saw them? They could have waited and topped him on the island."

"Sloppy?"

"I'd say brazen. They're probably already back in Beijing."

Björn shook his head. "We don't think so."

"Really?"

"No one matching either of them has flown out of the country, and we've had positive ANPR hits of the car they're driving in the Highlands."

"So where are they?"

"We're not sure. We have to assume they're still in theatre."

"Do we know what they want?"

He shook his head, but that was a lie. Control had briefed him early this morning when she had given him the new file. She had explained that there were several actors involved in this matter who had no independent knowledge of one another: a Scottish entrepreneur, Chinese state security, an ex–special forces soldier, and various sundry locals. They were all pieces on the chess board, and Twelve did not need to know the invisible relationships between them. All he was required to know was that he needed to remove some of those pieces; Björn would maintain the strategic view and direct the game as he saw fit.

"What's the plan for this morning?"

Björn had already given thought to how they might carry out their orders. "The meeting between Sutton and the target is at midday in Tobermory, but it'll be too exposed to do anything then. We'll observe from a distance and then follow."

"And?"

"And we'll find a quiet spot and do it then."

81

Milton watched. The CalMac ferry slowed as it moved toward the harbour; passengers gathered on the observation deck to enjoy the view of the town and the colourful buildings that made up the seafront. Milton, Ox and Flash had returned to Tobermory at ten and taken up their positions. Milton had made his way into position on the headland that looked down onto the harbour. It was the same spot from which he had observed Flash the first time, and, as then, it offered excellent sight lines of the immediate vicinity. He could see the ferry terminal to the left and, to his right, the concrete jetty onto which the visiting fishing boats would unload their catches. The smell of salt was strong, and the air was crisp, although the wind was strengthening in anticipation of the coming storm.

Milton adjusted his EarPods. "It's docking now. Are you both ready?"

"Ready," Ox replied.

"Yep," said Flash.

Milton put his binoculars to his eyes and scanned the

quayside. Flash's boat was tied up to a bollard on the right-hand side of the jetty, between two small fishing boats that had arrived within the last hour. Flash was out of sight, sheltered from view in the alleyway between the convenience store and the post office. Ox was leaning against the clock tower at the landward side of the jetty; it was the rendezvous that Milton had suggested for the meet, perfect on account of being busy enough to dissuade any move against Flash yet close enough to the boat for their own plan to be viable.

He looked back to the ferry as it bumped up against the dock. The passengers were still on the observation deck, and, now that they were closer, Milton was able to scan them with the glasses. Flash had described the man who had first recruited him, and Milton saw a man on the observation deck who could have been a match. He looked to be in his thirties, wore a beard and was wearing dark glasses to shield his eyes against the low sun. He was too far away for Milton to be sure, but it looked like a possibility.

Milton looked at his watch: five minutes to twelve. He put the binoculars in his bag, took out the pistol and slid it into his pocket. It was time to move, and, with a final look from his elevated vantage, he made his way to the path that would bring him down to the harbour.

BJÖRN HAD NEVER BEEN to Tobermory before and would have liked more than the thirty minutes' grace that was afforded by their late arrival. They had disembarked the ferry at Craignure and then driven along the coast of Mull, delayed for thirty minutes by an overturned lorry just outside Pennygown. The driver who had been transporting sheep to the slaughterhouse just a mile or two down the road had somehow misjudged a corner and overturned his vehicle. The scene was chaotic, with bleating animals and irate drivers remonstrating with each other and with the police who were arranging for the obstruction to be cleared. Björn had turned around and taken an alternative route, but it had added time to their journey that they could ill afford to spare.

He had found a spot for the car on the main street, fifty feet from the clock tower that had been suggested for the meet. They had set up two observation posts: Björn was inside the car, and Twelve was farther down the road, next to the public toilet. The two spots allowed them coverage of the main street in both directions, as well as a clear view of the bay should Connor Gordon arrive by boat. The street was busy with locals and passengers who had just arrived on the ferry. Cars were parked at right angles to the white-painted railings at the edge of the quay, and tourists posed for selfies against the bright façades of the buildings. A postman got out of his van to empty a post box; an elderly couple shuffled out of the Co-Op; a tour bus edged back into a space next to a fish and chip restaurant; a large man with cauliflower ears walked along the stone jetty and untied one of the ropes that held a rigid inflatable in place.

Björn tapped his radio receiver to transmit. "See anything?"

"Nothing yet."

"Stay on it. The ferry just got in. He'll be here soon."

MILTON LOITERED on the corner of the road that led uphill from Main Street, the road sign advertising the villages of Dervaig, Calgary and Gruline. There were shops on either side of the junction: the red-painted Tobermory Gift Shop on one side and a shop advertising tackle and books on the other. Passengers from the ferry started to make their way along the road to the centre of town. He waited with his back to the wall of the gift shop, hidden from view as the passengers turned a gentle corner. Two men in Lycra went by on their bikes, then a family with three squabbling kids, then a lone woman dressed in clothes that were too insubstantial for the brisk sea breeze, and then, finally, the man with the shades. Milton only got a glimpse at his profile, but, now that he was closer, he was confident that he fitted the description that Flash had provided.

Milton let him walk on and then followed.

"He's on his way," he reported. "Status?"

"I'm by the boat," Ox said.

"Still in the alley," Flash said.

"Sixty seconds out," Milton said. "Get ready."

Björn reached into his jacket and touched his fingers against the butt of his holstered pistol. There was no prospect of carrying out their orders here; there were far too many witnesses, and exfiltrating would be difficult. Their plan was the right one: wait for Sutton, observe the meeting and then act accordingly. Björn doubted that they would be presented with an opportunity this morning, but that wasn't of any concern. Even if they were to lose him, Gordon's file contained everything that they would need to know to track him down: his home address, the address of his business here in Tobermory, the marina at Tarbert where he kept his boats, the pubs he frequented. They would just need a little patience and the moment would come.

"Eyes on Sutton," Twelve reported. "Coming up behind you."

Björn looked out of the rear-view mirror. The spook was walking south along Main Street. "Copy that. I've got him."

Sutton walked to the right of Björn's car and crossed the road to the clock tower. There was a raised plinth around the tower, and he sat down, looking up and down the road for Gordon.

"Where is he?" Björn muttered.

He looked in the rear-view again, saw nothing, but, as he turned his attention forward once more, he saw him. There was an alleyway between the Co-Op and the post office, and a large man had made his way out of it.

"Eyes on," Twelve said.

Gordon's file had reported that he was a large man, but it hadn't done him justice. He was big—well over six feet tall—and heavy with muscle. He was dressed in waterproof trousers with a bright orange jacket. Something about that bothered Björn, although he couldn't immediately put his finger on why.

"Hold position," Björn said. "We observe and then follow."

"Copy that."

82

The spook went to the clock tower and waited there, following Flash's instructions for the meet to the letter.

"It's him," Flash muttered over the line.

Milton quickened his pace. "Sure?"

"One hundred per cent."

"Copy. Ox?"

"Ready."

Milton walked along the pavement, passing a line of parked cars as he drew nearer. He turned between two of them and was about to cross when Flash emerged from the alleyway. The two of them shared a quick look; Milton nodded and jogged out between two slow-moving cars to get to the other side.

The spook looked at his watch, then turned away from Milton and looked out over the bay as the ferry that had delivered him here set off on its return voyage. Milton reached him before he could turn back, pulled the Chinese pistol from his pocket and pressed it into the small of the man's back, stepping up close enough to use his body to shield it from anyone behind him.

"Take it easy," Milton said.

"What? What are you doing?"

"I have a gun against your back."

"Who are you?"

"Doesn't matter. Do as you're told and I won't have to use it. This way. Down the jetty."

The spook's fright made it obvious that he was not a field agent. Milton grabbed his left elbow with his left hand and turned him, pushing him down the jetty to the boat. Flash reached them and took his other arm, helping to move him away from the clock tower to the boat. Ox had untied the mooring line at the back and had moved to the front, stepping aside as Milton and Flash manoeuvred the clearly terrified man to the edge of the pier.

Flash climbed down the ladder and went to the console.

The spook stiffened. "No. I'm not getting into that."

"You are," Milton said, tightening his grip on his arm. "We're going on a little trip. You climb down yourself, or I'll throw you down. It's up to you."

The man's toes were right up against the edge and, with the gun hard against his spine, he decided that doing as he was told was the best choice. He turned and climbed down, losing his balance and stumbling against the console. Milton jumped after him and, after untying the second line and tossing it down before him, Ox followed.

"Go," Milton shouted over the buzz of the engines.

TWELVE SAW what was happening and moved on instinct. He pushed away from the wall of the public toilet and walked quickly toward the clock tower. He unzipped his jacket and reached in to rest his fingers around the butt of his pistol. A man Twelve had never seen before had intercepted Sutton, taking his arm with one hand while he held a gun in the other. Twelve kept up a steady pace, then slowed as Connor Gordon appeared from the alleyway next to the convenience store and hurried across the road to the clock tower. He and the other man hustled Sutton down the jetty toward a boat. Twelve looked over to the car and saw One sliding out.

"What do we do?" Twelve said.

"Stay back," One said.

"They're going for the boat. We'll lose him if they get him onto it."

"Stay back."

Twelve pulled his pistol out of its holster, keeping it hidden inside his coat. "I have a shot."

"Not here. Too many witnesses. Just get photographs."

Twelve gritted his teeth and pushed the pistol all the way back into the holster. He took out his phone and reached the clock tower as the boat moved away from the jetty. There were four men aboard: the target, Sutton, the man who had helped the target apprehend Sutton, and another large man who had untied the boat. Twelve aimed his camera and started to take photographs. The RIB carved through a sharp turn, sending wash to slap against the wall of the quay. It cut through the choppy water and raced away toward the mouth of the bay and Calve Island beyond.

Number One joined him at the clock tower.

"What just happened?" Twelve said.

One ignored the question. "Did you get photographs?"

"Yes."

"Including the man who grabbed Sutton? Not the target—the other one. The one with the gun."

"I think so."

"Show me."

He tapped the screen to open his gallery. He had a series of pictures, but, for most of them, the man One was interested in was facing away from the lens. He swiped left and then left again until he found a shot where the man was looking directly into the lens.

"Give it to me," One said.

Twelve had only met Number One today, but had been impressed by his steadiness. That implacability was missing now. It looked as if he had seen a ghost.

"What is it?"

"We need to contact London."

"Why? Do you know who that is?"

Number One looked out to sea. The boat had picked up speed, bouncing over the waves as it passed out of the shelter of the harbour. "That was John Milton," he said. "And we have a big problem."

83

Flash steered to port and opened up the throttles. The RIB shot ahead eagerly, leaving Tobermory behind and racing ahead of the Coll to Oban ferry, the captain of the larger boat sounding his horn in annoyance as they bounced across his path.

The spook gripped onto the console for dear life. "What are you doing?" he yelled at Milton. "Who are you?"

"It doesn't matter who I am. Give me your wallet and your phone."

"No."

Milton held up the gun. "I'll just take them otherwise."

The man had the good sense not to quibble and handed both items over. Milton tossed the phone overboard.

"Hey!"

Milton flipped open the man's wallet and looked through his credit cards. They were in the name of William Sutton. "Is this your real name or a legend?"

"It's my real name," he said.

"MI6?"

"I'm not talking to you about that." He glowered angrily,

then turned to Flash. "What *is* this? What are you doing? You know how much of a mistake this is?"

Flash kept his eyes ahead. "No," he said. "It's not a mistake. Shall I tell you what was? Everything I've done since I met you—*that* was a mistake. This is the first right thing I've done since I agreed to taxi your murdering Chinese friends around the islands."

Sutton turned to Ox, then to Flash, then back to Milton. "Do you have *any* idea how much trouble you're in?"

Milton ignored the threat. "You should probably get comfortable. How long until we get there?"

Flash looked down at the dials. "I can push her up to fifty-five knots before she starts to complain. It'll take three hours from here, maybe four if it gets any rougher."

"You heard him," Milton said. "Sit down and hold on to something."

"Sea's going to be a bit bouncy," Flash added with a grin. "I hope you didn't have a big breakfast."

84

Control had been busy: a new file had arrived overnight, and she had been working with her XO, Benjamin Weaver, to select the most appropriate agent to take it. It was overseas work, dealing with an avaricious government official in Lagos who was blackmailing a trade attaché who had fallen foul of a honey trap. The man had been warned off by an anonymous caller, but, blinded by the money that he believed he could extort from the attaché, he had ignored good sense and, instead, had doubled down on his threat to pass his incriminating evidence to the attaché's wife. That had prompted the file on Control's desk and had sealed the official's fate.

"Number Three?" Control suggested.

"Perhaps a little too senior for a job as simple as this."

"Twelve is still tied up in Scotland with Number One."

"Eleven, then. Or Ten?"

Control's screen flashed with an incoming call. "Speak of the devil," she said. "It's Number One."

Weaver half-stood. "Do you want the room?"

She waved the suggestion away. "No, no. It'll be an

update. They might be done, in which case we can send Twelve to Lagos straight from Edinburgh."

Control accepted the call and waited for the encryption to be confirmed.

"Number One," she said, "I'm here with Weaver."

"Ma'am," he said, "we have a problem. Twelve and I were at the meeting as planned. Sutton arrived on time and made the rendezvous with the target. But then he was forced into a fast boat and taken away. That's bad enough, but it gets worse."

"Go on—spit it out."

"There were two other men involved—we have pictures of both. I'm sending them now."

Two emails landed in her in-box. She clicked on the first, waited for the decryption to run, and opened it. The photograph that was revealed showed four men in a rigid inflatable: she recognised the driver as Connor Gordon, the target that One and Twelve had been sent to eliminate; Sutton was there, too. The third man was big, too, but unfamiliar. The fourth man was turned away from the camera.

"The man behind Gordon—do we know who he is?"

"No, ma'am. I've requested expedited analysis by Group One. But it's not him I'm concerned about. It's the man looking away from the camera."

"Do we have a better shot of him?"

"Open the second picture, please."

She clicked on the second file. The angle of the boat had changed so that the man who had been turned away was now facing the lens. She stared at the screen, unable to credit what she was looking at.

She angled it so that Weaver could look at it, too.

He stared, open-mouthed.

"Is that who I think it is?"

Weaver nodded grimly.

"Ma'am?" Number One said. "Have you seen it?"

"Yes," she said. "We have. I just can't quite believe it."

"I've sent it to Group One for confirmation."

"No need," Control said. "That's him. That's John Milton."

85

The crossing to the Flannans was much rougher than the first time Milton had made the trip. The RIB pitched up and down as they bounced over the tops of the swells, and Sutton had thrown up whatever he had had for breakfast within minutes of them reaching the open sea. Ox looked a little pale, too, and Milton would have been lying if he had said that it was a pleasant experience. He had ridden in boats like this and in conditions like these many times before, but he had never really found his sea legs. Only Flash was unaffected, gripping the wheel tightly and expertly angling the prow so that they attacked the waves at the safest angles.

The island loomed over them through a shroud of drizzle.

"We'll use the eastern landing," Flash yelled over the splash of the water and the thrum of the engines. "It's more sheltered. Still not going to be easy to get ashore, though. The swells are going to make it bloody difficult."

Flash navigated around the outside of the collection of smaller islands that broke the surface of the water to the southeast of the main island. The sea was a little calmer in the shelter of the leeward side, but the swells were still significant. They approached the island, the landing stage revealing itself through the spray. Two large seals lounged on the rock as spume blasted over them both.

"I'll get us as close as I can," Flash said. "Someone needs to jump onto the platform and tie us up."

"I'll do it," Milton said.

"Be careful. We'll be going up and down on the waves, and the water will push us away from the rock. I'll come in prow first—you'll need to jump from there."

Milton nodded that he understood and moved to the front of the boat. He took the end of the mooring line, looping it around his waist and then tying it in a double knot.

"I'll drag you out if you end up in the drink," Ox said, reaching for the other end of the rope.

Milton climbed onto the prow and knelt down, holding onto the cleats on either side of him as the boat pitched up and then plunged down. Flash applied the throttle, trying to judge the point where he could nudge them forward against the tide without crashing them into the jagged rock.

"Get ready," he yelled.

Milton leaned forward onto the balls of his feet. The landing stage was ten metres away, and the tide did not want them to get any closer. Flash opened the throttles a little more, and they closed the distance in bursts—two metres closer, one metre back—until they were two metres away and, as the prow tipped up at forty-five degrees, Milton leapt. His legs windmilled through the spray, and he knew he was going to fall short. He prepared himself to go under, but was wrong; his chest slammed against the wet rock, knocking the air from his lungs as he slid down. The sea swallowed his legs and would have dragged him down, too, were it not for the loop of rope that snagged around a sharp upthrust of granite. He kicked the water as he stretched out with his arm, his finger sliding into a cleft that offered him enough of a handhold to yank himself up and out. He slithered forward, lying on the wet lichen and moss that carpeted the surface of the rock.

"You okay?" Ox yelled over to him.

Milton turned over and sat up, giving a thumbs up as he untied the rope from his waist and looped it through one of the iron cleats that had been fixed into the rock. He pulled on it until it was taut, working in tandem with Flash as the boat drew nearer. Ox threw over the second line, and Milton secured that, too. Flash killed the engines as Ox leapt across the gap, his feet slipping on the moss as he landed so that he crashed into the wall on the other side of the stage. Sutton came next, tottering on the edge of the boat until Flash muttered something into his ear that, Milton guessed, might have been the option to jump or be pushed. He made it across safely.

"We need to move the equipment," Milton said, pointing down to the breaker, spades and pickaxes at the stern of the boat.

The hand tools were easy enough. Flash picked them up one at a time and tossed them over. The hydraulic breaker and its power pack were much more difficult. The engine was heavy—Milton guessed that it must have been over a hundred pounds—and the breaker would have been half the same again.

"We'll use the hoist," Flash said, pointing.

A long metal arm had been fitted to the rock. It was hinged at one end and had a chain and hook at the other and looked as if it had been there for decades; the metal was scabrous with rust and, as Milton tried to swing it out, the unoiled mechanism protested volubly. It was not quite long enough for the chain to drop down straight to the boat, but Milton was able to lower the boom just enough so that Flash could fasten the hook at an angle. Milton and Ox were able to swing the arm around enough so that they could bring the engine, and then the breaker, safely onto the platform.

Flash jumped across as Ox looked down at the heavy equipment and then up at the steep incline that ascended to the plateau above.

"How are we going to get them up there?"

"There's a winch and a trolley at the top," Flash said.

86

They had been up on the plateau near the lighthouse for three hours. The wind whipped off the sea, and fine rain fell as mist, but the work was physical, and Milton and Ox had quickly stripped to the waist. The two of them and Flash had settled into a routine: they would take turns with the breaker, using it to shatter the concrete enough so that they could use the pickaxes and shovels—and their bare hands—to clear it out of the way. A pile of rubble grew behind them as they worked, gradually digging down into the pit that had been dug and then filled. Sutton had stood to the side until Flash tore a strip out of him, threatening to toss him over the cliff if he didn't pull his weight. It reminded Milton of how his squadron commander had been during their time together in the Regiment; it was good to see, very different to the shame that had characterised him since Milton had found him again. His barked fulminations had the desired effect, and Sutton had picked up a shovel and set to work on excavating the pit with the rest of them.

The concrete pad was around ten by six, and they had

dug down three feet before they found earth, and then, beneath that, the bedrock that comprised the island. They continued, breaking up the concrete into chunks and heaving it onto the pile behind them.

"This is pointless," Sutton moaned. "They built a wind turbine here. That's it."

"Keep digging," Flash snapped.

"We're just digging up the foundations. There's nothing here."

Sutton raised the pickaxe above his head and was about to bring it down when Milton saw something.

"Wait."

Sutton lowered the pickaxe and looked ready to complain again when he looked down and saw what Milton had seen.

"Oh God," he mumbled.

Milton used the blade of his pickaxe to carefully scrape away the chunks of concrete that had just been disturbed by the breaker.

Sutton took a step back. "Is that... Oh, shit."

Milton could see the back of a head, and, beneath that, the discoloured flesh at the nape of a neck. He reached down and used his hands to remove the debris, uncovering a pair of shoulders. He stood to get a better look; he saw brown hair, with black, dried blood matted around the entry or exit wound made by a bullet.

Ox muttered a curse. Milton looked up at him and then at Flash. Ox looked as if he was about to be sick. Flash's face was curdled with anger; a vein bulged in his neck, and his hands were bunched into fists.

"Who is it?" Ox said.

"One of the workers who put up the turbine," Milton said. "I don't think he'll be the only one in there."

Flash took a step toward Sutton and, before Milton could stop him, fired out a right-hander that caught the spook on the chin. Sutton dropped to his knees.

"This is on you," Flash spat.

Blood dribbled down Sutton's chin from a cut lip. Milton reached out, put his hand on Flash's shoulder and drew him back before he could strike him again.

"They'll pay for what they've done." Milton nodded to Ox. "But we'll do it properly—we'll expose them. Not just him. Everyone."

Sutton hung his head. "I didn't know."

"Get up," Milton said.

"I didn't know. I never... I..."

"You've got two choices. One of them is much better than the other. Cooperate with me or deal with Mr. Gordon. I think you know what he'd like to do with you."

"Put it this way," Flash said. "You wouldn't be coming back in the boat."

Sutton was broken. "What do you need me to do?"

"Answer my questions."

"And what if I don't have what you want? I didn't know about *that*."

"Let's see how we get on. Chinese intelligence is involved in the bidding process for the wind farm out at St. Kilda. Correct?"

He looked away. "Yes."

"Why?"

"We're giving them a chance to install surveillance gear. They're already all over North Lewis. This is their chance to do the same out here."

"But you're manipulating the equipment?"

"We give them the signals so that they think what we want them to think."

Ox cursed under his breath. The story had already been spectacular, and now it was something else entirely. Milton didn't say anything, but he knew that at least some of it would never see the light of day. A government D-notice would put a stop to anything about the involvement of Chinese state security. Milton guessed that there would be an asset somewhere in Beijing, and that he or she would be burned if the full story were ever allowed to be told.

"How's Johnston Hannah involved?" Ox asked.

"He's the face of the project. The figurehead."

"He doesn't know about your involvement?"

"No. He's been dealing with a Chinese oligarch. He doesn't know what the Chinese are really doing."

"One more question," Milton said. "They've abducted a woman."

"Who?"

"Johnston Hannah's ex-wife. I think they're using her for leverage against him. Where is she?"

"Hannah's place," Sutton said. "His castle. Amhuinnsuidhe—it's on Harris. They took her there."

87

Sutton watched the boat with the three men as it raced away from the island. It headed due east toward the Isle of Harris, passing behind a slow-moving second boat that was chugging southeast toward North Uist. He turned away from the cliff and looked back at the island. He forced himself to look away from the excavation, knowing very well what he would see if he went much closer. They had continued to dig until they had found another body, and only then had they stopped. The man who had questioned him had suggested that they would find more, but that it was a task better suited to the authorities. He had obviously wanted to get off the island, too, and the weather was closing in now like a fist.

The lighthouse loomed at the head of the hill and, nearby, he saw the rusted old gear wheels that would once have driven the tram that worked the old tracks, long since abandoned. The weather was grim, with heavy rain slamming onto the grass and rumbles of thunder rolling in with the waves. He wondered how he was going to get himself out of this mess. The man who had questioned him had promised that they would alert the authorities in due course, and that, in the meantime, he should shelter from the wind and the rain in the simple dry-stone building that had been erected on the grassy sward before the lighthouse. Connor Gordon had suggested that it had once been a chapel, and, as such, he might spend a little time praying for forgiveness for what he had allowed to happen here.

Sutton knew that he couldn't just wait to be rescued, and, once the boat was well out to sea, he had climbed to the top of the hill. The lighthouse was lit, its beam sweeping around and around, the glare piercing the mist that seemed as if it would never shift. The door looked as if it had once been secured by way of a padlock, but it had been forced and was just hanging loose; other bits of the lock lay scattered on the ground next to it. Sutton removed the lock, pushed the door open and crept into the dark room beyond. He couldn't rid himself of the image of the bodies that they had uncovered beneath the concrete. He guessed that those two men, and whoever else was buried with them, had all been inside this lighthouse; perhaps they had sheltered here as they had worked to erect the turbine, before the others were moved to St. Kilda for the second test. The thought was macabre, and, although he knew that he had to be the only person on the island, it did not stop him from imagining what might lurk in the shadows. Sutton knew the story of the missing lighthouse keepers who would also have sheltered here. The locals said that the islands were cursed; Sutton wondered whether the blood shed here in the preceding weeks might be evidence of that.

He had no torch or other means of lighting his way, so he picked his way through the debris that had been left behind until he found the door that opened onto the tower itself. It was open and, as he pushed it aside, he was greeted by a wash of light from the huge bulb above. It lit the spiral staircase beyond as it wound its way up the inside of the tower. He had entertained the idle hope that he might find a radio or some other means of communicating with the mainland, even as he knew that the Chinese would have removed anything like that in order to prevent the immigrant workers calling for help.

He was about to climb the staircase when he saw a small storage cupboard that had been fixed to the wall. He opened it and saw a bright orange gun in the shape of a revolver, with similarly garish cartridges. A flare gun. He pulled it out of its mountings, stuffed three of the cartridges into his pocket and hurried outside into the wind and the rain. He began to run, stumbling over a rock and tumbling for several feet before he was able to arrest his momentum. He still had the gun, but two of the cartridges had fallen out of his pocket; he had one left, and, not wanting to waste time looking for the others, he staggered back to his feet and continued down the slope to the cliff.

The second boat had continued on its way, its running lights winking in and out as it rose and fell on the gathering swells. Sutton shoved the cartridge into the launcher, aimed above his head and pulled the trigger. The explosion jarred the launcher out of his hand, but the flare flew straight and true and ignited several hundred feet overhead. It burned bright as it slowly fell; Sutton squeezed his eyes shut and prayed that someone on the boat might be looking his way.

88

The boat bounced over the waves. The wind was still strengthening, and Milton found himself gripping onto the cleats and hoping against hope that they would be able to get ashore before it grew much stronger. The boat was fast, and Flash was a skilled driver, but Milton had seen the concentration on his old friend's face and knew that the voyage would demand all of his experience. The craft wasn't built for conditions like this.

Ox carefully manoeuvred himself around the edge of the boat until he was next to Milton.

"What's the plan?" he shouted.

"You're going to go and write your story."

"What about you?"

"I'm going to go and find Hannah and the Chinese."

"On your own?"

Milton glanced back at Flash. He knew he would want to help, and he wasn't about to tell him he couldn't. He had taken the discovery on the island badly, and Milton could see that he bore a weight of guilt that he would want to expunge. Beyond that, Flash was a soldier. Milton wouldn't insult him by telling him that he would go after the Chinese operators and their Scottish stooge alone.

"I'll be with him," he said. "You need to get the story written as soon as you can. It's not just the Chinese we need to be wary of—the people Sutton works for are just as dangerous. You'll be insulated if you can write it and get it out. Open an email account, paste the story into an email and schedule it to send to a newspaper. If they pick you up—"

"What do you mean? Is that likely?"

"They'll definitely be in touch as soon as our friend on the island gets back to the mainland," he said. "When that happens, you tell them that unless you go into the email account and change the time when the email will send, the story goes out into the world. That's your insurance."

"Like a dead man's switch?"

"Just like that. They won't be able to touch you then."

Ox nodded. Milton was impressed with him. He was gruff and difficult, but he hadn't signed up for anything like this, and he had accepted his lot with determination and without complaint. Ox knew how big the story could be, and what it could do for his career, but his determination wasn't driven by selfishness. He had worked as hard as any of them on the island, and his anger and disgust and horror had been obvious as they had exhumed the bodies that had been abandoned there. His career would benefit from the exposure that a story like this would bring, but it wasn't why he would write it. He wanted justice, the same as Milton and Flash.

Milton was looking at Ox when his face was lit by a sudden red glow.

"Milton!" Flash yelled, pointing astern.

Milton turned and, to his dismay, he saw a red distress flare slowly drifting down above the silhouette of the islands.

"Faster," Milton called back.

PART XII

SATURDAY

89

They knew they had to move quickly, especially given the sight of the flare that lit up the sea above the island. Milton cursed himself for his mistake. He had forced the lock on the lighthouse on his first visit to the Flannans and had forgotten that it would still have been unsecured, and that there could have been all manner of equipment inside that Sutton could use to raise the alarm. Flash told him to get over himself and that they were fortunate; there had been a radio set there until recently, and it would have been much easier for the spook to raise the alarm if that had still been the case. As it was, he would have to hope that someone aboard the trawler they had passed on their way back to Harris had seen the flare, and that, *if* they had, there was some way for Sutton to get aboard their boat in conditions that were becoming increasingly treacherous.

"What's the plan?" Ox yelled over the roar of the outboards.

"I'm going to go and find Chrissie O'Sullivan."

The big man gave a definitive nod. "I'm in."

"No," Milton said. "You're not."

"I'm not backing out now. I want to see this through to the end."

"No," Milton said firmly. "We don't know what we'll find when we get there. They're definitely armed, and they won't take kindly to me putting my nose in their business. You're more valuable writing the story. That's how we hurt them—how we *really* hurt them."

Ox looked away to the stern in the direction of the island. "All right," he said.

Milton waved to attract Flash's attention. "We'll need to land him somewhere before we get to Hannah's place. Any ideas?"

"Depends how long you want our diversion to be. We could run back to Luskentyre, but that's fifteen miles extra we'd need to do."

"I don't think we can spare much time."

"Just put me down anywhere," Ox said. "I'll sort myself out."

"There's a caravan park at Hushinish," Flash said. "That's on Harris—it's on the way for us."

"That'll do," Ox said.

MILTON HAULED in the sea anchor and raised his hand in farewell. Ox returned the gesture and made his way up the sandy beach to the collection of buildings that Flash said belonged to the farmer who kept sheep in the fields nearby. There were lights on in the house, and Milton guessed that the occupants would have seen them as they made their approach.

Flash gunned the engine, and they sped away, bouncing

over the shallower waves closer to shore before heading into the larger swells farther out.

"How long from here?" Milton called out.

"Seven or eight miles. We'll stay close to the shore where it's less rough."

It was less rough, Milton observed, but that didn't mean that the conditions were easy. Flash stood at the console and gripped the wheel tightly, his brow furrowed with concentration as he maintained a bearing to cut through the waves rather than allowing the surges to buffet them to the point where they might be at risk of capsizing. They were fifty metres offshore and, despite being a strong swimmer, Milton knew that it would be a challenge to get to land in such inclement weather. The coast here was rocky, and there were no lights that might have indicated buildings or passing vehicles.

"How much longer?" Milton yelled.

Flash turned to port and aimed the *Perseverance* between the arms of the headland and into a small sea loch. "Nearly there," he called back. "This is Leosavay. The castle's to the north. There—you can see the lights."

Milton looked through the spray from the prow to the building that slowly appeared out of the darkness. Amhuinnsuidhe Castle was impressive. It was more country house than keep and was composed of three storeys, sharply angled roofs and rectangular windows. A circular tower had been built at one end and behind the building loomed a steep hill of bare rock. The loch came to an end against a wall with an anchorage and stone steps that led up to a grassy lawn. Some of the windows on the ground floor and one on the second floor were lit. As Flash pulled back on the throttle, Milton saw a line of vehicles parked against the house. It was hard to be sure in the dark, but there was enough light from an adjacent window for him to be confident that at least one of them was a Range Rover.

"What do you think?" Flash said.

"It looks like they might be there." Milton squinted through the dark. "We'll need to come ashore somewhere they won't see us. We can't use the anchorage."

Flash stared across the water and pointed. "There. There's a second pontoon just behind the bend in the road. They won't be able to see us if we land there."

He opened the throttle again, turning to starboard so that they could follow the rocky coast and stay out of direct sight of the castle. He killed the engines completely as they reached the wooden pontoon, Milton jumping out to tie up the boat. Flash grabbed the shotguns and the bag of ammunition that Milton had taken from the hotel and clambered out after him.

"We're here," Flash said. "Now what?"

Milton split the shells between them, pouring a double handful into his pockets. "I'm going to go in and get Chrissie."

"And if Chen doesn't want her to leave?"

"Chen doesn't get a choice."

Flash cracked the shotgun and loaded two shells into the breech. "I'm coming, too."

"No."

"You can't go in alone. Chen won't be on his own—you saw how many he had with him when they took her. That might not be all of them, either."

"I don't plan on making a lot of noise. In and out, nice and quiet. I'd rather you stayed here and kept the boat ready."

"No, Milton."

"All right. How's this—stand guard outside. I'll go in, and if there's any trouble, you're my backup."

Flash looked ready to disagree, but Milton held his eye and gave a little shake of his head. Flash had saved Milton's backside once before, and it had cost him. He wasn't about to ask him to risk his life for him a second time.

"Aye," Flash conceded. "We'll do it that way."

90

They made their way from the pontoon, across the lawn and then onto a paved road that looked as if it was the main way in and out of the property. The terrain climbed steeply on the other side of the road, a mantle of gorse and bracken clinging to the rock. The castle was a hundred metres away. Milton held up a fist to indicate that they should wait for a moment while they were out of sight, and checked for any sign of guards posted outside. There was no reason to suspect that there would be any, and he saw no one. He pointed to the castle, drawing a circle in the air with his finger to indicate that would be their next rendezvous point, and set off.

The road descended along a shallow slope until it reached a wider area that was used as a car park. There were two Range Rovers there, and they looked very much like the vehicles that had been used in the abduction of Chrissie at the hotel. Milton looked inside the first and then the second, seeing nothing of particular note. He took advantage of the shelter offered by the cars to once again listen for any sign of movement, but he could hear nothing save the roar of the wind and the crashing of the waves against the stone wall to his right. He pointed to the next RV and set off once again. He stayed low, the shotgun cradled in both hands, and scurried across the open ground until he could press his back against the wet stone of the castle's wall. Flash arrived alongside.

"I'll go in through here," Milton said quietly, pointing to a door to his left.

"If I hear anything, I'm coming in."

Milton nodded. He reached around and tried the door. It was unlocked. He turned the handle and pushed the door back, then, with a final nod to Flash, he went inside.

THE CASTLE WAS LARGE, and Milton had no plan to work off. The view of the exterior suggested that it was built to an L-plan, with a tower at the other end from where he was now. He remembered the lights at the windows and concluded that if *he* were keeping someone prisoner, he would put them in an upstairs room with a guard to make sure they didn't go wandering. He would start at the top and work down.

The door he had used to get inside opened into a small hallway next to the kitchen. It was empty, as was the dining room next to it. He paused at the end of the hallway and listened; he heard voices, but they were too far away for him to make anything out. He cradled the shotgun in a relaxed two-handed grip and used the muzzle to gently push open the door at the end of the hallway. He found himself in the main hallway, with vaulted ceilings and a wide staircase that ascended to the floors above. There was a generous fireplace and the remains of a fire in the grate. Milton paused again and listened. The voices were a little clearer and were coming from the room on the other side of the hallway. The door to that room was ajar; Milton couldn't understand what was being said, but he recognised the language: they were speaking Mandarin.

Milton stepped away from the door and crept across the hall to the stairs. The middle portions of the treads were covered by a runner, and he used it to muffle the sound of his footsteps as he climbed. Despite his caution, though, the stairs were old and the wood creaked noisily as he put his weight on it. He quickened his pace, reaching the half-landing and surveying the top of the stairs above. Only once he was satisfied that there was no one there did he continue, reaching the top and pushing back against a wall where he could again check that he hadn't aroused the attention of anyone else in the castle.

The stairs continued up to the next storey, but Milton remembered that a window on this floor had been lit and decided to check that first. He turned around the corner and walked quietly along an opulent corridor, oak-panelled and with a thick blood-red carpet that looked as if it had been in place for years. There were doors along both sides of the corridor, but only one of them—the third on the left—revealed light between the bottom of the door and the floor.

He listened at the door and heard the sound of a conversation: a man whose voice he did not recognise and a woman—clearly angry—whom he did.

Chrissie.

He waited and listened intently.

"You're such a greedy gobshite, Jonty. You're as thick as manure but only half as useful."

"How many times? It wasn't supposed to go like this. The

first time was a piece of piss. We were together when those turbines went up. I made a fortune from it."

"It's not all about the money."

"I didn't hear you complaining about it when I bought your wee hotel for you."

"You bleedin' *eejit*," she spat back at him. "You get into bed with people like those bastards downstairs and eventually it's going to come back and feckin' bite you. Only now it's bitten me, too."

Hannah sounded frightened, and his wheedling tone suggested that he wanted her forgiveness for what had happened; Chrissie, for her part, was evidently furious. Milton was content that they were alone. He saw that the key to the door was in the lock and, with the shotgun in one hand, he turned it.

He opened the door and looked into a bedroom. There was an ornate four-poster bed, a fire burning in a marble fireplace and portraits in gilt frames on the walls. The window looked down onto the loch and, as Milton stepped inside, a fork of lightning lit up the sky.

"Who are you?" Hannah said. Milton put his finger to his lips as Hannah remembered him. "From the hotel. The chef."

"Keep your voice down," Milton said.

Chrissie looked at him across the room with an expression that mixed disbelief and shock. "You came after me?"

"I did." He closed the door. "I'm going to get you out, but you'll have to do exactly as I say and trust me. All right?"

Chrissie nodded.

"First things first—have you seen a guard up here?"

"Not for an hour or more," she said.

"They locked the door," Hannah added. "I suppose they thought that was enough."

"How many of them are there?"

Hannah answered. "There's Zhou and Chen."

"Who are they?"

"Zhou works for an investor I'm involved with. Chen is his muscle."

"Besides the two of them?"

"Three?" he said. "Maybe four; I can't be sure."

"There were four of them who came to get me," Chrissie said.

"I saw," Milton said. "Are they all armed?"

Hannah nodded. "Yes."

"With what?"

"I'm no expert..."

"Pistols, like this?" Milton held up the handgun he had confiscated from the man on the island.

"I... I'm not..."

"Yes," Chrissie cut over him. "Submachine guns, too. That's what they fired at you at the hotel."

"Good. Thank you."

"What are we going to do?" Hannah said.

"We're going to leave through the door near to the kitchen."

He winced. "But they're downstairs."

"They're in the room to the right as we come down the stairs. If we're lucky, they won't even hear us leave."

"And if we're *not* lucky?"

Milton raised the shotgun. "That's why I have this. I'll get us out, one way or another."

"Just you?" Hannah said. "You heard what we told you—there's at least five of them."

"I have a friend standing watch outside. He'll back us up if anything happens."

"And it won't, will it," Chrissie told Hannah sharply, "if you listen to Eric and do as you're told."

Milton felt the urge to correct her with his real name, but he fought it. It wouldn't do her any good to know his real name, and it would just add another layer to a situation that was already complicated. Maybe he'd tell her later, but it could wait for now.

"This is what we're going to do," he said. "I'm going to go first, and the two of you are going to—"

Milton stopped mid-sentence. He heard the sound of heavy footsteps approaching along the hall. The door was unlocked. If it was a guard come to check on them, he was going to realise something was amiss very quickly indeed.

"Get him to come inside," Milton hissed to Chrissie and then, before she could answer, he pressed himself up against the wall next to the door.

91

The door opened, and Milton watched the faces of Chrissie and Hannah as they looked to the man who must now be standing just inches away from him.

"Why is the door unlocked?"

Milton clenched his fists. Chrissie's face was blank, as if she had no idea that the door was unlocked, but Hannah was struggling to maintain the same deceit. His fingers twitched, and Milton caught a quick flick of his eyes from right to left to right again and hoped that the man was not looking.

"The door?" the man repeated. "Why is it unlocked?"

"I have no idea," Chrissie said. "But don't go blaming us if you or your pal dropped the ball. I'll tell you this—if we'd known you'd fucked up, we wouldn't be here, and that's the god's honest truth."

"I locked the door," the man said.

Lightning crashed outside and rain slammed against the window. Milton looked beyond Chrissie and Hannah and watched in the glass as the man stepped forward, his reflection running with the water that slid down the outside of the glass.

"Maybe you didn't lock it, you shite hawk," Chrissie goaded.

Her tactics were blunt and ought to have been obvious, but perhaps this guard wasn't the sharpest tool in the box. He came farther into the room with his fist raised and, as he did, Milton stepped out from behind the door and closed on him before he even knew he was there. He put his right arm over the man's right shoulder and his left arm over the man's left shoulder, clasping his left hand with his right, and then pulled back hard. The guard had no opportunity to defend himself. Milton was able to cinch the choke in good and tight. The guard clawed at Milton's forearm and tried to pull it away from his throat, but Milton dropped his left arm down so that it was braced against the man's back.

"Eric," Chrissie said.

Milton tightened the hold and, as the man started to fade, he looked past him to where Chrissie and Hannah were watching in horror.

"Stop!" Chrissie said. "You'll kill him!"

Milton knew that he didn't really have an option; he could choke the man out, but, if he regained consciousness before they were able to get out of the house, he would raise the alarm. Chrissie's face had become fearful, and Milton didn't want her to see that part of himself. He waited until the man stopped struggling, maintained the choke for another three seconds, and then released it.

"Is he...?"

"Unconscious," Milton said. "We need to move. We don't want to be here when he comes to."

92

The castle was dark, with corridors and doors that could easily shelter an enemy. Milton led the way along the corridor, and they reached the top of the stairs. He could still hear the sound of the men's voices coming from behind the door below. That, at least, was good, but he wasn't about to relax until they were aboard the *Perseverance* and away from the castle. Chrissie had a look of grim determination on her face, while Hannah betrayed his fear with frequent glances over his shoulder.

Milton held his finger to his lips and listened. He heard nothing save for the sound of the men's voices, the ticking of a grandfather clock and the steady hiss of the rain as it fell outside. He nodded, pointed down and moved off again.

Milton was on the penultimate stair when the door opened and a man stepped out.

He looked up, saw Milton and the others, and his mouth fell open.

Milton acted by way of reflex: he raised the shotgun, aimed it and fired. The shotgun boomed, the report filling the space, and the man was stitched from head to toe with lead shot. He stumbled back into the room and dropped to the floor.

"Move!"

He led the way across the hall, into the corridor and out of the main door. Flash was there, soaked to the skin and his hair plastered to his head.

"What was that?"

"They're on to us. We need to get out of here."

Flash nodded his understanding and, after checking the way ahead, he set off. Milton waited for Chrissie and Hannah to follow, waved them on, and stopped a moment to cover their retreat. He could hear the sound of angry voices over the falling rain and stepped a little farther out so that he could cover the front door. A man appeared: Milton pulled the trigger, and the shotgun boomed again. He was too far away to be accurate, but the shot peppered the front of the building, and it looked as if at least some had struck the target. The man staggered back into cover, and Milton ran.

He caught the others up on the grassy bank that separated the road from the loch. Flash had stopped, and Chrissie and Hannah stood uncertainly beside him. Milton slowed, ready to ask what the problem was, but it was quickly apparent: the *Perseverance* had loosed its moorings and was drifting out into the loch.

"Bollocks," Flash said.

"The swells," Milton said. "Could they have pulled the ropes loose?"

"No way. I knotted them tight."

"This is unbelievable," Hannah said. "I've been rescued by the Keystone Cops."

Chrissie shoved him hard. He slipped on the wet grass and fell to one knee. "Shut up," she said. "I don't know why they didn't just leave you here."

"That's still an option," Flash said.

Milton looked at the rapidly departing boat and knew they did not have time to dawdle. He turned and pointed at the parked Range Rovers. "We'll take one of those."

He grabbed Hannah by the shoulder, hauled him upright and turned him around, pushing him toward the parked vehicles. Chrissie followed, with Flash in the rear. They were halfway to the nearest car when Milton saw movement from the house.

"Run!"

The sound of automatic gunfire crackled through the storm, and a starburst of muzzle flash competed with a fork of lightning that sizzled overhead. He heard the *thwip* of the bullets and saw Hannah flinch as one of them crunched into the windscreen of the nearest Range Rover. The shooter had some sort of spray-and-pray SMG and, from over a hundred yards away, the chances of a hit were remote.

They reached the vehicle, and Flash guided them into cover behind it.

"Keys?" Hannah said.

"We'll jump-start it," Milton said, but then stopped.

Chrissie must have seen his dismay. "What is it?"

Milton pointed. Both tyres on this side of the vehicle had been punctured. Milton looked at the frontside wheel more closely and saw that the rubber had been sliced open with a knife.

Another volley of gunfire clattered from the direction of the castle. Bullets thumped into the bodywork of the Range Rover, and another drilled through the glass. Milton looked around the front wing of the car and then back through the rain: he saw two figures inching along the wall and, as he watched, one of them fired his weapon. The bullets struck the wing and door, each impact ringing out loudly. Milton shuffled back into cover, wiped the rain from his eyes and looked at the second Range Rover.

"It's the same," Flash said. "Someone's slashed the tyres."

He was right. The vehicle was angled toward them, both offside tyres sliced open.

"We can't stay here," Milton said. "And we can't leave. They'll pick us off as soon as we leave cover."

"I'll stay and cover you."

"No."

"What else can we do? They'll just flank us otherwise."

Milton knew that he was right. They did have to go, and someone would have to cover their six until they were out of range or they'd be sitting ducks. On the other hand, there was something about what had happened to the *Perseverance* and the Range Rovers that gave him pause. Flash wouldn't have made an error in tying up the boat, and the Chinese wouldn't have disabled their own vehicles. Someone wanted to keep them here; Milton had no idea who, and it concerned him.

Another volley of small-arms fire studded the other side of the Range Rover.

"You need to go," Flash urged. "I'll cover you, and then I'll make a run for it."

Flash was right, but only about the need to move. Milton owed him, and he wasn't about to let him take a risk for something that was his own responsibility.

"You get them out of here," Milton said. "*I'll* cover *you*."

Flash shook his head. "No."

"No arguing. That's how it's going to be." He loaded the shotgun and shuffled across so that he was at the corner of the wing. He looked around the car and saw that a third man had come outside.

Flash indicated the point where the castle's approach road climbed the hill and turned to the left. "Cover us until we get up there, and then I'll cover you."

"Not with that shotgun," Milton said. "You won't have the range."

"What are you going to do, then?"

"I'll swim for the boat."

"In a storm like this? You won't be able to get to it."

"I will," Milton insisted.

They both knew that Milton's chances would be slight, but Flash let it go. "Get ready," he said to Hannah and Chrissie. "We're going to run for it. John will cover us."

"*John?*" Chrissie said. "Who's John?"

Milton closed the breech. "I'll explain when I see you later."

He took a breath and made sure that he had shells in his pocket ready to load.

Flash moved Hannah and Chrissie to the rear of the Range Rover so that they would at least be covered until they were ready to sprint up the road.

"Go!"

93

Milton stood, turned and stepped out from behind the Range Rover. He saw a man against the wall of the castle, twenty-five metres away, a submachine gun aimed and ready to fire. Milton pulled the first trigger, absorbed the recoil against his shoulder and then pulled the second trigger. The man fired, too, but his aim was off, and the volley went harmlessly high. Milton slid back into cover, broke the shotgun and thumbed in two new shells. Flash had reached the second Range Rover and was ready to break cover. Milton swung out again, isolated a second target—a man a little farther away than the one he had just shot at—and fired again. The shotgun boomed, the smell of burnt propellant from the discharged shells heavy in the air. The man ducked into cover, and Milton encouraged him on his way with a second blast.

He slid back into cover and reloaded again. He could see up the road and held his breath as Hannah, then Chrissie, then Flash came out of cover and ran pell-mell for the protection that would be offered by the bend in the road.

He heard a loud crack. It echoed off the rocky hill and, as he watched in horror, he saw Flash go down. He crashed to the ground, out in the open. Hannah kept running, but Chrissie stopped, turning and backing away, caught between the urge to flee and the desire to help Flash.

Milton cursed. The report he had heard hadn't come from an SMG.

It was from a rifle.

He turned out of cover and blinked into the driving rain, trying to find who had taken the shot. He saw movement, saw muzzle flash and heard the bullet as it lanced through the wet air just above his head. He fired back, but the shooter was well out of his range, and all Milton could hope was that he might cause enough of a distraction for Flash to crawl behind a rock and take cover.

He looked back up the road. Flash was trying to move, slithering through the run-off rainwater as Chrissie dragged him by the shoulders.

It would be easy for the man with the rifle to pick them off.

Milton loaded again and was about to try to put down more covering fire when he heard the sound of something approaching them over the loch.

It was the sound of an engine echoing back at him from the castle and the slope behind it.

Milton recognised it.

A helicopter.

94

Milton couldn't locate the helicopter at first, but a crack of lightning lit up the sky and cast it in silhouette: the chopper was running dark and coming in low, swooping thirty or forty feet above the water. Milton recognised it now that it was closer: it was a Merlin, the medium-lift helicopter used by the Commando Helicopter Force. The pilot pulled up the nose so that it slowed to a hover. It was over the water, buffeted by the wind, its downwash throwing up plumes of spray that competed with the rain. The fuselage door slid open, and a soldier swung out the Browning heavy machine gun that was mounted in the aperture. He fired at the castle, the big gun roaring and ejected shells cascading onto the water as a shower of brass. The man with the rifle went down, cut in half by the .50-calibre rounds. The gunner switched targets and fired again, blasting at something or someone out of Milton's sight.

The soldier swivelled the HMG again. A voice boomed out through the amplified speaker. "No one move or you'll be shot."

Lines were tossed out of the fuselage doors. The pilot

edged the helicopter toward them just enough so that there was space beneath him, and three soldiers wearing night-vision goggles fast-roped down on both sides, each of them pulling sidearms as soon as their boots hit the ground. The machine gunner covered them from above. Two of the newcomers scurried toward the castle and disappeared inside.

The third soldier aimed at Milton's hiding spot.

"Come out with your hands above your head," he yelled, struggling to be heard over the roar of the helicopter.

The man was big, and his voice was accented.

Scandinavian, Milton thought.

"We have your friends," he shouted. "And Mr. Gordon needs a doctor. Surrender without any trouble and you have my word they'll be well treated."

Milton heard the sound of gunfire from inside the house. He tightened his grip on the shotgun. He might be able to take out the man who was speaking to him, but what then? Flash had been shot and needed help. And there was no reason to bluff about Hannah and Chrissie. Someone had been on the ground to untie the *Perseverance* and disable the Range Rovers. There was the helicopter, too. How was he going to outrun that?

He was trapped.

95

There was another rattle of gunfire from inside the castle. Milton couldn't tell whether it was from the Chinese men or the newcomers, but doubted it would matter very much. He had a good idea who had arrived in the helicopter, and he didn't rate the chances of anyone who went up against them, including himself. He laid the shotgun on the ground and raised his hands.

"All right. I'm coming out."

He stood. The soldier was ten metres away and had a bead on him square in the chest. There was a confidence about him that did not suggest that he was likely to miss.

"Step forward."

Milton did as he was told. He looked to the left and saw that Hannah's flight had been arrested; he had been sent back down the road and was now next to Chrissie and Flash again. They were faced by another man. He, too, was armed, toting a Glock with a laser sight that planted its dot in the middle of Flash's chest; he also wore night-vision goggles.

"Any weapons?"

"Just a pistol behind my back."

"Take it out and toss it away."

The man was considerably bigger than Milton, had pale skin and very light blond hair. He held his pistol in an easy, relaxed stance, with elbows bent just enough to absorb the recoil should he have to open fire, but not so much as to compromise his accuracy. Even with the goggles obscuring his face, Milton recognised him at once. He had last seen Björn Thorsson outside Kansas City. He had had the chance to put a bullet in him, but had decided against murder in favour of having him deliver a message. He wondered about the good sense of that choice now.

Milton took the pistol and threw it to his left. "Well done, Number One. You've got me."

"Face down on the ground, please, Milton."

Milton lowered himself to his knees and then lay flat on the wet tarmac. "I'm not going to fight."

"I know you're not."

"You don't need to worry about the others. Let them go."

Thorsson ignored him. "How many in the house?"

"Minimum of four."

"How many did you kill?"

"None," Milton said. "Didn't you hear? I've turned over a new leaf."

There was another rattle of gunfire from inside. "You can leave them to us," Thorsson said.

The helicopter started to descend on a diagonal track that brought it down on the grass between the road and the water.

"Where are we going?" Milton asked.

"I'm sure you can guess." Thorsson stepped closer and took out a pair of Flexicuffs. "Hands behind your back, please."

Milton didn't struggle. "Help Gordon and let the others go."

"Behave yourself and we'll see."

Thorsson put his knee in Milton's back and, with practised hands, looped first one and then the other cuff around his wrists and yanked hard, tightening them. The others were being shepherded back down the road to the castle. Chrissie and Hannah were supporting Flash, one on either side of him.

"Up," Thorsson said, hauling Milton to his feet.

"Leave him alone!" Chrissie yelled.

"I'm fine," Milton said. "Just do as they say. Don't worry about me. Flash—you okay?"

"Got me in the thigh," he said. "Wouldn't have made any difference, though. He was waiting for us around the corner."

Thorsson gripped Milton around the bicep with strong fingers, leading him into the downdraft from the chopper's blades. The second man backed up, covering Flash and the others. The fuselage door slid back, and two men in black coveralls grabbed Milton on either side and hauled him into the cabin. Thorsson followed, and then the second man.

"Go, go, go!" Thorsson yelled over the sound of the engine.

Milton stayed where he was on the floor of the cabin. He knew there was no point in trying to fight, but, he realised, he had no fight left in him. He had been running for years, and the effort of always staying out of sight, in the shadows, had taken a toll on him. He had done as much as he could to right the wrongs of his career. He had done his best. He could live with himself if this was the end of the road.

The big engine grew louder, and the floor tipped a little as the helicopter lifted into the air.

"Is that him?" one of the airmen said.

"That's him," Thorsson replied. "How long to Northolt?"

"Four hours, sir."

"Radio ahead. Tell them we're on our way."

Milton felt the bite of the plastic cuffs around his wrists. It looked as if they were going to leave him on the floor of the cabin. He tried to relax. He didn't know what the next few days would hold for him, save that it wouldn't be good. He closed his eyes and focussed on his breathing, and found himself recalling something that had been said in a meeting that he had attended in London at the start of his recovery.

If you want to hear God laugh, tell him your plans.

It was apt. A symptom of his addiction was the belief that he controlled the things that happened to him. He knew now, beyond doubt, that that was false. He was a passenger, with no more control of his direction than a feather blowing on the breeze.

EPILOGUE

Flash quickly lost track of time. It was dark in the boot of the car, and there was no way of telling how long they had been driving; it might have been fifteen minutes, or it might have been an hour. He was too big for the limited space, and his leg was killing him where he had been shot. He knew what they were doing: they were going to take him out into the middle of the countryside and put a bullet in his brain. Operators like this lot didn't take chances, and they didn't leave loose ends.

The car slowed, turned onto a rough track, and then accelerated again. Not long now.

He didn't know exactly who it was who had intervened at the castle, save that it was some sort of intelligence-led operation. It was extremely well resourced, and the two men and single woman who had taken out Chen and his men, captured Milton and then questioned him, Johnston Hannah and Chrissie O'Sullivan were serious players and not people it would be wise to test.

The three of them had been taken to a safe house. They had tended to Flash's wound, applying a local anaesthetic and then digging out the round that had lodged in his thigh. They had questioned him after that. Sutton had been involved in the interrogation; the spook was still seething from being left on the Flannans, but there was a shame beneath his prideful anger that Flash knew was caused by what he had seen there. He might not have known quite what the Chinese were prepared to do to win the bid for the western lease, but he could not have been left in any doubt that his work on the project had, at least indirectly, led to the deaths of one local and at least five immigrants. He had tried to use bluster to mask his guilt and disgrace, but Flash had seen right through it and had stared him out until he had left the room, and the interrogation, to the others.

Flash knew there was a good chance that they would never leave the safe house, and had decided to play the only card he had. He told them about Ox, about what he had seen and heard, and about—most importantly of all—what he would publish. Sutton must have corroborated the presence of a third man on the island during the exhumation of the dead workers. Flash had warned them that he was a journalist and that he would publish what he knew—together with photographs and other evidence—in the event that he felt unsafe. Flash had had to manufacture a closer friendship with the taciturn Ox than really existed, but he knew the bluff would have to be successful if he wanted to walk out of the building in one piece. They had demanded Ox's details, his address, and whom he worked for, but, since Flash really didn't know any of that, there was no way that he could give him up.

He had hoped that his bluff might have worked, but now, stuffed into the boot of the car, he had to assume that it had not. The operation to ensnare the Chinese had been valuable enough for British intelligence to turn a blind eye to the blood that had been spilled to further its aims; the operation to prevent the public becoming aware of those grubby transactions would require the same sacrifices.

The wheels rolled over loose gravel, and then, at last, the car stopped. Flash heard the sound of the doors at the front opening and then closing, a conversation that was too muffled for him to catch, and then footsteps crunching on the gravel. The boot was opened, and sunlight poured inside, blinding him. He felt hands on his shoulders and didn't resist as he was hauled out and dumped on the ground.

"On your knees."

Flash knew there was no point in arguing, but, if it was his time to go, he wasn't going out like a dog. He was a soldier. He had served in some of the world's worse shitholes, and he wasn't about to give these nameless bastards the satisfaction of seeing him beg. He knelt, his wounded leg throbbing, but, instead of looking down, he raised his chin and looked up at the man who stood before him. It was the black guy, the one who had been at the castle, the one who had—Flash guessed—been responsible for untying his boat and slashing the tyres on the Range Rovers. The woman standing next to him had a pistol in her hand.

"Get it over with," he said. "If you're going to shoot me, shoot me. I'm not going to embarrass myself in front of the likes of you."

"We're not going to shoot you, Mr. Gordon."

"So what was all this about? Putting me in the back of the car? Just making a point? Telling me what would happen if I didn't play ball?"

"You already know what'll happen if you make things more difficult. You want some free advice? Get on with your life. Go back to your business. Provided you do that, there's no reason why we'd ever have to meet again. And that would be best for you."

The man turned on his heel, leaving Flash at the side of the road as he and his associate went back to the car. He struggled to his feet and tried to work out where he was. They had stopped at the side of a track that overlooked a steep descent to a large body of water. He recognised the old postman's path that led to Port Reinigeadal and Loch Trolamaraig. He could see the Shiant Islands out in the Minch, with the Isle of Skye and mountains of the Scottish mainland beyond.

The car started, and it slowly turned around and drove back up the track. Flash watched it go and then started to limp down to the loch.

CHRISSIE LEANED against the wall that she had built with Eric—or John, or whatever his name was—and smoked the last of her menthol cigarettes. It had been one step forward, two steps back. She had finally managed to get the electricity running again, but she couldn't open the restaurant without a chef. She had placed another advert on the site that she had used before, and there had been a couple of applications that seemed promising. One, a woman from Glasgow, was due on the ferry later that afternoon. But, even if Chrissie liked her and she still wanted the post, she would still need to make arrangements to leave her present job and move to the island. Eric had been so much easier; she guessed that she might be waiting for another two or three weeks before they could open again.

It had been a difficult day and a half. They had been taken to a house directly from the castle. The three of them

—Flash, Hannah and herself—had been questioned separately for hours about what they knew. She couldn't speak for the others, but was able to honestly say that she knew very little indeed. The questioner had focussed on Eric, or John, as Flash had called him, for some time, but all she had been able to tell him was that he had applied for a job at the hotel and had turned out to be not quite what he had seemed. She told them about Alan Caine, about how Eric had been looking for him and about her own role in what had happened. She explained that she had reported Hannah to the charity that employed Caine and that he had been sent to investigate her allegations that he was using—and abusing—illegal migrants in his business. She didn't know very much else besides that, and after going over the ground again and again, they appeared to have come to the conclusion that she was telling the truth. They had told her that she was free to go, but that she was not to discuss what had happened to her or anything that she knew about Hannah or the immigrants or anything else. She had been happy to be able to leave and had promised that she would never speak of it again.

She finished the cigarette and stood just as Bobby made his way down to her from the kitchen door. He looked pale.

"What is it?"

"I just heard on the news—I'm sorry. I know the two of you didn't get on so well, but..."

"What are you on about? Eric?"

"No. Not him."

"Who didn't I get on with?"

"Mr. Hannah. You don't know? You haven't heard?"

He handed her his phone. The screen showed the BBC iPlayer, the shot frozen outside an industrial building bearing signs that read HANNAH FISH. The chyron at the lower third of the screen bore a headline for the story—'Boss Worried About Criminal Investigation Takes His Own Life'—and announced the reporter as Alexandra Marshall.

She felt sick as she tapped the icon to unpause the footage.

"A local businessman arrested yesterday on suspicion of using illegal labour in his fish factories is dead. Police tell us that he took his own life. Johnston Hannah had interests in the food, tourism and renewable energy industries, but it was his alleged willingness to use immigrant labour, often keeping the men and women in terrible conditions, that led to his downfall. His body was found this morning by staff at Amhuinnsuidhe Castle, the luxury property he owned on the Isle of Harris."

She paused the screen and handed the phone to Bobby again.

"I'm sorry, Chrissie."

She left him and made her way out of the front of the hotel, across the road and down onto the beach. She took off her shoes and walked out into the surf, the icy water fresh against her skin. Money was going to be tight. Johnston had offered to advance her a line of credit, but she had told him where he could put his cash, and now he was gone. Chrissie knew that what had happened to him had nothing to do with his fish farms and everything to do with whatever he had been caught up in on the islands. She also knew that her ex-husband would have been too craven to take his own life, and that it was much more likely that he had been taken back to the castle after the interrogation and been murdered.

She found her thoughts going to Eric and wished that he were here with her. She knew that he had been lying to her about who he was and what he was doing here, but she also knew that he would have been able to explain something more of what had happened here. And, more than that, she had felt safe with him, even amid the chaos of their escape from the men at the castle. She looked out to sea and the rugged beauty of Taransay, the uninhabited island that Johnston had been trying to buy as a destination for guests who stayed at the hotel. She was angry with Eric for his deception, but she would have given quite a lot to have him in the kitchen again, and in her bed.

She knew, though, that he was gone, and she would never see him again.

OX SHUFFLED from side to side on the seat and tried to make himself comfortable. The offices of the *Guardian* suited the image that the newspaper projected—high tech, sleek, cutting edge—but did not encourage repose. He was nervous, too, and had been for all of the long journey south.

He had been staying in a holiday cottage that one of his old rugby pals rented on Skye for the last two days, working on finishing the story. Ox had tried to contact Eric Blair, using an old BT payphone in the town, but he had not picked up the call. He had returned to the same phone box the next day but had noticed a car parked on the other side of the road and two men who appeared to be keeping watch. He knew that he was probably being paranoid, but there was something about the two of them that arrested his attention, so, instead of going in and calling again, he had gone into the café along the road and ordered a coffee. The car, and its occupants, was still there when he had walked by again an hour later. From that point on, he had assumed that they were looking for him.

He knew that the story was explosive, and, remembering what Blair had said, that publishing it was the surest way of protecting himself and the others. Once it was published and out in the world, there would be no point in anyone who might be affected by it trying to stop him. To that end, he had contacted a friend who worked at the *Guardian* and had told him that he had something that had the potential to be enormous. His friend had arranged contact with his editor, and their eventual call had been about as productive as Ox could have hoped. Ox had given him the broad strokes of what he had found—British intelligence had colluded in the death of innocent men in an attempt to win an intelligence coup over the Chinese—and the editor had said that he was definitely interested and would look at the story once it was finished. That was what today's meeting was all about. Ox had insisted that he would not transmit the story by way of the internet, requiring a face-to-face meeting instead. The editor had agreed.

"Mr. Oxendale?"

Ox looked up. He recognised Wilkinson from the photograph in his by-line. He stood and offered his hand. "Good to meet you."

The editor took his hand. "Thank you for coming to see me."

"I've finished it," Ox said. "It's done. Are you still ready to publish?"

"I'm afraid things have changed a little at this end. It's become quite sensitive."

"What the hell does *that* mean?"

Do you know what a DSMA notice is?"

"I have no idea."

"It stands for Defence and Security Media Advisory. They used to call them D-notices when I was a cub. The government issues them when they become aware of stories that would be damaging to national security if they were published. I'm afraid they've issued a notice about what you say happened in the Hebrides."

"It's not what I *say* happened," he said, "it's what *did* happen. The state colluded in the murder of at least six men in an attempt to fool Chinese intelligence. It's not speculation. I have photographs. I have proof."

"I understand that, I do—and I understand why this will be frustrating for you, just as it is for us. But I'm afraid I have no choice."

"So don't tell them in advance. Publish it and deal with the consequences later."

"We might have done that," Wilkinson conceded, "but we were served with the notice two days ago. They know what you're writing about. They've pre-empted the story."

Ox stood, gathering his bag. "Fine. I'll take it to someone else. Someone with the bollocks to run with it."

"The notice wasn't just served on us, Mr. Oxendale. They served it on *everyone*—all of the newspapers, radio, TV, the well-trafficked blogs. They will all have received it. I would really, really love to be proven wrong, but I don't think I will be—no one is likely to ignore the government on something like this."

"Then I'll publish it myself."

"You could," he said. "But I'd just offer a word of caution. This is clearly a very sensitive issue. They don't do this sort of thing often. If it is as inflammatory as it sounds like it could be, I think you'd be putting yourself at significant legal risk—possibly even personal risk—if you were to publish. I can't tell you what to do, but please be careful."

Ox wanted to say more, but he knew there was no profit in it. He put his bag over his shoulder and, thinking about how much time he had wasted by coming here, stalked out of the office and onto the street again. It was lunchtime, and the pavements were busy with workers going about their business, but Ox still noticed the woman who came toward him as soon as he stepped outside.

"Mr. Oxendale?" she said.

"Who are you?"

"I need you to come with me, sir."

"No," he said. "Not until you tell me who you are."

The woman glanced over Ox's shoulder. He turned to see that a man had followed him out of the office and was standing just behind him.

"Please, Mr. Oxendale. We just need a moment of your time."

A car pulled up by the kerb.

"Do I have a choice?"

"I'm afraid not, sir."

~

MILTON HAD no idea where they had taken him. The helicopter had landed at Northolt, but, from there, he had been transferred in the back of a van with no windows. They had travelled for less than an hour, and that, together with the sounds that he could hear, suggested that it was somewhere in London. They had arrived in an underground garage that he didn't recognise, allowing him to rule out the headquarters of the Group in the building near the Thames. Apart from that, though? It would be some anonymous government facility where he could be held in secret for as long as they liked.

He had been taken to a holding area, where he had been instructed to strip for a full search, and then given standard-issue coveralls to wear. There followed a short walk along an anonymous corridor to a cell; the door had clanged shut behind him, and it had not been opened since.

He looked around the cell now. It gave him no clues, either. It was ten feet by eight feet, with concrete walls that had been scraped and gouged by the prisoners who had been held here before him. There was a simple bed with a miserly mattress that was so thin as to be almost pointless and a toilet. There were no windows; the light was provided by a naked bulb housed in a metal cage. A camera in the corner observed everything with its single, black, unblinking eye.

Milton had no idea of the passing of time. He felt sure that days had passed, the hours marked by the trays of food and drink that were slipped inside through the bean slot in the door. He didn't bother to try to engage the guard in conversation; he knew that would be pointless, and that, if he were patient, they would come to him. Milton spent his time meditating on the Steps and weighing up his progress from the time he had stopped drinking to now. He recited the words of the Serenity Prayer—*God, grant me the serenity to accept the things I cannot change, courage to change the things I can, and wisdom to know the difference*—and promised himself that he would live whatever time was left to him in their light.

He was sitting on the bed when he heard the sound of the locks being turned. It wasn't the bean slot with his food—that slid to the side, the metal scraping against the runners—but the door itself.

"Stand back, Milton."

Björn Thorsson was outside. He held a small Taser in his right hand.

"You won't need that," Milton said. "How far would I get if I got out?"

"Not far," Thorsson said. "But you've been trouble before. I'm not taking chances."

"Suit yourself," Milton said.

"There's someone who wants to speak to you. Will you behave?"

Milton held up his hands. "I will."

Thorsson stepped inside, his bulk suddenly making the cell feel even more restricted. Milton doubted that he would have needed the Taser. The Icelander was a powerful man and younger than Milton; he might have been able to give him a run for his money ten years ago, but not now.

Milton heard footsteps from outside and turned to see a woman in the doorway. He guessed that she was in her late forties. Her hair was cut short, shaved to the sides and styled on top, producing, when combined with her delicate features, an almost elfin effect. Her clothing tended toward the androgynous, too: pleated taffeta trousers, a cashmere sweater, a cropped blazer.

"Hello, Number One," she said.

"I think you're mistaking me for him," Milton said, pointing to Thorsson.

"I've been wanting to meet you for a long time," she said. "Ever since I took the job."

"You should've called."

She smiled at the suggestion. "Well, yes—I'm sorry about the unpleasantness, but we came to the conclusion that you wouldn't come peacefully, especially after you and Björn met in Kansas City. You had him at gunpoint, I believe."

"You're Control now?"

"I am," she said.

"What do you want?"

"This will probably feel like old times." She reached out with the folder. "I have a job for you."

"Not interested."

"You won't even hear me out?"

Milton shook his head and folded his arms. "It won't make any difference."

"What if I said that I would be prepared to wipe your slate clean? No more running. No more hiding. I don't have the same personal animus for you that my predecessor did. To be frank, I'd much rather have your file off my desk. But you'd have to do something for me first."

"Didn't you hear? I don't do that sort of work anymore."

"It isn't that," she said. "I don't have a file for you. That's not what we need."

"So?"

"It's quite the opposite, in fact. There's someone we need to protect."

Milton pointed to Thorsson. "So send him."

"I would have done, but the subject is very particular. He's asked for you."

GET EXCLUSIVE JOHN MILTON MATERIAL

Building a relationship with my readers is the very best thing about writing. Join my Reader Club for information on new books and deals plus a free copy of Milton's battle with the Mafia and an assassin called Tarantula.

You can get your content **for free**, by signing up at my website.

Just visit www.markjdawson.com.

ABOUT MARK DAWSON

Mark Dawson is the author of the John Milton, Beatrix and Isabella Rose and Atticus Priest series.

For more information:
www.markjdawson.com
mark@markjdawson.com

AN UNPUTDOWNABLE ebook.
First published in Great Britain in 2021 by UNPUTDOWNABLE LIMITED

Printed in Great Britain
by Amazon